Riley Pine is the com
contemporary roman
them before. Expect
swoons. To stay up to
head on over to riley
details and more!

New York Times bestselling author **Lauren Hawkeye**
never imagined that she'd wind up telling stories for
a living...though she's the only one who is surprised.
She lives in the Rocky Mountains of Alberta, Canada,
with her husband, two young sons, a pit bull and
two idiot cats. In her non-existent spare time, Lauren
partakes in far too many hobbies! She loves to hear
from her readers through e-mail, Facebook and
Instagram! Sign up for Lauren's newsletter here:
eepurl.com/OeF7r

If you liked *My Royal Sin* and
Playing Dirty, why not try

One Night Only by JC Harroway
No Strings by Cara Lockwood
Discover more at millsandboon.co.uk

MY ROYAL SIN

RILEY PINE

PLAYING DIRTY

LAUREN HAWKEYE

MILLS & BOON

First Published in Great Britain 2018
by Mills & Boon, an imprint of HarperCollins*Publishers*
1 London Bridge Street, London, SE1 9GF

My Royal Sin © 2018 Riley Pine

Playing Dirty © 2018 Lauren Hawkeye

ISBN: 978-0-263-26646-7

MIX
Paper from
responsible sources
FSC® C007454

This book is produced from independently certified FSC™ paper
to ensure responsible forest management.
For more information visit www.harpercollins.co.uk/green.

Printed and bound in Spain
by CPI, Barcelona

MY ROYAL SIN

RILEY PINE

MILLS & BOON

CHAPTER ONE

Benedict

MY KNEES ARE stiff against the cold flagstones. No surprise, seeing as I've been at prayer since before dawn. But my concentration breaks every time my gaze falls on the painting of the blonde angel, the one hanging above my head in the gilded frame. Instead of elevating my soul, she's become my secret torment, her innocent image taking center stage in my wicked fantasies.

Imagine if she were flesh and blood instead of oil and canvas. Better still…imagine those pouty red lips sheathing my shaft, her hot tongue taking me to heaven while I pump her greedy mouth.

During these brief daydreams, I'm not Brother Benedict, a holier-than-thou man in a white collar and black cassock. I'm just plain Benedict—a free man able to give himself to all perverted desires, damn the consequences.

I suppress a shudder. Freedom is the one possession I've never had in my privileged upbringing as the second son to the King of Edenvale.

It isn't only dangerous for me to lust, it's pointless.

Rising, I crush my fist into my prie-dieu. With a heavy grunt, I lean my weight into my split knuckles, leaving a small tattoo of blood on the polished mahogany, penance for my debauchery.

At that very moment, the rising sun hits my prayer room's stained glass window, and the pane glitters like so many jewels. I freeze, hypnotized as the multicolored shards cast reflections on my throbbing hand.

Hundreds of years ago, a long-forgotten artist had carefully selected each of these colors based on their symbolic meanings:

Red for courage and martyrdom.

Blue for heaven and the promise of eternal life.

Green for hope and victory over sin.

Gold for divinity.

White for purity.

I bow my head and retreat into the shadows, my stomach clenching like a fist, tight with guilt. I'm a seminarian and in one month's time I'm going to take my final vows for Holy Orders.

This is my duty. My life has been scripted for this moment since birth. I can't afford for my resolve to weaken.

I stride from my private prayer room to pace my austere apartment on the top level of a medieval watchtower that rises from beside the royal chapel at the edge of the palace grounds. From this vantage, I can see all the way to the river and to the north, the extensive manicured gardens of the castle, where my father, the King of Edenvale, resides along with my older brother, Prince Nikolai, and his new bride, Princess Kate.

A choking bitterness rises in my throat. I do not covet my beautiful new sister-in-law, but I do…covet.

Maybe it's pathetic to be turned on by a painted angel. But what can you expect from a twenty-seven-year-old virgin and almost-priest?

These days it feels like the Devil tests me at every corner, filling my waking hours with carnal urges. I am no saint, just another sinner.

And what's one more sin, to release the pressure in my thickened cock?

I make my way to my bathroom and flick on the shower, setting the dial to an arctic cold, and strip, maintaining eye contact with my reflection. My dark hair and arrogant nose reveal me as a member of the royal Lorentz family. My body is hard, but there is no pleasure to be derived from these cut muscles. They are products of long workouts designed to cleanse my mind.

The trouble is that nothing is working.

I step into the frigid spray and close my hand around my rigid shaft.

"Forgive me, Father," I mutter, beginning to stroke.

My actions are practiced. A firm squeeze at the root, twist at the head, grinding my palm against the crown. It doesn't take long until the bathroom fades and a fantasy takes shape. Today I'm grinding my cock between the soft orbs of a perfect ass, not penetrating the perfect rose-tinted pucker, but humping the silken crease. My imaginary lover offers a moan, pushing back her hips, urging me to quit toying and grant her release.

I slide my hand to her slick delicate folds and let out an agonized groan.

She tosses her thick mane of golden hair and regards me coyly over one shoulder. But her angelic eyes gleam a deep crimson red, alight with hellfire. Her wings extend and aren't white feathers, but ebony leather, and when she speaks, it is to promise to plague my soul for eternity.

My fantasies always end the same way. Troubled, to say the least.

My hand flies from my cock, and I fall to my knees, bracing myself on the tile. The shower spray pummels my slumped shoulders, but no baptism is on offer. Neither is physical relief.

In thirty days, I will stand before the high altar in the Shrine of St. Germain and fulfill the long tradition of my family entering the priesthood. My elder brother, Prince Nikolai, is the true heir of our people, and his recent nuptials mean—the Lord willing—that children won't be far behind.

For the good of the kingdom, I must step aside from the path to succession and consecrate my life to the cloth, as have all the second sons of our line.

Once it becomes clear our seed isn't needed to prop-
agate future kings and queens, we spares are quietly
removed in order to prevent any family infighting.

And I am to do so with a smile on my face.

If I ever chafed at fate or held dreams to fall in
love, to raise children, to have a life dictated by my
own choices, those days are finished.

If I pray hard enough, if I purify myself enough,
if I try harder… I will be the perfect priest.

Failure is not an option.

Our family has suffered enough in the years since
our mother's unexpected death and it's a worthy fate,
one that has the power to achieve so much good.

I need to suck it up.

Life could be a lot worse.

Rising, I flick off the water and towel myself off,
my actions rough with self-loathing and disappointment. The harder I try to resist my urges, the more
these lustful fantasies grow: orgies, BDSM, decadent
and forbidden acts, signs that a burning desire smol-
ders beneath my repression. I hate being a fraud, but
I can overcome it.

Fire needs oxygen to blaze, and I refuse to entertain this behavior for a second longer.

Exiting into my bed chamber, I move with purpose back to my prayer room—and the gift from
my elder brother—my golden angel. On the opposite wall of the gilded frame is a cedar chest, and inside is a black satin bag. I open the drawstring and
remove the knotted leather whip. The towel slung

around my hips drops, and I don't allow a moment's pause before grabbing the handle and bringing the cord between my shoulder blades with a biting blow.

Bright stars of pain explode behind my eyes. I recite the Lord's Prayer while continuing my self-flagellation, increasing the force of my swing as my gaze locks onto the angel's sorrowful eyes. She knows all, everything from my doubts to my hidden resentments about being the second son born into a mapped-out future. But I hope that she also sees my determination to bear the weight of family expectation.

After ten blows, my stomach churns and hot blood runs down my skin. Good. Now I shall fast until sundown. The gnawing hunger should dull any unwelcome thoughts.

I'm fastening my white collar when a bell rings, a sign someone has entered the chapel.

A quick glance in the hall mirror provides confirmation that I appear every inch the picture of a serene priest eager to tend to my flock.

No hint of the devil within.

Ruby

I straighten my Cleopatra-style wig and dip my head to make sure the girls are in place, assessing the cleavage and how my breasts threaten to spill over the top of my corset. I take my chances that my client is a breast man, because, really, what man isn't?

Clients tend to pay more when they salivate upon introduction. At least, that's what I've been told. In fact, I've heard some girls say they've taken home an evening's worth of pay from a man's ogling alone. But ogling won't be enough for this job. My instructions require far more than that, and though it's my first night of employ, I am required to give my client whatever he desires. And if he desires nothing, I must tempt him to want more. There is no work in this kingdom for an artist from a disgraced family, so I have to take what I can get. The Madam at The Jewel Box sought me out, and I couldn't refuse her offer, not when it meant I could provide not only for myself but also my brother's wife and child.

"They asked for Pearl, but I believe an ingenue will appeal so much more to our dear, inexperienced prince," the Madam had said before I left. "And you're the freshest of my pretty little blossoms. The flower not yet picked. Pearl's not desperate like you are. Plus, that damned bodyguard X would recognize her in an instant. I've been looking for a way inside the palace—and other buildings on the grounds— which means you get to be my little lookout."

"I don't understand," I told her. "You want me to spy for you? Why?"

I can still feel the sting of her palm against my cheek.

"And here I thought you'd been trained," she'd crooned. "Question me, and there will be consequences. Disobey me, and—consequences. All I need you to do is tell me if he owns a painting of an angel—until recently, one I was led to believe had been destroyed when your father passed—and report where the painting is." She smiled her mirthless smile, and I fought back tears at the mention of Papa—at the fear of being struck again. "Darling, you not only get to seduce a celibate prince, but you get to find me something very valuable. Succeed in gathering the prince's attention—and finding what I seek—and you'll be a jewel as prized as your name. Succeed, and you and your remaining family will want for nothing as long as you remain in my employ."

I swallow the threat of my own conscience trying to weigh in. What do I care about a stupid painting or what she wants with it? I have the chance to save my brother, Jasper. That's all that matters.

So I repeat her words over and over again to center myself in the moment—to remind myself of what I must do.

I nearly break an ankle climbing the chapel stairs in these boots, four-inch stilettos that cuff just below my short skirt. After almost two months of my apprenticeship, I'm used to the shoes and clothes, but my attire was not built for more than seduction.

There's also the small fact that I'm on the Edenvale Palace grounds—making my way to an apartment in the lonely-looking, ivy-covered tower next to the chapel. My phone rings, and instead of silencing it as I pull it from my pocket, I accidentally answer it.

"Hello? Are you there?"

"Shit," I whisper-shout as I scramble back down the steps. "Camille, I'm here. Just…give me a second…" I race outside and around the corner, through the first door I see, not wanting my client to catch me conducting any sort of personal business when I am supposed to be…working. Complaints equal a reduction in my take, and some, I've heard, suffer worse.

I freeze, though, when I realize where I am—in the Royal Edenvale Church itself.

"Is everything okay?" I whisper into the phone, and I hear my brother's wife sniffle before she speaks.

"You're…you're working. Aren't you?" Her voice breaks on that word, *working*, and I can hear her anguish, her guilt.

"Yes," I answer, trying to soothe her with the one word. "It's okay. Don't worry about me. But something is wrong with you. Tell me what it is."

She sniffles again. "I took Lola to visit her father today. It was the first time I brought her with me, the first time she would see Jasper in two months, and when the guards told him we were there, he refused to see us."

I suck in a breath, both at Camille's pain but also for my brother, Jasper. Because I'm at the Edenvale Palace, completely out of my depth, about to seduce a man I've never met—a prince, no less. I understand his shame.

"He loves Lola. You know that. And he loves you.

But prison is no place for a child. And you can understand him not wanting her to see him like that. Can't you?"

I hear the clang of heavy shoes on metal in the tower entryway next door, which can mean only one thing. My client is approaching.

"He wouldn't refuse to see his child," Camille weeps. "Something is wrong. I can feel it in my bones."

"I'm sorry," I say frantically, trying not to let my own worry about Jasper sink in but also not wanting the prince to find me hiding out in the chapel on my phone. "I have to go, but if tonight plays out as it should, I will have enough to pay this month's lease on the cottage. You and Lola are safe for now. That is all that matters."

"But—"

The door from the stairwell starts to slide open, and because I have no choice, I end the call and sneak past the pews and into a confessional. I'm still trying to calm my breathing when the shadow of a man appears on the other side of the lattice.

"Have you come to make confession?" a deep, gravelly voice asks.

I stopped believing in any higher power long ago. But I know why I'm here and what part I need to play. "Forgive me, Father. For I have sinned."

I open the screen on my phone that has my script for our introduction. I must believe in my brother's innocence, and that giving up my own will set him free. If I can earn the money the Madam is talking about, then I can buy the best legal representation and set my brother free. Jasper Vernazza is a world-famous art historian. He'd never dream of stealing anything from the museum to sell on the black market. Someone set him up, but for the life of me I cannot imagine why.

"You may proceed, child," he says. "The Lord is ready to forgive your sins."

I stroke a finger along the lattice grate and hum, reminding myself to play the part for which I'm being paid.

"What if I want to keep sinning?" My voice is breathy and soft as I infuse it with the need a client would ache to hear. It's practiced need on my part, of course. But if my training was a success, he won't know the difference. I glance at the screen in my palm. "What if all I want is to relieve you of that desire pulsing between your legs?"

"Who sent you?" he says, and I can tell he speaks between gritted teeth.

"Let me taste your thick, aching cock, Father," I say, my voice sweet as an angel as I try to sound less like I'm reading and more like this is what I truly want. "Let me take you so deep. I want to feel you throbbing, salty sweet against my tongue—"

I jump at the sound of what must be his fist thumping the wall between us.

"Who. Sent. You?" he interrupts, but I will not be deterred, not when my only choice is to succeed.

I scroll through the preplanned dialogue on the

screen. "Think of all those times you've come alone,"
I tell him. "Every fantasy you've ever had, every sinful act you've dared to let yourself imagine—I can
be that for you."

His breaths are ragged, but he does not speak.

I glance at the screen again as a text notification
pops up, catching me off guard.

"'Why did you hang up on me?'" I read, but then
realize I've read it aloud. And then I add, "Shit!"

He breathes in, and I can tell he's about to speak,
so I fast-forward to the next step to regain control of
the seduction, even if it is a lie.

I let go of the lattice and slip my free hand under
my skirt, closing out the text and returning to my
lines.

"Highness." I moan as I slip a finger beneath my
thong, working myself until I'm wet. "Do you hear
that?" I ask, plunging two fingers into my now slick
heat. "That's my pussy, so ready for you. Don't you
want a taste? Just a little lick?"

*You need the money. Your brother's life—the lives
of his family—depend on it.*

This silent reminder plays on a loop in my head
as I try to lose myself in self-pleasure before I get
swallowed by regret.

This is for your family.

I swirl a slippery finger around my clit and gasp,
the phone clattering to the floor. "Don't. You want.
To make. Me. Come?" I ask between pants, the words
all me now. I am lost in the moment just as if I were

in the tiny bedroom of my old flat, taking myself to a place that is not here, in this church, but somewhere I am safe. Somewhere I am wanted rather than paid. "Is your hand on that cock, Highness? Is it daring you to bury yourself inside me? Because all you have to do is step into my side of the confessional and sheath yourself to the hilt."

I try to bring myself to climax, but even I can't forget entirely where I am or why I ended up here. So I embellish, crying out in feigned ecstasy.

"Oh… Your Highness. Oh God! Your Highness, I can't—" I add a few more gasps before yelling, "Benedict!"

"Enough!" he growls, and I collapse onto my knees with a satisfied grin.

Yes. That was quite enough.

He waited until he thought I was done, which means he didn't want me to stop. If that's all that comes of tonight, I have succeeded in the first step for which I have been hired.

You must earn his trust and break him.

Because this is not just any client on the other side of the wall. He is a prince, second in line to the throne and brother of our future king. I've just attempted to get myself off in the presence of a man I've only ever seen on a television screen or staring at me from the pages of a newspaper.

I let down my guard for mere seconds and scramble for my phone on the floor, which is why I startle to see him standing in the opening of my booth.

"Forgive me, Father," I say, straightening the skirt that barely covers what lies beneath. The air smells of sex, and the man looming before me stares with beautiful green eyes. "Did I make you sin?"

He grabs me by the wrist, and I paint on my most wicked grin.

"Come," he says and pulls me from the booth.

I force a playful laugh. "But, Your Highness... I already have."

CHAPTER TWO

Benedict

THE WOMAN FROM the confessional booth is sin in stilettos. Her angled bob accentuates her heart-shaped face, highlighting porcelain skin and perfect crimson-painted lips. While her mouth slants into a coy smile, eyes are said to be portals to the soul, and her violet-blue irises hint at secret pain.

"For the last time, who sent you?" I ask her gently, a wolf in lamb's clothing. Because her unexpected performance has had the desired effect. My cock strains against the thick band of my boxer briefs, where I clamped it securely in place before pulling her out into the light. The air around us is perfumed by a salty, rich tang, a scent not unlike my own release, and yet beguilingly unique.

Is this what women smell like between their legs?

A muscle in my jaw twitches even as my nostrils involuntarily flare. My mouth waters.

"Sent me, Your Highness?" Her lilt reveals she is

from Rosegate, the disputed territory on our northern border with Nightgardin.

Interesting.

Rosegate whores are notorious throughout Europe, hothouse flowers offered to elite clients for the price of what most people make in a year. And I can see the appeal. If I wasn't planning on offering my inheritance to the church, I'd gladly use it to open this woman's petals, to press my tongue to her bloom and drink in her dew.

"What makes you think someone sent me?"

I bunch my hands into fists, will my lust into an internal dungeon and padlock the door. My duty is to provide this woman respite from whatever spiritual matters weigh on her soul.

Nothing else.

"You passed by no less than four guard posts, then over acres upon acres of landscaped ground covered in Europe's most state-of-the-art surveillance system. Yes, my child, someone indeed sent you to me." But who would want to tempt me from the righteous path? Was it a trick of some discontented servant?

"Oh please." She huffs a laugh but refuses to meet my gaze. "I'm no one's child."

She's right, of course, even as she evades my question. Her ripe body is pure woman, but she is younger than my own twenty-seven years. If I were a betting man, I'd wager she was at most twenty, a young woman who should be busy studying at university, not here at the royal chapel, being paid to seduce an almost-priest.

"You have two choices." I draw myself to my full six-foot-five-inch frame. "Either give up a name, or I'll be forced to take you upstairs for questioning." I don't exactly know what that entails, but she can't remain here in sight of Christ on the Cross. "Follow me."

"Are we going to your bedchamber?" She skims her hands over her breasts, the tops spilling over her tight outfit, the skin soft and succulent as a peach.

"Not a chance." I can't question this woman anywhere near my bed.

That leaves one option.

I begin walking, my pace fast and unfaltering. I might not be heir, but I took my first steps in the throne room and arrogance is my default. I was raised to lead, to expect others to follow. After a moment, the sharp clicks of her heels behind me confirm my assumption that she is keeping up.

We enter my personal tower and I lead her up the spiral staircase. "Do we have far to go?" she asks after the second floor. "These boots aren't made for walking."

I'll give her that, all right. They're made to draw the eye to the lush curve of her shapely thighs.

"In here," I say crisply as we stop in front of a carved oak door.

I open it, and the bright summer daylight shines

dimly through the slitted windows, an architectural holdout from when medieval archers used these openings while stationed in the turret.

She scans the floor-to-ceiling bookshelves and gasps. "I've never seen so many books in one place except at the royal library."

I swallow a smile. My personal collection is rather extensive."

Little does she know that hidden behind covers like *A History of French Cathedral Gargoyles* are entirely different reading materials: *Story of O*, *The Joy of Sex*, plus a stash of Greek and Egyptian erotic art. Studying sexual arts is something of a twisted hobby. While I may be inexperienced, I'm far from ignorant in the ways of giving and taking pleasure.

"Sit." I gesture to a leather chair. It takes all my willpower not to revel in the length of her creamy thighs, exposed beneath her tiny skirt. I walk to an antique globe on a desk and give it a spin. "Were you sent by Nightgardin?"

Nightgardin is the kingdom to the north of our borders. Like Edenvale, it is small by modern standards, more a Luxembourg than France, but our mutual enmity has spanned centuries. For generations our two countries have warred through battles and of late, diplomacy, to control Rosegate, a much-admired city that sits on our border, claimed by both kingdoms.

Desperation darkens her gaze. "That's not important."

"I disagree. Nightgardin would take pleasure in exposing me as a hypocrite right before I take my holy vows."

"Please, believe me." Tears fill her eyes as her delectable bottom lip tremors. "I don't know anything. The Madam simply informed me of my assignment. A town car picked me up and brought me here."

My brow furrows at the anxiety in her voice.

"Crap." She covers her face with her hands. "I am blowing this so hard. Madam will fire me without a second thought, and I will be royally screwed. Please, Highness. Father. Whatever. Let me suck you, fuck you. You can have me anywhere, penetrate any place." She drops to her knees and tosses her hair back from her face.

"Anything?" Her offer warms my belly like a shot of scotch. "You'll let me act out any fantasy? No inch of you is off-limits?"

Her pupils widen, the delicate vein in her neck pounds. "I am yours to command."

Someone is hell-bent on sabotaging me. But the joke could be on them. Tonight's encounter could grant me a path to redemption that no one has counted on.

This woman offers me the chance to break every rule. But what if I can withstand her angelic body?

Here is the perfect way for me to cast doubt aside and prove myself worthy of taking my final vows.

"Stand up. I have a proposition."

Ruby

I swallow hard. Whatever he proposes, it cannot be enough to sway me from my purpose. I must make him give in to his lust, make him trust me, or we will lose everything. I close my eyes and remind myself of the stories some of the other girls have told me, though these tales are nothing found in the books that line the library's walls. They claim it wasn't always like this, that the Madam had changed ever since she'd returned from a trip to Nightgardin a year ago. Now she punished her girls for losing a client—and let clients dole out whatever consequences they saw fit, as well.

I once lost a month's wages for not swallowing when my client came in my mouth.

I know a girl who had her nose broken for telling her client he needed to bathe more often.

One girl got caught by her client's wife. The Madam not only fired her but had them scar her face so no client would want her after that, just in case she tried to do business independent of The Jewel Box.

I don't want to know who *they* are or how they enact physical punishment, but the prince has not yet kicked me out, so I will humor him and listen to what he proposes.

"What do you want from me?" I ask. "I've already offered you everything I have to give."

Myself.

He walks along the shelves, running a finger over the spines of the books.

"I take my final vows in one month's time. If it is, in fact, my brother who has put you up to tempting me, then he shall get his wish. Just not as he thinks."

My brows furrow, and he turns to face me as he continues.

"This—" he points to his collar "—has always been my path. The eldest son will rule the kingdom, and the spare will keep the royal family and its subjects on a moral path. The third... Well, you've heard of my brother Damien's banishment. Our family has been disgraced enough. I will not add to it." He raises a brow. "I know the rumors about my mother."

My cheeks burn. Though the queen died many years ago, gossip of the second son—of the man standing before me—being a bastard has long circulated throughout the kingdom. The origin of his birth means nothing to me. All I care about is *my* duty. *My* family.

"For many reasons," he continues, "this is a responsibility I have never taken lightly. Until now I have not succumbed to the temptation of the flesh, but then, I've been careful not to let myself truly be tempted."

I rise to face him, but he still towers over me. "Stop speaking in code, Your Highness. I came here to do my job. Are you or are you not sending me home a failure?" I don't think the Madam truly cares whether I am able to seduce him or not. I just need to stay long enough to look around—to find the painting she's so convinced is on these grounds. I try to sound tough, not to let on what failure could mean, but the tremble in my voice betrays me.

He reaches a hand toward my face but squeezes it into a fist before his skin meets mine.

"Tempt me," he says, and a muscle in his jaw ticks.

"I don't understand," I tell him. "I thought I already tried."

He unfastens his collar and pulls it from beneath his shirt. "I am not worthy of the priesthood unless I truly can resist. Unless I am genuinely tempted. Whatever your fee is, I will triple it if you come here nightly to try to lead me from my virtue."

My breath catches. Triple my fee. Nightly. Surely the Madam will free me from my original obligation if he is willing to pay such a wage. And coming to him every night? Wouldn't that give me access and time to find what she seeks?

"Nightly? Would you send for me when wanted, or shall I show up and surprise you?" I laugh and bat my lashes at him. "Like tonight?"

He shakes his head. "If you need to do this to provide for yourself…" He nods at my attire, the small gesture filling me with more shame than masturbating in a confessional.

The Prince of Edenvale sees me as a whore. I have

to remind myself that is exactly what I am now. Once upon a time, I was the beloved daughter of a famous and respected man. But I am not that girl anymore.

I raise my chin in a futile attempt at defiance. "What?" I ask. "Say whatever it is you were going to say next."

He runs a hand through his thick, dark hair, and I realize that whatever he's about to propose, he's nervous.

This realization melts a little of the ice around my heart.

"There is a cottage past the gardens in the center of the maze. It's been vacant for months, but there is staff assigned to clean and maintain it in case of visitors. It is ready for you right now."

My pride begs me to refuse him, but the thought of another night in the brothel has me putting logic, comfort and safety first.

"I can't afford rent," I say coolly.

"There would be none, of course."

"And during the day?" I ask.

He nods. "Your days are your own to do as you please, on or off the palace grounds. I will send for you nightly at eight o'clock. Our work begins tomorrow."

On or off the palace grounds.

I can find that painting in a matter of days.

"What other rules are there?" I ask, waiting for the catch, for the other shoe to drop.

He clasps his hands at his waist, the collar be-tween them. "As long as your skin never touches mine in a sexual nature, there are no other rules. Do what you will to tempt me from my path."

He reaches a hand toward my face again, and just when I think he's about to break his own rule, he pulls my wig free, letting my blond waves tumble over my shoulders. Again that muscle tightens in his jaw, but he is otherwise unreadable.

"And never," he says, his voice gentle yet authoritative, "wear this again."

He wants to pay me triple what I'd make with any other clients—without him ever laying a hand on me. I swallow tears and extend a hand. "I'm Ruby." I give him my fake name from the brothel, and he hesitates, my wig in one hand, his collar in the other. "Shaking hands doesn't violate any rules, does it?"

The corner of his mouth quirks into something almost like a grin. Almost.

For a moment I'm tempted to tell him the truth. I am Evangeline Vernazza. Surely he would recognize my father's surname. But no. Prince Benedict and I are more similar than he thinks. I know family disgrace as much as he does. I am not a budding artist, daughter of a respected name anymore. I am Ruby, the newest escort from The Jewel Box, the most prized brothel in Europe.

He drops the wig to the floor and takes my hand. "It's nice to meet you, Ruby."

I smile enough for the both of us. "Your Highness, I'd say you've got yourself a deal."

CHAPTER THREE

Benedict

I HAVE NEVER laid eyes on this woman in my life, so why does a strange recognition thrum through me? Ruby's golden hair tumbles over her narrow shoulders, loose curls that skim the swell of her breasts as they rise and fall. Her unease is palpable, a problem when my own instincts are hardwired to provide comfort. I flick my gaze to the wall where a discreet intercom system blends into the sumptuous red-and-gold wallpaper. Never once have I summoned for the help of those who wait around the clock for my beck and call. But this woman is causing me to break all of my rules.

I cross the room, press and hold the small button. "X, I have need of you."

"Very good, sir." My bodyguard's response is cool, clipped and unsurprised. He had guarded my brother Nikolai for years but asked to be reassigned to me after my brother's engagement to his matchmaker, Kate. The request came as a surprise. X joked that he had grown tired of being surrounded by all the newlywed romanticism. If that's true, he came to the right place in heading up my security detail.

At least, until tonight.

He appears a moment later, seemingly conjured from thin air. His suit is impeccably tailored, his implacable features revealing no shred of shock to find a seminarian alone with a scantily clad lady of the night. Nor does his mouth so much as quirk at my next order.

"This is Miss Ruby. Please escort her to the gardener's cottage within the maze and see to it the quarters are well provisioned. It should go without saying that I expect a high degree of discretion."

"Of course, Your Highness." He is the consummate professional. No hint of incredulity. No second glance at the young woman's thigh-high boots.

"Spare no expense on food, beverage, clothing. Her wish is your command." I offer no further explanation. None is required. Being a prince of the blood means never having to give a reason.

"Understood."

He turns and offers his arm. "Miss Ruby."

Her hand trembles as she accepts his gallant gesture.

"But what about my things at my...workplace?" she asks. "I don't have much," she admits, and I wince at the thought—at the excess in which I was brought up—and suddenly I want to give this stranger everything she lacks.

"I see." X's steely eyes hold a hint of a twinkle. "Well, it just so happens that Monique Mantissa is an old friend."

She gapes. "The designer Mantissa?"

He inclines his head. "I believe her fashion line is rather popular."

Ruby's laugh deepens, a husky melody that makes my skin sing. "Um, if by popular you mean appreciated by those who shop at Versace, Chanel or Prada. You know Monique Mantissa. She is rock-star famous. Her shoes are... There are no words." Her eyes take on a glow that I've seen only in nuns after a rapturous spiritual revelation.

The fact X knows such a person is of no surprise. He worked for years as my brother's personal bodyguard before his abrupt reassignment after Nikolai's nuptials. That reminds me.

"Also there is to be no mention of this arrangement to my brother or the king," I command.

"Not a word. Perhaps it would ease your mind to know your father has decided to expand his current travel to fly to New York for a United Nations summit, and Nikolai and Kate left for the Hawaiian Islands on honeymoon this morning."

"I see." If a man deserves happiness, it is my elder brother, who finally found true love in a most unlikely place, with the matchmaker assigned to find him a wife. I do not resent his position. His future crown has never been my ambition.

And yet...

And yet nothing.

I swallow hard, refusing to allow any of my true dreams to float to the surface.

"It appears that you have the run of the place. Will you need anything else, Highness?"

"That will be all," I snap, my tone gruffer than intended. "Wait. Take my Black Amex for the shopping spree. And, Miss Ruby, I shall see you in my bedchamber tomorrow evening when the sunset fades from the evening sky."

Her expression loses some of its innocent pleasure. After the sound of their footsteps fade, I return to my room, guilt eating at my stomach.

They don't exactly teach "Obliterating Sexual Urges 101" in the seminary. I am a man with a man's needs. But I'm also a prince, a second son, who has a duty. I can't let Father down. Especially when my face is the one that looks nothing like his. I was raised surrounded by the whispers that my mother, the queen, rest her immortal soul, grew lonely during a long absence from my father twenty-eight years ago and took comfort in the arms of the Captain of the Guard. A man some might say is my true father, except to voice such a claim in public would invite charges of treason.

But my blood runs with hidden lust, and in my heart I know that is my legacy. Born in sin, forged by an act of fornication. Father has never acted on these rumors, but he has always kept me at a kingly distance, his touch always a little cold, a little distant. To admit me a bastard would be to admit himself a cuckold.

So I am allowed the titles, the acceptance, the palace life.

Now it is time to pay the piper.

I fall to the unforgiving floor. "Oh, Lord, please grant me the strength to face this challenge."

Ruby

A knock sounds on the cottage door promptly at eight in the morning. I lie in the unfamiliar bed, blinking away the best night of sleep I've had in ages. I burrow further into my pillow, hoping I imagined the sound, and let out a blissful sigh.

I think I want to marry this pillow.

Knock. Knock. Knock. Knock.

This time it is loud and unmistakably real. I rise from the bed and wrap the sheet around my naked frame. I know it will not be Benedict. He said my days were my own. He will not require my...services until nightfall. Whoever dares to wake me at such an hour is not worth the time it would take to get dressed.

"I'm up. I'm up," I groan as I unlock the door only to find a young man dressed in what I assume is the attire of a palace servant—a black double-breasted tuxedo coat and tails, a vest and white bow tie. Wow. I wonder what they're required to sleep in if this is day wear.

"Miss Ruby," the man says, wheeling in a silver cart with covered plates on top of it. "X has requested you eat and dress so that you are ready to meet him at the palace gates at nine. A groundskeeper will pick you up in a golf cart just outside the maze in fifty-five minutes to bring you to the car."

After being told I was free to do as I choose, I open my mouth to protest. But that's when I smell the buttery sweetness of baked goods, the aroma of fresh coffee. My mouth waters, so I close it before speaking a word and swallow.

"What does Mr. X need me for at nine in the morning?" I ask.

The man uncovers a platter of scones and croissants, another of fresh fruit. He then pours coffee into a porcelain cup and bows his head.

"Shopping, miss. That is all I was told." He smiles softly. "And you may call him, simply, X."

My eyes widen as I remember X's mention of Monique Mantissa, of Benedict offering his credit card. I have never been the kind of girl to get worked up over material things, especially now that I must do whatever I can just to make ends meet not only for me but for my niece and my brother's wife. But I just slept in a bed fit for a queen and am about to eat a breakfast fit for a king. Is there anything wrong with living like a princess for a day?

To avoid the guilt that threatens to take away my moment of joy, I remind myself that this is all part of earning triple my fee, all of which I will use to support Camille and Lola. Camille's teacher's salary alone barely covers their rent, let alone the legal fees piling up since my brother's arrest. With this job, I may be able to hire a proper advocate to represent Jasper—to prove his innocence.

"Thank you," I say. "And you may call me, simply, Ruby."

It's strange to speak this name, especially to this man who looks at me as if he knows me, as if he senses that behind this name and position is a whole other life, a whole other story.

He smiles another of his enigmatic smiles and bows before exiting the cottage, and I jump up and squeal at the sight of the feast before me. I lose my grip on the sheet, and it falls to the floor as I laugh and shrug. "When in preparation for seducing a priest yet not having to bed a stranger…" I joke to myself, and then I indulge in a chocolate croissant and the most decadent strawberries I've ever tasted—and try to forget the fact that I haven't seen a painting of an angel or what Madam will do if I don't find it.

I fire off a quick text to The Jewel Box messenger service, asking if Madam will allow me to spend more time on the palace grounds to find what I'm looking for. The response is almost immediate.

Enjoy your stay, Evangeline. I expect this means you will have good news for me soon, or else you know what to expect from me.

My palm flies instinctively to the cheek she slapped the first time I questioned her.

"Whatever it takes, Jasper," I say aloud. "I will not lose you, too."

When X extends a hand to help me from the golf cart and into a Rolls-Royce, he raises his brows.

"What?" I ask, skimming the length of my own body, afraid I'd forgotten to dress myself after my feast.

"Nothing, miss. It's just—I'm looking forward to finding you something more befitting a palace guest."

I lower myself into the car as my cheeks flame and my eyes prick with tears. I try to swallow it all back, to not let him see his judgment get to me. But when X situates himself in the driver's seat, the first thing he does is speak to me via an intercom.

"My apologies, miss," he says. "I meant no offense. It is just that if we are to be discreet, it is necessary that you do not stand out in a way that will make the staff ask questions."

I knock on the glass partition that separates us, and he lowers it as he turns to face me. His salt-and-pepper hair lies in neat waves, and that square, rugged jaw is both attractive and reassuring. Somehow I know that whatever happens today, X is on my side. Still, I need to set the record straight.

"I get it," I say. "I'm here to do a job. And I might not be entirely proud of what I need to do to earn a living right now, but I'm not ashamed of the way I look." It's a half-truth. Even if this wasn't always me,

I look and feel sexy in these clothes—in the boots. I just wish I was wearing it all for me and not as a means to an end.

His brows draw together, and his jaw tightens. When he looks at me, it is as if he wants to say many things but holds himself back. "If my comment elicited shame, miss, then again, my sincerest apologies. I am your ally. I do hope you see me as such."

I swipe away a tear. "Thank you, X. And can we please cut it with the 'miss'?"

He smiles. "Of course, Ruby. You remind me of Princess Kate."

With that, he turns back to his steering wheel and leads us away from the palace grounds.

Belladonna Square is not unfamiliar to me. I've driven past it. Walked through it. But never have I stepped foot into one of the shops. It was nothing more than a tourist attraction the few times I'd been in these parts.

"You know," I say as the car rolls to a stop, "even when things were good, they were never great. My father died when Jasper was fifteen and I was only twelve. Jasper grew up and found work doing research at the art museum and I— Well, there aren't many jobs out there for a girl who likes to paint." Especially when her résumé basically reads like a telenovela.

X nods.

"I don't know why I'm telling you this," I add. "I guess I'm just a bit overwhelmed is all."

He exits the vehicle and opens my door, offering a hand as I climb out. Then he holds out a black credit card.

"You're not coming with me?" I ask, eyes wide.

He offers a soft smile and nods toward the closest boutique, a place called Cheri Cheri. "I called ahead and had them put aside all their Monique Mantissa pieces for you. Just go in and tell them who you are, and they will take care of you. This is your day, not mine. Go enjoy."

I can't help but grin, a giddy electricity pumping through my veins. I reach for my bag and realize in all the excitement that I forgot it in the cottage, so I slip the credit card into the cleavage of my bustier.

X chuckles, and I shrug.

"Here goes nothing!" I say and let my confidence buoy me in the direction of the store.

As I enter, my boot heels click on marble floors, and the place smells of jasmine. I close my eyes and inhale, a smile spreading across my face when I'm greeted by a soft, lilting voice.

"May I...help you?"

My eyes open, and there she is, a tall, lithe woman with a chic pixie cut, her ebony hair shining like satin.

"Everything in here is Monique Mantissa," I say, stating the obvious.

She looks me up and down, her painted-on smile morphing into something more like a sneer.

"Are you lost, miss? The Mantissa knockoffs are on Market Street. This is Belladonna Square."

Heat seeps into my veins.

"I know where I am," I insist, trying to still the tremble in my voice. "I'm here to shop." I pull the credit card from my top and brandish it at her. "See?" I say, the volume of my voice escalating. "I have money to spend. On…on Mantissa. On whatever the hell I want."

She backs toward a marble counter, which must be where the transactions take place. "Miss, you have fifteen seconds to leave before I press the security button. After that, you'll have just as long before the Edenvale Police arrive."

My eyes widen. "You're serious. Aren't you?" I ask incredulously.

She snakes behind the counter. "You're down to five seconds, miss." Her eyes narrow. "Four… three…"

I stumble back through the door and bolt to where X dropped me off, pulling at the handle of the door. It's locked. Tears stream down my face as I yank at the door again and again until I feel strong hands grip my shoulders.

I scream as X spins me to face him.

He is my ally. He is my ally. He is my ally.

"I'm done shopping," I gasp between sobs. "I want to go home."

He nods and unlocks the door, helping me inside.

When he is back behind the driver's seat, he speaks in a calm, soothing voice.

"When you're ready, Ruby, I want you to tell me what happened."

But I shake my head.

"I will fix this," he adds, and then he picks up a mobile phone. He doesn't close the partition between us, so I hear every word.

"Your Highness, something unexpected has occurred." Pause. "Yes, I did exactly as we'd discussed." Pause. "No, she is too upset to speak. But I know how to make things right. Miss Mantissa owes me a favor. If she is in town, I can have her bring over a collection of samples." Another pause. "Yes, Highness. To the cottage this evening. It shall be done."

The call ends, and X pulls away from Belladonna Square, his eyes focused on the road.

"They treated you poorly in the store, yes?" Rage is clear in his voice.

I sniffle. "Yes."

"You told them I had called ahead, that you were on official palace business?"

"She didn't give me a chance." My tone is biting. "Maybe you didn't mean to shame me, X. But she did. I had money to spend, and her only intention was to make me feel worthless."

His jaw tightens. The muscle flexes at some deep, hidden emotion.

"I am deeply sorry, Ruby. You of all people did not deserve such treatment. I did not think…" He sighs. "Prince Benedict will join you this evening in the cottage for a private shopping spree of sorts."

I force a smile at this while wondering what he means by me of all people.

"It's okay," I say. "If she's not in town or whatever. I have other clothes back at my place..." My voice trails off. Because I was looking forward to this, to being a princess for a day.

But it took only seconds for that woman to remind me that she saw me as nothing more than a whore.

"You deserve better than what happened just now," X says in his mysterious tone.

I used to think that, too, but it's getting harder and harder to believe.

CHAPTER FOUR

Benedict

THE LAST RAYS of the sun blaze across the western horizon as I pad across the palace grounds, ignoring the royal pond with the swan-shaped pleasure boats, the marble fountains filled with ancient Greek and Roman statuary, and the lush hedges clipped into geometric shapes.

Earlier, X filled me in on Ruby's disastrous visit to Belladonna Square, and I'm still pissed. She was judged on an excursion meant to bring her innocent pleasure.

Acid gnaws at my core from my hypocrisy. After all, she's an escort on my payroll, which makes no part of our relationship innocent even if my motives are pure.

The first star appears as I enter the maze. Left. Left. Straight. Right. My footsteps are unerring, the result of a childhood spent chasing Nikolai through these twists and turns, and later both of us running from our youngest brother, Damien, who hurled himself forward, always intent on keeping up, even if it resulted in trip after trip to the infirmary for broken bones.

Damien.

Reckless. Impatient. Unstoppable. A force of nature. Nikolai and I had loved him, perhaps getting him into more trouble than befitting a much younger brother, but always getting him out of it again.

His birth ended our mother's life, yet no one could look upon our youngest brother's face and fail to see the arrogant, brutal features of my father, the king. My Damien may be many things, but no one would ever call *him* a bastard.

Unlike me...

These days, however, we see him only in paparazzi photos. After he bedded our stepsister— also Nikolai's first betrothed—he was banished from Edenvale. His portraits were removed from the halls. The press has a field day with his wild exploits. His fistfights in high-end nightclubs. His drinking binges. His tumultuous romantic affairs. His devotion to fast cars and racing.

My frown deepens as a shadow ahead takes shape, merging into the form of a man.

"Your Highness." X dips his head in his curt version of a bow. No obsequious gestures for him.

"Jesus." I am startled into taking the Lord's name in vain. "Where did you materialize from, thin air?"

A smug smile serves as his response. "Miss Ruby

anticipates your arrival. You will find Monique has treated her well. And I will see to it that the saleswoman who mistreated your guest is aware of the commission she lost."

The cobblestone gardener's cottage rises behind his broad shoulder, a scene from a storybook come to life, a dwelling that would look at home in one of Grimm's very own fairy tales. Every light is ablaze inside the small round windows. My Adam's apple bobs. What will I confront inside? Scraps of lace? Strategically placed silk? Leather?

It takes all my self-control to walk with a steady, measured pace. A young but capable-looking guard stands watch at his post. I recognize him as Gideon from the front gate watchtower, the one with the large strawberry birthmark on one cheek. Good. I'd ordered X to make sure Ruby remains protected during her sojourn, mostly from curious interlopers as our grounds are well fortified. Gideon's inquiring gaze veers in my direction as I rap on the door.

It swings open in an instant. An older woman, raven hair styled in an intricate chignon, sweeps into a curtsy. Monique Mantissa. "Miss Ruby is ready for your inspection." She sidles past me and out into the maze with a throaty giggle. "I believe that you will be most pleased with her selections."

"Allow me to entertain you while the prince makes his examination?" X's voice betrays no hint of innuendo, and yet the fashion designer's breathless sigh is audible as the door snicks shut.

My eyes adjust to the light. The air is rich with perfume: roses, jasmine and lilac penetrate my senses. A floorboard squeaks in the next room. I step forward, steeling myself for sin incarnate.

A fire roars in the hearth, the same color as her shimmering golden silk and lustrous hair. Out of all the possible sights, I never imagined to discover Ruby dressed in a formal gown, looking every ounce as regal as any queen in Europe.

She truly is a jewel.

Ruby

Heat warms my cheeks as the prince drinks me in with his eyes.

"It's too much," I say. "I told them it was too much. I'm not meant to wear—"

"That gown was made for you and you alone," he says, no hint of irony in his tone. No condescension or judgment. I'm not entirely sure what to do with that.

"Is there no pretense with you, Your Highness?" His dark brows furrow, the reaction endearing. "You say what you mean, mean what you say. You don't let any of the bullshit get in the way." I gasp and cover my mouth. "My apologies, Father."

He smiles and shakes his head. "That won't be necessary. Ruby, this is your home for the next month. I want you to feel safe to be yourself here."

No big deal. Just be myself and find some paint-

ing for the Madam. I try to tell myself this isn't a betrayal of my new benefactor but rather a step closer
to saving Jasper. It's not as if I'm going to do anything to the portrait. I just have to let the Madam
know it's here and where it is. What happens then
is beyond me.

I give the prince a once-over—my whole pre-
posterous situation rolling out before me—and then
burst out laughing. And there he goes again with the
crinkled brow, completely disarming me and making me forget, at least for now, how I ended up here
in the first place.

Damn this man for looking so beautiful when
he's befuddled.

"It would already be a tall order to ask me to be
myself while residing among royalty. But I'm meant
to spend the majority of my time here with not only
a prince but one who—though not yet a man of the
cloth—dresses like he's forever on a pulpit about to
give a sermon."

I'm still giggling when he does something so out
of character that it stops my laughter and catches my
breath all at once.

He smiles.

The whole kingdom—and the entire world for
that matter—has been known to swoon for the king's
firstborn, Prince Nikolai. They loved him when he
was a tabloid playboy, and now that he's proved himself worthy of ruling Edenvale, as well as worthy of
his future queen, the public swoons for him even

more, myself included. Nikolai Lorentz is a beautiful man who will do great things. But before me stands the man who has always lived in his shadow—who keeps himself there by hiding behind a collar before it is truly his.

And he's the most beautiful man I've ever seen.

"You're wrong, Ruby. This," he says, pointing to the white collar, "is my pretense." He unfastens it and pulls it free.

I smooth out a nonexistent wrinkle in the buttery-soft silk of my gown. "When you take your final vows—" something twists in my gut at the thought "—do you have to wear it all the time?"

Again he grins, though this time the expression is laced with a wistfulness I don't understand.

"No," he says. "Giving my life to the church is my duty. But presiding over the church is also my livelihood. When I'm not performing clerical duties, I'm free to dress as I please." He glances at his attire and then shrugs. "I guess this is easier."

Then he unbuttons his black shirt and removes it. I gasp until I realize that beneath it he wears a white cotton T.

"There," he says, hanging the garment over a high-back leather chair that faces the fire. "No more pretense." He then strolls to a tall oak cabinet against the wall. With wide eyes, I watch the sculpted muscles in his arms flex as he retrieves a decanter of red wine and two crystal goblets. The prince nods toward a small game table, ignoring the clothes strewn about the sofa.

"You can...drink?" I ask, and he laughs, a rich, deep sound that sends an unexpected shiver through me, goose bumps dotting my flesh.

He sets the items on the table and pulls out my chair for me.

"There are many things I can still do once I am a priest," he says. "But, of course—some I cannot."

His eyes darken before they dip to the table as he seats himself across from me. When he looks up again, he forces a smile, but I know the spell is broken, and it's time to get to work. I reach behind and start to lower my zipper.

"Stop," he says. "Not yet."

Because he is my prince and also my employer, I obey.

He pours two goblets of wine and hands one to me.

"Ruby." His voice is gentle. "I'm sorry for what happened in the Square this morning. That was unacceptable."

I press my lips together and shrug. "I didn't belong there," I say matter-of-factly.

He sips his wine and shakes his head. "You belong wherever it is that you want to be."

My throat tightens, and because I don't know how to respond, I take a long, slow swallow of the expensive crimson liquid, as well.

"I hope you did enjoy your private shopping spree of sorts, though."

I grin and stand, offering an exaggerated curtsy in my favorite of all the pieces Monique Mantissa herself gave to me.

"I felt like a princess," I say. "Thank you, Your Highness."

He clears his throat. "Benedict. Please, call me Benedict."

Sure. He's just a guy in my borrowed home, a guy in a great-fitting T-shirt that hugs an always hidden muscular frame, yet he's not hiding it from me. Still, he is more than just Benedict. I can pretend many things, but I cannot ignore his lineage—or my own.

"This gown is beautiful," I tell him. "But for what you've hired me to do, well..." I reach for my zipper again and pull to where it stops just below my hips. I stand, and the dress falls to the floor, revealing what I've been hiding.

No bra. No panties.

"No more pretense," I tell him, and though he stares at me with ravenous eyes, this feels nothing like the ogling, the leering of what I expect from a client. At twenty-two years old, I am not without experience when it comes to men, but that does not mean I ever thought this would be easy. But the prince is nothing like I expected.

I am comfortable—safe beneath his gaze. Whatever happens next, I trust the man before me.

After laying the gown neatly atop the pile of other Mantissa samples, I take my seat across from him, sip from my goblet and note the varying drawers in the small table. I open one up and pull from it a deck of cards. My teeth skim across my bottom lip. Then I smile and raise a brow.

"So, Benedict." I draw out his name, getting a feel for it on my tongue. "Would you like to play a game?"

CHAPTER FIVE

Benedict

RUBY CUTS THE card deck as my features settle into a bemused poker face.

"Truth or dare, my prince?" Her teasing tone intoxicates. Her nipples are the color of raspberries, a ripe red that ignites my appetite.

I've barely taken a sip of the vintage in my hand, yet the room feels like it does a slow spin. I dig my heels into the wool rug and fight back the growing sense of vertigo.

"You know this game?" Her mouth quirks. "Or were you too busy playing polo and competing in fencing tournaments as a child?"

"I preferred the contact sports, boxing and mixed martial arts." I set down my goblet and meet her surprised gaze. "And I choose truth."

Her brows furrow in concentration. "Hmm." She props two cards together, then adds a third and fourth. It takes a moment to realize what she is doing—building a house of cards.

Higher and higher her flimsy walls rise until she pauses, twirling a Queen of Hearts between her fingers. "Have you ever seen a naked woman in the flesh?"

"No." My voice is cool as a glacier. I refuse to play the role of a clumsy, naive schoolboy. This imperious mask is second nature, my default setting since I was a boy. How many years have I worn it? Probably since the time that I informed my private tutor that someday I intended to do great things, lead the Edenvale armies, explore distant jungles, fulfill any number of mad ambitions a young, imaginative boy might nurture.

Except Father had been listening from the doorway to our palace classroom. That night he had me escorted to the monastery that borders our palace ground, and there, in the nave of St. Germain, backdropped by the mournful sound of Gregorian chants, the head monk informed me that my path in life was chosen. He spoke of the honor I would bring our kingdom by serving as the spiritual advisor to the king himself.

He made it clear in no uncertain terms that this was the role of the second son, and that if I were to stray or reject the family tradition, it would break my father's heart.

Those were the words that he used.

Break. My father's. Heart.

I knew our mother's death during Damien's birth must have cracked that organ into a million pieces.

There was no chance that I'd be the one to deliver the death blow.

And so ever since, I've walked the straight and narrow without complaint. I have striven to do what is right, what is expected.

Until now.

"You are serious?" Ruby's eyes widen curiously. "Never?" Her legs part and she runs her fingers up her smooth inner thighs. My heart threatens to break through the bars of my rib cage. "Are you saying that you're an innocent, my sweet prince?"

A pause. "A virgin in the flesh." Not the mind.

Ruby's pussy is bare, utterly devoid of hair—soft, pink and fucking perfect. The second coming could begin outside the windows, and my gaze would stay fixed on her slick skin, the dew sheening the slit between her lips.

"Want to touch?" She flicks the tip of her finger over her mound.

"You know that I cannot." My voice is hoarse.

"But do you want to?" A sliver of curiosity enters her tone, as if she is actually interested in what I want. As if she is doing more than going through the motions of her profession. She is talented, indeed, to make me believe such illusions.

"Yes," I hiss through gritted teeth.

"How?" she pushes. "How would you touch me if you gave in to the temptation?"

I try to maintain my composure with a measured

breath, telling myself that voicing what I want is no more than putting words to a thought. It is not the act.

"So light at first," I say, "that you almost wouldn't know I was making contact, like a brushstroke and your body was a canvas. A butterfly wing against summer's first rose."

Her eyes widen, as if I've struck a hidden nerve, but then she relaxes into that coy smile again. "You wouldn't want to claim me?" There is a challenge lurking there. "Graffiti your name? Mark your territory with greedy thrusts?"

I shake my head. "I'd rather bring you pleasure."

She freezes, staring at me as if transfixed. "But why?"

"Because if it is good for you, it would be good for me," I say simply. "My pleasure must hinge on yours." I don't know why, but instinctively I understand that it's the way that I am wired.

A shudder runs through her as she lowers her lashes. "Mmmmm. My prince, you do say all the right things. For a man not experienced in the ways of the flesh, you certainly are getting me all worked up with just your words. Look how wet I am. It feels so good." She rolls her hand with wanton abandon, dips her fingers deeper inside until they circle an engorged, rosy bud. "So wickedly good." She pauses, arching a brow. "Dare me to offer you a taste?" She drags her hand free, shows me her glistening fingers.

Saints take my immortal soul. I burn as if with a fever.

But I sense she is hiding, that she's back to showmanship.

I wonder if she'd enjoy being stripped of her defenses?

I clear my throat. "You take a taste. Describe your flavor."

"Sir?" She pauses, hesitant, a flush heating her own cheeks.

I've caught her off guard. A flare of pleasure rushes through my veins. I get up from the small game table and saunter to the fireplace, resting my elbow on the mantel. "You heard me."

She obeys, and my own pleasure grows sharper than I'd imagined it could.

Ever so slowly, she raises her fingers to her mouth, full lips parting as she sucks on the tips with a deliberate lick.

Hunger flares in me. The tenor of the room shifts. Her coy, artful smile is lost, replaced by a look of shock. Of wonder. Her pupils grow wide, and a flush spreads in the delicate skin between her breasts.

"Describe it."

Her breath hitches at the dominating timbre of my voice. Her gaze turns thoughtful. Inward. And I know she is going to give me the truth.

"Sweet," she begins slowly, "almost like wildflower honey." Her voice is a shy whisper. "But slightly spicy with a salty tang."

My tongue presses against my teeth. It's absurd how natural this feels—me, fully clothed and standing, towering over a naked woman pleasuring herself at my command. It's like opening up a door and walking into a part of myself that's always been here, waiting for me to find the way. "Keep going," I grind out. "Tell me your darkest fantasy."

"You've already had a turn," she says with a fake pout. "I did the dare." Her hands are already sliding back as if of their own accord, spreading her most secret part, revealing every inch of the tantalizing landscape to my view. She is so wet I can hear it, the sucking slide of her fingers. Perhaps she has done this five hundred times to five hundred different men, but tonight, in this moment, she is mine.

And if her soaking wet pussy is any indication, she loves every second.

The fire beats against my legs but is a cool breeze compared to the blaze in my cock.

"This is my game now, angel. My rules." My voice is kind but inflexible. The log in the hearth hisses and pops, but hellfire doesn't scare me, not now when salvation lies between Ruby's parted legs. "I want you to expose not only your body to me, but also your mind."

Her thick lashes flutter. "You do?"

I incline my head. "I have a theory that you might be as desirable on the inside as on the outside. So tell me…" I lower my voice an octave. "What fantasy makes your thighs quiver, your nipples tighten into tight, aching peaks? Let me inside. Let me see."

"What?" Her voice quavers, her toes curl against the thick wool rug. "What do you want to see?"

I cross the small room as if in a dream. Then I'm standing above her, my hand tilting her chin, ensuring her gaze is fixed on me and me alone. "A glimpse of your soul."

Ruby

He holds a hand out to me, and I take it, letting him guide me from the chair, out of the hearth room—and to my bed. With a look, he tells me to lie on the plush duvet as he moves toward the rocking chair under the window.

"Relax," he says softly. "Close your eyes and let me inside you the only way I am permitted to do so. Show me what you'd want me to give you if only I could."

I swallow hard and nod, my chest tightening at the unexpected emotions brewing within me—my core burning with unbridled need.

This is not what I expected. Everything up until now has been a show. But what he's asking...

"Touch yourself, angel. Touch and tell me what it is you desire."

I think of his words, that his touch would be like brushstrokes on a canvas. He couldn't have known. Could he? That painting is my passion, but this—using my body for money—is the only way to save my family.

My lips part as my finger circles them softly. "I want featherlight kisses to start. Ones that tell me with each sweep of his mouth on mine that I am what matters. That for all I do to protect those I love, there is someone out there whose one true desire is to protect me. To love me."

The truth falls from my lips without pretense, and I don't know where it is coming from. I've never said any such thing aloud...to anyone.

"Continue," Benedict says, breaking the silence. So I do.

"His kisses trail down my neck to my breasts." I give one of my nipples a soft pinch and gasp. "He takes me into his mouth, his teeth nipping, tongue swirling." I lick my thumb and forefinger, rolling them around the peaked nipple of my other breast, pinching harder this time. My pelvis bucks upward, and I moan. "More," I say. "I tell him I need more, that the teasing is driving me mad, and the kisses continue, lower and lower. They are still soft, still sweet, and though he hungers for me, he is in control. And he will tease because as much as I beg, he knows I love every second of it."

I've never let my imagination run away like this. Fantasies aren't anything I have the luxury to think about, let alone voice.

My thumb presses my swollen clit, still teasing just as I wish he would—as I wish Benedict could— and I writhe.

"More," I whimper. "Oh God, more. Benedict, I need more!"

I gasp but keep my eyes squeezed shut. Because in my mind—in this never-before-realized dream— it is he who kneels over me. It is his hand between my legs, his fingers aching to pump inside me. It's this stranger who allowed me to sleep like a queen last night and dress like a princess today.

Prince Benedict wants to know my soul.

I know better than to think this fantasy could ever be realized by a celibate prince, by a man who does not get to touch, let alone love.

But for tonight I can pretend.

"Please. Benedict." I say his name again, using the cloak of darkness behind closed lids as my safety.

"Take control, angel," he says, his deep, velvety voice carrying an unmistakable ache. "Show me what you want me to do."

I suck two fingers down to the knuckle and then plunge them, wet, between my legs, sinking deep into my warmth.

I cry out.

The show is over. This is so real I can feel it in every nerve, every pulse of blood through my veins. So I do the unthinkable and open my eyes, propping myself up on my free elbow, so my stare locks with his.

His eyes burn into mine, veritable flames igniting something in me that refuses to be extinguished. As my fingers pump harder, his hands grip the armrests of the chair, knuckles white and nails digging into the wood.

"This is what I'd have you do. With your hands. Your mouth. Your cock." I slide my fingers out, drenched in my own arousal, and swirl them fiercely around my clit. My head falls back, and the arm that supports my weight begins to shake. "I can't—" I say. "I can't last much longer. Make me come," I plead. "Make me fucking come, Benedict!" My voice is not my own. It is something savage, a need I didn't know existed until now.

"I cannot," he says, but the words are a primal growl.

"Do it!" I command, my eyes on his again. "With your words, Benedict. Just your words. Tell me what you would do to finish me off. They are nothing more than innocent words."

He leans forward, hands still glued to the armrests, and I can see that his pupils have grown so large his eyes look black. "Fuck." He grits his teeth. "Fuck."

But he says nothing more. So I collapse on the bed, one hand spreading myself open for him to see, the other sending me over the edge and into oblivion.

I don't hold back. I don't stifle my scream as I fill myself with one finger, then two, then three until I buck against my palm.

When I finally slide my hand free with a shudder, I lie there, limp and languid from the most perplexing orgasm I've ever experienced.

What does it mean that I enjoyed what just happened…or that I wanted it to be his hands on me instead of my own? I was prepared to give him a good show, but instead, despite the undeniable pleasure of the evening, I'm left wanting more.

"That was…different," I say, my voice back to its soft lilt. "I've never done anything like that before. I assure you." I laugh, my eyes still shut, lids heavy as the aftermath threatens to carry me off to sleep before he can respond.

I open my eyes to gauge the prince's reaction, to congratulate him on his restraint.

But the chair is empty. And when I hear the front door slam, I wonder if the first night of our arrangement will be the last.

Because Benedict is gone.

CHAPTER SIX

Benedict

I KNEEL IN front of the high altar of the royal chapel. The tabernacle is open, exposing the Eucharist, the consecrated bread transmogrified into the body of Christ. I need him to see what I have done this night, reveled in lust, taken pleasure in bending a woman to my will, woken my dormant craving for sexual domination. As Ruby undulated in her sheets, her pale skin flush with the intensity of her orgasm, a single refrain played through my mind.

What would her wet pussy feel like throbbing around my own fingers?

Would she enjoy it as much as what she'd just done to herself? Would I?

"No!" I don't realize that I've spoken out loud until the word echoes through the marble-walled nave. Even now, even here, my thoughts are polluted. I cover my hands over my face. How can I be what my duty demands? Why can't I conquer these urges?

If I stray from my path, where will it lead?

A frustrated moan escapes my gritted teeth. I am so fucking weak.

"Can I be of assistance?"

I'm on my feet before my next breath, hands braced against the altar rails. "Who said that?" The voice comes from near the pulpit. Could it be the miracle I'm looking for, the gift of salvation? "Lord? Is that you?"

The low, deep chuckle is familiar. X steps from the shadows. "Careful, Highness," he says with a wry smile. "You want to give me a God complex?"

"Where'd you come from?" I snap, embarrassed at my error.

"Couldn't sleep, and you were otherwise…occupied." He shrugs. "So I took a stroll through the catacombs."

I blink. "Where?"

He saunters down the altar steps and sits in the first pew, crossing a foot over his knee. As always, he is dressed in an impeccable suit. It would be tempting to dismiss him as continuing to have fun at my expense, but the dust coating his hair makes his salt-and-pepper locks appear saltier than normal.

"The ancient catacombs beneath the chapel. As far as I can tell, they've been sealed up since the early seventeenth century by your nine-times great-grandfather King Ivor the Protector."

I cross my arms. "I haven't been down there. We

were thought too young to attend my mother's funeral."

He gives me a look of sympathy. "Many of the tunnels are in disrepair, and I encountered a rat the size of a cocker spaniel. That's when I exited through a secret passage here beneath the high altar beside the statue of Saint Everly, the patroness of our realm."

X has been a fixture of the castle since I was a teenager. And yet he is an utter mystery to me. "What were you doing there if it is so dangerous?"

"The more interesting question is whether you are enjoying the company of Miss Ruby. You might not be aware that she comes from The Jewel Box, a Rosegate pleasure house valued for its discretion but also quality. All the girls there go by the names of precious stones." He gives his chin a musing rub. "I've had the good fortune to while away many a pleasant afternoon with a most diverting escort named Pearl. She used to insist on wearing nipple clamps and would do anything to get a chance to go under my flogger."

I am ashamed to realize that I know little about Miss Ruby. I can describe every inch of her perfect body, but I haven't the first clue about her actual life. I clear my throat, deciding to hide my discomfiture behind a question. "You consort with escorts regularly?"

My bodyguard is an enigma. I knew my brother was a favorite of the ladies, but apparently, when it came to his most trusted bodyguard, the apple didn't fall far from the tree.

Not for the first time, I wonder why he requested a transfer to my security detail.

X's laughter is amused, not unkind. "I consort with women regularly. Some of them are escorts. Some are not. All of them are quite skilled at...consorting."

I stare blankly for a few seconds, struggling to process his words. Again, I can't help but wonder, Who is this guy? Like Ruby, I have never wondered much about X's past. He was my brother's bodyguard, but it seems there is more than meets the eye. The tabernacle bores into my spine, the eyes of the Lord waiting to judge my next move. I have questions that require answers, but I can't ask them in here.

"We will continue this conversation out of the church."

I stride toward the thick carved doors as X replies, "Very good, sir."

Outside, the night air is crisp. The wind blowing over the surrounding snowcapped peaks cool my heated face, but I won't lie to myself. My shiver has nothing to do with the temperature.

"You do not tie yourself to one woman?" I know not everyone believes in monogamy. My elder brother, Nikolai, certainly didn't...until he met his Kate that is.

X adjusts his tie, his expression blank. "I am not opposed to...tying," he says, the corner of his mouth quirked into a knowing grin. "But I'm normally the one who makes the knots."

Envy hits me with blunt force. "The stories you could tell," I mutter, but my tone does not escape him.

"I know you are well-read, but there is something to be said for experience, for true knowledge. You aren't a priest yet, Your Highness."

Though X is overstepping, I do not call him on it. Instead, I swallow hard at the idea. I have so many questions. They press against my skull, threatening to crack the bone.

I want to know more, but I need to resist.

"The choice of celibacy is not one to take lightly," X says, his voice firm. "You can yield to her. There is no harm in seeing what you'd be missing."

But I can't afford to give in to the bonfire of my sexual urges. If I do, I might burn down my carefully scripted future. Instead, I turn wordlessly and escape back to my tower that tonight feels more like a prison than ever before.

Ruby

The drowsy aftermath of my orgasm is replaced by something unsettling, something that not only keeps me from sleep but drives me from the cottage altogether. The summer night is cool, but my body is still alight from the mere thought of Benedict's touch, so

I wear nothing but a long silk dressing gown, another gift from Monique Mantissa.

Thanks to X's coaching this afternoon, I've learned my way out of the maze—well, with only having to backtrack twice. I'd say that's pretty impressive for my first day. Though the sun has long set, the brilliant moon lights the palace grounds in a soft glow. I make my way to the gardens behind the palace itself, not sure what I'm hoping to find. Benedict on an evening stroll, trying to clear his thoughts just as I am? But all is quiet but for the guards on patrol. I stare up at the tower where I know the prince resides, and for a second I consider climbing that spiral staircase and knocking on his door.

For what? He does not want to see you. That is why he left.

Yet I cannot deny that I wish to see him.

Instead, I decide to give him space. Back at the cottage, I can call Camille to check in, see if we have any new leads on Jasper's case. This, I remind myself, is why I am here. For my family.

So I make a hasty retreat. Once there, it takes me only one try to get through the maze and to the cottage. I only now realize there is no guard on patrol at this hour, and once I'm inside, that unsettling chill returns. Though this time it is different.

Something is different. I can feel it. And it is in my room where I find it.

I flip on the light, the space brighter than it was before, and then realize Benedict and I were lit only by the moon. The rocking chair, the one from which he watched me—was it not closer to the window before? Benedict himself had leaned forward for a better view, but had he actually moved the chair?

I circle the benign piece of furniture, sure that there was no room to step behind it before, and a floorboard creaks, a sound I should have heard had Benedict rocked against it.

I bend to examine it, and the wooden slat comes up easily in my hand.

I scramble backward, gasping at what cannot be real, but I peek over into the open space again and see not the foundation of an architectural structure but what looks like a cavernous hole with no end.

Then, as if from the bowels of hell, comes the terrifying yet distant sound of a woman's triumphant laughter.

Without another thought, I am running—out the door, through the maze and straight to where I swore I would not go. I don't even remember climbing the stairs when I'm already pounding on his door. Maybe I hallucinated it. Maybe the sound was just the wind. But my skin is covered in goose bumps and my heart is threatening to crack my sternum.

"Benedict!" I cry, no time for propriety. "Benedict, please. Open the door!"

In seconds he is there, bare but for cotton pajama pants, his chest beaded with sweat, but I'm too frightened to react to his body the way I know I would have only a short time ago.

"Ruby," he says, his eyes widening. "What is it?"

I hug my torso, shivering now—from the chill in the air? Fear? I'm not even sure.

"Did you go to the cottage?" I ask, hoping for logic to rearrange my frantic thoughts. "Did you go to my room?"

His brows furrow, and he shakes his head.

"I— After you left, I went for a walk. And…" I take a shuddering breath. After what my life has become these past two months, I'm starting to trust that things will only get worse. "I think someone broke in while I was gone."

A muscle in his jaw ticks. He looks over his shoulder and then at me.

"Come in," he says. "You are safe here." He steps aside and closes the door. "Follow me."

He moves in front of me, and I gasp as he leads me from the entryway, as my eyes rest on the raised welts that cover his back.

He says nothing until we are in a modest bed-chamber. The walls are bare but for a crucifix on the wall by a lone window. The bed is large but without any trappings of royalty. Just plain white sheets and a quilt. He sits me on the edge of the bed and moves a good distance from me, crossing his arms.

"Tell me what happened," he says, not bothering to acknowledge the new elephant in the room.

"Tell me what happened to you," I say.

He sighs. "Nothing," he says softly. "Nothing more than purging myself of my guilt."

My hand flies to my mouth as I stifle another gasp.

"My tormented soul isn't your concern, Ruby. I hired you to do a job, and you performed as expected. Now tell me what you are doing here."

His words bite, though I know they shouldn't. They are nothing more than the truth.

"When I got home," I tell him, "something felt wrong. And when I went to my room, the chair—your chair—was not where you'd left it. At least, I don't think it was." As I speak, I realize I sound less convincing by the second. But then I remember the floorboard. "There was a squeaky piece of wood in the floor behind the chair, and I thought it odd that it hadn't sounded when you were there, because I swear your chair was right over it, so I pulled it up and—"

"Let me guess. And you found the catacombs?" He raises a brow and grins.

I stand up in a huff. "I just ran here frightened for my life, and you're joking around?" I ask. The idea of laughter seems too ridiculous to mention. It must have been the wind and my own overactive imagination.

I turn to storm out, realizing I won't find comfort here, but Benedict grabs my wrist.

"Wait," he says.

I face him but say nothing more.

"There is a chance I may have moved my chair closer to you." His expression darkens. "I don't remember. You bewitched me with that show you put on—inserting me into your fantasy. I probably couldn't have told you what day it was while I was in that room, let alone whether or not I moved a chair."

"But the catacombs? That dark hole under the floor?"

He nods, a soft smile taking over his features. "There is not only a maze above the ground but one beneath it, as well. They run from under the palace to the far reaches of the grounds. I assure you that is all you saw beneath the cottage, and I can almost assure you it was I who moved the chair."

I sigh, and he finally drops my wrist. "I guess that all makes sense." And it does, though I'm still uneasy. "I guess... I'll head back and go to sleep."

He reaches for my cheek but stops short.

"You are still frightened."

I nod.

"Then you will sleep here." He gestures toward the bed. "I was going to sleep on the floor anyway," he adds.

At this, I want to reach for him, to ask him to forgive himself for nothing more than wanting what he cannot have. But I know that will only cause him further distress. And because I do not want to be alone in what now feels like too strange of a place, I agree.

"I do have one condition," I say, and he bows his head slowly. "You need to let me tend to your wounds. There are so many bruises." For a moment I wonder if this is the hardest he's punished himself yet. "I don't want you marred on my account." He opens his mouth to protest, but I shake my head. "Let me—let me do something good," I say.

His shoulders relax, and he points toward the direction from where we came. "The bathing room is on the left. You will find supplies in there, healing salves and such."

I smile and turn toward the door, and that's when I see what's on the wall...what wasn't in my line of sight when we entered the room.

This is what I was sent to find, but now that I see it, I realize that whatever the story is behind the painting, it's more than I anticipated.

It is not only the image of an angel...but it is one who wears my face.

CHAPTER SEVEN

Benedict

THERE IS A loud thump as my bedroom door slams shut. I whirl around to find Ruby crumpled against it, hands pressed to her face, her cheeks drained of all color.

"What is it?" I demand. My heart is in my throat. She seemed fine a moment ago, composed even.

"The portrait…" She keels forward as if to swoon. "You own one of Vernazza's Guardian Angels paintings?"

I blink slowly, unable to comprehend the depth of emotion in her voice. "You're a fan of Giuseppe Vernazza's work?" Vernazza was regarded as the great artist of our age until his unfortunate death a decade ago, losing control of his car and wrapping it around a tree along the Nightgardin border. A waste to lose such a gifted prodigy before his time.

Her laugh is without humor and goes on and on, the hysterical edge slashing my peace of mind. "You could say that," she gasps. "Vernazza was my father. Look closer at the painting. Tell me, does it remind you of anyone?"

I transfer my gaze from her beautiful face to that of the angel, the one that has so often served as both my temptation and my salvation—and my heart gives a dull thud. What a fool I have been not to see what was right under my nose. Ruby's face…the angel's face, good God, they are one and the same. No wonder she appeared so familiar the moment she removed the wig. My insides churn.

"He painted my features as he imagined they would one day look. His imagination came close to the truth, right?"

It's as if my world has flipped its axis and down is up and up is down. "I didn't know."

How could I have been so blind?

"Of course not." She winds her arms around her legs, hugs her knees to her chest. "Who would imagine the daughter of Europe's most famous painter since Pablo Picasso would make a living by selling her body?"

"Why do *you* work for The Jewel Box?"

Her eyes darken. "My father died."

"Rest his soul." I make the sign of the cross. "A terrible accident. I shall pray for him."

"Accident?" She pushes herself to standing, her features fierce, shining with hidden fire. "My father drove that same route between Nightgardin and Rosegate at least once a week to deal with patrons.

He took expert care of that car. No. That wasn't a mere accident that claimed his life. The weather was calm. The sun shining. He was murdered. Someone tampered with his brakes!"

My shoulder blades slam together. "You have proof?"

A sob escapes her. "Only the truth in my heart. There is no proof. No motive. Mother died not long after my birth, and all I had after Father was my brother. J-J-J-Jasper." As the name leaves her tongue, her weeping grows.

"Jasper Vernazza." I frown. "This name, it's familiar to me."

"His fate wasn't as dramatic as Father's. He still lives, if you can call being locked in a cage like an animal a life. He was a minor news story this past year until we lost his case and they locked him up. He was an art historian caught stealing a painting from my father's collection in the Musée des Beaux-Arts. They say he wanted to sell it to a black market dealer in Hong Kong, but my brother reveres museums and Father's legacy. It doesn't make sense." She wipes her eyes. "The portrait he was accused of stealing was another angel, actually. My father painted a whole series of them."

"And each one is superb. I've studied his works." I've seen most of them over the years. They are all of Ruby's dreamy, heavenly face contrasted with a different hyperrealistic dystopian cityscape.

"My brother was set up, I just don't know why."

With one shuddering inhalation she composes herself. "Anyway, this is not your concern. I remember your library. Art is not the only thing you study. You are fascinated by tales of pleasure, as well. I swear on my life you know more about the erotic arts than Madam herself."

I nod. "I seek to understand beauty, for to know beauty is to know the face of God." Strange. Until this moment I've never articulated this idea, either in thoughts or words.

She ducks her chin, a little shy, and stares up between her curtain of golden hair. "And to you, pleasure is beautiful?"

"I believe there is a sacred union of the body and soul when it comes to sex." I begin to pace, assuming the tone of the professor, not a stretch considering I hold a PhD in Sacred Theology from the University of Edenvale. "Sexuality has the power to be as explosive as dynamite, and when used properly, it can be a tool that moves mountains. And if used improperly, it can grow volatile and wreak untold destruction."

Her brows knit. "Yet you deny yourself."

"I have what you could call an arranged marriage," I say wryly. "My intended bride is to be the church."

She lets out a frustrated huff, opening the door and disappearing for a moment. There is a rustling from the bathroom, and she emerges clutching a small vial. "I found arnica." She uncorks the lid and takes a tentative sniff. "It appears to be mixed with lavender oil."

"A medicinal ointment." I nod my head. "Useful to treat all manner of aches and pains."

"Let me do this." She clutches the bottle, eyes wide. "Heal you."

I take a step backward and find myself in a corner. "Why do you want to?"

"Because I think you are a good man. And the marks on your back make me want to cry. They also make me angry at God because why would He demand you to punish yourself for feelings that you admit are natural?"

"Sacrifice is holy," I tell her, repeating the lessons I've been taught my whole life.

"If lust is an impulse that must be literally beaten from your flesh, then you are giving God something that is unclean, unholy. Why would He want such an offering?"

I bite the inside of my cheek, impressed at the depth of her impassioned response. "You'd make quite the scholar, Miss Vernazza."

"Don't call me that," she snaps. "Not anymore. Now I am simply Ruby." She strides forward, pouring ointment into her open palm. "And you are trying to distract me from my task like a naughty patient. Sit." Her tone brokers no dissent.

I move to a wooden chair and sink to the seat.

"Let's see how extensive the damage is." She peruses my back, her long hair tickling my bare skin.

Her silence stretches for the length of a minute. "Benedict," she says, my name a sigh from her lips. "So much pain." Her fingertips press on my throbbing skin, the welts from the whip. The lavender scent of the ointment floods my senses, but is nothing compared to the intense vibrations sent out across my flesh from her soft, circular massage.

"Let's see if we can make you feel better," she whispers in my ear.

Ruby

His skin is like fire under my touch, the raised welts tearing at my heart as my fingers travel over each one.

"Benedict," I say, but I don't know what comes next. His name falls so easily from my lips, yet I know the skin I touch blazes not only with the heat of desire but that of intense, overwhelming guilt. It is the skin not just of a man but of royalty; a world in which I do not belong, save for my likeness hanging on his wall.

His head droops.

"Have I hurt you?" I ask, afraid I am doing more harm than good.

He gives his head a soft shake. "The way you say my name," he says.

"I'm sorry," I blurt. "I meant Your Highness."

"No," he assures me. "It is not that." I listen and continue to massage the salve over his wounds. "The way you say Benedict, it makes me feel...known."

"Oh," I say, my hands pausing but never leaving his skin. "I'm not sure what to do with that," I admit.

"Nothing." He lets out a bitter laugh. "Only God can truly know me," he says. "That is my chosen path."

I step around the chair to face him, and he lifts his head.

"Did you really choose that path, Benedict? Or was it chosen for you?"

His green eyes are a storm of emotion, yet his words are the picture of calm.

"How I got here is of no matter," he says. "This is my path, and I shall not stray."

I kneel and place my hands on his thighs. He takes a ragged breath, and I expect him to push me away. But he doesn't. So I decide to push. Not because of what the Madam assigned me to do and not to push Benedict toward failure if, in fact, this is not what he wants. The entire realm envies the royal family, yet I wonder what anyone in a position such as Benedict—or any member of his family for that matter—gets to choose.

"If you had a choice right now," I ask, "if you could have something you wanted that you thought you didn't deserve, what would it be?"

He leans against the chair and winces. He is in more pain than he's letting on.

"Is this more truth or dare?" he asks, forcing himself to smile through the pain, but his feigned attempt at levity does not work on me.

"No games," I say. "We already did that, so I'm technically off the clock. I want you to choose something for you."

He places his hands atop mine, his fingers circling my wrists.

"To voice such a thing would be selfish."

I laugh even as tears prick at my eyes. How many times have I wanted something just for myself only to give it up for someone else? To have the luxury of acting on one selfish wish? I would take it in an instant.

"Then be selfish, Benedict. You are not a priest, not yet. And from what I know of your religion, until you take your final vows, you may do as you please. This is a new millennium. You're young, fairly easy on the eyes." I grin. "You could have any woman you want, and yet you deny yourself. Why?"

He grips me tighter, lifting my palms from his legs.

"To save myself for God," he says through gritted teeth.

"No." I shake my head. "I don't believe that. After what you had me do tonight, I know you want. I know you are tempted. Why not act on those temptations while you can?"

Now he does throw my hands from him, and he springs from the chair, pacing the length of the room. He runs a hand through his hair, tearing at it as he does.

"Benedict," I say, standing and heading toward the wall. "Benedict, you're scaring me."

He stops before me, chest heaving and his emerald eyes wide.

I squeeze my eyes shut and try to burrow into the wall to escape whatever is coming. I have forgotten myself tonight—forgotten who I am and what it is that I do. I have forgotten that this man, this prince, is nothing more than my client, and a displeased client takes his frustrations out on the whore. I have heard the stories. I have seen the aftermath. It's more than a surprising slap across the face from the Madam.

I just didn't think it would happen to me so soon.

"Ruby," he says, his voice as gentle as a whisper, and I open my eyes. My hands are still balled into fists, and I realize I'm holding my breath. "Heavens, Ruby, no. Did you think— I could never—"

A tear escapes the corner of my eye, my fear finally getting the best of me, and he swipes it away with a thumb. Only then do I exhale.

"Madam leaves punishment up to the client. If he is not satisfied…"

But I also factor in her own dissatisfaction—what she will do if I don't let her know about the painting now that I know where it is.

He brushes my hair from my face, each stroke of his hand telling me that he is different. That I am safe.

"I am not a client," he says. "Not for the rest of this evening."

I exhale. "But you were so angry. And it happened

so quickly, I thought... I mean, I was getting myself ready for the worst."

He raises his head to the ceiling—or, most likely, the heavens—and whispers Latin words I do not understand. Then his eyes find mine again. The storm is gone. He is once again the picture of calm.

"There are two reasons why I deny myself the pleasures of the flesh though I've not yet taken my vows. I would like to tell them to you."

He is so close, his woodsy, earthy scent intoxicating me. If he is not a client right now, then what is he? Why is it that in his presence, I long for him to know me, as well?

I nod.

"First," he says, and his hand skims the silk sleeve of my robe until he finds my clenched fist. I relax and let him take my hand in his. "To maintain my virtue until my vows—it is the ultimate test of strength and will. I want to be strong enough for this. I want to give myself to the Lord wholly and completely, which means I will not give myself to another."

"Okay," I say softly, accepting that this is a choice he gets to make, and if anyone can understand that, I can.

"The second reason," he says, his head dipping toward mine, "is that I am terrified to know what I am missing."

"Oh," I say, eyes wide.

"I will not give you my virtue," he says.

"I know."

"But for just a moment, I do want to be selfish."

"What do you want, Benedict?" His nearness is almost too much to bear.

"A kiss," he says.

I know without asking that I will be his first, and I know the slippery slope down which this could lead.

But I want to be selfish, too, just for a moment.

"Take what you want," I tell him.

"First tell me your name. Your real name."

And because I want to be known, too, if only for tonight, I say it.

"Evangeline."

"A beautiful name." He grins. "My angel, Evangeline." And with that, his fingers circle my wrists again, sliding my arms up the wall so he holds my hands over my head. I am captive to my prince, and yet I've never felt more free.

My nipples harden beneath my silk dressing gown, and I cannot ignore the throb between my legs.

His head dips farther until I can feel his warm breath against my skin, and when his lips brush hesitantly against mine, I thank whatever God there is that Benedict is holding me in place, because my knees give out. I whimper, and my prince takes what he needs.

CHAPTER EIGHT

Benedict

I PRESS MY forehead to hers. Evangeline Vernazza. I kiss her again, deeper this time and more urgent. She responds with a hunger not unlike my own, her sweet tongue flicking and caressing mine until I groan. My hands leave hers to tangle in her silky hair. Our breath mingles, feverishly hot.

At last I give in and allow myself to cup one of her perfect breasts, soft as rose petals, and her body bows. So responsive. So passionate. I growl my approval, unable to get enough.

I'll never get enough.

How many times have I flicked through dusty leather-bound books of poetry, scoffing at the over-inflated metaphors and purple prose? Now…now I finally understand those poor poets, and pity everyone who attempted to capture this feeling of two souls merging with mere words.

I dip to kiss her arched neck, trace my tongue

along her pulse. Every inch of me burns, but this does not feel like hell.

No.

This is a heaven I never could have imagined.

Even though my control hangs by the barest thread, I refuse to let it snap. Tonight I have glimpsed what can exist between a man and a woman.

This moment must be enough.

As much as I want to forget the world and burn in her arms, I am bound to my duty, my destiny as the second son to Edenvale's king.

Ruby...no—Evangeline...my sweet angel and un-expected jewel, opens her eyes.

"Why did you stop?" she whispers, brows knitting.

Because if I didn't, I'd be inside you to the hilt. I would throw away my entire future.

But I don't say that. Instead, my features settle into a familiar mask. I might not look much like my youngest brother, but suddenly I understand the hard smile, the shuttered eyes that Damien used. My gut twists in understanding. My little brother hid the secrets of his heart just like I hide my own now, for I am falling for a woman whom I pay to tempt me. Common sense would say this feeling is nothing but lust.

But fuck common sense.

There is more to heaven and earth than what meets the eye, and the saints, I am sure, are laughing their holy asses off.

My lips twist into a bitter smile. Of course I'd

imagine myself falling head over heels after a mere two days. If she touches my cock, I might propose marriage.

"Go to bed," I bark, ignoring her questioning gaze. It's not fair. But it is my right. I am Prince of Edenvale. My word is law here.

She senses the authority in my voice and dips her head. "As you wish, Highness…but…" She dares to glance between her thick fringe of lashes, a glitter of mischief, as if she's not as subservient as her posture might pretend. "Don't you want to join me?"

She'll be the death of me.

"I will check on you later. For now, get some sleep Find some peace. One of us deserves that much."

Before she can ask another question, I turn on my heel and stalk from the room.

When I enter the library, I'm surprised to find the antique lamps are lit. X glances from his perch in a leather chair. He assumes a more casual pose than I am used to seeing, one of his legs slung over the chair's arm, and for once in his life, he looks startled.

"Benedict!" He bounds to his feet and clicks his heels. "Did I or did I not see Miss Ruby enter your bedchamber?"

I incline my head. "She is in my bed this very moment."

"And yet, you are here?" He does not ask the question he wants answered most, yet I know it hangs between us. "Have you gone mad?"

Perhaps I have.

I relax my shoulders, grateful for an opportunity to unburden my chaotic mind. "I needed space from temptation."

"Forgive me." His mouth purses. "But is that not the whole point of having her around?"

"I don't know!" I snarl through gritted teeth, then whirl and punch the wall. "I know nothing." The pain steadies me, so I do it again, three times in quick succession.

"Feel better?" X asks, the corner of his mouth curling up in amusement.

"No." I open and shut my hand a few times. "What are you doing here, anyway?"

He smiles lazily, but I swear I sense a troubled soul lurking behind his hooded eyes. "I am your personal bodyguard. And tonight I decided to do a little light reading while you were otherwise…ahem… occupied."

I cross the room and swipe the book from his chest. "*The Asca Mountains: A History.* What's this about? Do you plan to do an overland hike into Nightgardin?" The Asca Mountains provide the ancient border surrounding our old enemy to the north. In fact, the forbidding peaks have long kept Edenvale safe from the various feuds across Europe. Back when the great Carthaginian General Hannibal crossed the Alps during the Second Punic War, he ransacked the Romans because he wasn't able to breach the perilous Ascas.

"One can never know too much about local geography," X says enigmatically. "How about you? What brings you here when you have a willing woman warming your bed? Back before he met Princess Kate, your brother Nikolai would have disappeared for a week if he had struck upon such good fortune."

I set my jaw. "I am not my brother."

"No, you aren't." X appraises me with a shrewd eye. "You have too much of your mother in you."

My throat constricts. Perhaps if she'd lived, none of what has occurred in my family would have ever happened. Damien wouldn't have grown reckless and self-destructive from carrying the crushing burden of guilt for her death. Nikolai would have been saved earlier from his wanton bad-boy behavior. Perhaps she'd have even softened Father to my existence, encouraged me to walk a different life path despite my duty to serve the church.

But daydreaming about what-ifs is a luxury not afforded a member of the royal family. "You knew my mother?" I ask.

"She was a wonderful and kindhearted woman who loved her children more than life itself."

"How about my father?" I don't know where this rush of anger comes from, but it hits me with a tidal-wave force. "Tell me. Did you happen to be acquainted with the Captain of the Guard?"

X rises to his feet, the ancient book clattering from his lap. "Is that truly what you think of your mother? That she was unfaithful to her husband and king?"

Shame circulates in my veins.

"It's what everyone whispers," I challenge. "They say that my mother played the whore while my father the king was away on diplomatic duty. That I am the living, breathing testament to her transgression. Isn't that why my cuckolded father insists that I walk this lonely path, destined never to love or be loved, only to atone for the sins of a woman that I barely remember and a man that I have never met? My duty is atonement."

There it is, the bitter truth, out at last.

"Benedict…" X winces. "Is this what you truly believe?"

"It is what I know," I say with quiet resignation. "It is my life and has been since I was old enough to understand the burden I bear."

He looks as if he means to say more, but as he opens his mouth, a muffled but bloodcurdling scream pierces through the ceiling.

Ruby. Evangeline.

We race to the stairs and fly to my bedchamber.

Evangeline

I don't recognize the room or the bed, not even the thin silk gown that covers my otherwise naked form. But she stares at me from where I clutch the pillow to my body. The angel stares, and I can do nothing but scream.

"Ruby!" a rough voice cries, but I do not know

this name. I do not know the man who speaks it. "Go to her, Benedict. I will search for intruders."

A strong hand grips my shoulder, and I thrash against it, crying out until my throat is raw.

"Evangeline!" He is stronger than I am, pulling me to him even as I let go of the pillow and beat against his chest. "Evangeline!" he cries again, and something deep within awakens as recognition blooms, as the warmth of his touch breaks through the icy fear.

I stop fighting, and my shoulders droop as I sink into him, my arms wrapping tight around his neck.

"Benedict," I say, trembling, my senses returning.

"Shh, angel. You're safe now." He strokes my hair and cradles me in his arms as I try to catch my breath, the screams and sobs finally subsiding. "X," he says over my shoulder. "A glass of water, please."

"Yes, Highness," I hear, now recognizing the other male voice as that of Benedict's bodyguard. "All windows are secure, as is the door. I suspect it was only a dream."

Seconds later X returns, handing Benedict the water, which he gingerly brings to my lips.

"Drink," he says, and I do. My throat burns and my vision is still blurry from the tears, but I know where I am now, that I am safe, if only for the moment.

But the angel in the painting is still here—staring, judging. She knows I will betray my prince. And dream or no dream, I know I'm right. It's all too coincidental—what has happened to my family and now this portrait the Madam wants, a portrait so clearly of me.

"They will come for me," I say softly after a few sips. "They came for my father, my brother. Soon I will be next."

Benedict sets the water on the night table next to the bed, and I cling to him even tighter.

"This is not the first time you've had such a dream," he says, a statement rather than a question.

I shake my head. "It has been some time, though. I thought I'd rid myself of the nightmares years ago after Jasper found a wonderful doctor who helped me find peace with my father's death. He is a good big brother, you know. He's taken care of me since I was a young teen."

I bury my head in Benedict's chest, taking in his soothing woodsy scent, cedar and fresh-cut pine.

"His imprisonment has been difficult on you," he says, and I nod against him. Then I look up, my eyes meeting his. "You can tell me more," he adds. "If you want."

And because no man has ever looked at me as he does—with such protectiveness, such care—I want to tell him everything. Instead, I settle for the dream.

"When I was younger, it was always me standing on the side of the road where my father crashed. I would have to watch him slamming on the brakes while the car kept speeding toward its violent end. Toward his end. And every time, just before I'd wake up, the whole scenario would slow down. As his car would wrap around the tree, I'd hear his voice telling me, 'Find the map, Eva. Find the map and save us all.'" I let out a nervous laugh. "That sounds ridiculous, right? The doctor who helped put the dream to rest convinced me that it was my own subconscious wanting to find a way to save my father."

Benedict tilts my chin up and brushes a soft kiss over each of my tear-soaked eyes.

"And now, angel?"

I steady myself. "Now it is almost the same dream, but it is Jasper behind the wheel and not my father. Yet the message has not changed, only the voice that makes the plea." I straighten in my prince's lap, more sure of myself than I've been for quite some time. "I think that doctor was wrong, or that maybe he didn't want me searching for whatever map this might be. Because I know my father was murdered. And I know my brother was set up. And if I don't figure this all out before they do—whoever they are—they will come for me next."

X clears his throat, and we both turn to where he stands in the doorway. X's jaw tightens. "Let me return to the library to continue my studies. I assure you that you and Miss Rub—Evangeline Vernazza—are safe. I should have more concrete information for you by morning. For now, I think it best you stay with your guest."

Benedict opens his mouth to argue, but I interrupt.

"Please don't leave," I say to him. "If X can help, let him, but don't leave me alone here tonight."

He sighs and nods toward the doorway. "I will see you after my morning benediction, X. Meet me in the prayer room at ten. With answers."

X bows. "Yes, Your Highness." Then he dips his head toward me. "Rest well, Evangeline." And before I can thank him, he is out the door so quickly it's as if he was never there to begin with.

"How does he do that?" I ask. "It's like a magic trick."

Benedict laughs. "Just wait," he says. "I have seen him bypass doors altogether. Perhaps one day you will, too."

His tone is wistful, as if he speaks of a time in the future when our lives will still overlap, but I know this cannot be true as sure as I know that the way he holds me now is out of necessity, to wake me from the terror that threatens my sleep.

I swing my legs off his, but he does not let go of me.

"I'm sorry," I say. "This is most inappropriate. I should go clean myself up."

His only response is to dip his head toward mine and kiss me again. This time, though, there is nothing of the hunger from before. Just a sweet, gentle yearning as his tongue slips past my parted lips, as we both taste the lingering salt of my tears.

We lie down, his soft kisses continuing as we do. He pulls my body close and grins.

"What are you smiling at?" I ask.

"I didn't realize I could do that," he says. My

brows pull together. "Kiss a woman," he continues, "and have it not be sexual in nature."

I stroke his cheek, my chest tightening at what it would be like to meet such a man under any other circumstances than the ones we are in. That's when I know I have to break this spell. I thought the hard part would be living with myself if I succeeded in tempting him from his holy path—or if I betrayed him to the Madam. I realize now the difficulty lies in thinking I could fall for such a man and not get my heart obliterated.

"I think I'm okay to sleep now," I say, trying not to sound too cold.

"Of course," he replies flatly, taking the hint, and I know I've hurt him…or at least bruised his ego.

He slides his arm out from beneath me and leaves the bed, lowering himself to the hard, wooden floor.

"Don't you want a pillow?" I ask. "Or a blanket?"

He rests his head on his forearm. "Not tonight. I must remind myself there are certain comforts that are not for me."

Like sleeping with a woman in my arms, I imagine him saying to himself.

Like believing a prince could choose you over God, I think, realizing my own guilty wish.

"Thank you for making me feel safe," I say, staring at the ceiling.

I hear him let out a long breath.

"You will always be safe with me, Evangeline."

Tomorrow morning we will find out what X

knows of the map that must exist. Tomorrow night I will convince Benedict how dangerously tempting I really am—so that neither of us is seduced again into thinking there could ever be more.

So that my foolish heart understands there is no promise in a prince's kiss.

CHAPTER NINE

Benedict

NOT LONG AFTER she fell asleep last night, Evangeline cried out softly again. Another bad dream. Against my better judgment, I climbed in beside her, wrapping her trembling body in my arms and somehow silencing her whimpers. Her soft breaths must have lulled me to sleep before I could return to the floor.

Now, with the first morning light, I am warm, comfortable and unwilling to climb from the bed for a punishing cold shower and an hour of contemplation at my personal altar. Instead, I turn and find the reason still snoring lightly beside me.

In the soft light, devoid of her makeup, she is Evangeline. My blonde angel. My painting come to life—salvation and temptation all at once.

I can still taste the tender kiss we shared, the inkling that perhaps there is more inside me than animalistic lust.

Even now I don't want to ravish her. My cock

twitches in disagreement, but my heart overrides the urges. Instead, I want to...take care of her.

I slide from the sheets with a reluctance that she seems to echo as she emits a soft, purring moan of protest.

"Shh." I bend and kiss her forehead. She smiles dreamily and returns to peaceful sleep.

In my simple galley kitchen there is a used coffee mug in the sink. A sign X woke even before me and is already in the study poring over books, trying to get answers for Evangeline's many questions. I wonder, in fact, if the man slept at all.

There is time ahead to help her, to figure out if her dreams hold truth. But I am also convinced in the healing power of simple, kind gestures, like a fresh goat cheese and spinach omelet paired with thick slices of toast, the bread delivered fresh to the palace every morning.

I have always had a measure of talent when it comes to cooking, but food seemed like one more sinful pleasure, giving over to the body when I needed to focus on the spirit. So day after day I have eaten plain oatmeal for breakfast, a slice of whole wheat toast and a piece of soft cheese for lunch, and a simple root vegetable stew for dinner. It brings me joy to cut and dice these ingredients, put my larder to use to help plump Evangeline's cheeks, hollow from grief and fear.

When I return to the room holding a tray, she is

sitting, rubbing her eyes. "Where did you go?" Her jaw falls open as she registers what I carry. "Oh."

"I thought you would enjoy breakfast in bed," I say, suddenly shy. What if she wants to be alone, just as she urged me out of the bed last night? Perhaps I am a fool to assume.

"I'm starving," she says, interrupting my inner torment. "And this looks amazing. Like something out of a magazine or a reality cooking show."

"See if it tastes okay." I set it down and shove my hands into my pockets. "It's been a long time since I have prepared food for another."

She takes a bite and groans, the same sound I have heard her use when giving herself over to absolute pleasure. "This is wicked, Benedict."

Ice flows through my veins. "What do you mean?"

She bites her lower lip, eyes shining. "What is happening to my taste buds is a sin. I might require confession by the time I finish the toast."

I am unable to give voice to how much her small happiness brings me joy. So I offer her a soft smile.

She dips her fork into another bite, and this time her eyes roll. "I am serious. How do you know how to cook like this? I would think you'd have grown up with a hundred classically trained chefs waiting at your beck and call."

I nod. "This is true. But I was a curious child, also shyer than my brothers. I spent a lot of time in the palace library, which is even bigger than my collection here in the tower. I'd read everything I could get my hands on. Including cookbooks. Once Jean-Paul, the old royal chef, found me poring over a seventeenth-century collection of recipes from Versailles, and he invited me to the kitchen. It became my safe haven. I befriended the serving staff, the sous chefs, the pastry makers. They treated me as an equal, not as a prince or a future saint."

This is something I don't talk about, yet when I'm around her, my past spills out of me.

"It sounds like you have many happy memories from that time."

My smile fades. "Yes, until Father deemed it unseemly for a prince to perform what he believed were menial tasks."

She shakes her head. "But what you did here with food, it is art. No different than what I do with paint and canvas."

"I should like to see you paint someday."

She gives a wistful sigh, her fingers twitching as if holding an imaginary brush. "I miss it above all things. Except for, of course, Jasper and Papa." Her voice hitches.

"I'll tell you what." I clap my hands, inspiration striking. "Today you will do nothing but make art."

"But…" She is incredulous. "Aren't I supposed to be tempting you, giving you a taste of forbidden pleasure?"

"Forget all that. Your employ is only for the evenings," I say. "Let the days be your own. Besides, nothing would bring me more pleasure than seeing you happy," I say honestly.

She considers me for a long time before speaking. "You are a most unusual prince."

Another thought strikes, even as it causes me a glimmer of fear. "Of course, perhaps one bit of temptation before art."

"Yes?" I can see her eyes veil as she slips into her role of Ruby.

"On the roof of this tower, I have a claw-foot bathtub. It can only be heated by lighting a small fire beneath it. Normally I don't bother with it, but this morning, I want to give you a bubble bath. Wash your hair with fresh mountain spring water and watch as the sun rises over the peaks and turns to spun gold." I shall fill the tub with roses from the garden below.

"You are playing a dangerous game," she whispers, her hand rising to the side of her throat.

"How so?"

Her soft eyes gleam with a passionate intensity. "If you aren't careful, I might never leave your side."

Evangeline

Benedict leaves me to finish my delicious breakfast while he prepares the bath. My days are mine to do as I please, and as much as I know this will drag me deeper under his spell, I choose this. I choose to spend my time with him.

I'm practically licking the crumbs from my plate

when he bursts through the apartment door, almost racing to where I still lie in bed. He wears nothing but a gray cotton T-shirt and the pants he slept in—and a sweet, boyish grin spread across his face. When I first saw him the other night, he seemed like such an old soul, but this morning he is youth incarnate, a young man with the world at his feet.

He dips his head. "Forgive me if I seem too eager, but I don't want the sun to make it past the mountaintops before we get up there. If you're still hungry—"

"I am beyond stuffed," I tell him, setting my plate on the night table. So he reaches for my hand, and I offer it without hesitation.

In seconds we are out the door and bounding up a smaller staircase around the corner from the spiraling one of which I've already grown quite fond. He holds the door open at the top, and I step through to see the entirety of Edenvale stretching out in every direction, including the shimmering Royal River. I race past the tub until I'm bellied up against a notch in the tower's stone parapets.

"Oh, Benedict," I say, but I'm at a loss for words. I may not have been born in this kingdom, but I grow to love it more each day, despite the trials my family has faced. I reach for Benedict but realize he isn't there, turning to find him outside the door, back against it, watching me from afar.

"Join me, Your Highness!" I call to him, teasing, but he shakes his head.

Then he nods toward the tub, where I just now notice rose petals floating atop the steaming water.

"Your bath chamber," he says with a grin, "is as far as I go."

I give the landscape one more glance, the dawn breaking across this beautiful kingdom, and make my way to where he stands. This time I hold out my hand for his, and he laces his strong fingers around mine.

"I don't need any of this, Benedict."

"But you deserve it," he says. "You deserve a bright and beautiful morning after such a dark night. To bear witness to your happiness is enough for me."

I swallow the threat of tears and place my palm on his cheek. He was so good to me last night, taking me in when I had nowhere to go, soothing me from my nightmares. And the only thanks I gave him was to practically toss him out of bed and to the floor when all I wanted was to slumber in his arms.

He presses a soft kiss against my hand, and a ripple of warmth spreads from his lips to my very core.

Benedict leads me to the tub, where embers of kindling still glow beneath it.

"I will douse the remnants of the fire if it's too hot."

I dip a finger into the gorgeous copper tub, a fixture most definitely fit for royalty, and shake my head. "It's perfect." I lift the silk gown over my head, baring myself to him, and to my surprise, he does not react with shock. His eyes, green pools glow-

ing in the ever-increasing morning light, look upon
me with a reverence I have not seen before. Without a word, he holds my hand, guiding me into the
fragrant warmth, and I lower myself until I'm covered in ruby-red petals of the sweetest roses I've
ever smelled.

I hum softly as I try to convince myself this isn't
a dream.

"I don't need to see what lies beyond the walls of
the roof," he says. "Not when I have the most beautiful view of all of Edenvale right here. Just for me."

He kneels next to me and takes off his shirt, his
taut muscles rippling in the glint of the rising sun. I
run my fingers atop the dusting of dark hair on his
chest, and he sucks in a breath.

"I'm sorry," I say, letting instinct overpower logic.
"I didn't mean—"

"Don't apologize for putting action to your desires. You have the freedom to do so. I only wish I
had the same."

He dips his head toward mine and kisses me. I
taste the bitterness of coffee, delicious on his tongue,
emboldening me to wrap my arms around his neck,
tugging him closer. Water and rose petals slosh over
the lip of the tub, soaking his pants.

I let him go, and we both laugh, the sound of his
happiness something I have not heard before.

"Sorry!" I cry, my hand flying to my mouth as I
only laugh harder. "This is all just a lot—the roof,
the roses, the most beautiful man I've ever seen kiss-

ing me at sunrise. I'm a little out of my element, and I guess I got carried away."

His laughter subsides, and he collects himself. "Most beautiful man you've ever seen?"

I touch him on the shoulder, on his very muscular, naked shoulder. "Now you're going to tell me you don't read the papers or watch TV." He arches a brow. "Okay, fine. You probably don't watch television because it's pleasurable, and I get it. Deny, deny, deny. But come on, Benedict. Despite your holy calling, the women in this kingdom are mad for you."

"Ah," he says, leaning back on his heels. "So I am some sort of celebrity fantasy to you?"

I roll my eyes and groan. "No. I mean, yes. You are beautiful to look at, but two days ago that meant nothing more to me than having a pleasurable view while I tried to seduce you."

"And now?" he asks with a wry smile. "Everything has changed in a mere thirty-six hours?"

Impossible, I think. But yes.

I rest my hand on his chest and let his heart beat against my palm for several long seconds.

"So much of your beauty lies in here," I say. "And I'm honored to be one of the few who get to see it."

He stands, staring at the pants that are soaked against his long legs. Then he shrugs and steps over the lip of the tub, lowering himself in across from me.

I yelp with laughter. "What are you doing?"

He reaches over the edge for a copper pitcher and fills it with the rose-infused water.

"I'm going to wash your hair."

He scoots forward, his legs crossing over mine. Water sloshes over the edge, spilling onto the roof, and I swear I've never felt happier.

He pours the pitcher over my head, then massages my scalp with hands that are strong and full of purpose. Yet I also feel a gentleness in his touch, one I've not experienced since the days when my father was alive.

"What about shampoo?" I ask, even as I moan with pleasure.

"These roses are from the palace garden," he says. "There is nothing softer or more beautiful than the aroma of their perfume. I've also added some essential oils to the water, which will soothe and nourish your scalp."

I tilt my head into the cradle of his hands and sigh, the tension of last night evaporating with the steam.

"Benedict," I say softly.

"Yes?" His hand caresses my cheek.

"Thank you for holding me this morning." His eyes widen. "I remember the nightmare starting again, and I know it was you who chased it away. It's okay," I assure him as I watch his eyes turn dark with worry. "I'm glad you were there."

"You're welcome," he says, his voice hoarse.

"Come," I say, grabbing his shoulders and urging him to turn around. The welts on his back have gone down, but angry bruises remain. I kiss each one before pulling him to me, his back against my breasts, his head cradled against my shoulder. "Let someone hold you for once."

I kiss his temple, and he nods. Without another word, we lie there together, watching the sun crest over the snowcapped peaks. I'm certain we would have stayed there all day, or at least until the water was too cold to bear. Instead, just as the whole roof is bathed in the morning glow, I hear the door burst open behind us.

"Highness!" X calls. "I've found the map."

CHAPTER TEN

Benedict

EVANGELINE IS NESTLED in an oversize leather chair in the library. Her freshly washed hair streams over her shoulders. Her small feet poke from the bottom of my bathrobe. The red paint is chipped on her left big toe. Something about the sight is endearing, yet I can't explain why.

X clears his throat, an understated reminder of why he called us in from the tower roof. Even now my pulse pounds, making it hard to focus on the easel dramatically covered by a white sheet.

"You have our attention," I observe wryly. "Now on with the show."

He ignores my verbal poke and turns to Evangeline. "I have reason to believe that beneath this sheet is the reason why your father was murdered and your brother, Jasper, was taken prisoner." X pulls away the sheet and there is my painting of my guardian angel.

A confused silence follows.

"I was gifted this piece by my brother Nikolai last year for Christmas. He respects my interest in art collection even if he doesn't share the passion."

"Nikolai didn't realize what he was buying you— it is beyond the value of money," X says. "There are people who'd stop at nothing to own this piece."

"It is priceless," I answer. In less than a month I will take my final vows. This portrait of a younger Evangeline will be my reminder that our time together ever occurred.

X clicks his tongue in irritation. I've never seen him like this, as if reaching the edge of his legendary composure. "My sources have learned that Jasper, Evangeline's brother, intentionally sold it to Nikolai. We think it was intentional, to keep the piece from falling into the wrong hands. He must have decided that the well-protected walls of Edenvale Palace would make the perfect hiding place."

Evangeline rises and pads across the room, her mouth creasing in a small frown.

"My God. Look!" Her hand flies to her mouth. "The necklace."

"Yes!" X exclaims. "Yes, exactly. You see what I mean!"

"It cannot be," she says. "It's a legend."

X's face is dark with repressed emotion. "Is it?"

"Do you two mind speaking plainly?" I rise and join them. The image is the same one that I've seen on my wall a thousand times. A sad-eyed ethereal beauty rising above the wasteland of a terrified populace fleeing a handsome young man.

"The angel is wearing a necklace with a vial. A vial of golden water," Evangeline says slowly. "Look, it's there, half-hidden amid the folds in her robe."

"Golden water?" I chuckle. "From what? The Spring of Youth? That's an old story. Surely if there were such mineral compounds in nature that could keep a person looking young while prolonging life, they would have been patented by major American pharmaceutical companies. They would be worth billions, if not trillions of dollars to a society devoted to worshipping youthful beauty."

The fabled Spring of Youth was said to exist beneath Edenvale in a cavern deep beneath the earth. The specific combination of minerals were said to delay the effects of aging, but it came with a price— whoever drank the elixir would live longer but slowly lose their mental faculties, descending into paranoia and madness.

"Edenvale is a land of ancient secrets. Perhaps this artwork provides a rare answer," X says.

Evangeline touches the corner of the painting. "Father loved symbology. Look at the street signs— Detour and This Way. The angel also raises two fingers. I had always assumed it was in benediction, but it could also be read as—"

"A sign of The Order." X's expression is deadly serious.

"The Order?" I frown at their excited faces. "As

in the Knights of The Order?" They cannot be serious. "The secret society of legend?"

"Charged with protecting the realm. The best knights of Edenvale once vied to be selected for the honor. This painting somehow links to The Order and provides a key to the map. But how?" Evangeline speaks almost to herself.

I feel as if we are discussing the existence of Santa Claus or the Easter Bunny. "The Order hasn't existed since the Dark Ages."

"Some say the members have gone underground," X says gravely. "Secretly protecting the realm to this day."

"From what?" I ask. "Magical water?" I would think he was teasing me except for the fact his lips don't twitch.

X nods at the dystopian landscape, the violence. "That." His tone deepens with a strange intensity. "To live on young and beautiful, even with the threat of madness? Many despots would be tempted by such an opportunity."

Evangeline blinks. "My father is hiding something here behind the canvas. If only I had something sharp to open it in the back..."

"Like this?" X pulls a four-inch steel blade from his trouser pocket, the edge sharpened to deadly perfection.

Evangeline's mouth opens, then closes. I chuckle and shake my head.

"Do not try to make sense of a man such as X," I

say, then turn my gaze to the man himself. "Nikolai needed a bodyguard with all his public escapades. I'm not sure I need protection from anything at all, but it's good to know that if I do, you're more than prepared."

Evangeline clears her throat. "Perfect." She reaches for the blade and raises her brows in a quizzical expression. "May I?"

"It would be an honor to watch Vernazza's daughter at this moment." X's voice is grave.

She slides the knife along the back of the frame. Her movements are quick and assured. At last she pauses, wipes her forehead. "Here goes nothing."

Peeling back the paper, she reveals what I never could have fathomed—a map written in black ink, the paper yellow with age...and in the center is a symbol of a spring, and written beneath it in gold leaf script are the words *aquas vitam aeternam*.

"Waters of Eternal Life," I translate.

Evangeline

"Waters of Eternal Life." Tears spill from my eyes, but I'm careful not to let the salt water drip onto the map. Benedict has his prayer books, but this—for me—is the most sacred of texts.

"Oh, Papa," I say, my fingers carefully skimming the parchment. "What did you die to protect?"

A warm hand caresses my shoulder, and Benedict presses a soft kiss on top of my head. I want to turn to him, to bury my face in his chest, but I'm transfixed by the vision before me. An angel, ageless faces and the key.

"It's like losing him all over again," I say, sniffling. I run the sleeve of Benedict's plush bathrobe across my eyes. "And now to know that I'm not crazy, that this wasn't all some terrible nightmare that has plagued me for a decade…" I spin to face both of them now. "It's real, right?"

X nods, and Benedict runs his fingers through my hair.

"Realer than real," he echoes, but my prince's words are not a question.

"What now?" I ask.

X takes a step forward and carefully pulls the map from the frame.

"Well," he says, brows raised as he holds the map out for all of us to see.

I squint at the lines of text above a map that leads who knows where. "Are those even letters?"

"It looks more like code," Benedict says.

X shakes his head. "In all my linguistic studies, I've come across this but once. Were it in Portuguese or Uzbek, I'd have had this translated before you finished peeling back the painting. But this—this will take some time."

I nod, but I cannot hide my disappointment or the new wave of tears it brings.

"So that map is real," I say, "but we don't know

where it leads or what my father and brother were protecting?"

What does the Madam want with this map? Or worse—who is she working for? I've heard many whispers of her connection to Nightgardin, Edenvale's centuries-old enemy.

It's up to me now to protect what my father sacrificed his life for. I must protect the wonderful, caring prince who's been protecting me, which means keeping this map to the legendary Spring of Youth from falling into the wrong hands.

X bows his head toward Benedict. "Your Highness, I can decipher this code. It may take a few days, but it can be done. Take Miss Ruby—I mean, Evangeline—to your brother's old quarters in the palace. I do believe both of you will be safer within its fortified walls."

The prince scoffs. "The tower has never been breached."

"This is no time for pride, Highness. You may not think you need protecting, but she does."

He nods and snakes his fingers through mine. "You're right. We will head to the palace at once."

He squeezes my hand and starts to lead me from the library, but I stop in my tracks.

"My family," I say. "Jasper's wife and daughter. They could be in danger, too."

All Benedict has to do is give X a look, and the other man nods.

"We will send men from the Palace Guard to keep watch."

This is enough to satisfy me. Benedict retrieves a coat from his chambers and throws it over my shoulders before I finally let Benedict lead me away. By the time we get to the future king's annex, the one where he lived before he and Kate married, all of my belongings from the cottage are already there.

I call Camille to check in and breathe out a sigh of relief when I hear her voice.

"I think we can help Jasper," I tell her. "Maybe even free him."

She gasps. "But—how?"

"I can't say too much right now, but know that the prince and his guard are helping us, and we will have Jasper home soon. Just promise me you and Lola will lie low until I call again in a couple of days, and speak nothing of this to anyone. I love you both."

She agrees, and I decide not to tell her about the guards being sent over, since I don't want to frighten her. They'll be there, surrounding their apartment building but hidden, looking after her and Lola, and that's what's important.

When I end the call, I notice I'm standing alone in the annex's kitchen, that Benedict has given me privacy to tend to my family matters. I swallow the knot in my throat and send a message to the Madam.

Haven't found it yet, but the prince and I are grow-

ing closer. He's beginning to trust me. I should have
what you need soon.

The response is immediate.

I am growing impatient, girl. If I find out you're
lying, you'll have more to worry about than me mar-
ring that pretty face of yours. I have very influen-
tial friends. It won't take much for me to get to the
people you care about.

I wrap myself tightly in the oversize coat, breathing in Benedict's scent as I realize the gravity of my
lies—that one misstep could mean Jasper's life…
or my own.

I take off the coat and pad down the hall to what
I know will be a lavish bedchamber compared to
Benedict's, but what I'm greeted with is far beyond
my expectations.

My hand flies to my mouth, and Benedict grins.

"I thought maybe this would help get your mind
off the map for a bit."

He stands next to an easel, a blank canvas leaning
against it, and beside it, a table full of paints.

"How?" I ask. It's more than what he's given me.
It's that his gift is exactly what I need right now.
How can this stranger somehow know me so well?

He shrugs. "The palace does have its perks. It's
simply been a long while since I've wanted to take
advantage of them."

I stride toward him and don't even hesitate when I wrap him in my arms and squeeze.

"Thank you," I whisper into his chest. "Thank you, Benedict."

He stands frozen before pulling me in even tighter.

"Anything for you, angel," he says, and for the moment, I actually believe it.

I look up at him, his eyes an enchanted forest of green.

"But I don't want to paint the canvas," I say, and his brows draw together. "I want to paint what I see in your eyes—paint you."

He says nothing as he removes his T-shirt, baring his chest to me.

"You have not put your collar on since the other night," I say.

He shakes his head.

"And this is okay?" I ask, reaching for a tube of green paint and squeezing it onto a palette. I dip a brush in, swirling it around, and then bring it to his chest, where I paint one single leaf.

Still no words, but he nods, backing toward the four-poster bed.

"But the linens," I say.

"Fuck the linens."

He lowers himself to a ruby-red duvet.

I gather the colors of my forest onto the palette and lay it on the bed. Then I climb over him, brush in hand, parting my robe so I can straddle his legs.

He is hard beneath his pants, and I... I am bare

but for the material draped over me, on fire for my prince, for this man.

"Stop me if it's too much," I say, and he grabs my wrist.

"Paint first. Then I'm going to tell you what I would do to you if I could." He unties the robe completely, letting it fall off my shoulders. "How many times I've looked at that painting, wondering if such beauty truly existed in the world. Now here you are. An angel in disguise. In another time, Evangeline—"

"Don't," I say, swiping the brush across his jaw. "Just for today. Please. Don't talk about what we can't have. Instead, let us enjoy what we can."

He nods and reaches for my breast, cupping it gently in his palm. He gives my peaked nipple a soft pinch, and I writhe against his hard cock.

"Benedict."

I feel him flex against me.

"It's not a sin," he growls, squeezing his eyes shut.

I drop the brush on the palette, then lean over and kiss him, the paint on his jaw smearing against mine.

"You're still just a man, Benedict. This is your choice. I won't take anything you are not willing to give."

His hand slides along my torso, skimming over my belly, and resting between my legs. He stills for several seconds, time lengthening between us. And then, there it is, the tiniest of movements—his thumb brushing my clit—but it's enough to make me cry out.

"I—" he says, his deep voice hoarse with need. "I want to know what I'm missing."

Then he slips a finger inside me, and I'm certain that I see stars.

CHAPTER ELEVEN

Benedict

I'VE FOUND HEAVEN on earth. It is tight, wet and perfect. My index finger has been inside Evangeline's pussy for only a few seconds, but it's as if I've lived five hundred lifetimes in the span of each one. When I start to withdraw, my fingertip slides over a small ridge near her entrance.

"Oh God!" Her inner muscles clamp as her neck arches. Her skin is so delicate that her veins are visible, her pulse rapid-fire fast.

Ah, the infamous G-spot. So it does exist.

My answering groan tears the fabric of my soul. I'm not meant to touch. But now that I am here, it feels holy to give her the pleasure she craves. I crook my finger and smile as her lids flutter.

"Benedict," she murmurs, hips undulating. "My God, Benedict."

"Your mouth was made for one thing," I growl, flipping her and bending over her.

"What's that?" She squeaks on the last word as I stroke her hidden secret again.

"Saying my name." I slip in another finger and still another.

"Yes, feels so good," she purrs, taking hold of my forearm, urging me to drill deeper. "Fill me. Fill me up."

"But this is too much." I pause and try to hold on to a shred of sanity. "I don't want to hurt you."

Our gazes lock and her pupils are dilated so much that I can see my own reflection in their onyx depths. "This is incredible."

"You're so tight." The walls of her tunnel are like slick satin. "I had no idea it would be this tight."

I brush her G-spot again and hold it as she mewls.

"Yes, there, don't stop. Don't ever stop, Benedict." Her pussy clamps my fingers, milking my hand with her orgasm, and I am humbled to my bones by this unexpected gift.

I've given a woman the gift of pleasure, and not just any woman, but one who is conquering my mind, body and soul. I have overcome my years of hard-earned repression and done the forbidden, and what's more? I've fucking loved every second of it.

As I move to withdraw, she frowns. "Don't go."

I have heard of this, a woman's ability to keep attaining pleasure. "You want to come again?"

She hums a sexy laugh. "All day if I can. You're quite talented, Highness. Your fingers are very... nimble."

"Must be all those years I spent kneading bread."

But her laughter ceases at my attempted joke. Instead, she looks hesitant.

"What is it?" I murmur. "Don't hide. You know you can tell me anything."

"The other night, you asked me to touch myself and tell you my fantasy. I didn't know until I cried out your name that you had somehow infiltrated my dreams. And now that I trust you—now that I know you'd never do anything to hurt me—I want something more."

My eyes widen. "I am part of your fantasy?" I ask.

She nods. "I've never asked this of anyone, but…" She trails off, and I nod, offering her encouragement to continue. "I… I wonder if you'd be willing to try something." She pushes an errant lock of hair off her cheek and nibbles her plump lower lip. "Something that I have never done before with any man."

"What?" I rasp, my throat threatening to clamp shut.

"I want to feel your whole hand inside me."

I freeze. "I… I am not sure that I understand."

Her cheeks are the color of flame. "I'm sorry. I know I shouldn't have asked. It's just that I feel so connected to you, and I've always had this fantasy but have never trusted anyone enough to give it to me."

"You truly want this?"

She gives a hesitant nod. "As you can see, I am not…loose. My vagina is incredibly tight, so the pressure feels amazing. Most women can't get off from penis-to-vagina sex."

I nod. "Yes, I've read about this. They need clitoral stimulation."

"Exactly. And while I enjoy such stimulation, I can come without it…if my partner is able and willing. I realized as a younger girl… Oh my gosh, I can't believe that I am telling you this…" She trails off.

"Evangeline, nothing you say could ever shock me. Your body is made to feel pleasure, to have desires. You can trust me."

She stares at me as she worries her bottom lip between her teeth. "I know I can. At first I thought it was because you were an old soul, but now I wonder if it's due to something deeper." She covers her face with her hands. "I feel—oh God, don't laugh—but I feel as if our souls recognize each other."

I let out a long, shaky breath. "You are saying we are soul mates?" With a few words, she has moved the rock long crushing my heart. At last, real heat pumps through my cold veins, returning me to life. I've become a flesh-and-blood man…with a man's needs.

"You want me to put my entire hand in your pussy, to fist you." My thumb twitches at the idea of giving her such depraved pleasure.

She peers through her fingers. "I have heard other girls at my…work…say it can bring about the most intense pleasure. But it is not something to do with a paying client. The trust factor is huge. You must open yourself up to another in the most intimate way possible."

I remind myself that, while I am at a precipice, taking the leap will still leave my own virtue intact. It is a selfish rationalization, but it is one that comforts me nonetheless.

"I will do what you ask," I say after a considered pause. "Except I don't have lube. As wet as you are, I would be required to exert a great deal of pressure and couldn't bear the thought of giving you any pain."

"A little pain can be a pleasure." Dark lust flashes in her eyes. "But I appreciate your consideration. I happen to have a bottle of lube with me in my red suitcase there on the chair across the room."

I arch a brow. "You travel with lube?"

She arches one right back. "This is my job, Benedict," she reminds me, a truth I've tried to bury. "And part of the Madam's requirements is that we are prepared with whatever a client might need. I travel with a great deal of lube, and a host of flavors: pineapple, raspberry or cinnamon." She dips her head, looking up at me through hooded lids. "I've also been told this type of...creativity...can also serve as a diversion, interesting a man in something more playful than..." She trails off, then sets her gaze on me directly. "You aren't like the others would be, Benedict. I am sure of it. I trust you...with everything."

I rise and cross the room, open the suitcase and select a small unscented vial that promises warming sensations and guarantees to delight. I slather my entire hand until it's well coated. It seems so big, and she is so tight. Three fingers felt like I'd packed her full. But I take my place next to her on the bed again. If she trusts me, then I will trust what she desires.

"Thank you," she says in a quiet voice. "For not judging me. I felt a little silly admitting this fantasy to you. But this isn't something I wanted to ever share with a client, only a man I knew would treat me with care, who'd fill me with a loving touch."

"Never apologize for wanting what you want." There is a small wet sound as I slide my fingers in. "I've read about this."

"Of course you have." She offers a sweet, teasing smile. But as I fill her, her hands grip the sheets.

"The word itself sounds fast and hard, but in reality it requires patience and a great deal of arousal," I say.

Her mouth forms a perfect O. "We have both of those factors on our side."

"Relax," I tell her. "You are in charge of the situation." I press my thumb beneath my four fingers to make my hand as narrow as possible. "If you need me to stop at any time, for any reason, I want you to tell me."

"Yes. Yes." Her thighs tremble.

I go slow, and the knuckles are the trickiest part. She takes deep, measured breaths, urging me on, then with a slight rotation of my wrist over her pubic bone, I'm all the way inside, my hand naturally forming a fist. Her muscular walls quiver around me.

"How do you feel?" I whisper.

"Vulnerable," she breathes. "Impossibly full. Stretched to my limits. I'm close. So close, Benedict."

With my free hand, I lick my fingers and circle her clit. It takes the barest whiff of pressure, and she reacts with tidal force, bearing down on my enclosed hand with an orgasm that threatens to cut off my circulation. I continue to worship her clit, letting her ride through two, then three orgasms.

They can probably hear us from the guard towers to the servants' quarters, but nothing, including the Big Man himself, could make me stop.

"Benedict," she squeaks, toes curling, as she grabs a handful of hair. "I never knew. I never knew it could be like this. So full. So good."

My heart threatens to burst. "Neither did I, angel. Neither did I."

Evangeline

We lie there in silence, me coming down from a high I never thought possible, and Benedict beside me, his jaw tight and body anything but relaxed.

Both of us are staring at the ceiling when I ask, "Benedict?"

"Angel," he responds, and I smile at his use of my nickname. At least what just happened hasn't changed that.

"Please tell me you are not quietly chastising yourself. If I've made you feel guilty in any way, I won't be able to forgive myself."

He props himself up on an elbow and faces me, the hand that gave me pleasure like I've never known now tracing lazy circles around my belly button.

He kisses my temple. "Guilt?" he whispers. "Surprisingly, no. I've been trying to figure out how to put a voice to what I have decided. More so, I hope it will not be too much to ask of you."

I take his wrist and guide his hand from my torso to my breast. Still, after what I've just asked of him, this elicits from him a ragged moan.

"Let me do something for you," I say. "Trust me like I trust you."

He rubs a thumb over my raised peak, and I gasp.

"I know where this road will lead me," he says. "What awaits me at the end of this path."

I swallow. "Your vows," I say, realizing that a tiny part of me had the nerve to hope that whatever he is going to ask of me might involve some sort of future for us beyond the end of our month together.

"Yes. My vows. My vows are my future—but you said something before that hit me." My brows rise, and he continues. "Right now?" He rolls my nipple between his thumb and forefinger, and I let out a soft moan. "Right now I am just a man."

I prop myself up so we are eye to eye. "What are you saying, Benedict? Do you want to…?"

"God can have my virtue," he says. "But you, Evangeline, you can have everything else."

It is not the answer I was hoping for, but it's close enough. I slide closer to him and let my fingers tickle the flesh above his pants.

"May I have this patch of skin?" I ask, itching to follow the trail of dark hair to where it leads.

"You may," he says with a grin, and I dare to keep traveling south, beneath the seam of his cotton pants—where there is no undergarment for me to tease any further.

He's right there, within my reach. All I have to do is stretch my pinkie, and then I feel it—the warm, slick precum on his tip.

Benedict lets loose a growl.

"This, my prince. Is this mine? Does this fall under everything else?"

"Yes," he says through gritted teeth, and I know that today will be a day for many firsts.

And that's all it takes for me to slide my hand the rest of the way, to wrap my hand around his thick, hard length and stroke him from root to tip.

"Evangeline!" He bucks against my touch, his reaction making my pulse quicken.

I climb over him, tugging his pants to his ankles and then off completely.

I gaze upon his naked form, speechless for a few erratic beats of my heart.

"What is it?" he asks, and I shake my head.

"You're…quite the specimen," I say, feeling a rush

of heat from my core to my cheeks. "To think that this will be hidden away forever…and that I am the only one who will have seen it? Why me?"

The corner of his mouth curls into a grin that lights a fire within me.

"Because you are the most exquisite soul I've ever known."

My breath catches. "You don't know my soul, Benedict. You couldn't possibly. This—" I motion between us "—this is fantasy. This is two strangers giving each other what they need." I have to say this because to believe otherwise is too much. To believe otherwise is to want what I could never have.

He grips his cock, tilting it toward me so his wet tip slides against my clit.

I hiss, exhaling in a sharp breath. "Benedict!" He does it again, and I shudder.

"You said our souls recognize each other," he says. "Then believe that it's more than recognition—that I know yours. That I know *you*." He caresses my cheek. "This is not fantasy," he says. "It is me giving you everything I possibly can before it is no longer mine to give."

I drop over him, sliding along his length until that naughty tip nudges me again. He clamps his jaw shut, groaning as I writhe. This man—he may be preserving his virtue, but he will drive us both mad in the process.

He slips two fingers inside me, and I sink down to his knuckles, pretending it's his cock filling me instead. I imagine taking him so deep, forgetting where I end and he begins.

I manage to maneuver my body while he vibrates within my walls, so that now his cock is in front of me, and I lick my lips before sucking him down to the base.

"Fuck!" he cries out as I grip him, my hand trailing my mouth as I slide up his long, slick length. Again and again I do this, and he answers by adding a third finger, by fucking me the only way I think he can until he slides his hand free and replaces it with his mouth.

His tongue is warm, lapping between my folds, and I am a lit fuse about to explode.

I cup his balls and squeeze, all the while bucking against him as his tongue swirls around my throbbing clit.

I said I didn't need this to come. But I never said it couldn't take me to the edge of the universe. That he couldn't take me there. Because he can, as will I for him.

"Fuck!" he cries again as I start to tip over the edge. "God. Evangeline." But he loses his words completely, exploding inside me, and I drink him in. Every last drop. Because this is the only way we will ever be as one, and I want to savor the taste of him, the intimacy, the knowledge that while his seed will never grow inside another, I am nourished by it nonetheless.

I collapse, and he rises to his knees.

"You're not finished," he says.

I shake my head.

"Good. Because I need to taste the nectar of the gods one more time."

"Gods?" I ask, raising a brow. "Why, Benedict, I believe that's blasphemy."

He pushes my knees apart and gives me a wicked grin.

"Then forgive me, Father, for I'm about to make this angel take your name in vain."

He drops between my legs, and though I do cry out for God in heaven, I do not think it is in vain. Instead, it is a prayer…or maybe a plea.

Let this man remain just a man. Let him have all that he's denied himself. Let him find happiness where he wishes to seek it and not where he's been told to find it.

And then I add on one selfish request.

Let him be mine.

CHAPTER TWELVE

Benedict

FOR THE NEXT WEEK, I barely make it out of bed, except to take quick showers. I enjoy all manner of delights off Evangeline's delectable body: greenhouse strawberries covered in lashings of whipped cream, a drizzle of wild clover honey, dark sea salt chocolate. Once I've devoured my fill, I feast on her instead. The sweetness between her legs puts even the most gourmet Belgian chocolatiers to shame.

This morning we are still in bed even though the sun is nearly at the sky's apex. Her small foot nestles between my hands, and I give her a massage with almond and cherry scented oils. Another of my angel's secret delights? Getting her feet rubbed.

And here's one of mine—I love giving her exactly what she loves.

I'm riding a dopamine high, satiated physically, and even more important, experiencing true intimacy with a woman for the first time in my life.

"What are you looking at, Highness?" she asks, coyly circling one of her rosy nipples. The unself-consciously sexy action sends a shock wave through my core.

"Why, I'm looking at you, angel."

I increase my pressure, kneading the ball of her foot. Her lids flutter in a sort of ecstasy. I love that my touch brings her joy on so many levels, from carnally depraved acts to these gentle moments of tenderness. In fact, this is what surprises me most. I never doubted that physical pleasure with another would be anything less than addictive and amazing. But it's these quiet interludes where we aren't suck-ing and mouth-fucking, grinding and groping, that make me happiest.

I could watch Evangeline sit naked and cross-legged on the bed all day—doing nothing but sip-ping Earl Grey and sketching me—and consider myself contented.

She has filled almost an entire notebook with my nude form.

I'm not sure what she'll do with it when she even-tually leaves. I stiffen, my jaw tight as always when I think of such impossibilities as our eventual sepa-ration. I am arrogant enough to assume that she will take my images with her and on some lonely night in the future look at them with a smile playing on her lips of the sweet time we shared, these magic hours when the world seemed to stop for us.

We haven't taken things all the way. Christ, I smirk at myself. I sound like an earnest virgin.

But if the shoe fits…

I'm a virgin who has fucked a woman with his whole hand, allowed her to trace her tongue over every acre of my cock, kissed her from her aroused clit to her rosebud ass.

But I have not truly entered her.

Nor will I.

For as real as this feels, we still are playing a game of pretend. And for all intents and purposes, I am her client. No matter what emotions I think are tugging at my heart, I hired her from that Rosegate madam to be mine for a month.

If I enter her now, one thing is for certain… I won't ever be able to fulfill my destiny. If we join together, we will never be put asunder.

So I hold back, and though it seems to disappoint her, I have made sure to make it up to her in other ways that cause her immeasurable pleasure—and multiple orgasms. My current record is five in one session.

And it's one that I'm determined to break.

"What shall we do this afternoon, Your Highness?" she asks idly.

"I was thinking of trying that trick with my tongue that made you claw at my shoulders like a she-cat," I answer with a studied nonchalance.

She tosses a pillow at me, laughing. "A she-cat."

I point at the claw marks on my shoulders. "Do you have a better description?"

"I plead innocent," she says, opening her eyes extra-wide for emphasis. "I was driven out of my mind by lust."

"I'll drive you out of your mind," I cry and lunge at her, hooking her around the waist and tickling beneath her ribs.

There's a knock at the door.

"Did you order room service?" I ask, willing to let her go if she is famished. We've kept up quite the athletic horizontal routine.

"No, you?"

I frown. "No."

The knock sounds again with increased urgency, and I get the sinking feeling that our happy time here sequestered from the world has come to an abrupt end.

Evangeline lets out a huff of annoyance and wiggles into a pink silk nightshirt crumpled beside her. I get up and wrap a towel around my waist, sauntering to the door. It's a disappointment but not a surprise to see X there, hands clasped, face serious.

"I apologize for disrupting you, but this couldn't wait."

X has been hard at work deciphering the language of the map. What he thought would take him a mere day or two has lasted the week.

"Of course." I beckon him forward. "One moment so that I can get decent."

I duck into the bathroom, where I tug on a pair of sweatpants. My chest is covered in love bites. It turns out Evangeline likes to mark her territory, and for the time being, she considers my body hers.

I love seeing them there, a reminder of some of the happiest times in my life thus far.

When I come out, X is still standing, and Evangeline kneels on the edge of the bed covered in my robe.

"I couldn't get him to crack," she says. "He refuses to tell me a single word."

"That's because I didn't want to share this information without Benedict close by to provide support." X's voice is calm, cool, but also kind.

"What does that mean?" Evangeline rises up off her knees, her cheeks blanching with alarm. "Oh my God, Jasper. He's not… He isn't… Oh no, no, no—"

"No, not Jasper. Your sister-in-law, Camille, has been arrested, and your niece, Lola, has been removed to a government-run orphanage."

Evangeline

I crumple into a ball on the bed, convulsing with sobs. Here I've been basking in pleasure for the better part of almost two weeks, as if in denial of the danger my family still faced. Whoever started this has already taken from me my father and my brother. Now a mother and her child? Who could be so hateful? So merciless?

"Shh, angel. It will be okay," Benedict whispers as he rubs my spine.

I can barely speak through the tears. "This is my fault," I tell him. "I came here to do a job—to earn enough money to take care of them. To save my brother. Maybe I have been doing this for them, but I've also been indulging my every fantasy." I nearly choke on a hiccuping breath. "Because of my selfish whims, my niece—" I can't bear to think of it. "Oh, Lola," I cry. "Why didn't Camille call me? Prisoners are allowed a phone call, aren't they?"

X shakes his head. "This place is…different."

Benedict continues to try to soothe me, but I push him away, scrambling off the bed to where X stands.

"I have to help Camille—and get Lola out of that place!" I tell him. "You can help, X. I know you can."

He swallows but just stands there. Then I feel Benedict's hands on my shoulders.

"Evangeline," he says. "Of course X can help. We both can. But this is beyond our jurisdiction. The mother…she is imprisoned in Rosegate, yes?"

My whole body trembles as I nod.

"Your Highness," X says. "Despite our years of diplomacy with our territory, we have no direct oversight of their courts or laws. This is part of the Rosegate Compact of 1702."

I learned about this in primary school as a child. Our small kingdom was a simple city, smaller than Monaco and more akin to Vatican City, a country once walled off from the rest of Europe, with a focus on pleasure-making and the arts. At last, feeling the looming threat of war from the aggressive Nightgardin, Rosegate gave up much of our independence to be protected by Edenvale—but not all. And we never lost pride in who we were, a cultured people with a storied history.

"And, of course, the fact that last year your brother spurned the Baron of Rosegate's sister and blew up their planned engagement means we can't go through any direct route," X adds.

Through puffy eyes, I watch a silent conversation transpire between my prince and his guard. Benedict narrows his eyes at X, his jaw set in quiet obstinance.

"Your Highness," X says again, but nothing comes after.

For a long, drawn-out beat, neither man says a word. Benedict simply stares the other man down until X finally grumbles something.

"What was that, X?" Benedict asks with the authority of a true royal.

X crosses his suit-clad arms. "It was Sanskrit. I'm afraid the true meaning of my sentiment will get lost in translation. But if you are determined to try your dealings with Rosegate in this matter, then I must assist you."

I throw my arms around X's neck and kiss the man's cheek. "Thank you!" I cry. "Thank you! Thank you!"

Then I turn to Benedict, and he looks at me with a measured gaze.

"I have not forgotten our arrangement," he says, his voice calm. "I have sent two weeks' worth of payment to The Jewel Box already—and I've put some extra in a private account for you to access once you leave this place."

The muscle in his jaw ticks, and I want to reach for him, to assure him that as much as I need the money, he has become so much more than an assignment. But I can't lose focus again. So when my fingers twitch, and my hand begins to move, I stop myself before I can feel his stubble against my palm.

"Thank you" is all I say. "I'm going to clean myself up. Then have to leave for Rosegate at once."

Benedict is quiet for much of the three-hour ride to Edenvale's neighboring territory—to the place I truly call home. Though in the back of the Rolls-Royce that X drives, the prince sits with my hand in his, every now and then giving me a gentle squeeze to let me know he is still there.

I've gotten so used to seeing him in plain clothes—or nothing at all—that to see him in the habit of a priest once again is so jarring that I wonder if the man sitting next to me is the same one who has tasted every inch of my body.

"This is who I am," he says softly when he notices me staring.

I nod, and my throat tightens. "But is it who you want to be?"

"Evangeline," he says, but nothing comes after the utterance of my name.

And I get it. He has a duty to fulfill, whether he wants to or not. It is the way of his family, and despite his carnal needs, Benedict Lorentz is a man of honor. We are so much alike, the two of us. Bound to family in a way that choices seem to be made *for* us rather than of our own free will.

"This sure as hell isn't who I wanted to be," I say, forcing a laugh. But he doesn't respond. "I'm not proud, you know. Of what I have to do to take care of the ones I love." I swipe at a tear under my eye. "But there aren't many options for me in the art community at the moment, not with our family name being dragged through the mud like it is. It's funny, though. If the other girls knew I was a *prince's* whore—"

"Stop!" he growls. He drops my hand and grabs me by the shoulders. I see the pain in Benedict's dark green eyes, and I know that I've hurt him somehow.

"Never, Evangeline. Never do I want you to call yourself such a name again. Do you understand me?"

I open my mouth to answer, but he doesn't wait for me to do so.

"That account I set up for you—it's not just for the month you'll be with me. It is to take care of you and your family after we go our separate ways. I will not send you back to that place. I will not let another man—"

This time I interrupt him.

"I am not yours to save," I say, though I know

I'm a hypocrite. Here we are, entering the city of my birth, where I'm fully willing to let him leverage his power as a priest to get what I need. Because the truth is, if anyone could rescue me from the life I never wanted, it would be this man.

I would choose him. But he can't choose me.

"Highness, we are here," X says over the intercom, and I look out the window to see a sign that reads Rosegate Institution for Female Confinement.

Benedict and X both convinced me that trying to see Jasper is too risky. With me being the only one to solve this puzzle and save my family, whoever is after us—and I know the Madam fits in here somewhere—cannot know that I've found the map.

But a recently imprisoned woman who has called upon her personal priest for confession…

Benedict is our ticket to Camille.

"Do you remember the plan?" X asks, and Benedict nods.

"How can you be sure they will not recognize me?" the prince asks.

X lowers the partition and turns to us, grinning. "Because your brother is the face of Edenvale right now, and while I know living in his shadow might be unpleasant at times, you will now use it to your advantage. It would be wholly unexpected for Edenvale royalty to walk into this institution unannounced— and that is precisely why it will work."

I raise my brows, my gaze volleying between the two men.

"X," I say, "you speak as if you do this kind of thing all the time."

He winks. "I assure you I do nothing of the sort, Miss Evangeline." Then he turns to Benedict again. "They have a chapel on the premises. That is where they will bring her to meet you. It's imperative that you take her to the confessionals on the second floor. Should anything go wrong and you have to abort the mission early, there is a zip line that runs from the second-story window straight over the outer stone wall. We'll pick you up there if necessary."

Benedict squints at something in the far-off distance. "Do you mean that wall out there with the barbed wire at the top?"

X nods. "That's the one."

"And I'd have to jump out of a second-story window to attempt traveling over that wall?"

X nods again. "Yes, exactly."

"And if I ask how there came to be a zip line from the chapel to the property beyond the prison?" Benedict asks.

X gives him a crooked grin. "I'm afraid I'm not at liberty to divulge that information."

Benedict clears his throat. "Well, then. Nothing will go wrong," he says.

He kisses me quickly and exits the vehicle.

CHAPTER THIRTEEN

Benedict

"Father John?" A weasel-faced guard frowns at the roster. "I don't seem to have you here on my list of approved visitors."

"I arrived at the Rosegate Monastery last week." My tone is mild but firm, velvet stretched over steel.

"From Edenvale?" The guard cocks a brow and scratches the side of his pointy nose.

My accent gives me away as expected. I keep my face a gentle mask, the model of a simple priest come to hear prisoner confessions. "Yes, I'm here in your lovely city on a sabbatical."

The guard grumbles under his breath but seems reluctant to grill a man of the cloth.

"On your way," he mutters, hitting a buzzer that allows me entrance, and picks up a pornographic magazine.

Charming.

I pass through the thick stone walls topped with

barbed wire. No woman has ever broken out of a
Rosegate prison and lived to tell the tale. X must
have been joking with his talk of zip lines. Despite
Rosegate's reputation as a city of beauty, art and
learning, it has a dark underbelly, not unlike many
old European cities. In this case, it's home to an old,
but notorious, penitentiary.

A grim-faced female warden greets me with a
downturned mouth. "Morning, Father. This is an
unexpected visit."

I give her the sign of the cross. My hand does not
betray me with a tremble. My features remain as
calm as with the guard out front.

"There is no right or wrong time to find succor in
the mercy of the Holy Spirit," I say mildly.

She snorts and flexes her large fists. She looks
like the sort of person who drowns puppies for fun.
A steely-eyed woman for a coldhearted place. The
air is sour with hopelessness, as if those behind the
bars have been abandoned by God Himself. Through
one of the barred windows high above comes the unsettling sound of sobbing.

"No one has signed up to hear confession in
weeks," she growls. "Besides, what good will it do
'em?"

From somewhere deep inside the prison bowels
comes a terrified scream. "No, please! No!" It's cut
off with an abruptness that makes my throat tighten.

"For those who are of the faith, the sacrament is
an opportunity for atonement, to cleanse the soul

from the stain of sin." It's all I can do to steady myself in the face of so much casual cruelty.

"Ha! Hope you've come armed with bleach and industrial cleaner to deal with this filth." She whirls and sees a female prisoner scurrying past clutching a stack of books. "You there, where are you going?"

The woman flinches as if expecting to be struck with the billy club hooked to the guard's utility belt. "I'm Prisoner 35495, assigned library duty."

"Well, I don't like the look of you, 35495," the matron snarls. "What was your crime against the city?"

The woman bobs in an awkward curtsy. Her cheeks are gaunt. It looks as if she hasn't eaten a proper meal in months. I feel sick to my soul. This is what passes for justice in these parts? I'm part of the royal family and therefore culpable in this mistreatment. Rosegate might be a special city with special rules, but prisoner mistreatment is a violation of international law.

"Begging your pardon, miss," the woman stutters, her Rosegate accent making me wince. She sounds so much like Evangeline, who is now outside, waiting for me to send word of her sister-in-law's fate. "I'm a pirate."

"But there's no ocean near Rosegate. If you take me as a fool, I'll show you who laughs last around here." The warden's eyes are slits as her hand, the one that reads hate, slinks to the club.

"Begging your pardon again, I mean no disrespect," the prisoner says hastily. "See, I was convicted of piracy, not with regards to the ocean or ships, but for stealing." She hangs her head, her grimy face stained with shame. "I pirated a great deal of intellectual property. Books, to be specific. Hundreds if not thousands of them. That is why I work in the library now. I only have another month on my sentence, and I am trying to atone for the error of my ways."

The warden looks flabbergasted anyone would steal an item such as books. "Be gone from my sight, worm," she commands. "Now, where was I? Oh, you..." She looks at me as if I'm dog excrement stuck to her combat boots. "Like I said, no one signed up for confession. Sorry you hiked your holy butt out from the monastery, but we can't help you none."

I think fast. "But surely you have new prisoners. My monastery informed me that your new intake occurred this week." The lie flows so smoothly off my tongue that I almost convince myself.

She eyes me warily. "What's it to you?"

I'm setting off her internal alarms. "New prisoners might not have time to have requested confession."

She shrugs. "We only got one this week. Treason."

I don't blink an eye. "Then it sounds like she must have much to unburden. If you would be so good as to show me the way to the chapel, I'll wait for her there."

The warden blinks but finally grabs her radio. "Main Yard to Solitary, Main Yard to Solitary."

There is a crackle over the walkie-talkie. "This is Solitary, over."

"Yeah, I have a priest here who needs to hear the confession for the new prisoner you have on the floor."

"Prisoner 54329?"

"That's our girl."

"She started a hunger strike. She might be weak."

The warden's smile chills my blood. It is a promise of torture and cruelty untold. "Tell her to get moving or I'll drag her out myself...by that long ponytail of hers. She is scum, just like her thieving husband."

"Copy. She will be sent to the chapel. Over."

The warden smacks her fleshy lips with satisfaction. "You do-gooders don't know. These people are criminals. You have to treat them with a heavy hand. Fear is what will save them in the end. Not love."

I draw myself to my full height and allow a glimmer of my royal arrogance to gleam through my eyes. "That's enough."

She gasps and takes a few hurried steps back. "These lives, Father. They don't matter."

"I disagree," I say firmly. "Now take me to the chapel."

Evangeline

I pace outside the car while X leans against the front bumper, relaxed as if the prince sneaking into prison—unrecognized—is something that happens every day. Every few paces I stop and glance up at the stone wall that must be twenty feet high, the menacing barbed wire tracing the perimeter.

"Do you really have a zip line set for Benedict to escape if need be?" I ask.

X nods.

"How? This place is a secure fortress. And you didn't even know we were coming here until you walked into the annex this morning."

The man merely straightens his tie. "*You* didn't know we were coming here until I walked into the annex this morning."

My mouth opens and closes as I try to decide whether or not he is playing me. "You know heights are not his favorite, right?" I ask, sounding like a petulant child. Though it's not X who is deserving of my chastisement. I am. Because if anything happens to Benedict, it will be because of his involvement with me.

X simply nods again. "It is amazing what one can overcome when he has no choice but to face his demons."

I cross my arms and set my jaw. "Haven't enough choices been taken from him?"

X raises a brow, like he knows that my desire for Benedict to choose his own path is sprinkled with my own selfish hope.

Just then a crackling sound comes from the open window of the Rolls-Royce.

"What was that?"

He grins.

"That, Miss Evangeline, is our royal highness, Prince Benedict."

I run to the window and peek inside. "Did you tap into some sort of internal audio system?" I ask, expecting to see computer equipment that would alert me to X's possible hacking abilities, but all I find is a fancy digital watch sitting on the dashboard. I brandish it toward X. When my eyes meet his again, he takes the watch, fastens it to his wrist and shakes his head.

"A bug," he says, and I swat at the air around my head.

"Where?" I ask. "Is it a wasp? I think I might be allergic." My eyes dart from side to side looking for the would-be attacker. X steps around the nose of the car and grabs the hand that tries to shoo away the invisible insect.

"Not that kind of bug, Evangeline." He points to the watch. "This kind of bug."

"You have five minutes," a faint but distasteful voice speaks. "Then this one can get back to starving herself."

Someone makes a soft grunt, and then I hear him speak.

"Are you ready to make your confession, my child?"

It's Benedict, loud and clear. But it's the next voice that stops my heart.

"Forgive me, Father, for I have sinned. It has

been…a long time since my last confession. I've done many things, told white lies, taken the Lord's name in vain, been envious of other people. But you have to believe me that I'm innocent of any crimes that have landed me in this godforsaken hellhole." She gasps. "Forgive me again, Father. But someone is trying to hurt my husband and is now using me to do it. And our girl…" The woman sobs softly, her words muffled but understandable just the same. "They have taken everything from us. Just, please, find my darling girl."

"Camille!" I cry, but X covers my mouth with his strong hand.

"Listen," he whispers. "But do not call out, for either of them. Do you understand, Evangeline?"

I nod, trying to calm myself. But I cannot, not after I hear the desperation in my sister-in-law's words, not now that this is all too real. Jasper. Camille. Lola. Even Papa. They've all been taken from me, punished one by one, all for some stupid map hidden behind my painted face. A painting I was sent to find—one I may now give my life to protect.

"What if I said I could take you to her?" Benedict asks, and my whole being stills. What is he talking about? We came to talk to Camille, to find out what happened to get her locked up. Benedict couldn't possibly have the means to do what he's offering.

"Then you would be more powerful than God himself," Camille says. "I have prayed, begged, beseeched the Lord with my pleas to save my daughter, but I see no way out of this horrid place."

"Not out," Benedict says. "Over."

My eyes widen. Benedict went in there alone, but he plans to come out with Camille.

"I'm going to remove my hand now," X says. "That is, if you think you can behave."

I nod again, and he steps away, lowering his palm from my mouth.

"He came here to get her out?" I ask softly. "We came here to save her? Is this why there's a zip line?"

The corner of X's mouth quirks into a devilish grin.

"How can you possibly smile at a time like—"

But X isn't listening to me. Instead, he brings his wrist to his mouth, touches something on the watch and then speaks to it.

"Now, Highness! Grab the girl and get out of that place at once!"

I hear Camille yelp, and almost immediately after, shouts ring out across the prison yard.

"There's a jumper at the chapel!"

"Prison break!"

"Is that a…flying priest?"

"Holy shit. Sound the alarms!"

And then the alarms do sound. Just as quickly I hear a whistling and whirring noise, which is when I notice the nearly invisible line that skates over the sharpened wire that follows the perimeter atop the wall.

"They aren't going to make it!" I cry, caring nothing for the volume of my voice at this point.

"Get in the car!" X cries, forcing me toward my door. "Now! Now! Now!"

He throws open the door and hurtles me inside. I barely have time to right myself before we are careening away from the prison wall.

"What are you doing?" I scream, frantically clawing at the glass partition. "You can't leave them!"

My hand is on the door handle, and I'm ready to throw it open, to tuck and roll and run back to do... I don't know what! I am helpless to save Benedict and Camille, just as I was helpless to save my father. My brother.

X slams on the brakes hard. I'm thrown from my seat and onto the floor of the vehicle. I scramble for the door, but it opens before I can get to it. There stands my prince, dusting off his priestly habit with one hand, his other entwined with Camille's.

"Eva!" Camille cries when she sees me.

"Highness, we must get to the safe house. My associate will meet us there with the child."

Benedict helps my shell-shocked sister-in-law into the car, and she hiccups on a sob. "Evangeline...did he just say 'the child'? Does he mean my Lola?"

As soon as everyone is in the car, X races off again.

"He does, miss," Benedict answers her question.

"Wait, I know you." Camille's eyes bug out of her head. "I thought you looked familiar in the prison.

But it can't be... Am I dreaming? Has that terrible prison made me mad already?"

"You're safe. Just breathe." I grab her hand and give her a warm squeeze. "But how?" I ask my lover. "Did you know? I mean, I thought we were only going to get information."

Benedict shrugs. "This is X's doing, angel. All I knew was that eventually I'd have to jump. The rest is X's secret to reveal."

But the man behind the wheel stays silent, so I wrap my brother's wife in a hug and squeeze as I whisper, "I'm sorry," over and over again.

Then I check both her and Benedict for any barbed wire–related injuries and see nothing to give me pause until I find a tear in Benedict's pants above his outer thigh, blood staining the edges of the fabric.

"You're hurt," I say, my throat tightening.

"I'll live."

Then I launch myself into his arms and kiss him hard.

Camille gasps, and Benedict smiles against my lips.

"Camille Vernazza," I say, "meet Benedict Lorentz, Prince of Edenvale."

CHAPTER FOURTEEN

Benedict

"WE'VE GOT COMPANY," X says grimly, interrupting the family reunion taking place in the back seat of the Rolls.

A squadron of sirens fills the air. I twist around, my gaze narrowing. A dozen patrol units are in hot pursuit, speeding up the steep mountain switchback below. If I had any illusions they were hoping to bring us in for questioning, it's shattered when a flurry of gunshots erupt in staccato pops.

"Get down!" I fly over Evangeline and Camille, shielding them with my body. Dull metallic thuds shudder through the car as bullets riddle the bumper.

"I've never heard of law enforcement behaving in such a way," Evangeline breathes. Her body trembles, sending my protective instincts into hyperdrive. There is nothing—no damn thing—that I wouldn't do to keep this woman safe and free from suffering.

My body would happily endure any torments, as long as she makes it through this ordeal alive.

"Law enforcement would never act in this fashion," X snaps.

"These thugs are going through a hell of a lot of trouble trying to appear as rank-and-file police officers. The sirens are an especially authentic touch. But no." His voice hardens. "There is nothing legal about the men pursuing us. They are here for one thing and one thing alone. The map to the Spring. And they will stop at nothing until it is in their possession."

Evangeline grips her now sobbing sister-in-law.

"This is all my fault! We'll be caught for sure." Her eyes, sheened with her own tears, meet mine over the top of Camille's head. "I'm so sorry for dragging you into my mess. My brother and I are cursed. We hurt everyone we come in contact with and—"

"Don't say that!" Camille cries. "Your brother is a hero to Rosegate—"

"Hold on." X takes a bend at over one hundred and thirty kilometers an hour.

Jesus Christ, he isn't breaking a sweat.

Who is this guy?

Evangeline brushes an errant strand of hair. "The danger that you're all facing is because—"

"Of our choosing," Camille interrupts. "I knew what your brother was before I agreed to marry him."

"What?" Evangeline's laugh is incredulous. "A

mild-mannered art historian? What danger did you think he'd get you into? A narcoleptic state where he waxed on for five hours on the birth of French Classicism or inquiries into Gothic architecture?"

Camille's brows smash together. "But surely you know."

"She doesn't," X says in a steady voice, increasing the speed as he pushes the throttle into fourth gear. "Evangeline hasn't been informed of a great many things. Her brother and father left her in the dark, hoping to keep her safe. I'm sad to say it's had the opposite effect."

Outside the Rolls's windows, the mountain wildflowers blur into a single hue of pinkish purple. The engine hums. We're going too fast. There's no way we can hope to take the next turn.

Sweat prickles my chest. X meets my eyes in the rearview mirror. He silently asks for my trust. The sirens grow louder. My brother Nikolai trusted this man with his life day after day, and also the life of his true love. Now I must do the same. I give a single curt nod, and I swear the man smiles.

"Your brother? Mild-mannered?" Camille gives me a disbelieving laugh. "You really don't know!"

"Know whaaaaaaaaaaaa!" Evangeline cries out as X misses the next turn altogether and flies straight off the asphalt.

My stomach turns in a sickening somersault as the Rolls soars through space. No one screams. The two women must be in shock, because there is only stillness. It reminds me of the time I flew in a glider with Damien and Nikolai, back when we were three brothers united by love and laughter.

The sirens fade behind us, but below a mournful whistle cuts through the valley.

A train.

"Excellent." X checks his watch. "The 5:55 express from Geneva is running right on time."

"You can't be serious," I say as the Rolls descends faster and faster. Outside my window a bird of prey soars past and does a double take.

"Serious is my middle name." X grips the wheel. "I've timed it perfectly. Everyone stay calm, and— that's it, really. Just stay calm."

A twelve-car commuter train stretches out beneath us.

"You've done this before?" I shout.

A small muscle in his jaw twitches. "Of course not! Who'd be insane enough to drive a Rolls-Royce off a mountain and try to land on a moving train?"

The next three seconds go fast and slow all at the same fucking time. I feel as if I live a thousand lifetimes in fear, not for myself but for the woman beside me. She's going to survive this no matter what happens. There's a thump and X slams the brakes.

We are balanced in the center of the car.

He dusts off his shoulders. "Well, I have good news and bad news."

"After the stunt you pulled, I'll take the good

first, thanks," I snap, fighting to keep my heart in my chest.

"We're alive."

"That is always a bonus," I comment wryly. "Now for the bad news."

"We're about to go into the St. Georges Tunnel." He gestures to the looming black hole in front of us. "I'm afraid that the Rolls is lost. A pity. I love this car."

Evangeline and Camille grip each other tightly.

"The train will slow going into the tunnel." I go into hyper-focus. "We'll need to jump."

"Yes." X doesn't hesitate because we are obviously out of time. "An unconventional but necessary outcome, I'm afraid, Highness."

"Jump?" Camille moans. "We'll break our necks. I'm going to leave Lola an orphan."

The whistle blows as the engine car disappears into the mountain tunnel. The train begins to drop in speed.

"Here's what we'll do." I'm utterly calm, my protective instincts taking over. Nothing bad will happen to Evangeline. I will do whatever it takes to see her safe. "Stay loose. Fear makes you tense. If you stay relaxed, you'll have a better chance of not being injured."

Evangeline gives me a surprised look.

"Before I was in the seminary, I was a black belt student of jujitsu. I even trained in Brazil for a summer. We learned how to fall properly through hours of relentless practice."

X nods. "Yes. Good advice. We're going to all jump off the left side."

"The key will be to land on the balls of your feet, press your knees together and keep your chin tucked at all costs," I order. "When you hit, twist so that your calves and thighs hit the ground before your head and shoulders."

Evangeline is shaking as Camille hyperventilates.

"There is no choice. The tunnel is here!"

Evangeline

"Now!" X cries, and before I can react, he throws the driver's-side door open and leaps from the vehicle.

Tears stream down my face as I look at Camille. "Go!" I say. "You must get to Lola!"

She nods, and Benedict flings open the door. She doesn't look back—scared as I know she is—and jumps.

A strange silence holds Benedict and I suspended in this final moment. Logically, I know that the train's engine alone is deafening, but my world has boiled down into his eyes.

"I'm not leaving you," I say with a sob.

His green eyes shine as he forces a smile. "We cannot jump together, angel. It is too dangerous. You must go first." He takes my hand and squeezes it. "If I could give my heart to any other than God, Evangeline, I would give it to you. Whatever happens, know that this was never about what I hired you for, not after that first night."

I open my mouth to say something in response, but the whistle blows violently, the final alarm.

"Jump!" he cries, and as I hurl myself from the door, I whisper words he cannot hear.

"I love you, my sweet prince."

I try to remember Benedict's directions as the ground speeds up to greet me, as I hear the sickening crash of metal hitting the tunnel walls—the Rolls.

Balls of my feet, bend my knees, twist. But I twist the wrong way, and I cry out as something feels like it snapped in my knee. The pain makes me gag.

I roll, my limbs now tucked to my chest as my cheeks scrape against branches strewn across the small clearing in the woods. When I finally stop moving, I lie there for a minute or two catching my breath, checking myself for any other injuries. I touch my cheek, and my fingertips come away with a light smear of blood. But everything else seems intact. That is, until I stand, forgetting about the whole knee-twisting-on-impact incident.

I crumple to the ground again and hiss from the gut-twisting agony, but I cannot stay here. Once whoever is chasing us finds the wreckage from the Rolls—and doesn't find us wrecked inside it—they'll know we escaped.

So I crawl to my feet, balancing on my left leg

while I attempt to put the slightest bit of weight on my right. It hurts like nothing I've ever felt before, but I'm able to limp, slowly. I cross my fingers that it's just a sprain and hobble in the direction of where the tunnel opens, which I know will eventually lead to a main road. We had no time to discuss where we would all meet after the jump, so I assume this is my next logical move.

I want to call for Benedict, Camille or X—not just because I'm afraid to be alone out here but because I need to know that they're okay—but if whoever is after us is already searching the woods, that is the last thing I should do.

So I limp for the tracks, gritting my teeth each time I put pressure on my right leg. This is the only way I'll find Benedict again.

It feels like a lifetime when I finally make it to a road, but there is no one there to greet me. I can't walk any farther, though, and am about to collapse when I hear the faint rumble of a car's engine. If X had this whole prison break planned, then he must have foreseen us needing alternate transportation.

Adrenaline courses through my veins, and I'm filled with a renewed sense of hope when a black limousine with tinted windows rolls to a stop where I stand.

"Benedict!" Happy tears fall as the rear door flies open. But my elation turns to horror when a woman I don't recognize steps from the vehicle. She is sturdy and strong with an unforgiving sneer on her face and a billy club in her utility belt. She raises a brow and gives me a studied gaze, that sneer morphing into a terrifying smile. She cracks her knuckles, and I read the words *love* and *hate* tattooed across the fingers on each hand.

Without a word, she backhands me across the face, on the already split-open cheek, and my teeth clatter. I cry out and stumble. But she catches me by the wrist before my knee gives out, her steely grip nearly pulling my shoulder from its socket.

"Get inside, whore. Madam would like to have a little word."

That voice. I've heard it. I swear it is the same one I heard speaking to Benedict inside the prison, but there is no time to ask questions.

She jerks my arm, and I pitch forward into the vehicle, my hands and knees bracing my fall as I hit the floor. Stars dance across my vision, and I think I might be sick, but my attacker follows me in, hauling me onto the seat before my body has a chance to react. She yanks my hair so I'm facing my employer, a woman I know only as the Madam.

Once the limousine door is closed, the Madam removes her black hat and with it the short, netted veil that covers her face. She is frightening and beautiful at the same time, with her porcelain skin, jet-black waves falling over her shoulders and lips as red as blood. She stares at me with eyes so dark I almost think they are black, but I decide I must be hallucinating from the pain.

"Ruby, Ruby, Ruby," she lilts in a soft voice that could lull me to sleep if I didn't fear for my life. "You were hired to do a job, and so far you have failed."

She smiles, her lips curling to reveal perfect white teeth.

My captor gives my hair a swift tug. "This is the part where you ask what you can do to make it up to the Madam," she says in a gruff tone.

I swallow hard. "I... I thought you would be pleased with the new arrangement," I say. "The prince is sure his brother only meant for me to tempt him for the night. Now I have the rest of the month to find—"

The Madam cuts me off with a terrifying laugh. "Prince Benedict still thinks his brother, the future king, brought you to him? Then he's more naive than I thought. Yes, Prince Nikolai is the one who requested Pearl. But that simply gave me my in to use you."

"He tripled my fee—" I start, but I almost choke when my head jerks again.

"You're done speaking until I say," the other woman says.

The Madam is impatient. "This was never about money, sweet jewel," she says, then leans forward to caress my cheek with an icy finger. "It was about trust. I knew that prince would never be able to resist another reluctant sinner. Now that he's risked his life for you—and dare I say fallen in love—we have our trust." She brushes her hand across my bruised and bloodied cheek, and I wince. "Stop. Wasting. My. Time. I know you've found it. But that's no longer enough. Bring me the map, Evangeline, and your family will suffer no more."

She knew. This whole time she knew that painting was me—that it belonged to my family.

I grit my teeth, even as I tremble. "Never," I say, and the brute of a woman next to me threatens to scalp me with her grip. "I will not betray him."

There has to be another way.

The Madam sighs, pulls a phone from a clutch beside her on the seat and hands it to me.

"Just press Play," she says, and with a trembling finger, I do.

What I see is worse than any nightmare that has plagued me for the past ten years. It is my brother, Jasper, tied to a chair as someone dressed head to toe in black, an executioner of sorts, punches him again and again in the face until all I can see is blood where his eyes should be. I hear the horrifying crack of what must be his nose breaking, and I shriek when the person in black removes a dagger from their boot and holds it to my brother's neck.

But Jasper doesn't say a word. I cannot even tell if he is conscious. But he was at some point. He took that beating without making a sound, and I realize this is not the quiet, reserved man I know. This is a man with a strength I never knew he possessed, strength these people are trying to test, but he does not give in. And just as it looks as if I'm about to

watch my brother's murder, I hear the Madam's unmistakable voice say, "That will be enough."

The screen goes black.

I tremble, barely able to speak. "Did you... Did
you kill him?" I stammer.

"Not yet," she says with measured calm. "He
claimed not to know where the map was, but thanks
to your correspondence with dear Camille, we realized that you do."

Camille's phone. They've been listening to our
conversations the whole time.

"But I never said—"

The Madam waves me off. "You said enough for
me to know that you already have what I need and
have the audacity to think that you can stall for more
time. The Order can't stop us now. Simply bring it
to me, and all of this goes away." She reaches for
the phone still clutched in my hand. "And if you
disappoint me again? Well, let's say that the police
guard outside your brother's hospital room can be
easily persuaded to turn a blind eye while we finish
the job." Her lips part into a bloodred smile. "And
remember—if we can get to you in your little royal
residence, we can get to your prince, too." She leans
close, her breath caressing my cheek, and my body
convulses. "Imagine the pious second son found
murdered in his chamber by his filthy whore. Think
of what that would do to his family—to his memory."

I shake violently, but I won't beg this monster for
mercy. I already saw what she did to my brother. I

have no doubt in her threat—at how easily she could end Benedict's life and point the finger at me. And though I'd never raise a violent hand to my prince, his life is in danger because of me. I would, in essence, be his killer.

The Madam places the veiled hat back on her head and nods to the woman next to me.

"You get to return to your prince now," the other woman says with one final tug at my hair. "If you know what's good for you—and your friends—you won't breathe a word of our little encounter. And at midnight tonight, you'll bring the map and anything else you've learned to that sweet little fairy-tale cottage of yours. One of our people will meet you there to collect it."

She throws open the door and steps out, grabbing my wrist and forcing me to follow.

"I know you won't disappoint the Madam again," she says.

When she lets go of my hand, I crumple to the ground, my strength and my resolve flooding out of me all at once. The tires crackle as the car rolls away, and I squeeze my eyes shut trying to erase the vision of my brother sitting in that chair, broken but unwavering in his purpose of protecting the location of the map.

And now I have to betray him—and the man I love—to save them all.

"Evangeline!" I hear in the distance, but I decide it must be a dream, so I keep my eyes shut.

I don't want to wake up now, because the nightmare doesn't just exist when I sleep. "Evangeline!"

"Benedict?" I whisper, but it's too late. Pain, ex-
haustion and fear pull me under as strong, sturdy
arms scoop me up, my head cradled into a warm
chest.

"It's okay, angel," he says. "You're safe."

But we're not. We never were. So I'll do what I
have to do to save Jasper's life—to save all of them—
even if it means losing Benedict for good.

CHAPTER FIFTEEN

Benedict

"BENEDICT, BENEDICT. Is it really you?" Evangeline burrows deeper into my chest, murmuring my name over and over like a prayer.

"I am here, angel." I kiss the top of her head, inhaling her sweet scent. "I'm right here. Everything is going to be all right. We're back together."

"No!" She gasps. "Nothing is ever going to be all right ever again!" Her eyes are unfocused. Her cheekbones have been slashed by brambles, and there's a sickening bruise on one temple. "The whole world feels on fire. All dreams nothing but fire and ash." And with that her body goes limp as the darkness again consumes her.

A crow calls somewhere deep in the forest. I shudder. In our country, the crow is an omen of death and dying.

I step off the road in favor of the tree cove, my feet padding the detritus fallen from the towering pines. The air is thick with sap warming in the dappled shafts of sunlight slicing through the ancient branches. This place feels primeval, beyond time and almost holy.

A branch cracks, and a frisson of awareness skims my skin. We are not alone.

I turn, ready to fight to protect the beautiful woman who lies unconscious in my arms.

"X!" My shoulders slump at the sight of my guard. "Jesus Christ, am I glad to see you."

He raises a brow, the man looking relaxed and ready for a night on the town, no worse for the wear after jumping from a speeding train. "Thought you weren't supposed to commit blasphemy."

I narrow my gaze. "Today I have busted a woman out of prison via zip line, taken part in a high-speed chase in a luxury vehicle and held on as said car broke through guard rails and landed on top of a commuter train. Oh, and then I jumped off that train to avoid being decapitated by a mountain tunnel. I believe the Holy Spirit is willing to cut me some slack given the circumstances."

X's broad shoulders shake with a rumble of soft laughter as he passes a hand over the top of his head, removing a stray pinecone. "Fair enough."

"Two questions," I say. "How do you look as if you've merely been out on a stroll, and where is Camille?"

X ignores the first question and answers the second. "Camille has been picked up by friends from

The Order. She will be taken to a safe house while we attempt to locate the daughter in the orphanage."

Evangeline gasps.

My eyes widen. The men and women of shadow. Secret assassins and ancient defenders of the secrets of our realm.

"You heard a crow earlier. That was the signal she had been located. The crow is their symbol."

"The symbol of death?"

"For their enemies. And also themselves. They must kill off the parts that know fear."

I glance through the underbrush. Are these secret soldiers watching us even now?

"It is just us here," X says, cuing into my thoughts. "No easy solution like a safe house for a member of the royal blood, I am afraid. But not to worry. Help is on the way—or at least will be once I fetch the chopper."

"A helicopter?"

X cracks his neck. "My apologies, Highness, but there isn't time to explain. Four hundred meters down the hill you will run into a stream. Follow it for a kilometer, and at the junction look up. You will see a small cave. It is one that hermit monks once used as a shelter to avoid the temptations of the world. You will find it stocked with medical supplies to tend to Evangeline, food and a warm bed. Look to the west when the last light of the sun falls. I will come for you. You and Evangeline will be safe within the palace walls well before midnight."

Evangeline

I bolt upright in bed and cry out, my cheek burning with pain. A hand reaches for me, and I swat it away, expecting to see the word *hate* tattooed across knuckles about to make contact with my skin.

"Evangeline!"

I'm not strong enough to fight him off as his hand wraps around my wrist, and that's when my vision clears. I'm not being held captive in that limousine anymore.

"Benedict," I say, and I stop struggling. "I wasn't dreaming."

He shakes his head, but his emerald eyes are a storm of worry. "You're okay, angel. But I think the jump was the hardest on you."

He reaches gingerly for my face with his other hand, a hand that holds a cotton swab doused in some sort of liquid.

"I thought I could clean the wound while you were unconscious, that I could spare you the pain. I'm sorry to have startled you."

Even though I know it's coming now, I still wince.

He pauses. "You took quite a beating out there," he says with a forced smile.

I close my eyes and nod, bracing myself for the sting. With it comes the reminder of what really did happen out there—and that I cannot tell him any of it.

I take a shuddering breath as he swipes the cotton

across my skin. Tears stream from the corners of my closed eyes, and almost as quickly as they begin, I feel Benedict's lips kissing them away.

"I'm sorry," he whispers. "I'm so sorry." He drops the cotton onto a tray beside the bed.

I blink and take in my surroundings, realizing we are not at the palace.

"What is this place?" I ask, voice trembling. "Where are we? Are they still looking for us? What… what about Camille? And X?"

"Shh," he whispers. "We're safe. X led us here, and he'll return this evening to take us home. Camille is on her way to be reunited with Lola. Everyone is okay."

Benedict tucks my hair behind my ear and swipes at a falling tear. I exhale, daring to let my shoulders relax.

"Everyone's okay?" I ask, remembering the one person who isn't.

Jasper.

He nods, but his brows pull together. "I thought—" His mouth clamps shut, the muscle pulsing along his jaw. "I thought I might lose you," he says, his voice rough.

You will, I think, and swallow a sob. It is the last thing I want and yet the only way to make sure Jasper lives. That all of us do.

"I'm right here," I say, because whatever time we have left together, I want to give him my full attention—to give him whatever he needs. Because despite what must happen when we get to the palace, I love him.

I slide back to rest against the headboard of the bed, hissing as I put pressure on my leg.

"What is it?" he asks, his eyes wide with alarm.

"My knee," I tell him. "I twisted it when I landed."

He pulls away the blanket. "Jesus," he whispers. "You need help. The swelling is bad."

I nod. "I know. And did you just take the Lord's name in vain?" I ask, trying to smile.

He lets out a bitter laugh. "Yes. And it's not the first time today." He moves to the button on my jeans, and I gasp.

"What...what are you doing?"

He continues his movement as he speaks, pulling down my zipper. "I grew up with two brothers," he says. "I know enough about sprains and breaks to be able to determine how serious the injury is. I'm not sure how to get X here with the helicopter any quicker, but if we need to get you to a hospital, we'll find a way."

"No!" I cry, knowing that if I don't complete my task tonight that Jasper may not be alive tomorrow. "No hospitals—not until we know they're not looking for us anymore." The lie comes so easily, but I know to tell him any of this would be to risk his life as well as my brother's.

I cooperate, though, as he tugs my pants over my hips and to my ankles. He must have already removed my shoes, because a second later my jeans are on the cave floor.

His brows pull together, and he rests a warm hand on my knee. I squeeze my eyes shut, too scared to look.

Benedict's relief is in his voice. "Nothing looks out of alignment." I open one eye to peek at him... and at the swelling. "Can you bend it?"

I slide my heel just enough to raise my knee off the bed, biting the inside of my cheek to keep from crying out. But I can move it. That has to be a good sign.

He leans over and kisses the bruised skin. "It needs ice," he says against me. "We won't be able to tell much more until the swelling goes down, and I worry that we won't be able to tend to it for some time."

I touch his face, his stubble scratching my palm, and finally let the tiniest bit of relief flood through me.

"I thought I'd lost you, too," I tell him. "You made sure everyone else got out of the car first. We were so close to the tunnel. I didn't think there was enough time—"

He crawls up beside me and kisses me, soft at first and then with a fierceness that tells me that whatever's been happening between us this past week, we've crossed over a threshold today, and I'm not sure we can go back.

"I'm right here," he says, echoing what I said to him.

"I know." He kisses me again and again, each one hungrier than the last. "But I feel like I can't get close enough—like I cannot satisfy this need to keep you safe. I don't want to let you out of my sight again."

My hands cradle his face as our lips meet once more. Our tongues tangle and dance, and I know what he means. Because I pull him closer, kiss him deeper, but it's not enough.

He lifts his head, his chest heaving, and his gaze bores into mine.

"What's wrong?" I ask.

"I don't want to hurt you."

I skim my hand along his temple. "I don't feel any pain when you're kissing me," I say.

He shakes his head. "That's not what I mean." He takes in a long, measured breath, then lets it out. "I want to tell you something, but I'm afraid that in the long run, all it will do is hurt you. Hurt both of us."

And because I know what he wants to say, I decide to relieve him of his burden and say it first. To let him know that it's okay. To follow his destiny, he must break my heart. And for me to protect the ones I love, I must also break his.

So I beat him to the punch.

"I love you, Benedict." His eyes widen. "I love you, and whatever happens after this, it's okay. I'll survive it."

I watch his Adam's apple bob as he swallows. Then he grasps for the hem of my shirt, lifting it over my head.

"I love you, Evangeline. With every beat of my traitorous heart. With every shred of my sinning soul."

He flicks open the front clasp of my bra, fingertips skimming my breasts as he removes it from me completely. Then he slides my panties down my legs until I'm completely exposed—bare, trembling and so much in love with this tortured man whom I will betray to protect. But not now. Not here. Until we leave this place, he is mine to care for.

"God can decide what to do with my body and soul once it is his to govern. But today I give myself to you. My angel. My love. My Evangeline."

My breath catches as he removes his own shirt, his pants and what he wears beneath. All that is left is a gold chain with a cross dangling like a pendulum above me.

"Benedict," I start, but I don't have the right words to say to this beautiful man who has given up everything, who is giving himself over to me. As much as my heart cries out for him, my body responds by welcoming him, my clit swelling between my legs, causing me to writhe against the sheets.

"You were my first client," I blurt, needing him to know that I did what I did out of necessity. That I was never practiced in this art.

"And there will be no more," he says, his voice laced with a type of possession I wish would last a lifetime. "But I'm afraid I don't have— I was not anticipating—"

I let out a bittersweet laugh. "I am protected," I say, understanding his worry. "I have to be. In case anyone…" But I don't want to think about being with anyone in this way but him. I don't want to dwell on what might have been if I was not sent to Benedict first.

I reach for his cock, my thumb swirling the precum over his tip, and then I pull it toward my opening, letting out a soft moan as he rubs against me. I'm already slick between my folds, ready to take him in.

"Are you sure?" I ask. "This is what you want?"

Without another word, he sinks inside me to the very hilt, a primal growl tearing from his lips, and I arch against him as I cry out his name.

"Christ," he says through gritted teeth, but his word is not meant for prayer.

And he does not ask for forgiveness.

CHAPTER SIXTEEN

Benedict

My world is Evangeline, and Evangeline is my world. I hold still and absorb the magnitude of this moment, savor the fact that I am inside a woman—and not just any woman, but one whom I love. It is not just the eight inches of my body inserted into her wet, tight heat like a well-fitting glove, but it is our very souls connecting. There is no she or me, just a communion of sweat, salt, love and desire.

"Please," she begs, making near-inarticulate purrs. "Please."

What we share is as old as the stone surrounding us, an ancient dance that my body understands, despite the fact this is my first time. I roll my hips, unable to bear exiting completely, and then rock back in.

As much as I want to look at her face until her image is seared into my mind like a permanent tattoo, I close my eyes, needing to feel her more. Every sweet square inch of her silken folds and satiny tunnel. No fabrics at the finest dress shops in Paris, New York or London can compare with the exquisite softness of my Evangeline's gorgeous pussy.

She lifts her hips to meet my next thrust, and my thick shaft traces over her hardening pearl-like center. At the same time, her inner muscles clench my cock, milking me hard. Fuck. She blows my mind.

"Do that again," she murmurs.

"Oh yeah. Again and again," I rumble. This time I clench my ass and put more force into my glide, ensuring her swollen clit gets every inch of my royal treatment. The slapping sound fills the cave, our lovemaking hot and raw. This isn't mindless fucking, but savage joining, bittersweet because it cannot be forever.

But it is now.

And it must be enough.

She wraps her thighs around my hips, her heels finding grip against my ass, and I know that I am lying.

This will never be enough.

This is what I was born to do.

Desperation explodes within me. It's like I'm in a candy store and have been told I can have anything I want, but only for the next ten minutes. My mouth fastens on the peak of her nipple, and I suck, then let my lower teeth graze the pale skin, and she arches against me. As I turn to give my attention to the other, I lower my hand, grasping her ass while I roll over, letting her be on top.

I remain in a half-sit, laving her nipples while she rides me buck wild. It's all I can do to hang on to her undulating body. The scruff from my five-o'clock shadow skims her wet, flushed flesh. She leans into me with a cry, and my fingers slide into the cleft of her backside. I skim her tight rosebud, not entering, but keeping up a light pressure as I enjoy the show.

She raises her arms up over her head, twining her long hair through her fingers, luxuriating in the feel of me filling her with everything I have to give. I use my other hand to thrum her clit in relentless circles that echo the rhythm of her hips.

She's so wet and I shove her backward, mouth-watering, needing a taste of that sweet pussy. I'm rough, but no less rough than she, as I part her folds with my thumbs and drag my tongue over her tangy slit, her nails biting into my shoulders.

"God. Benedict. Oh my God, yes, right there."

I drink her like she is a sacrament, like she is salvation, and every lick is heaven.

"Inside me," she begs. "I want you to feel me come for you."

She doesn't have to ask twice. I throw her on her stomach, burying myself back inside. Her ass nestles again my abs. I brace myself with one hand and use the other to skim over her beautiful bouncing breasts, the concave dip of her belly, the flare to her hip, and I nestle at the apex of her need.

I can go deeper in the position, but what I don't count on is how much deeper I can go into myself. I am discovering a wellspring of powerful love and tenderness that I never knew I was capable of feeling. My entire body feels like nothing more than a vessel to worship this woman until the end of time.

But we don't have that long, and I need to make every second count. I bend and run the underside of my lower lip between her shoulder blades. I breathe in her scent. There is so much that I need to tell her, but I am not sure if I have the words. So I turn to the vocabulary of gentle kisses and teasing clitoral swirls.

"Come with me," she urges, her voice cracking with urgency. "Now."

Evangeline

Benedict stills inside me and pulls out, and for a second I wonder if he's already regretting this, stopping before we can finish.

"I need to see you, angel," he says in a hoarse whisper. "I need to look into your eyes when we take this leap together."

I roll over, any physical pain I might have felt now nothing more than a distant ache, and there he is, towering over me with such love in his eyes I wonder how I'll ever survive the fallout of what I must do tonight.

I stroke a finger over the cut on his thigh, telling

myself that the wound is only superficial. But how deep will the hurt go when I break his trust?

"Benedict," I say, my voice cracking, and I think I might tell him everything.

But he reaches toward my face, his thumb brushing away a tear when I hadn't even realized I was crying.

"Let me take the pain away, Evangeline."

Then he bends over to kiss me, his lips sweet and featherlight against mine before he fills me anew. I cannot stop the tears as he thrusts inside me, again and again, his eyes locked on mine.

"I love you," he says. "Always."

Then he plunges deeper than I knew any man could go, filling not only my body, but my entire heart and soul.

"Always, Benedict." He presses a hand between us, his thumb on my clit, and I buck against him, insatiable. Our short time together can never be enough.

Together we fly off the edge in undeniable ecstasy, a savage growl tearing from Benedict's lips as I cry out his name.

He collapses next to me, chest heaving as he cradles me in his arms. He kisses me, and I taste the salt of tears, not sure if they are his or mine—or maybe both.

"I didn't know it could be like this," he whispers, and all I can do is nod, to speak to him only through lips touching lips, or else I will crumble to a million pieces, my heart trampled to dust.

Hours later, we sit in a helicopter, piloted by X, as he tells us what should be good news. Camille and Lola have been reunited and are hidden in a village until it is safe for them to return. But my chest is heavy with the weight of what's to come—of what I still stand to lose.

"Also," he says into his headset microphone, "I did not want to mention it this morning." He raises a brow. "I felt the whole breaking your brother's wife out of prison situation was enough to focus on."

"What is it?" Benedict asks, squeezing my hand.

My mind wanders, wishing we were far away from here. "I've deciphered the map."

X's voice comes through loud and clear in my own headset, but his words do not register.

"What?" I ask, my eyes widening.

Benedict leans forward toward the cockpit. "Where does it lead?"

X holds up a hand, signaling for the prince to wait, and my stomach feels as if it has leaped to my throat. Maybe this will be good news—something that will mean I won't have to betray my family or the man I love.

We're landing.

Minutes later we touch down on the royal helipad, and we wait several minutes for X to power down the beast and for the propellers to stop.

X exits the aircraft, and then Benedict follows so the two of them can help me to the ground. I limp to a waiting vehicle, a BMW SUV.

"Ah," Benedict says. "Damien's car that he left behind. Father gave this to him before he was even old enough to drive it—legally. Now, from what I know, he only drives the sleekest of racing automobiles. And he's quite good, I hear."

Benedict says his banished brother's name in a wistful tone, and I realize there is so much of this man's history I do not know.

"We should at least get you to the palace doctor," he says as I wince lowering myself into the car.

I shake my head. "I want to know what the map says. I want to see what my father and brother were hiding."

X pulls his door closed in front and turns to face us.

"What we were hiding," he says. "I know Jasper Vernazza well. And I think it's time I tell you everything, Miss Evangeline."

Benedict gets his wish—as do I. We sit in his private library, X laying out the map on a table before us as the palace doctor does his best to examine me.

"It seems to be a nasty sprain," the man says as he props my foot on a pillow and places a cooling pack on my knee. "You should stay off it for a few days."

Benedict stands above me, arms crossed. "I'll see to it, Doctor."

"But this gash on your cheek..." he adds. "Are you sure you merely scratched it? The bruising says otherwise."

Benedict's eyes darken. "What do you mean?"

The doctor strokes a short, dark beard. "The severity of the bruise and the swiftness with which it has appeared speaks to blunt trauma."

"I think I might have bumped it on my fall, as well," I blurt, remembering the force of that woman's hand against my face. It takes all of my will to keep myself from shaking, to convince everyone that what I speak is the truth.

The doctor lets out a sigh. "I do recommend X-rays for both injuries. The fact that you can limp suggests a sprain, but the swelling can be hiding something we can't see. And that bruise?" He shakes his head. "I'd hate for there to be a chipped bone in that beautiful face. Promise me that you will get to the hospital in the next day or so after you've rested."

I nod, seemingly appeasing all three men, and the doctor bows to the prince before taking his leave.

Benedict sits on the couch beside me, softly stroking my battered cheek with the tips of his fingers.

"Is there anything you're not telling me?" he asks.

I swallow the lump in my throat and shake my head.

"I jumped off a moving train," I say. "I think that's enough to do a girl in."

And watching my brother almost get beaten to death.

He kisses me softly. "Of course, angel."

I let out a breath. "X," I say. "Tell me everything."

CHAPTER SEVENTEEN

Benedict

"Everything?" X arches a brow after showing the doctor out and locking the door behind him. He then heads to the windows and pulls the blinds, even though we are on an upper floor in the tower library. His shoulders heave in an inward sigh. "Very well. Why don't we start here?" He blows across the map. Dust motes fly off the parchment, filtering through the lamp-lit air.

I rub my hand over my thigh, trying to subtly knead out the muscle tension. Of course there is a bad feeling welling inside me. Only hours ago I buried my shaft in the silken cleft of the woman beside me, this amazing and devoted sister and aunt who is going to stop at nothing to reunite her brother with his wife and child.

"Where is *here*?" Evangeline asks, oh-so-naturally lacing her fingers with mine. She has no idea that she destroys me with the gentle caress.

"At the start of all good stories." X jabs a finger in the top left corner of the map. "The beginning of everything."

Beginning.

The word seeps into my skin like vitriolic acid. We sit and discuss beginnings when too soon my time with Evangeline will come to an end. Perhaps this is my great spiritual test, to be confronted by my heart's desire, be offered it freely and without equivocation. But I must lead myself not into temptation and instead deliver myself from evil.

Except there isn't an evil bone in Evangeline. She is an angel in female form. Good to her core. Why can't I have her? Why can't I walk a different path than the one paved for me by expectation and family tradition?

I know the answer, and it lies deeper than a boy so desperate for his father's attention. The sins of the mother. That is what I must contend with. So much has gone wrong in our family and it's up to me to do my part to put things to right.

I grip her hand tighter than intended, and she is alarmed.

"Benedict...are you all right?"

"Sorry, angel," I mutter. "Please proceed, X."

"I have to make a confession. When we discovered the map behind the angel, I was not entirely truthful on a few matters." He meets my gaze and holds it steadily. "Allow me to rectify. This forest stretches from beyond the palace walls to the peaks that separate Edenvale from Nightgardin." X waves a hand over a dark shadowed area on the map. "Here is where our story begins. The Tale of The Order."

"Let me guess," Evangeline says in a teasing tone. "You're one of them, a covert secret soldier charged with guarding and protecting Edenvale."

"Do not laugh," X orders. "This isn't a game. Our neighbors to the north want something very badly. The Spring of Youth."

I blink. "How do you know if the old story is real? Have you ever seen the Spring?"

"Highness." X regards me a long time. "Recall the story of Doubting Thomas? He doubted the risen Christ until he was able to touch the wounds with his hands, look upon the Lord's face with his own two eyes."

"Of course I do," I say testily. "But what you ask me to believe is…is…"

"A matter of faith," Evangeline breathes.

X nods. "Exactly. There are things at work around us that most never see, nor need to understand. The Order prefers it that way. No member since the original cohort who made the map have ever set eyes on it. Better to keep away."

"Lead us not into temptation," I murmur.

"So let me get this straight. The Order protects… access to the *actual* Spring of Youth?" Evangeline says slowly.

"Yes," X replies. "Among other things."

She knits her brows. "And my brother and father were members?"

X nods. "Who performed their assigned duties with distinction and valor. They embody the very spirit that makes The Order the last line of defense against evil temptation in the world. Nine hundred years ago King Randall the Fair discovered the Spring. He was consumed by beauty and youth even as the waters began to corrode his mind. Eventually his brother, King Humbert the Just, overthrew him in a coup. And it is from Humbert that the Lorentz line descends. Disgraced, Randall moved to Nightgardin, where in his addled state he revealed the secrets of the Spring. Nightgardin began making incursions into our realm to find it and The Order was subsequently formed by King Humbert to seal the Spring forever and defend it against those who wish to exploit its power. After all, aging is as much a part of life as is youth, and beauty is more than skin-deep."

I swing my gaze to X. "You know a great deal about The Order."

"Like I said, I wasn't entirely truthful in your library the night we discovered the map." X closes his eyes a moment before removing his suit jacket and placing it neatly on the closest chair. "I couldn't tell you about my membership without securing permission from our leader." Then he rolls up his shirtsleeve and there, on his bicep, over the defined ridge of flexed muscle, is a tattooed crow's feather.

Evangeline

I hold in my surprise. "Jasper and my father always maintained the crow tattoo was a Vernazza family symbol. I never questioned it as all the men in my family bore the mark."

X nods. "Some women as well, but never both spouses. Dedication to The Order is an honor and a privilege—but the dangers are also quite great. To allow a husband and a wife to serve together—"

"Could mean leaving your children orphans," I interrupt as my throat feels like it's closing in. "Yet here I am an orphan anyway. My brother and his family are all I have."

Benedict pulls me to him and buries his face in my hair. "I'm so sorry, angel. We will get your brother back. I'm not sure how, but it will happen."

I let out a shaky breath against his strong chest. I know how to get him back. By betraying that which Jasper almost gave his life to protect.

"Members are gathering," X says. "I assure you we will bring him to safety. And we will ensure the Spring's protection, as well."

I pull away from Benedict and nod. "I'm tired," I lie, trying to keep my voice steady. "I think I'd like to lie down."

X bows his head. "Of course. This is a lot to take in. There is more to show you about the map, but it can wait for now. We will make our move when the nearest members of my brethren arrive. It will not be long."

Benedict helps me out of the library and up the spiral staircase to his apartment.

"Too much has been thrown at you today," he says as we make our way to his bedroom. "I will leave you to rest while X and I figure out what's next."

"Stay with me?" I ask, voice trembling now. It is too early to say goodbye, and I need to take my fill of him before I leave.

I sit on the edge of the bed, and he settles next to me.

"Anything, angel. Anything you need."

I can hear a similar sorrow in his own words, one that says he knows we will be parted all too soon. But he believes we have weeks left, while I know this night will be our last.

"Make love to me," I say, a simple plea, and he does not hesitate before kissing me.

His lips are soft and gentle, as if he understands we need to savor this experience. He undresses me, his movements slow and deliberate, kissing every inch of my skin as he bares my body to his loving gaze.

He lays me on my back and runs a finger from my chest to my stomach, and then down between my legs, entering me with one soft glide.

"I could touch you like this every minute of every hour of the day," he says, his voice rough as gravel.

"And I would let you," I tell him, my words barely

heard. He slips another finger inside me and dips between my bent knees. His tongue is warm as it expertly swirls around my swollen center, like he's done this a hundred times. But my body is the only one he's ever truly known, and it is as if he was born to touch me like this.

I let out a whimper, and Benedict responds with a savage groan.

"To taste you," he says, peering up to look at me, "is second only to breathing."

His fingers pump inside me, and I arch. My fingers curl into his sheets, but I feel like I cannot get any purchase. He will send me over the edge in mere seconds, and I am powerless to stop him.

"Benedict," I cry. "I don't want to do this alone."

He pulls his hand free, only long enough to remove his own clothing. And then without another word, he sinks into me, and my heart threatens to explode.

I wrap my arms around his neck and pull his lips to mine, the taste of him and of me mingled as one.

Deep as he is, every inch buried to the hilt, it's like I cannot get enough.

"More, Benedict," I say. "I need more."

He lifts his head and then dips it toward my breasts, where he licks and nips at my sensitive peaks, all the while pounding himself straight through to my core. I arch into him, raking my fingernails down his no-longer-welted back, though I'm sure I now draw blood.

A thunderous roar rips from his chest as his arms snake under my back. He lifts me to him, our bodies slick with sweat, and I truly do not know where I end and he begins.

"Come for me, angel," he says against my lips, and then his hand slides to the place where we're joined, his thumb against my swollen clit, and he takes me to the brink and straight over the edge with him.

Tears stream as wave after wave of ecstasy takes over me.

We collapse onto the bed, Benedict still inside me, as my muscles contract around him.

"I love you," I say as we lie there entwined, our limbs exquisitely tangled.

"And I will never know love such as this again," he says. "You are my world, Evangeline. I would trade my soul not to leave you—if I could."

And I would give my life for him—for all those I love. And soon that is exactly what I will do.

I'm not sure how long we stay that way, but eventually Benedict nods off, and I am forced to leave the love of my life.

When I have dressed and put myself together as best I can, he is still in the deepest of sleep. So I kiss his forehead—one final connection—grabbing the supplies I need and taking my leave.

In the library I do what is necessary before I roll up the map and tuck it under my arm. Then I do the best to explain myself, to pray that the man who nearly gave his soul to love me will someday also grant me forgiveness. Someday—when I can tell him everything. But I have to save his and Jasper's lives first.

My Dearest Benedict,
Please know that I have no choice. The last thing I want to do is betray your trust, but this is the only way to save the one other person I love most—my brother. They will kill him if I don't deliver the map. They may kill him anyway, and me, but at least I'll know I tried. And I'll know that you are safe from this mess I've dragged you into. Be sure of one thing, though. I love you to the depths of my soul. Whether my time on this earth ends tonight or several years from now, it will be you who lives within my heart until the very end.
I love you. Always.
Evangeline

It takes me nearly thirty minutes to limp to the cottage in my condition, but I make it just before midnight. When I enter, I see my time with Benedict in flashes of scenery—trying on beautiful dresses, teasing him at the game table, watching him watch me in the bedroom.

I sit in my chair at the game table, imagining Benedict sitting across from me. I reach underneath, feeling for what I know is there, the one pullout compartment that was empty of game pieces. In it I leave my gift to Benedict. Then I retreat to my bedroom and wait.

My body convulses with a shudder. This man trusted me with everything, and I have kept him in the dark when I need him most. At least he has X and The Order to keep him safe.

X.

The Madam couldn't possibly know about X being a member. There's no way she would have let me stay here if she knew I was under the protection of The Order. She threatened Benedict's safety if I told him what was happening tonight. But maybe he and X can help.

I sit on the bed and pull out my phone. For so long I've felt the burden of protecting those I love. Perhaps it's time I lean on someone else for a change.

I dial the number X gave me in case of emergency, but just as I hit Send, the floorboard creaks behind me.

I gasp as an arm snakes around my waist, then drop the phone when a hand covers my mouth.

"No time for second thoughts, dearie," a gruff female voice says. "Looks like we can't trust you to keep quiet after all."

I don't have a chance to protest as she drags me and the map toward the trapdoor. I scrape my hand against the floor, snagging my phone and shoving it in my pocket before we slip down, down, down below the surface.

When we reach solid ground, she throws me to the dirt floor, my head landing at a steel-toed boot. I look up to see the Madam, dressed in all black, a thief who blends into the night. All that lights my vision is a torch she holds in her right hand.

She nudges my injured knee with her boot, then presses her toe into it until I cry out.

"Welcome to the catacombs," she says. "Now let's go find us a magic spring."

CHAPTER EIGHTEEN

Benedict

MY ENTIRE BODY is slick with sweat. A nightmare. I've had a nightmare. One where Evangeline was lost in the dark, afraid, in danger, and no matter how hard I tried, I couldn't find her. I roll over to gather her close, steady myself with the rhythm of her breath. But her spot in the bed is empty. My stomach muscles contract in time with my jaw. The sheets are cool as well as the goose-down pillow, no lingering trace of body heat. She's been gone for some time. I sit and rake a hand through my hair.

"Angel?"

No soft, lilting voice answers.

I rise from my bed, tug on my black boxer briefs, a pair of gray sweats and a white T-shirt. The clock reads just after midnight. Where are you, Evangeline? I walk through my apartment and find no sign of her. I freeze as I open the door and gaze at the staircase.

The library. The map.

Hairs bristle on my nape. Every step down to the second floor heightens the strange, foreboding sensation in my soul. When I enter the library, it is empty. A faint smell of perfume wafts through the air beneath the dusty scent of ancient books. Slowly, as if caught by a magnetic force, my gaze swings to a small envelope on the center table.

Benedict. My name is written in a small neat script.

I bite on the inside of my cheek, a metallic taste flooding my mouth as I take the envelope in hand. Letters left in the dark of night seldom contain good news.

I read her hastily written farewell, and her betrayal. The words lance me like a hundred knives. Joy can fill the deepest caverns of one's heart and soul, but that is also how great the sorrow is when that joy is gone.

I am alone in an abyss. Forsaken by love.

She has left and taken the map to make a devil's bargain.

"No!" I sweep my hand across the closest shelf. Glass baubles and trinkets fly to the floor and shatter into a million pieces, impossible to put back together, just like my heart. "No."

Metal grinds and creaks behind me. I whirl around to see one of the bookcases swing open. X emerges from the shadows dressed head to toe in black tactical gear.

"Angel..." It is all I can say.

Evangeline has betrayed me, X, this kingdom. But

I cannot bring myself to hate her for a decision made out of love for her brother, her only living family.

"I will go into the catacombs to get her. Alone," X says. "She has her phone with her." He lifts his own and the Find My Phone app shows a small dot on the move.

"The fuck you will," I growl. "As if I'd allow you to leave me behind."

"I know you want answers as to her choices." He shoves a hand in his pocket. "I also know you wouldn't want to see her hurt, or worse, but remember. You're determined to enter the priesthood. This is a way to let me get Evangeline out of your life—safely, of course. Once gone, she will tempt you no more."

My whole body stills. X offers me two distinct paths for the rest of my life. If I take the former, then I will not let my father down. I will be the good bastard who atones for the sins of the mother. I will be the dutiful second son who doesn't rock the boat. Who accepts the destiny mapped out for me. If I let him seek Evangeline alone, I will be able to consecrate my life to good works. No one will know what happened. How I gave my heart—and so much more—realizing what can take place between a man and a woman is more than mere lust, but a holy act of union.

But it all feels like a choice offered to another. Not me.

Because it isn't a choice at all.

You can't choose to breathe. Or have your heart beat. And that's how loving Evangeline feels to me. It is a basic, primal part of who I am. And if she has truly betrayed me, I need to hear her explanation with my gaze fastened on her face.

"Let's go. We don't have a second to lose."

X nods. "Follow me." He leads me out of the tower and across the grounds, through the maze to the gardener's cottage. There are signs of struggle in the bedroom, fingernail marks on the old wooden floor. Rage rises within me, red-hot. When I get to the people who took Evangeline, they will see no mercy from me. I will be an avenging angel raining fire and brimstone. Even if she stole from and lied to me, I can't cut off my feelings.

The door in the floor is still open, and we enter the catacombs, trading the world of the living for that of the dead.

X lights a torch I didn't know he had with him, but then again he never ceases to surprise me. The air down here is strange, dense. Our footsteps make no echo. We occasionally have to duck and weave around thick roots, and every once in a while there is a sound of dripping water or a rodent scurrying from our approach.

I try not to look upon the walls, lined with skulls, the hollow eyes and gaping teeth seeming to mock my intentions.

We reach a T-junction.

"Left or right?" I mutter.

X checks his phone. "Right."

I turn to go when something stills my step.

"Your mother's tomb," X says in a reverential tone.

A weight presses on my chest as I stare at the marble-faced statue of a woman in front of a large sarcophagus covered in fresh flowers. The crypt is candlelit but cold, a lonely place to spend eternity.

"What kind of man would she have wanted me to be?" I ask, my throat tight.

X regards me with eyes that are twin pools of black ink. I cannot read what is written there.

"One who was happy," he says curtly.

Then a memory slams me with the force of a bullet. A kiss on the forehead in the middle of the night. A whisper in my ear, a voice I haven't heard in over two decades but know to my bones is that of my mother.

Be brave in the days ahead. And above all else in your life, find joy—and do good. You can have everything if you choose wisely.

My eyes burn as I stare at her statue. She said I had a choice. But the choice ahead? My joy lies not in consecrating life to God. It is to live to the end of my days beside the woman I seek. To her I shall consecrate everything, my days, my life, my soul.

Perhaps I've known this for some time, even if I couldn't fully articulate the thought. My heart pounds. "How can I abandon the woman that I... *love* for the church? It's an impossible choice for me to make. I might let down the king, but I would be honoring the wishes of my queen, and in that I find strength."

"Your mother loved you very much, Benedict. More than you can possibly imagine."

I want to ask more, ask how he knows, but now is not the time.

We set off again, this time in a dead run. Sweat slicks my back, my T-shirt clinging to my skin. Each gasp shreds my lungs. I lose track of the minutes as my legs pump in a sprint. How long have we been here? Five minutes? Five hours?

Then in the distance, I hear a sound that isn't water or rats. A sound that turns my veins to ice.

Evangeline's scream.

Evangeline

I taste blood, coppery and warm, before I spit and see crimson spray across the stone floor of some chamber they've dragged me to beneath the palace grounds.

"You already know what the map says," I growl. "Otherwise we wouldn't be here."

She clucks her tongue. "Ah, ah, ah, my dear Evangeline," she lilts. "You're holding out on me. What I seek is down here. Yes. But only the map's hidden text can tell us exactly where." She nods to a slab of rock where the map is laid out for her to study.

"You've found what I seek—you and your precious prince. Surely you've deciphered it, as well."

I'm hauled to my feet now by my old friend the warden while the Madam says, "Again, Gideon."

Gideon, the third member of our party, is the soldier with the strawberry birthmark on his cheek who'd been assigned to guard my cottage in the maze. If I had to guess his age from his eyes, I'd say he'd lived several lifetimes, and none of them good. But his features are that of a young man, possibly even younger than me.

His lips curl into a sneer before his stony hand makes contact with my face once more. I shriek as my head snaps back, and I see stars. And though I stumble, ready to welcome hard, unforgiving ground, my captor doesn't let me fall. Instead, she pulls me tight against her as my knees buckle, forcing me to stare straight ahead with an eye that is quickly swelling shut—into Gideon's lifeless gaze.

"Perhaps that jogged your memory?" the Madam says with the demeanor of one enjoying her afternoon tea.

She steps forward, an ominous laugh dribbling off her lips. She swipes a thumb under my swollen eye, and I draw in a sharp breath. Her skin comes away slick with my blood. She stares at it before wiping it clean on her black pants.

"Young, vital blood runs in those veins of yours. And soon, when I taste the eternal water, it will run through mine. Only then will I be able to dispose of you. But first I have to tell you the good news. It seems that Jasper—despite his severe and life-threatening injuries—has taken to talking in his sleep. And hell if he isn't trying to tell us what we need to know now that it's almost too late." She hums. "By the light of the moon, Evangeline. Remember. By the light of the moon."

The words might as well be another language. All I ever knew of my brother was his quiet nature, his love of art. This Jasper she speaks of is a stranger to me. But he is still alive. It is this thought alone that keeps me from going under. I can still save him. Somehow. Even if it means lying through my teeth to do it. All I need is to buy myself time and hope that my call to X went through, that he knows I'm in trouble.

I try to feign a look of realization but doubt anything can be read from my expression other than pain and fear.

"You know what he speaks of. Do you not?" the Madam asks.

I nod.

"And yet you would have me believe otherwise?" She leans close enough that I feel her on my skin. "Evangeline—it seems you need to be punished."

She nods toward the woman who holds me upright, and in a flash I'm on the ground, the heel of the brutish woman's boot pressing into my knee. Something cracks, and I scream, the pain white-hot as it shoots through me.

But then the pressure is gone, and I hear the

sickening sound of flesh being pierced before the woman who was towering over me pitches toward the ground. I have to roll out of the way to avoid being crushed.

My vision clears to show her lying beside me with a dagger protruding from her chest.

The Madam hisses, and she jumps in front of Gideon, her eyes darting from left to right.

"Come out, come out, wherever you are," she singsongs, but there is a heightened edge to her tone. "Surely you know I have your angel," she says. "If you want me not to finish her off, you'll be smart and show yourself."

I try to scramble backward, but the pain in my leg is too great.

That's when I see him. As if born from the darkness, Benedict emerges, haloed in a pool of light.

I'm dead, I think. I'm dead, and my prince—my love—has come to welcome me into whatever afterlife will have me. This can't be heaven. I don't deserve it. The sight of the man I betrayed must have been sent to torment me.

"Release her," Benedict says. "You have committed enough crimes against Edenvale. I'm sure you don't want to add another murder to the list."

He speaks so calmly and of such things as sparing me that I almost believe he might be here to rescue me.

The Madam cackles and steps aside, revealing Gideon.

"No," I croak. If Benedict really is here, I will not watch him perish, too. "No!" I cry louder, pushing myself up to my elbow.

My prince's eyes find mine, and I watch the color drain from his face. His jaw clenches.

"You," he says to Gideon. "You did that to her?" He moves to strike, but not before his gaze falls on me again. This is all it takes to give Gideon his opening, and he delivers a swift kick to Benedict's ribs.

He grunts and stumbles, but he does not fall. Instead, he straightens, his face split into a knowing grin.

"You're going to have to do better than that, boy," Benedict says. "Because I'm not leaving here without Evangeline—without making you pay for hurting her and betraying your sworn duty as a royal guard."

Gideon strikes with his fist this time, but Benedict ducks the blow, taking Gideon by surprise as he punches him in the face. Gideon's head swings to the side, and I see crimson streaming from his nose.

He laughs, his tongue lapping at the liquid as it flows over his lips. The Madam crosses her arms and grins at the display before her.

Gideon strikes again, this time catching Benedict in the jaw, and I yelp as I see a spray of blood fly from his mouth. But he still doesn't fall, this time sweeping his leg across Gideon's, the boy falling to his back.

Benedict sneers at him, but Gideon rises with lightning-quick speed, as if he thrives on the pain.

Because despite his bloodied face from what must be a broken nose, he acts as if it is nothing more than a scratch.

After one of Gideon's blows, Benedict calls out. "A little help now, X?"

And out of the shadows walks the prince's guard, twirling another dagger in his hand.

Gideon freezes, as does the Madam.

"I thought you were doing quite well. But if you require assistance, I am, of course, at your service."

X points the knife at the Madam, and she takes a step away. Then he points it at Gideon.

"No!" she yelps.

Benedict shakes out his hand, his knuckles bloodied. X nods toward the stone slab and the map.

"Your choice," X says. "You can leave with the map or with your progeny."

Progeny? Gideon is the Madam's son? But how? She couldn't be more than a decade older than me.

"Look at me," the Madam says, a certain desperation in her tone. "Do you know how many procedures, how many injections it takes to keep myself looking like this? I was the most beautiful woman in The Jewel Box, but now I'm surpassed by all those girls with their youth and dewy skin. I've had enough of doctors and needles. Nightgardin came to me last year. They made me a promise. Deliver the map—deciphered—and I'd get to drink from the waters. No more going under the knife!"

"Not tonight, you're not," Benedict says with quiet confidence.

The Madam's lips curl into a wicked grin. "She will never be safe. Your precious Evangeline." She spares me a glance. "Not as long as we still seek the Spring and she holds the answer."

X strolls toward Gideon, touching the pointed steel of the dagger to the boy's chest. He traces a small circle over his heart, and the Madam takes a deep breath.

X pulls up his sleeve to reveal the mark of The Order. Behind him, several more men and a few women—all dressed in black from head to toe—step forward, as well.

"As long as we are here," X says, "and we will always be here, Nightgardin will not harm the children of Vernazza again—or any member of the royal family. If so, we will seek retribution, and I do not think your benefactors want a war. You've lost. Accept what is true. The location of the Spring will never fall into Nightgardin possession."

The Madam reaches for Gideon's hand and tugs him to her side.

"We are not through, X," she hisses, then turns toward a passageway I had not seen before.

"I'm through with you," I say, then despite the pain that rips through every muscle, through the bones in my leg I know are broken, I launch myself forward and grab the Madam by the ankle.

She pitches forward, landing face-first on the stony ground.

A guttural roar rips from her chest as she scrambles to her feet, blood streaming from her now misshapen nose.

"I'll kill you!" she cries, lunging for me, but she is intercepted by one of the hooded women of The Order. Gideon is subdued by one of the men.

"It's fake," I say, knowing this woman will kill me if she ever gets the chance, but I need Benedict to know. "The map is fake. I painted a replica and hid the original." My eyes meet Benedict's. "I needed you to believe the betrayal so you'd be safe. She said they'd kill you if..."

The last of my adrenaline seeps from my pores, but before I slump to the ground, Benedict is there. He scoops me into his arms, and tears stream from my eyes when I see his bruised and battered face.

"You came for me," I say, my voice trembling. "After what I did, you came."

He nods. "And I almost lost you," he says through gritted teeth. "Evangeline—" But he stops himself, his voice cracking on my name.

The Madam—shouting furiously—and Gideon are dragged away, hopefully where they can never harm my family again.

"We need to get her to the hospital at once," X says. "I've just received word that Jasper is there, too. My brethren will stand guard at his door. No one else is to be trusted now."

"Of course," Benedict says, pulling me closer to him. He opens his mouth to say something more, but no words come.

"We got here in time," X says to him. "That is what matters."

Pain courses through my bones, through every nerve ending, but I wrap my arms around Benedict's neck, afraid if I don't I will lose him forever.

"The game table," I whisper into his ear. "I hid it beneath the game table. Please forgive me."

Then darkness pulls me under.

CHAPTER NINETEEN

Benedict

THE DOCTORS SAY she should have regained consciousness by now. They come by on their rounds and examine her with furrowed brows. I dislike their thoughtful, pensive frowning. Once, not so long ago, I, too, was a man of pondering, of reticence. Now the time for measured thinking seems too slow.

I am not the person that I once was.

I want action. Fuck it. I want *them* to take action, and bring her back. But the choice to wake is hers and hers alone.

"Evangeline, angel, please. Open your beautiful eyes," I urge her. "I have so much to tell you, my love. So many things are now in perspective."

"Love?" a deep voice says from the hospital room doorway. "What the hell is going on here, son?"

I glance up to see a man standing there, watching me with a stunned expression etched into the weathered lines of his face.

"Father," I say. What is he doing here?

"X rang me," he says, answering my thoughts.

He steps forward, posture perfectly erect. "I say, it was presumptuous for a bodyguard to use my personal phone line, but he seems to think that you and I have some talking to do. I didn't know what he meant, except now I can see. While I've been busy handling Edenvale diplomacy at the United Nations, you've been busy with a whore." He snorts. "I was skeptical about your older brother choosing his matchmaker, but at least she made an honest living. This woman... Son, you employed her to tempt you from the cloth, and she has succeeded. Why should I rejoice?"

I cross the room in a flash. "That woman you are so quick to disparage almost died to protect me—to protect Edenvale. Tread carefully here, Father. Because if you call her a whore one more time, I will make sure it's the last word you ever utter."

The two hulking men who stand at a short distance behind the king make menacing sounds deep in their tattooed throats. I ignore their little alpha charade with a sneer. If they want to bark, then I'll show that I have bite.

"Evangeline is not a whore," I say. "And even if she were, it is of no matter, for I have given her my heart forever and more."

Father's mouth opens and closes. "Impossible."

"I am not going to join the priesthood." The words

aren't as difficult to speak as I feared. In fact, they feel like the most natural thing I have said to him since I can remember. "You will have to punish me in a different way."

His brows raise. "Punish?" He crosses his arms in a gesture that makes him look, for the barest second, exactly like our missing youngest brother.

"For being the bastard," I snarl. "For being the living embodiment of mother's shame. But all she wanted for me was happiness. And making the woman I love the happiest woman on God's earth is my new mission in life. If you knew what she did for our kingdom's protection—"

"Bastard?" Father retreats a step. "You can't mean to say you believe those discredited old rumors. We never were sure of the source, but they seemed to have been started by our enemies in Nightgardin."

Rumors? All my life I'd grown up with whispers. Worse yet, I heard no one deny them. So yes. I believed in the stain that I thought I bore, in my responsibility to cleanse it.

"I am truly your son?" The impact of his words hits me with unexpected force. I physically brace myself with the door frame.

He inclines his head, a look of shame crossing his face. "If you ever heard lies and believed them, the fault is my own. I'll admit I once had a brief moment of doubt, to the point where I requested a paternity test from the doctor who delivered you. It was the only serious fight your mother and I ever had. The tests showed that you were my son, and I spent the rest of our short marriage trying to make up for my lack of faith in her loyalty and love."

"But I look the least like you," I murmur.

"Yes," he agrees. "You are your own person. But if you are willing to fight for the woman you love, I can see that we have something in common." He clasps me on the shoulder. "I won't deny that family tradition is important to me, as is my faith. To have you become a priest would have filled me with great pride. But I also want you to choose the path that is right for you, my son."

Pounding feet echo up the corridor. There is shouting. My brother Nikolai bursts around the corridor, his new bride, Kate, hot on his heels.

"Jesus, Benedict." He pulls up short. His skin is tanned a golden brown from their Hawaiian vacation. "X sent a Learjet for us and a dossier bringing me up to speed." He looks over my shoulder. "We go on a short island vacation and the whole palace goes to hell. Is that her? The woman?"

"The woman I love," I correct. "The woman I hope to make my wife."

"Benedict?"

My throat tightens as I slowly turn around.

Evangeline's lids flutter. Her pupils are dilated, but her gaze is strong and intense.

"Angel—you're awake."

Evangeline

I try to sit, but everything in me screams in pain. I shudder, and Benedict is at my bedside before I can exhale.

"You need more morphine," he says. "I'll call a nurse. I... I need to let the doctors know—"

I use what little strength I have to rest a reassuring hand on his—a hand now adorned with medical tape, an IV and a pulse monitor on my finger.

"No medicine yet," I say, my swollen lip making it hard to speak. "I want to think clearly. Are we... Are we safe?" I ask, the events of the late-night hours coming back with unforgiving force. The pulse monitor starts beeping, and Benedict leans over to smooth my hair.

"You're safe, angel. They cannot hurt you again. I promise you that."

"And Jasper? Did you find Jasper?"

He nods. "He is not conscious yet, but members of The Order stand guard outside his room, and the doctors say his body is healing. You both are under The Order's protection for the entirety of your existence. You will not be harmed again."

His voice catches, and I run a thumb over the bruises and small cuts that pepper his face. He leans into it, pressing a soft kiss to my palm.

"I'm fine." He answers my questioning look. "In fact, I've never felt better."

I laugh, even though it hurts. "We're quite a pair. Aren't we?"

He nods. "I would do it again, angel. For you I would do anything."

I open my mouth to speak, but the words catch in my throat.

He kisses my palm again. "I know why you didn't tell me the truth. You felt it was your only choice. But know this, Evangeline. You can trust me. You need not put yourself in danger for my sake. Not now or ever again."

I peek over his shoulder to the three people standing outside the door, and despite my blurred vision from the eye still swollen shut, I recognize them all—the king, the heir apparent and his wife.

"Did you really mean what you said to your father, or was I still out?" I ask, not sure I'll be able to take his answer either way. If I dreamed it, it means I will still lose him in a matter of weeks. If what I heard was real, then Benedict is giving up everything. For me. And I cannot ask him to do that, no matter how much I want him for myself.

I glance the length of my body to see the plaster extending from the bottom of my thigh to my ankle and clench my stomach muscles.

"You're not okay," he says. "But you will be. And I will spend the rest of my days making sure of it."

"But I can't ask you—"

Benedict doesn't let me finish. "You aren't asking. I'm choosing, Evangeline. I choose happiness. And my happiness…is you." He clears his throat. "That is, if you'll have me."

I pull him to me as best I can, kissing him regardless of the pain. Because he is my prince.

"You saved my life," I say against his lips, tasting the salt of our mingled tears.

"And you saved mine right back."

He kisses me with such tenderness, such carefulness, and my heart bursts with a love I never knew could exist.

"I love you, Benedict. God, I love you," I say but then gasp. "I'm sorry. I didn't mean to use the Lord's name in vain."

Benedict leans back and raises a brow. "I am still a man of faith, angel. Always will be. But you are my earthly ruler. My very own heavenly body. I pray to your altar now and expect no apologies from my soul's savior."

"All right. All right," I hear from over Benedict's shoulder. "I've waited long enough. It's time I thank the woman who tempted my brother from the cloth."

"Nikolai!" the princess calls out, following on her husband's heels. "I'm sorry, Benedict," she says from where they stand at the foot of my bed. "You know your brother is impossible." She flashes me a warm smile, and my heart swells at the sight of the future king and his bride, the way he looks upon her with unrivaled adoration.

I swallow hard when my gaze falls on Benedict. Because he gazes at me with that same reverence.

"Tell me, brother," Benedict says as he stands to greet our visitors. "Is it I who should be thanking you? Did you send Evangeline to my tower?"

Nikolai cocks a dark brow and gives his brother a crooked grin. "I did call The Jewel Box, yes. Does your lady love go by the name of Pearl? I called on an old friend for a little favor."

"Pearl?" Benedict says with a tone that makes me feel like I'm missing some private joke. "No. The Madam gave Evangeline the name Ruby, but no one will ever call her that again."

Nikolai crosses his arms. "Fair enough." Then his eyes fall on mine. "Benedict and X have filled me in on your family's history. I am sorry for all you've suffered in the name of your father's legacy. The kingdom is indebted to the work he did—to the work your brother will continue."

I nod. "And I, as well," I say.

"What?" Benedict asks, his eyes wide.

"I'm an artist," I say. "I want to use my talent to further protect the kingdom. I'm not saying I want to join The Order. But I want to help in any way I can."

The king steps forward and bows his head. "It seems I was quick to judge. Please accept my deepest gratitude, Evangeline."

"Thank you, Your Highness," I say.

X strides up behind the king, his sons and the princess. "Actually," he says, "I'm quite impressed with your forgery of the map and the speed with which you produced it. The Order could use someone like you as a friend—in case we ever need such services." He glances toward Benedict. "I swear she will be safe, Your Highness. Any work she might do for us would be highly secure and confidential. Though the Madam will not be able to harm you, Evangeline, Nightgardin still seeks the Spring and will try again to find the map. And if she relayed to her employers what your brother said in his unconscious babblings…"

"By the light of the moon, Evangeline," I say. "You know what that means?"

X walks to the window on the opposite side of my bed, pulling open the shade with a gloved hand. It is not yet dawn. He takes a map from beneath his arm—one I know immediately is the real deal—unrolls it and holds it up to the moonlight. The only sound is a collective gasp as we all peer at an image coming into view, an illustration superimposed over the map of the catacombs. It looks an awful lot like a small body of water—the Spring.

As quickly as he shows us the moonlit image, X clears his throat and rolls the map back up.

"Your father's angel kept this map safe for years, and while I trust the palace is the best place to continue hiding it, I will leave it to The Order's discretion. For everyone's safety, the final location will be kept a secret from all but our members."

Everyone nods their agreement.

"Also, Miss Evangeline, Jasper is awake and asking for you. I've already sent for his wife and daughter to travel from their safe house."

New tears spring from my eyes as I look to Benedict, my love.

"Take me to him. Please."

He nods. "I'll have a nurse come with a wheelchair." He turns to X and his family. "Can we have a moment alone?" he asks.

With that, the whole party bows their heads and takes their leave.

And then my prince takes my hand once more— and drops to his knees beside my bed.

CHAPTER TWENTY

Benedict

"BENEDICT, WHAT ARE you doing?" Evangeline asks in a stunned voice.

"Angel, you have brought me to my knees," I say simply. "My entire life I have walked about with a sense that something was missing inside me. For a long time I had hoped that joining the church would bring me that sense of purpose, but I was wrong. While I will always have a strong faith, I know now that what was missing was you."

Her eyes fill with tears and shine with such love that for a moment I am unable to speak. Finally, I clear my throat and move on.

"You are my soul's mate, Evangeline. My darling. My forever. And I don't want to waste another second not giving you everything your heart might desire. I am nothing but a second son, with no hope of inheriting our kingdom's ancient throne, but I will devote my existence from this moment forward to giving you the happily-ever-after that you deserve."

"What are you saying?" Her voice cracks.

Even in this hospital bed, after all those monsters did, the sight of her takes my breath away.

Carefully, I engulf her hand in my own. "I am saying that I love you. And you would make me the happiest of men if you'd be willing to take me as your husband."

She gasps. *Marriage.* Her lips form the word, but no sound escapes.

I incline my head. "I wasn't quite prepared today. I don't have a ring, but we can get one made, any type of stone, any setting, you say the word and it's good as—"

"Yes!" She pushes herself into a half-sit, tossing her head, her hair pouring over one shoulder like a waterfall of golden silk. "Yes, a million times over."

I let out a shaky breath. I have chosen, just like my mother said I should. I have chosen happiness. But I will still do good—by this woman and by all who shall cross our path. Because she is goodness incarnate, and in her angelic light I shall not stray.

"You mean it?" I ask.

She giggles. "Don't look so shocked. Have you looked in a mirror? Loving that face for the rest of my life isn't exactly going to be a hardship." She presses a palm over my heart. "And loving this?" she says with a reverence I'm not expecting. "It's not within my power to do otherwise."

I rise up and kiss her softly, given her bruised and battered state. My lips brush hers, and as I move to pull away, she reaches out and grabs my head, pressing my mouth firmly to hers. When her sweet tongue tangles with mine, I growl with repressed desire. She tastes like peaches and brown sugar. I want to devour her but first must get her well.

And that is exactly what I do. For the next two weeks, I spend every waking second in the hospital as she recuperates behind the safety of The Order. We're still trying to sort out the breach within our guard—how Gideon came into royal employ and if there are others such as him within our midst. During the periods when Evangeline rests, I stand watch with the brethren. When she tends to personal needs or is taken for therapy, I wander the wards. Mix with the people. See the operations of this remarkable institution, the dedication of the doctors, nurses and other staff.

"You are wonderful with the children," I tell her one evening after watching my love, from her wheelchair, teach a painting class in the pediatric wing. "You are everyone's angel, it seems."

She slides over in her bed, patting the spot beside her, and I crawl in to cradle her healing body like I've done so many nights before.

"I told you," she says. "I want to give back. I always thought my art didn't mean anything to anyone but me, but I can help The Order. I can help these kids." Her eyes shine with the happiest of tears. "I never thought I could make a difference, but—"

I silence her with a soft kiss, and she melts into me.

"Everyone you touch, angel, is better for it. Don't you see that?"

She sniffles and smiles. "I think I'm starting to," she says.

"What if we can make a difference together?" I ask, and her brows furrow. "I've been invited to serve on the board of directors. The royal family will be contributing a sizable donation to spearhead a campaign to build a specialty hospital just for children. The vote has been finalized, and it seems the board has accepted my proposal for what to call it." Her eyes widen. "The Giuseppe Vernazza Hospital for Children."

I was wrong. The tears that stream down her face, these are the happiest I've seen, though I know this moment is bittersweet. If I could give Evangeline her father back, I would. Instead, I will see to it that we honor his name with work that will take care of our future generations.

"Oh, Benedict," she says, and I kiss her sweetly on the forehead. "I didn't think it was possible to love you more than I already do, but you keep surprising me. Ever since Jasper, Camille and Lola went into hiding, I've felt so lost without them. If not for you, I don't know how I would have survived their departure. You are my family now, and you've given our future such purpose. I don't know how I could be happier."

I pull her close and breathe in the sweet scent of her. "This is only the beginning, angel. There is so much more to come."

At last the day Evangeline is to leave arrives. I find her in her hospital room, sitting in a chair by the window.

"All set?" I ask.

"Yes, but we have to wait another hour," she says with a pretty pout.

"Why?"

I am the prince. If my future princess is ready to leave, there should be a team of porters assembled to cater to her whim.

"Because X said that he had to talk to you and Nikolai together."

She runs a hand over my chest. "We have sixty whole minutes to kill. Whatever shall we do to pass the time?"

There's no mistaking the naughty tease to her tone. My cock strains against my pants. I have been so focused on her healing that for weeks we have not been able to connect in such a way that acknowledges our simmering chemistry.

But now our attraction is bubbling over.

"Are you sure?" I murmur, bracing her face between my hands.

She licks her lips and then, grabbing my wrist,

lowers her mouth over my index finger, sucking it hard. When she reaches my knuckle, she gives a gentle wink.

"Fuck me hard," I rumble.

"Gladly," she purrs. "Lock the door, my liege."

Because when I give her this, the most intimate part of me, I am not just giving her my body and heart. She owns my soul.

Evangeline

This is my future. This man who is finally able to see his true potential. This man who never thought his life was his own choice, yet once he realized it was…he chose me.

"I love you, my prince," I say as I sink over him again, burying every inch inside me yet never feeling like I can truly get enough.

"And I love you, my angel. My soul's keeper. My Evangeline."

He kisses me, then tilts his head to offer me a wicked grin. This man is so full of goodness, but, oh, how I love it when he's bad.

"What?" I ask, and he answers by slipping his hand between us, spreading my slick, wet heat over my swollen clit.

I cry out, but he whispers a soft "Shh. Remember where we are. You don't want the nurses thinking you need help. Do you?"

I shake my head, then bite my lip to keep from making another sound.

"And there will be reporters waiting for our exit. Everyone wants to catch a glimpse of Edenvale's newest princess-to-be." His words are measured and calm, but I can tell he's barely keeping it together. Just to test him, I clench my inner muscles around his cock, and he hisses through his teeth.

I raise my brows in silent victory, but all he does is grin.

"I'm going to make you come now, angel. I'm going to make you come so fucking hard, so do what you have to do so as not to give us away."

And because I believe him, I nod. Then I bury my face in his neck and bite on his skin, hoping I don't draw blood. Because as I lift my hips, allowing him to slide out slowly, his hand slips between us again so that when he plunges back inside, hitting me precisely where he knows he should, I all but come apart at the seams as the orgasm rocks through my core, both inside and out.

I shudder against him as he growls into my hair, his climax taking its grip, and he finally loses control, savagely crying out like I've never heard him before.

I burst into a fit of giggles, my head still hiding in the crook of his neck.

"Well," I say through sharp pants. "At least the nurses won't think I'm in any danger."

He throws his head back and laughs, my beautiful, wonderful, soul-stealing prince.

And just as predicted, an impatient fist pounds at the door.

Benedict and I clean ourselves up in record time. I seat myself on the side of the hospital bed and smooth out my skirt while he finally unlocks the door.

Nikolai raises a brow and clears his throat.

"What?" Benedict asks, running a hand through hair I notice is dampened with sweat at his nape.

The corner of Nikolai's mouth quirks up. "Nothing, Your Holiness. I just usually wear my clothing with the tags on the inside. And in the back."

That's when I see the stitching on Benedict's pants—because it's on the outside. Inside out and backward does, likely, give us away, and it's all I can do to stifle my laughter.

Benedict simply shrugs. "What can I say?" he asks. "Evangeline gets to go home today. To *our* home. We decided to celebrate early."

Nikolai looks at me and winks, and my cheeks turn red-hot.

"Well," Nikolai says, "fix yourself up, because X will be here any minute. I'd like to know why I was summoned when I should be home ravishing my own wife. Again."

Benedict drops his pants right then and there, turning them the way they should be before pulling them on again.

"Really?" he says to his older brother. "We're

going to take sibling rivalry to this level? Because I've got decades of virginity to make up for. I don't think you could keep up, old man."

"Boys," I say, and they turn their attention to me. "As much as I'm enjoying this little cock fight..." I nod toward the door, where X stands in one of his impeccably tailored suits. Sometimes I wonder what goes on when he's not saving our lives. Actually, no. I always wonder. As much as X has opened my eyes these past months, so much about him, The Order and my family's history is still a mystery.

"Come with me" is all he says.

"I'm not leaving Evangeline," Benedict tells him. "She's not yet been released."

X nods. "We are not leaving hospital grounds. Bring her, as well. This will affect her life, too."

Benedict reaches for my hand, and Nikolai's playful smile disappears. Both men follow their guard with measured calm, but the way Benedict squeezes my hand tells me of his unspoken fear. What are we about to walk into?

X guides us to an elevator, where we ride up several floors to the intensive care unit. I swallow hard. This is where Jasper was before he came out of his coma. I breathe deeply, and it's as if X reads my mind.

"Your brother and his family are safely hidden, Evangeline. This...is something new."

The doors open to the quiet floor. We pass the nurses' station and travel down the hall until its very end. Room 7104.

The door is cracked, but we cannot see inside.

"What is this, X?" Benedict asks, but X just holds a finger to his lips.

We listen to the murmurings going on inside.

"He's lost consciousness again," a female voice says. "But he was awake long enough for me to get some answers. His name, which we will have to verify by calling the family, and enough evidence for me to conclude this is quite the traumatic brain injury."

"What do you mean?" a deep male voice asks.

"Doctor, our patient has no idea how he ended up in Edenvale. When I asked him to recall the most recent national event he'd seen reported on the news—he spoke of a tabloid headline concerning Prince Nikolai's sexual exploits upon a French heiress's yacht."

Benedict gives his brother a knowing stare.

"Hey," Nikolai says. "While I do remember that exploit fondly, that was the old me. I exploit no one other than my wife now." He quirks a brow.

"What's the matter with that?" we hear the male doctor ask.

The woman clears her throat. "Sir, the headline is just over a year old. If the last thing he remembers is a story about his brother, our patient seems to have lost a year of his life."

"Brother?" Benedict says, his palm damp against my own hand. "X, what the hell is she talking about?"

X steps back as the door flies open, startling the man and woman in white lab coats.

Finally, I see a young man lying in bed, his face bruised and swollen, a strip of gauze taped over what must be a gash on his left temple and the telltale scar down the side of a face as famous as his brothers, who stand before me.

"What the fuck is he doing here?" Nikolai asks.

"So it's true," the female doctor says.

Benedict nods.

"Benedict?" I ask. "Is that really…?"

He pulls me close and squeezes me to his side, as if I am the only thing grounding him right now.

"Yes. That's Damien," he says softly. "Edenvale's banished prince. Our brother."

X finally lets out a breath. "I don't think it's a coincidence he was found the same day Evangeline is set to be released. This is a message from Night-gardin. It seems they will use any means to gain the location of the Spring."

EPILOGUE

X

IT'S BEEN A fucking day—escorting the royal family back to the palace. All the family. Even Damien, the youngest of the Lorentz brothers and no longer a complete persona non grata, is in the palace for the first time in years since betraying his eldest brother, Nikolai, by first seducing his fiancée—and then causing the accident that took her life and scarred him forever. He bears not only a spiritual stain…but the physical reminders, as well.

I have more business to get through, but as I park my bike in front of The Jewel Box, Rosegate's finest brothel once more now that the Madam is gone, I smile at the thought of mixing in a little pleasure first.

A window slides open at the entrance, and I show my lifetime pass. The door clicks open, and I stride inside, barely noticing the sumptuous red velvet furniture, the golden wallpaper or the runway-caliber women sauntering about wearing nothing but the jewels for which they are named. With Benedict being her one and only client, Ruby—or Evangeline—never worked the floor, never bore the jeweled mark of her trade. She was not meant for this line of work, and for her I am happy that with His Highness she found something more fitting. But the women here now—they are consummate professionals, more than adept in their skill. And they take pleasure in their craft.

I see Diamond, Amethyst and Topaz. Emerald is leading a patron up the stairs by his tie. Opal is putting on an old-fashioned burlesque show on a small stage in the room to my right. A trio of Danish businessmen stare in rapt attention.

But my Pearl is waiting for me on the third floor, in a room designed to look like the sea. I climb the stairs with slow purpose, my cock stirring in anticipation.

It's been too long.

The door to her bedchamber isn't latched, so I push it open—and frown. The giant oyster-shaped bed is empty. Instead, there is a Bluetooth earpiece resting in the center of an overstuffed pillow.

Shit.

Looks like business is coming first.

I hate it when that happens.

I pop in the earpiece. "White Knight is in the castle," I say, using the old code name for Damien.

"They're saying amnesia," the husky female voice answers in my ear. "Is it real or an act?"

"Hard to say." I cross my arms. "Seems legitimate, but we've seen good actors before."

"This would be just the sort of diabolical ruse Nightgardin would attempt to try to gain access to the Spring. Corrupt one of our own, and turn him into a plant to betray us from the inside."

"Or he really has lost his memory."

"Figure it out," she snaps. The line goes dead.

"Good night to you, too," I say wryly, removing the earpiece and throwing it out the open window. It self-destructs before it hits the ground in a staccato crack, like a car backfiring.

I don't take it personally. The Order prides itself on absolute focus on the mission to prevent a cataclysmic world war over the Spring. But we're all human. Even her, once my protégé and now my boss.

We all have feelings.

The floor creaks behind me, and suddenly I am having a hell of a lot of feelings. I turn to find Pearl dressed like Holly Golightly from *Breakfast at Tiffany's* right down to the cigarette holder, little black dress and pearl choker.

She knows she's killing me slowly.

"You done with work yet?" She pouts. "Not very nice, kicking a girl out of her room."

"Sorry, babe," I say. "You wouldn't believe the day that I've had."

She drops the cigarette holder and crushes the

ember with the toe of her stiletto before undoing her dress. It falls to the ground, and my cock responds with unbridled need.

Even my self-control has limits.

She stands with her legs spread, wearing fucking garters, and I spy a small wet spot in the apex of her sheer thong.

"Forget about saving the world tonight." She kneads her breasts in the push-up bra. "Let me save you for once."

"From what?" I lick my lips. Ready for the feast ahead.

She arches a brow and drops her gaze to the giant erection in my suit pants. "Yourself."

* * * * *

PLAYING DIRTY

LAUREN HAWKEYE

MILLS & BOON

For the incomparable Suzanne Rock and Julia Kent, for not judging me when I said "Little Women" and "erotic" in the same sentence.

CHAPTER ONE

Then

THIS COULDN'T BE RIGHT.

Ford Lassiter tore his gaze away from the blocky brown house that sat on a large lot shaded by leafy green trees. Looking down at the GPS on his phone, he squinted at the blinking icon that told him he had reached his destination.

"That's just great." He had paid a lot of money for the best that technology had to offer, and now when he really needed his GPS to work? It took him to some run-down estate on the South End instead of the garage he desperately needed to fix his car, which was making a rather ominous rattle.

He was going to miss his meeting outside the city. Nothing to be done about that. Still, he was not accustomed to things not running according to his plan, and it was like an itch that he had no way to scratch.

"Damn it!" Slamming a hand into the center of the steering wheel, he jolted when he accidentally set off his horn. It sent a surge of adrenaline through his system, a shot of caffeine to his blood, and he couldn't help but roll his eyes at himself.

"You can run a small empire without help." Scrubbing his hands over his eyes, Ford took a moment to lean back in his leather seat. "But you can't get your car fixed without an assistant."

The very notion hurt his pride. He had an MBA, for heaven's sake. He was a very intelligent, very rich man.

He could get his own damn car fixed without a babysitter.

Scowling, he once again punched in the name of the garage that the old man at the gas station had recommended—Marchande Motors.

Arrived at destination.

"Okay, then." Either he was going to kill the designer of Google Maps or there was something he wasn't seeing.

He pushed his way out of the low-slung silver Porsche Turbo and took a moment to stretch and look around. He was parked on a quiet street in an old neighborhood, one that looked like it might have been fancy once upon a time but now had clearly seen better days. Unlike the neat grid of downtown Boston, where he spent most of his time, this area was…confusing.

Well-worn family homes were interspersed with the occasional newer model, probably things that had been built after tearing down older ones that just couldn't weather the elements another day. Then there were residences that were little more than shacks. The one that was supposed to house the garage and the one next door to it were stately old estates, though the neighboring house was in far better repair than the one he was currently standing in front of.

Cars were parked on lawns on some of the nicer houses, and pretty flower boxes lined the sills of the poorer places. None of it made sense to Ford. He supposed that it might hold some charm for someone more whimsical than himself, but all he saw was chaos.

He'd had a meeting in a suburb south of the city, and his car had started to make that ominous sound once he'd entered the South End. He'd never actually spent any time here, and, looking around, he could see why.

Pressing his lips together, he rounded the sidewalk of the place he'd been directed to.

"There we go." The old, twisted trees had hidden the fact that the building was on a corner lot. Once he rounded the corner, he could see a driveway and cars lined up in a more or less neat row.

More than seeing that there was more to the house, he could *hear* it—music was blaring, loudly enough that he wondered how it hadn't reached his ears before. He got his answer when he pushed through the verdant greenery and the volume only increased—it had acted as a barrier.

Now that he was through? He winced as the thunderous bass notes threatened to make his eardrums explode.

He recognized the din, just barely, as Metallica, and though he'd so far resisted the urge to look down his nose, this choice pushed him past the point of no return. Who listened to "Enter Sandman" when there were so many more *civilized* options? Like Coldplay.

The plastic sign with crooked letters that identified the garage as the place he'd been looking for did nothing to improve his opinion. It was stuck into the lawn with a wooden stake, and while he thought the words might once have been red, they were now the peachy pink of salmon.

"No way am I leaving my car here." Ford knew he was a bit of a snob, and he was okay with that. He worked hard to live up to the family name—more than his own father had ever done. So what if he enjoyed the perks that came with wealth?

"You dropping off keys or are you going to stand there all day?" a female voice shouted out from the shadowed depths of the garage, jolting him—he hadn't seen anyone inside. Ford squinted into the bright midday sunlight, but he couldn't see the speaker.

He wasn't used to being put on the spot, and he didn't appreciate it.

"It seems I've come to the wrong place." A garage attached to a ramshackle house, music loud enough to deafen him, a woman yelling at him instead of smiling, like he usually encountered—no. Just no.

Spine straight, Ford turned on the heel of his hand-tooled Italian leather shoe and started to walk away.

"If you're looking for another garage, I know for a fact that Jimmy's place is overbooked." *Ov-ah booked.* The speaker's voice had more than a little hint of the Massachusetts accent that he'd tried hard to eradicate from his speech. It should have only served to further annoy him, but he couldn't focus on her voice, not with what she'd just said. "He sent me the job I'm working on right now because he was full up."

Shit. The rattle in his Turbo sounded pretty bad, especially when compared to its usual near-silent purr. Still, he might have risked it…if he could have remembered when he'd last had it serviced.

Turning on his heel, he pulled out his phone and tapped out a text to his assistant, never mind that he'd wanted to prove that he could do this himself. Jeremy replied within a minute, efficient as always.

You're not going to like this, but don't shoot the messenger. It's going to be at least twelve hours until you can get a tow. There's been a huge pileup by the harbor and every truck is there, cleaning up the mess.

Ford ground his teeth together.

What garage are you at? Could you leave the
Porsche there and I'll send a car to pick you up?

Down the street a rough engine growled, roaring
to life. Ford jolted, nearly dropping his phone.

The engine was followed by coarse language and
shouts that had south Boston dripping from their
every word.

The Turbo was his baby, the first big purchase
he'd made when the money started to roll in. No, he
wouldn't be leaving it here overnight.

"Where do I leave my keys?" His voice was tight
as he turned yet again and stalked forward. He entered the open door of the garage, scanning the ap-
pallingly disorganized shelves and inhaling the
heavy scents of motor oil and gasoline.

He still couldn't find the person who'd spoken.
Infuriating.

"Leave them on the counter there." The voice was
coming from below him. Taken aback, he looked
down to find a pair of absolutely filthy work boots
sticking out from beneath a rusty old Contour—his
mystery voice.

"Could you please come out of there so I can
speak with you for a moment?" Ford wasn't accustomed to having to ask for things like this, either.
When he entered the high-rise in downtown Boston
that served as the headquarters for his hotel conglomerate, people snapped to attention. The security
guard would smile and wave him through. People

held the elevator. On his floor, one assistant would hand him a cup of perfectly brewed black coffee and the other his tablet, the day's schedule already open for him to peruse.

A very unfeminine snort issued from the area of his feet.

"If I come out to talk to you, I'll have to stop working on *this* car. And that will just put the next car behind, and consequently yours." The voice, otherwise sweet in tone, dripped with sarcasm. "And I'm guessing you're the type who's in an all-fired hurry to get out of here, so no, I won't be coming out until I'm done. Leave your keys on the bench, fill out a form, and come back in three hours, or have your car towed back to the north side."

Jeremy had said that towing wasn't an option. This was unacceptable.

"Three *hours*?" Ford was indignant. "That won't work at all. I'll pay extra to have it bumped up the line, but I expect this car to be finished as soon as possible."

His tone was the one he used on the battlefield of the boardroom—the one that always, *always* got him the desired results. Instead?

The feet, which had been tapping in time to the music, stilled. A breath of honeyed vanilla hit his nose seconds before the woman rolled out from beneath the Contour.

He had a brief impression of dark hair and incredibly blue eyes, and then the navy jumpsuit–clad creature was on her feet, not just glaring at him, but actually poking her finger into his chest.

He knew that he wasn't going to win any feminist awards, but he was a bit taken aback that the mechanic was a woman—he'd assumed that the voice belonged to a receptionist or assistant of some sort. Not that he thought women couldn't do any job they wanted—he just hadn't expected it.

"Now just a minute—" He wasn't going to tolerate this kind of treatment from a service provider, not even if she was a woman. No way, no how.

He didn't get a chance to say so.

"*As soon as possible* will be as soon as I finish this car, and the one after that." Those eyes shot out licks of cerulean flames that threatened to incinerate him. "Around here we do what's fair, and what's fair is for you to wait your turn."

"I'm not sure you understand how much money I'm willing to pay—" Ford tried to speak, and the damn woman poked him in the chest again.

"What kind of person bends the rules for money?" She sniffed, tossed back a long dark braid, and Ford again caught that intriguing whiff of vanilla. The scent was so out of place, layered over the engine grease, it made Ford think of cupcakes.

An odd thought for him overall, since he rarely indulged in dessert.

"So you're saying there's nothing I can do to speed this process along?" Ford shook aside thoughts of sweet baked goods and grasped his irritation. He found it especially annoying that he couldn't really see her, this strange creature who had the gall to yell at him—couldn't see the person in the shapeless coveralls or the skin beneath the thick layer of engine grease. She looked like she'd been grubbing around in a coal mine.

The woman gave him a sweet smile, but Ford noted that her eyes—the only part of her that was clearly visible—were still glittering as she did.

"Like I said." She pointed at the desk. "You've already put me behind. So for the love of God, if you want your damn car fixed, go put your keys over on that bench and fill out the form."

"I can't believe I'm stuck here," Ford muttered as he turned to do as the woman said, and he heard a snort of laughter that made him turn back to her.

"Actually, you'll be stuck at the café down the street." Now her expression was mocking. She clearly didn't think much more of him than he did of her. "I don't have a waiting room."

With the smooth movement of someone who had much practice, the strange person lowered herself back down to the rolling thing—what was it called?—and again disappeared beneath the Contour.

Ford's mind quickly sorted through words and phrases, searching for a witty comeback that would put this impudent woman in her place.

He had nothing. Nothing that would convey the deference he was used to receiving to this grease-covered imp who clearly didn't care.

Scowling, he stalked over to the workbench and all but threw his keys down on the unfinished wooden surface. He took up the stubby-nosed pencil and the order form, then shook his head and instead pulled out a business card, which had all of his relevant information. He clipped it to the form.

Marchande Motors
Proprietor, Beth Marchande

So she was not just the mechanic—she owned the whole garage. Ford didn't quite know what to do with that information—the woman didn't fit into any of the preconceived slots he had to classify the female of the species. And he needed to classify—to classify everything.

What was life without order?

It seemed that this strange, vanilla-scented woman would force him to take a taste and find out.

CHAPTER TWO

BETH DIDN'T HURRY the work that needed to be done on the Contour, or on the massive old truck that came after it. When she hurried she made mistakes, and mistakes hurt the reputation of her business.

One customer lost meant money lost, and she and her sisters and Mamesie didn't have a penny to spare. They all hustled to keep them in their family home, and sometimes that meant servicing the cars of assholes when she'd rather tell them to take a hike.

It was late afternoon when she finally scrubbed the grease off her face and arms, then grabbed the keys that the fancy man had tossed onto her workbench—tossed with more than a bit of temper, which made her lips curl up into a grin.

She was laid-back by nature, so her sisters always said, but when someone threatened her notions of right and wrong, she did tend to lose her grip on control. And even the fact that the offender was jaw-droppingly gorgeous didn't ease the weight of his offenses, at least not in her eyes.

"Of course." Lizzie huffed out a breath when she noted the Porsche logo on the key chain. The breath turned to a whistle when she trotted around the corner and saw the sleek silver Turbo parked on the side of the quiet, tree-lined road.

The fancy man was not only sexy...he was *loaded*. She'd just known it—everything about him had screamed north side. What the hell was he doing out here in the South End?

Actually, what was he doing with a ten-year-old Porsche? She was pretty sure he could afford a new one. Still, a Turbo was a Turbo, and she couldn't quite suppress the thrill when she opened the car door. She was halfway in when she realized that while she'd cleaned off her skin, her coveralls were still soaked with grease. And she'd just bet that Mr. Tight Ass would have something to say if she dirtied up his buttery leather seats.

Shucking her dirty coveralls, she rolled them into a ball and tossed them onto the passenger's seat. Clad in the ribbed white tank top and bright pink yoga shorts that she wore beneath, she finally slid behind the wheel.

She couldn't quite hold back the moan as she ran her hands over the steering wheel. Her joy at being behind the wheel of something like this was almost sexual, it felt so damn good.

She grinned as she briefly considered giving herself a handsy little ride on the seat, picturing the man's face if she told him about it after.

Tempting, but not professional. So instead she eased the vehicle forward, wincing as she heard the death rattle.

"Transmission." She didn't have to look—she was a damn good mechanic, and she'd heard that sound before. But she wanted to give the Turbo a full diagnosis, so after pulling it into the garage, she popped the hood, sighing only a little at the whisper-soft swish of the automated lift.

Without bothering to put her coveralls back on, she started to poke at the guts of the beautiful machine.

She was more than a little disgusted with what she saw.

The main problem was, as she'd known, the transmission. The filtration system was clogged, the seals were hardened and the fluid had been neglected. The Turbo was going to need an entirely new part.

Wear and tear was part of owning a car. But this combined with the sludge that passed for oil, the corrosion in the cooling system, the clogged fuel injectors…

She'd bet that the man…what was his name? She grabbed for the form, leaving fresh smudges on the white paper.

Ford Lassiter. Of course. Fancy name for a fancy man. And all those fancy college degrees listed after his name. Anyway, she'd bet that Ford Lassiter had only serviced his car a dozen or so times in the ten years he'd had it, assuming he was the original owner, and she assumed he was.

Irresponsible.

"Is it fixed?"

Beth turned and found the man in question standing in the entrance of her garage, silhouetted by the
late-afternoon sun. He was tall, probably a good
eight or so inches taller than her own five feet six.
His hair was the tawny kind of color that made her
think of a lion, and it offset the surprising chocolate
brown of his piercing eyes.

He was lean, but his body looked hard, like he did
more with it than just hit a gym. The suit he'd been
wearing earlier was well cut and clearly expensive
and showed off that body quite nicely.

In the hours since she'd sent him away, he'd removed the suit jacket, loosened the tie and unbut-
toned the top few buttons of his white shirt. And in
sharp contrast to the sleekness of the outfit, he now
had an open can of Coke in his hand. Beth highly
preferred this look. In fact, as she met his stare and
leaned back against the sleek door of the Turbo, she
found herself wanting to purr a bit as she took in
the view.

Not that he was her type. At all.

"It is most certainly not fixed." Even through her
annoyance, she felt a little quiver in her belly when
she looked at him—really looked at him. She'd have
to have been dead not to.

"What do you mean, it's not fixed?" That handsome face schooled itself into a disapproving frown,
and Beth arched an eyebrow.

Sexy or not, he'd best keep some respect in his tone when she broke the news to him.

"When's the last time you had a maintenance check done on this car?" Pushing off from where she lounged, she beckoned for Ford to come look under the hood with her. He hesitated, and she didn't miss the way those dark eyes meandered down her body, which was far more exposed than it had been earlier in the coveralls.

Interesting. Beth had always had a knack for reading people, probably since she preferred to hang back and study them rather than dive right in. That knack was telling her that Ford Lassiter was a man who kept everything in his world under rigid control.

She would have bet money—if she'd had any— that he wasn't that deliberate in checking out a woman unless some part of him wanted the woman to know.

He hadn't moved but was instead regarding her intently.

Well, well, well. The rich man wanted to go slumming, did he? Smirking, Beth crooked her finger again and deliberately swayed her hips as she bent over the open hood.

That leonine power, that tightly coiled control— he would be fun to tease. And, she noted when he finally deigned to saunter over, not bothering at all to bank the combination of curiosity and attraction in his eyes, she couldn't deny that little click that she felt in her gut when their eyes met.

Chemistry. Couldn't make it, couldn't fake it. It was either present with another person or it wasn't... and it seemed that she and Mr. Ford Lassiter had it on the most elemental of levels.

Beside her, he leaned a hip against the Turbo and regarded her with an amused smirk on his own face. Oh, yes, he felt it, too...and unless she missed her guess, he was entertained by the notion of being attracted to a woman like her.

Beth had made it a point to live her life without worrying about what others thought of her, but it still stung when someone, even a stranger, looked at her like she was one of those wild Marchande girls from the wrong side of town. Well, fuck that. She was going to make him want her so badly his head would spin...and then she'd send him packing.

"Can't remember? Even with all those fancy letters after your name?" She tilted her head, looked up at him, waited while he thought back to her question.

"I don't recall." He didn't even have the decency to look ashamed about it, though she noted that his spine stiffened a bit in defense. "I'm a busy man."

"Seems to me that a busy man like you would have people who could take care of little details like car maintenance for him." Though Beth's lips curved in a smile, inside she went from irritation to anger. "This fancy machine here? Most people in this neighborhood have to work for five years to earn that kind of money."

She wouldn't focus on what she and her sisters

could do—could pay off—with that kind of cash. Replace the furnace that threatened to quit every winter. Patch the place in the roof that let the rain in. "Some of those people might think that you'd want to take care of something like that. Take some responsibility."

"You're right." There, finally, was evidence that he was human—the tiniest flicker of guilt. It was enough to melt her anger away.

Likely he hadn't ever thought about how long other people would have to work to pay for one of his toys…and why would he treat it as anything special when he probably had a garage full of others at home?

"Can I get that in writing? I think it's probably not something you say very often." Beth arched an eyebrow. Ford blinked at her, seemingly stunned, before bursting into laughter.

It was a rich laugh, not the carefully controlled chuckle she would have expected from him, and it cut her off at the knees. To her, nothing was sexier than a man who could laugh at himself.

"Don't get used to it. It probably won't happen again." As if he realized that he'd let his control slip, Ford's grin quickly morphed back into stern lines. "In all seriousness. Now that we've established I don't take proper care of it, what is wrong with it? Do you not have a part that I need?"

Beth couldn't hold back the snort of sarcasm that slipped from her throat. "Well, that's a start, but no,

I don't typically carry parts for cars like these. Not much call for them around here."

Doing her best not to roll her eyes—they were clearly from such different worlds—she rubbed her hand over her cheek. The return of his smirk told her she'd likely left a smear of engine grease behind on her clean skin, but she didn't care. That was her. Take it or leave it.

"Your transmission is shot. That needs to be replaced. I can call in a favor and have the part couriered in for the morning, since I figure you're probably willing to pay the rush fee. But replacing it is going to be a full-day job." She held up her hand as he opened his mouth, looking like he was prepared to argue. To her way of thinking, there was nothing to argue about here. "But if you stay consistent with the way you treat this car, then I would suggest you let me fix everything else that's wrong with it while you've already got it in the shop. Your fuel and cooling systems need work, you've got some corrosion… and you need a basic damn oil change."

"I see." Ford gazed at her steadily, his expression unwavering. Beth stared right back, startled when he was the one to break away, huffing out a sound of exasperation and waving his hands in the air. "*What* are you listening to?"

"Sitar music." She loved this playlist as much as she'd loved the heavy metal one she'd been playing earlier. Music was so deeply ingrained in who she was, she felt it was a shame not to appreciate as much of it as she could.

"Right." This, finally, this was what seemed to throw him off his game—the music blasting from her phone.

Beth felt her breath catching as he reached out and sifted his fingers through the end of her braid. Her breasts pushed forward as she exhaled, and Ford looked her over again with that hungry stare—not lecherous, just an acknowledgment of that strange little click between them.

Beth didn't believe in love at first sight…but oh, she sure believed in lust.

"Sitar music. Heavy metal. Purple in your hair, and the scents of vanilla and engine grease on your skin." He sounded bemused. "Has anyone ever told you you're a very unique woman?"

"All the time." She was pretty sure it was a bad idea, but the way this strange man was looking at her made her very, very hot. Riding on instinct, she reached for the cherry-red can of Coke that still dangled from his fingers and lifted it to her lips. "But you've only scratched the surface. There's a lot more to me than the color of my hair."

"I can imagine." He watched her with painstaking attention to detail as she lifted the can to her lips and sipped. The rush of sugar burst over her tongue, and she imagined she got just the slightest taste of him, as well.

"Are you always this forward?" He tracked her tongue as she ran it over her lips.

"Afraid of catching girl cooties?" Beth handed the can back and arched an eyebrow. "And yes, I often am. I'm usually pretty clear on what I want."

Stepping away from where they were still curled together beneath the hood of the Turbo, she laced her hands together and dipped her head. "But sometimes I like to be told what to do, too."

Her heart pounded as she made the admission. Had she judged wrong? She couldn't have. She liked to go after what she wanted, true enough, and she felt no shame in wanting what she did. But she usually felt the subtle little click that she had with Ford when the dynamics between them were just right—as in, the other person wanted to be in control, and Beth wanted to relinquish it.

"I…" Ford took a step back, not the reaction that Beth was expecting. He looked her over again, and her skin felt on fire everywhere his gaze touched.

No, she wasn't wrong. She felt it in her gut. But he didn't seem to be all that pleased by the notion.

"I'll tell you what to do, then." The struggle to regain control was evident in his voice. One blink of her eyes, and the stern businessman mask was back in place, shuttering the hint of passion that she'd glimpsed below. "Order the part. Fix the car. And call me when it's ready for pickup."

Beth felt the same slight chill that she had when she'd noted that he seemed uncomfortable with whatever this was sparking between them—felt it and resented it.

She wasn't asking for a ring—she was just embracing her needs and desires, like she and her sisters had always done.

"You didn't ask how much the parts and work are going to be." Beth's temper rose, so she unlatched and slammed the hood of the Turbo closed, hard enough that most people would have turned to check that she hadn't taken a golf club to the metal.

He didn't turn, didn't look back—not at the vehicle and not at her.

"Like you've pointed out already... I can afford it."

Well, then. Clearly he wanted to highlight the differences between them. Beth cocked her head and watched as he headed out of her driveway and back in the direction of the café, probably off to research his accommodation options, which she could have told him were few. She suspected he wasn't going far.

His gait was easy, the stride of a man who knew that he had the world at his feet. As if pulled by her gaze, he finally cast one look back in her direction.

The intensity of the connection when their eyes met nearly brought Beth to her knees. Yes, that attraction was there, burning brighter than any she'd ever felt.

So why was he turning away from it? From her?

She could dwell on it, could go cry into a bottle of wine with her sisters over the rejection, but she'd never seen the point. Sex was supposed to be easy, fun. And to her it always would be.

If Ford Lassiter was uncomfortable with being attracted to her, well, that was his problem. Beth was just fine with who she was. Still, it was a damn shame he was a stick-in-the-mud, she thought as her lips curved.

A man who looked that good *in* clothes? He would surely look even better out of them.

CHAPTER THREE

THE SURFACE OF the bar was sticky beneath his hand as Ford placed his whiskey glass back down. It was his second of the night, and he felt like he needed to indulge in at least one more, just to get his head back on straight.

He'd been feeling off center ever since the interlude with a certain little mechanic that afternoon. Damned if he could entirely understand why.

"One more?" Even in the dingy bar that was connected to the equally dingy motel he'd had no choice but to book a room in, the bartender who approached him was still more his type than the woman who'd laid into him about responsibility that afternoon. Tall and slender, with icy-blond hair and a neat sleeveless blouse, she more closely resembled the women he dated back in the city.

Neat. Proper. Nice.

He considered for a moment, contemplated indulging some of this frustration in a flirtation with the blonde. Maybe it would lead to a nice dinner and some equally nice sex.

Before he could consciously decide, his hand covered his glass. "Not right now, thanks."

There was a flicker of disappointment in the blonde's eyes as she nodded and walked away, and Ford cursed himself. *That* was the kind of woman he should be attracted to.

Curvy mechanics with rainbow-bright ink snaking over their pale skin didn't belong in his life. Not even for a night. And not because of that brightness...but for other, darker reasons.

Settling back on the stool where he'd been seated since the need to escape the shabby motel room had clawed at his skin, Ford blocked out the thunderous music from the old-timey jukebox and allowed his mind to pull up the image of her—of Beth Marchande.

Nothing about her made sense.

She moved like she couldn't care less about anything but was quick to speak up when she had something to say. Confident—she was quietly confident, owning her curves in a way that stick-thin women he knew back home didn't seem capable of.

Her hair, in that long, thick braid, was midnight black up top and twisted with bright purple below. *Purple*...what kind of woman had purple hair?

And yet he couldn't stop imagining it wrapped around his fist as he thrust into her.

Jesus. He needed to get a grip or he'd embarrass himself in the middle of this dive bar.

He'd been in her presence for less than an hour, and yet he already knew he'd never forget her. She was too vibrant to ever be erased.

"Forget about it." He'd fucked it up that afternoon by being an asshole, he knew that. It would be best to signal that sweet blonde bartender and order another drink, to forget all about Beth Marchande of Marchande Motors.

But damn it...when she'd stood there, hands clasped submissively in front of her? When she'd issued that invitation, had said she liked being told what to do, while he could just make out the outline of a barbell piercing her right nipple, pressed against the tissue-thin fabric of that skimpy shirt?

She'd pierced right through to the core of his basest desires, the ones that he tried with an iron fist to keep locked away and buried.

Lots of men with his power, his position, indulged in all sorts of hedonistic things, and he didn't judge them for that. But after seeing his father go through wife after girlfriend after mistress, treating them all like his possessions?

As far as Ford was concerned, nice men didn't have the urge to tie their women up. Didn't have their palms tingle with the need to redden white skin, to leave a mark of mastery.

The tattooed little mechanic made every one of those latent desires come roaring to the surface, threatening to boil over.

That just wouldn't do.

And yet here he was. He hadn't been willing to be far away from the Turbo, sure, but that wasn't the only reason that, instead of calling a car to take him home, he'd taken a room in the one small motel he'd been able to find close to the shop.

The woman had hooked him. He was interested, even if he didn't want to be.

Bad idea, Ford. Very bad idea.

"Excuse me?" Lifting his head, Ford raised his hand to signal for the bartender again. He'd have that third drink, and then he'd go take a long, cold shower. He'd work from his motel room until his car was ready, and then he'd go, as fast and as far as he could.

Out of reach of temptation.

The volume of the music increased with the next song, something slow and sultry that he didn't recognize. Down the length of the vinyl-covered bar, a large young man wearing work boots stumbled onto a stool and slapped a fiver down. "I need a beer, Sallie, and I need it now. There's one hell of a show goin' on over there, and I'm thirsty."

"Coming right up, Ned." Ford watched as Sallie— the cool blonde—slid a longneck across the bar to the rough-looking man. The bartender then leaned against the length of covered wood, looking off in the direction the man had come from, and the man looked that way, too. Both seemed to be settling in to watch a show.

Ford followed their gaze, and lust was an instant, heated punch to the gut.

His sexy little mechanic was on the dance floor, and she was working it.

Torn, faded jean shorts cut off high on her shapely thighs, barely covering an ass that was curved enough for a man to get a good grip on it. A white lace camisole on top revealed enticing flashes of skin as well as a black bra that held her full breasts up nice and high.

Black leather boots with high spiked heels wrapped the length of her calves and all the way over her knees. He could imagine her with nothing but those boots on, hands clinging to his headboard as he moved, hard and fast, between sweetly spread thighs.

She was gorgeous. Not his type at all, with the crazy hair and the tattoos spilling over her collarbone and arms. But on her, it worked. He shifted uncomfortably and noted that it seemed to work just fine for him, too.

"Damn." Ford couldn't hold back the groan as Beth shifted, stepping into the light, and he realized that she wasn't alone. No, she had a woman at her front, a man pressed to her back and her eyes closed, her expression dreamy as she rocked between the two bodies, every movement sensual and sure.

The man behind her was dark and swarthy, and Ford might have thought to be jealous if he hadn't been so fascinated with the way the man fisted Beth's hair and pulled her head back. What he'd seen of her today said that she'd protest being forced to do anything, but her lips, shiny with red gloss, opened with a moan that he couldn't hear but that resounded in his head regardless.

The woman in front of her, a redhead in a tight dress, rubbed her breasts against Beth's own. Ford shifted on his stool, his cock hardening fully as the woman dipped her head and licked a slow trail down Beth's neck.

Damn.

As if he'd spoken out loud, Beth's eyes fluttered open. Lifting her head, she looked across the bar, over to where he sat, aching...and right into his eyes.

Earlier today her eyes had been the color of the afternoon sky, but now they were sapphire fire, the flames licking along his skin. His gut tightened as she smiled lazily, then slowly, sensually disengaged herself from the tangle of limbs.

Behind her, the couple continued their dance, but Ford didn't care—his eyes were on the woman who was crossing the room toward him with slow, deliberate undulations of her hips.

"Fancy meeting you here, Sir Lassiter." She stopped well into his personal space, and that vanilla perfume made his mouth water and his jaw clench.

"*Sir?*" He arched an eyebrow and tried really hard not to do what he wanted, which was to reach out and place his hands at her waist, to slide her shirt up and feel the warmth of her skin beneath.

"Mmm, you seem like a *sir*." Beth smiled and inched closer, stepping right between his spread thighs. He felt his expression darken—she knew exactly what she was doing, what she was asking for.

"What makes you say that?" His instincts told him to tug her flush against his body, to press her to him so she could feel exactly what she was doing to him.

He did not.

"You seem all proper and noble...like an aristocrat. A knight. Sir Lassiter." Beth nudged forward just a whisper, and he felt the curve of her hip press into his inner thigh.

His mouth went dry.

"Like you're trying so hard to do what you think is right. But tell me something." Tilting her head back, she looked up into his eyes, searching. "Why is denying yourself something that you want, that we both want, the right thing? I know you feel it, too."

Her open question gutted him. He'd been in the boardroom with billionaires, with sheikhs, with sharks, and he'd bested them all.

The little woman who smelled like cupcakes? She was bringing him to his knees.

"I—" He started to explain, but she cut him off, stepping back, her sudden frown breaking the spell.

"I see." Her lips pinched together in a mockery of a smile. "I'm not the kind of woman you want to get involved with, right? Not even for a night. Let me assure you, that's your loss."

Wait...*what*?

"Wait just a damn minute." When Beth would have turned, Ford did as he'd imagined, catching her by the waist and hauling her back into the vee of his legs. This time her pelvis connected with the steel length of his erection, and he savored her sharp little intake of breath. "What do you mean?"

"I think it's pretty self-explanatory." Beth regarded him coldly, though she didn't back down. "My hair, my tattoos… I'm far too wild for you."

"Oh, do you think so?" The way she was looking up at him, so certain she was right, was a challenge, and he felt something inside him roaring to life to meet it.

She thought he was turned off because she wasn't his usual type? Well, he couldn't deny that she was not at all the kind of woman he was usually drawn to, and his instant attraction to her puzzled him more than a bit.

But that wasn't the problem. The problem was what she made him *feel*.

"I don't give a damn about the color of your hair or the ink on your skin. Got it?" The need to prove that she wasn't the problem was quickly overriding his sense of restraint, the only other thing that had held him back from accepting her sweet offer that afternoon.

"I don't know you, yet you make me want things I'm not comfortable wanting. Make me feel things I shouldn't." His hands at her waist squeezed, hard, to emphasize his point, and he savored her resultant shudder, which ratcheted up his own excitement.

"Why would you be uncomfortable wanting something if it doesn't hurt anyone else?" She was watching him again, lids heavy over those big eyes. "Or maybe you think that it *is* hurting someone?"

He kept his stare on her face, absorbing every nuance of her expression, which was open, honest.

Something told him that Beth Marchande wasn't going to be disgusted with the demands he might make of her.

"Sometimes a little bit of hurt is good, Sir Lassiter...especially when I'm begging you for it."

"Fuck." Dragging his hands up her sides, over her rib cage and the swell of her breasts, Ford clasped Beth by the shoulders and tugged her forward, crushing her smirking lips to his own.

Rather than offering him a kiss as sweet as the vanilla she smelled of, she moaned beneath the pressure and opened, her tongue surging out to tangle with his.

One hand slid behind her head and fisted in the long mane of raven and amethyst hair, just as his fingers had itched to. He tugged her head to the side roughly and then dragged his lips down the column of her throat, settling over her pulse and sinking his teeth in to claim.

"Well, what's it going to be, Sir Lassiter?" Beth's breathy question rasped in his ear, and she shuddered when his teeth marked her skin. "Are you going to be good? Or are you going to be bad? What do you think?"

Shoving his glass aside—he felt intoxicated just from being near her—Ford stood, making sure that every plane of his body glided against hers as he did.

Her eyes glittered with the same need that he felt as he quickly pulled a fifty from his wallet and tossed it onto the surface of the bar.

"I think…" Ford deliberately wrapped his fingers around her own, drawing them up to his lips to nip. "I think that we're going to go back to my room right now. And I'm going to find something better for that smart mouth to do."

CHAPTER FOUR

WHAT AM I DOING?

This woman was different. Exotic. Wild. Not like anyone he'd ever been drawn to before, and he wasn't sure why he was attracted to her now. He didn't do exotic, didn't want wild.

And yet when he placed a hand at the small of her back to guide her out of the heated bar, he swore he almost felt a physical shock from just the press of his fingers to that small dip in her spine.

The Turbo had been his first acquisition on the road to success. He'd kept it because nothing had ever felt as good as that first achievement. That first marker of success that he'd earned on his own, not riding on his parents' coattails.

Over the decade since its purchase, he'd bought and sold cars, property, investments. Had pursued some of the most interesting and beautiful women in the world. Had grown his small hotel chain into something internationally renowned.

Nothing had come even close to recapturing that

thrill, the high of knowing he'd achieved something on his own.

Nothing, that was, until now.

Beth said something to the giant man standing by the door as they passed, making the other man laugh. Then they were outside, the cool air of early fall in Massachusetts as refreshing as a swim on a hot day after the beer-soaked heat inside the bar.

He watched as she shook her long fall of wavy hair back. The bright purple seeming ethereal and mysterious in the fading light.

What was going on with him? Purple hair wasn't sexy. Full-sleeve tattoos weren't sexy.

Except that on her, it was.

He stuffed his hands into his pockets as she looked him over. Those blue eyes of hers seemed almost to glow, full of wicked intent as she took her time regarding him from head to toe.

His body responded, dark need curling tightly in his gut. No, he had no idea why he wanted this woman so badly, but he did, wanted her with a craving that seemed primal in its intensity.

"I'd invite you back to my place, but I could tell this morning it wasn't exactly your cup of tea." She smirked at him, a knowing little smile that made his mouth water. She was provoking him deliberately.

That exchange they'd had earlier in the garage. The dynamic between them. Unless he'd read it very, very wrong, she wanted the very thing that he tried hard not to offer.

"Clearly you didn't think I was serious about finding something better for your smart mouth to do." He couldn't help it. The needs that he was usually fine ignoring were clawing beneath his skin, begging to tear their way free to be with her.

The sharp inhalation of her breath was confirmation. An ache spread through his core.

Nice men don't want this.

Then maybe he wasn't a nice man.

"Coming?" Arching an eyebrow at him, Beth turned and started to walk in the direction of the motel. He couldn't have stopped himself from following.

The small rectangle of parking lot was bordered on three sides with rooms. He'd been assigned to room twelve, and when he'd checked in earlier he'd been unimpressed by the cheap floral bedspread, the rough green carpet and the dated lighting, though at least the place was clean. Now he noticed nothing but Beth as she kicked the door closed behind them, seating herself on the edge of the bed and looking up at him with a hint of mockery in those insanely blue eyes.

He wanted to fist his hands in the long waves of her hair and taste her lips again, to touch her until she was breathless and all traces of that mockery were gone. He wanted to flip her over and bury himself inside her.

He needed to get a grip, needed to take the control back. So far she'd hinted at what she wanted but had been the one in the driver's seat.

No more.

"Do you like wine?" The hinges on the small minifridge whined as he opened it. Earlier he'd refrigerated a bottle of the best chardonnay he could find at the tiny grocery store on the corner. He was stymied when he realized that he didn't have a corkscrew.

Frustration mounted. He was supposed to be in charge here. Why couldn't he grab hold of it?

"Need this?" Not bothering to hide her grin at his discomfort, Beth opened the bedside drawer. There, next to a worn copy of the Bible, was a waiter's corkscrew.

"Spend much time here?" He held back a growl of frustration as he took the offered tool, expertly pulling the cork from the bottle of wine. There were so many feelings, so many sensations pressing on his chest from the inside out that he couldn't even raise an eyebrow at the fact that he was pouring the pricey wine into water glasses.

"I've been here before, yes." Beth took the glass from his hand. Lifting it to her nose, she inhaled, then looked up at him. "And probably for exactly the reason you're thinking. Does that bother you?"

Did it bother him? The idea of her with other men?

He wanted her, but he didn't know her. He shouldn't care what she'd done before.

He didn't care for the thought of other men touching her when his own cock was aching to be between her soft thighs.

"Drink your wine." Deliberately, he refrained from answering her question. Crossing in front of her, he watched as she took a sip, puzzled by the expression that crossed her lips after she'd sipped. "What is it?"

"I'm more of a beer girl." Lips twitching, she set the glass aside. Then she crawled to her knees on the bed, making herself right at home. Rising so that she was almost at eye level with him, she looped her arms around his neck and ran her tongue over her lips. "But I'm not here for a drink."

"What are you here for, then?" Reaching behind his head, he caught her hands in his own, holding her there. He countered her direct stare with one of his own, triumph surging when she broke, looking away first.

"Well, Sir Lassiter." Licking her lips again, she tried to pull back, her breath catching when he held tight, keeping her in place, her breasts almost brushing across his chest. "I think we've established that there's chemistry here. I'm here to see what you want to do about it."

His control snapped, the last whisper of wariness evaporating in a sizzle of flame. *Sir.* That mocking mouth, calling him *sir.*

He didn't want to analyze why he wanted her or why he shouldn't. He didn't want to hold back.

"I—" Still, the words stuck in his throat, even as his hands slid along her upper arms, over her back, tracing a line down her spine.

"I think you told me you had something for my smart mouth to do." Arching into his touch like a kitten in the sun, she fisted her hands in the hem of her top, lifting it up and over her head. He broke his hold long enough for her to toss it to the ground, then groaned when he saw what had been hiding beneath.

Her breasts were perfect. A little more than a handful, soft globes that sat high on her slender torso. The bra she wore was black lace, a pattern that let him clearly see the outline of full pink nipples beneath. One was pierced through with a small silver bar, and the sight of that naughty bit of jewelry, rubbing against the lace, was sexy as hell.

He wanted to place his cock between those sweet curves and let go.

Real men didn't do that.

She noticed his hesitation. Making a sound somewhere between a hum and a sigh, she cupped his cheeks in her hands, forcing him to look right at her.

Like he could look anywhere else.

"Look." Her eyes searched his face, and there wasn't even a hint of hesitation in the blue depths. "I'm here because I'm pretty sure that we want the same thing—a night of incredibly hot sex. *Dirty* sex. Why don't you stop thinking so hard and just let go?"

God, she was demanding. He didn't usually like that, either, but at her words, something inside him surged to life—all of the wants that he usually kept buried down deep.

She had made it clear that this was what she

wanted. What would the harm be in letting himself revel in it for just one night?

"This mouth of yours." Dipping his head again, he brushed his lips over hers, taking the kiss deep fast. His tongue probed at the seam of her lips, and she opened for him, humming with approval as he stroked it over hers. "I think I had something for it to do."

"I think you did," she agreed, planting her hands on his pec muscles. She squeezed a tiny bit, scoring him lightly with her nails as her hands traveled down. Stroking over his stomach, she hooked her fingers in the waist of his suit pants.

"Mmm." Her touch brushed over the head of his cock, which was fully erect and caught in the waistband of his boxer briefs. "Yes, I think we very much want the same thing. Unless you're this happy about something else."

"I'll be happier when you do what you're told." Had he really just said that? He'd been raised in Boston society. The women he usually dated would be horrified. He might have even gotten slapped.

Beth just grinned.

His stomach muscles quivered when she undid the button at his waistband, then slid the zipper down. The metallic rasp grated at air that was suddenly thick with tension. With need.

He tugged at his pants, pulling them down around his hips. His cock sprang free, and, going on instinct, he took his shaft in his fist.

"That's a good look for you, Sir Lassiter." Pushing him away from the bed with a gentle shove on his hips, she slid to the floor. Rising to her knees, she rested her palms on the tops of his thighs. "I bet this is a good one for me."

Lust centered in his groin, a physical ache. When was the last time he'd had a woman on her knees for the sole purpose of sucking his cock? High school, probably. He enjoyed getting head, but he never demanded that a woman get on her knees for him. It was one of those things he wanted so badly that he didn't dare let himself ask. That he assumed a woman did only because she wanted to please, not because she got anything out of it.

Looking down at Beth on her knees, her lips wet and ready, he knew that she was getting just as much out of this as he was.

Their stares locked as he slid a hand into her hair. Massaging her scalp, he guided her head forward until her lips brushed the head of his cock.

They both shuddered. Before he could take a breath, her fingers joined his, wrapping around the length of his shaft.

Her mouth closed around him, a hot, wet embrace. She sucked him in, and his eyes nearly rolled back in his head.

He never let himself play like this, edging onto something shadowy that both tempted and terrified him.

But it felt so damn good.

"You're good at that." His voice was raw. She looked up at him, and though he couldn't see a smirk on her lips, it was there in her eyes. He couldn't help but grin in return. "Of course, sassy as you are, I'm probably not the first to want to keep it occupied."

As if he'd challenged her, she slid her hand down his shaft, nudging his fingers out of the way. She worked him up and down with a tight grip as she took him deeper into the silky heaven that was her mouth.

His free hand joined the one fisted in her hair, and soon he was helping to guide her movements as she worked his shaft. Pleasure started to build at the base of his spine, and his hips started to thrust.

He needed to stop her before he came in her mouth. Needed to see to her pleasure first. He wanted to make her come before he took her, wanted her weak and wrecked because of what he did to her.

He wasn't at all expecting her to cup his balls in one hand and tug gently. Her nails scored a light path over the tender seam, something no one had ever done to him before, and he saw stars.

"Beth. Beth!" He tried to pull her head back. She hummed around him, the vibration working through his cock, and scraped those nails gently over his seam again. "Oh, fuck."

His release shot from his very core. He pulsed into her mouth, and rather than being repelled, she wrapped her lips around him tightly and swallowed him down. He watched the lines of her throat, transfixed.

Who the hell was this unearthly creature? And where had she been hiding his whole life?

She continued to lick him as he softened against her tongue, finally letting him slide from her mouth. The air of the room was cool after her heat.

Panting, he took a moment to simply look down at her, searching her features for some hint of discomfort.

Instead she grinned up at him, then climbed back up onto the bed. Crawling across it on her hands and knees, she sat back on her heels and looked over her shoulder at him as she undid her bra and tossed it aside.

"My turn."

CHAPTER FIVE

WHY WOULDN'T HE just let go?

The man was a caged beast, his dominance rattling the bars. Beth couldn't understand why, after all the reassurances she'd given him, he seemed to think he still needed to hold back.

She huffed out a breath of surprise when he caught the bra she'd just tossed aside.

"Nice reflexes." She smirked at him, wondering if she was going to have to keep hold of that dark edge of his all night to keep it from sliding back beneath the surface. She exhaled sharply when he lifted the scrap of black lace and let it dangle.

"I like this." He tossed it to the floor, then with a move she didn't see coming, pulled at her feet, making her tumble to the bed. He rolled her so that she was lying across the bed face up, and then he was straddling her hips.

His cock still hung free, swollen, red and damp from her mouth. Her stare moved between it and the way he was undoing the front of his shirt, each button revealing another inch of rock-solid torso.

He'd been hiding one hell of a body beneath that suit. Whatever he did for work that required that suit, he countered it with some serious sweat at the gym.

She wasn't about to complain.

His expression was so intense as he looked down at her that she almost—almost—felt the urge to cover her naked breasts. The piercing through her right nipple. She didn't, though, instead waiting to see what he would do. If she would have to prod him, or if he would let go.

"Do the bottoms match the top?" With a wicked grin, he worked a hand underneath her, sliding up along the back of her thigh to cup her ass beneath the abbreviated hem of her cutoffs. He squeezed, and she pressed into the sensation of her bare skin in his palm.

"Doesn't seem to be much of them, whether they match or not." He moved his hand around to the front of her hip, then to the crease where her thigh met her torso. He grazed the silky fabric of the thong she'd changed into along with this outfit, and she let out a shaky moan.

"Lift." The cutoffs slid down easily when he tugged. Leaving them at midthigh, he sat back on his heels and took his time looking her over.

"They do match." He arched an eyebrow, and she felt flushed everywhere his stare traveled—her

breasts, her belly, her hips, her thighs. Her center. "I
didn't think they would."

"You make it sound like a bad thing." She wanted
to part her thighs, to feel his weight between them,
but with the shorts still halfway down her legs, she
couldn't. "You seem like the type to send full sets of
matching lingerie to your girlfriends. Garters, stock-
ings and all."

"Oh, it's a horrible thing," he agreed. With steady
movements, he tugged the shorts the rest of the way
down her legs. Propping herself up on her elbows,
she reached for the zipper on one of her boots, but
he stopped her with a raised eyebrow.

"The boots stay on." He worked the shorts down
over the leather that stretched all the way up over
each knee. "But those matching panties have to go."

"Obviously," she agreed, her voice breathy as he
tugged the scrap of fabric down to her ankles, then
helped her free each foot. Letting the thong fall to
the floor, he surprised her by tugging her across the
bedspread until her ass was flush with the edge of
the bed.

Oh, yes. Her thighs quivered at what was to come.
This was going to be good.

Some men didn't like dropping to their knees for
a woman, but Ford did so as he did everything—with
confidence. Hell, even when she damn well knew
that he was holding back from really delving into
that streak of dominance that kept slipping out of

him, he still carried himself with ease. A man who was sure of his place in the world.

Beth was comfortable with herself, but her place in the world still hadn't been defined. His confidence drew her like a bee to pollen.

Arching her back, she tilted her head, enjoying the sensation of her hair against the heated skin of her back before letting herself fall back to the mattress. When he closed his large hands around the insides of her thighs, she sucked in a breath and shut her eyes.

"You keep those eyes open." He squeezed, the pads of his fingers digging into her skin. She did as he said, looking down the length of her naked body to where he knelt. He'd tugged his pants back up around his hips but left them undone. She could see the head of his cock, which was on its way to hard again, sliding out the slit of his boxer briefs.

His taste was still on her tongue, and yet her mouth watered. She wanted everything he had to offer.

"Eyes open," he reminded her sharply when her eyelids started to flutter again. "I want those eyes on me. Want you looking at me when you come, fully aware of just who it is that's making you feel so good."

"I'm not likely to forget." She let out a shaky laugh that quickly turned into a moan when he slapped that same soft skin.

She thought he would talk more, would continue with those dirty little words that seemed so strange coming from a man like him and yet suited him perfectly. Instead he pushed her thighs open wider, catching one ankle and arranging one of her legs over his shoulder.

She quivered as she waited for that first touch of his tongue, his breath fanning hot and damp over her folds. She caught his gaze as he lowered his head, and the intensity in those stormy eyes took her breath away.

He could deny it all he wanted, but the bossiness suited him. Dominance suited him. And if he'd just grab hold of it with both hands, he could blow both of their minds.

His mouth descended. He pressed a hot, open-mouthed kiss to the cleft between her legs, and she shifted her hips beneath him. Nuzzling his nose between her folds, he licked her from top to bottom, then bottom to top, and a soft cry escaped her lips.

"You're wet. Soaking." He swirled that tongue around her clit. "You liked sucking my cock, didn't you?"

She moaned, then cried out when he delivered a light slap to her inner thigh again. "Answer me."

"Yes, I liked sucking your cock." Her voice was hoarse, her hips undulating beneath his attentions. "I wouldn't have done it if I didn't."

"No, I don't think you would have," he agreed, pulling away just long enough to look at her. She protested, her hands sliding down to tangle in his hair. "I doubt very much that you do anything you don't want to do."

"I don't." She raised her hips. "God, go back to what you were doing."

"Hmm." He hummed against her, and the vibrations traveled to her belly, which was knotted tightly. "What part of it do you like, I wonder? The actual cock sucking? Or pleasing your partner?"

She parted her lips, trying to gather her thoughts enough to formulate an answer, but it seemed that his question was rhetorical. He pressed his mouth to her flesh again, but this time it was with an intensity that stole her breath.

When she'd flirted with him earlier, at her shop, she'd thought she would have to be the one to seduce him. The one to convince a man in a suit to take a walk on the wild side.

As he slid a finger inside her and continued to circle her clit with his tongue, she admitted that she wasn't the one doing the seducing. And she was just fine with that.

"Fuck, yes." He flicked his tongue over her clit, and she felt the shock of sensation all the way to her toes. "Right there. More."

"Greedy girl." He chuckled as she tried to close her legs to get away from the sensation, and at the same time arched her hips to meet his mouth. "I like it."

Pulling his finger out of her slippery folds, he surged back in, this time with two. He scissored them inside her, stretching her swollen tissues, and Beth felt the tension inside her start to coil tighter and tighter.

"That's it." He slapped her inner thigh again, right in the same place. The skin there was starting to burn, in the best possible way. It heightened the pleasure that was threatening to break. "You're going to come for me, right now. If you do, then I'll give you my cock."

"God." No, this man certainly didn't need to be seduced. The more she writhed against him, the filthier that look on his face got. It was like he'd been covered in a fine sheen of ice—colorless and tasteless, it had still only given her an impression of the man beneath. His orgasm had shattered that ice, and now she was getting glimpses of the full thing.

The real thing.

And she liked it.

She ached to see it all.

"Come on." He scraped his teeth over her clit again, and the wave inside her rose higher and higher. "Let go."

He crooked the two fingers inside her, rubbing them over a spot that made her see stars. At the same time he used his other hand to rub roughly over the skin he'd smacked, reigniting the burn. It was that burn that made the wave finally crest. Beth cried out, Ford's name tumbling from her lips as she shook around him, grinding her face into his mouth.

He licked her through the shudders, sending her

reeling into an aftershock. When the waves finally ebbed, she lay back on the bed panting, a sheen of sweat trying to cool her feverish skin.

"You're awfully good at that."

"She wiped a hand over her brow.

"I'm good at lots of things." He stood, and she struggled to prop herself up on her limp arms so that she could see him. He stood at the end of the bed with his shirt open, his pants around his hips and intent in his eyes.

It was a good look.

She watched, her mouth dry, as he peeled the shirt away from that defined chest. It fell to the floor as he hooked his hands in the waistband of his suit pants, slowly pulling them down. His cock, now fully erect again, popped free, and she couldn't help but suck in a breath.

Most men stripped themselves out of their clothes as fast as possible. She usually did the same, so she'd never found cause to complain. It had never even occurred to her that watching a man disrobe could be so hot.

Ford knew exactly what he was doing to her. He knew just how good he looked. And damn if the arrogance on his face wasn't hot as hell.

He let his pants fall to the floor, kicking them to the side. He stood there completely naked, smirking as she looked her fill.

Yeah, he knew she liked what she saw.

"You look awfully pleased with yourself," she

managed to pant as she crawled backward on the bed. She swallowed hard when he placed one knee, then the other, on the bed. He closed the distance between them quickly, and she expected him to range his lean body out on top of hers. Instead he placed his hands on her shoulders, stroked them down to cup her breasts. She arched into the touch, rising up on her knees to offer herself to him.

"I've just made a sexy woman scream my name," he replied, rubbing his thumbs over her nipples with a soft touch that only made her crave more. "What's not to be pleased about?"

He caught her piercing in the fingers of one hand, rolling it. The pleasure snapped through her as he explored the silver bar, growling out a sound of pleasure that told her how much he liked it.

"I'm going to play with this more later," he promised, dipping his head to run his tongue over the bar and her nipple in one slow lick. Then with swift movements, he released her breasts, sliding his hands down to her waist. Grasping the soft curves tightly, he rolled her, settling himself with his back to the headboard. Her knees were on either side of his, straddling his lap, and she gasped as her wet, swollen cleft pressed against his erection.

"I'll be more pleased when you ride my cock." His voice was low enough that she had to duck her head to hear him.

"I like the way you talk to me." God, did she

ever. It made her hotter, wetter than she could ever
remember being.

Something sparked in the brown of those wraith-
like eyes, and she responded to it. Lifting her arms,
she looped them around his neck, and she watched
as his stare tracked along the colorful ink that ran
from her wrists to her shoulders.

"Why have you chosen to mark yourself like
this?" She stiffened for a moment, but there was no
censure in his voice. Just curiosity. It made her relax.
She truly didn't care if other people didn't like her
ink, but it still pissed her off when they judged her
for it.

Yes, she had tattoos. She also had a brain. A family. A business. The ink on her skin was just one
small part of her.

Ford wasn't judging her, though she'd bet her non-
existent funds that he'd never been so up close and
personal with inked skin before.

"Two reasons." Her voice was husky, and she
paused to clear her throat. "First. My sister Amy is
a tattoo artist. When she started getting into it, my
sisters and I were all drawn toward marking things
that are important to us on our skin. Claiming it, I
guess."

Releasing him with one hand, she trailed her
newly free fingers over her oldest tattoo, which slith-
ered across her left forearm. It read Music Soothes
the Savage Beast. She'd gotten it at eighteen, when
she'd been full of emotions she didn't understand and

the only thing that had assuaged them were the hours that she spent at the battered old piano in their house.

It had been almost ten years, but the words still fit.

"And second?" He sank his teeth into her lower lip, sending a thrill through her veins. Almost like he knew what she was about to say.

"Second?" Planting a hand on his chest, she dug her nails in, just the tiniest bit. He hissed, but the wildness on his face told her he liked it.

"Second is that I liked the pain."

He exhaled, something that sounded like a curse word but wasn't fully coherent. He seemed to be struggling with himself again, with that need that he didn't seem to want to fully acknowledge.

She couldn't have said if the need in his eyes meant he'd won or he'd lost. She knew which side she was coming out on, though, when he nipped at her lip again, this time sinking his teeth in hard enough that she knew the soft curve would be swollen tomorrow.

"That shouldn't be so hot," he muttered, closing his eyes and tipping his head back. She took advantage of the moment to trace her tongue down the column of his throat. He shuddered.

"Why are you lying to yourself?" Studying the cords of his neck, she licked her lips, then sank her teeth into the spot where they met his shoulder. He reared up beneath her, his cock sliding through the slickness of her folds and grinding against her clit.

"You like it, too. As long as we're both into it, what's wrong with that?"

He didn't answer, at least not with words. Instead his hands found her hips, squeezing before delivering a sharp slap to each side. The heat spread beneath his fingers, and she rubbed her taut nipples against his chest in response. Her piercing caught on his skin, making her shudder.

"Yeah, like that." He wasn't even inside her yet, and she could feel the pleasure rising. "Feels so good."

He cursed again, under his breath, but didn't argue. He agreed without words, slapping her hips again, then rubbing roughly over the heated skin.

She ground down against him, savoring the tease of his hard length against her wetness. She was reaching a fever pitch.

"I want you to do it now," he growled into her ear. "Sit on me. Now."

It was on the tip of her tongue to tease him, to glide back and forth over his rigid cock to show him who was really in control here.

The look in his eyes told her that the time for playing was over. Her pulse sped, and something dark and needy started to gather in a tangle in the depths of her belly.

"Condom?" She spoke against his lips, then sank into the kiss when he pulled at her hair and held her in place. Little nerve endings sparked along her scalp. And she couldn't hold back a purr of satisfaction.

He'd been listening, and he was giving her what she wanted. What she craved. Every minute that they were together, skin on skin, seemed to bring out more and more of the beast inside him.

She was dying to see what he would be like if that creature escaped.

"My pants pocket." He didn't let go until she tore herself away, crawling across the bed to reach for the suit pants he'd left on the floor. When she was bent over, rummaging in the pockets, he took the opportunity to rain three quick spanks down on her ass, all on one side, and she reared back, gasping.

"Yes." She hissed it out between her teeth as wetness surged in her cleft.

Grabbing her by the waist, he hauled her back to the head of the bed, again situating her across his lap. She reached for the condom, and he held it up to her lips. Grinning, she caught it in her teeth, biting tight. He pulled and the foil ripped. She plucked out the latex ring and, pinching the tip, pulled his cock away from where it rested against his belly and rolled the sheath down to the root.

A low growl of satisfaction slipped from his lips at her touch, and his hips rose from the bed. His movements became bossy—bossier—and within seconds he had her positioned over his cock, the head nestled between her lower lips.

"Take me." It was an order, one that made her melt. She sank down just enough to take the tip inside her, meaning to consume him slowly. He had other ideas, his hands driving her down so that he impaled her in one hard thrust. She cried out, rocking on top of him, both trying to get away and to get closer.

"You're tight." He grunted beneath her as he gave a series of short thrusts, trying to work the rest of the way inside her. She couldn't catch her breath— Jesus, but he was big. "Open for me, baby."

She wasn't sure she could. They rocked for a moment, her body fighting him but wanting more pleasure. Claiming her lips, he slid his hand from her hip around her backside, sliding between her legs from behind to tease at her full folds.

Slickness surged. She moaned, rocking on him, and he sank in another impossible inch. Her fingers grabbed at his shoulders, searching for purchase.

He returned his hand to her hip, pulling her bodily up. His thick cock dragged over her tight and now incredibly sensitive inner walls, sparking nerve endings with every pulse.

"That's it." He worked her back down, and she felt that storm of pleasure gathering again. When he spanked her hip again, she felt herself melting into something dark and dreamy, more decadent than she'd ever felt before.

"Ford." She wasn't a beggar. Usually. Right now all she wanted was for the sensations to continue. To grow.

She rocked back and forth on his lap, had the pleasure of watching his own expression grow hazy. His stare caught hers, intense and sure, and she found that she couldn't look away. That look was her anchor in the intensity she felt as he guided her up and down.

It was too intense. A tendril of affection unfurled in her chest, and it would have made her panic if she had room left to feel anything else at all.

She started to squirm, desperate for the release that remained just out of reach. His eyes, his hands on her hips grounded her, and her breath started to come in pants.

"Ride me." He trailed a hand up her back, tracing her spine before tangling in her hair yet again. She didn't know why she liked that so much from him, but every little tug had her growing even wetter. "Take what you need. Do it now."

When he commanded her like that, she couldn't have done anything else. Sinking her teeth into her lower lip, she centered her weight on her knees, her palms splayed out on his broad, hard chest.

Slowly, she rose, shuddering at the pleasure. As wet as she was, she still had to work her way back down, the sting melting into need with the delicious drag of his cock over her inner walls.

The way they fit together, the connection that snapped in the air between them, God, just the way he held so perfectly still, letting her do as he'd told her to—to ride him. It all mixed together into a tangled knot of pleasure that was sending her higher than she'd ever been. She'd meant to keep her movements slow, deliberate—to savor the climb to what she knew would be one of the best releases of her life.

She couldn't be slow. Her movements quickened until she was rocking back and forth on his cock with abandon, grinding her clit against the solid planes of his abs. He couldn't seem to remain still anymore, either. One of his hands was digging into her hip, urging her to move faster. His pelvis rose up every time she slammed down, and they both shuddered every time he bottomed out inside her.

Her body started to shake. She was so close, and it was like she'd been caught in the wake of a tsunami—she was powerless to do anything but be pulled wherever the storm wanted to go.

Back slamming into the headboard, he ground up into her so hard that she saw stars. The bite of pain was a crimson ribbon snapping through her, and the storm inside her started to break.

With a growl, he slid a hand up to grasp her breast. She arched into his palm, crying out when he rubbed a thumb teasingly over her pierced nipple.

She needed more than that. As though she'd said it aloud, he tightened his hold until he was tugging lightly. She felt the pull all the way down to her core, and when he tugged again, her entire body snapped.

"Ford!" She hadn't meant to say his name, but it spilled from her lips as her orgasm broke. Clinging to his shoulders, she rode the edge of her release, crying out again when he tugged on her nipple one last time, sending an aftershock coursing through her.

"You have no idea how good that feels." She could tell from his ragged breaths and the sweat beading his forehead that he was close. She stared down at that gorgeous face, fascinated as it contorted with pleasure yet retained the fierceness that had sharpened with every little bit that he'd let go. "I can feel every ripple of your pleasure. Pleasure that I gave to you."

With most men she would make some kind of pithy comment at that, something along the lines of being able to pleasure herself just as well as they could, but here and now, that would have been a lie. A big one.

She'd had some good sex before. Great sex, even. But this? This was something on an entirely new level.

"You gave me this," she moaned softly into his ear, still writhing against him even though she was losing control of her muscles. "Let me give you what you want."

He groaned, a wrenching sound like he was in pain. Deliberately, she clenched around him, and his breath caught. Beth thought it was the sexiest thing she'd ever heard—this big, powerful man brought out of his mind with pleasure because of her.

"Fuck." He ground the word out between clenched teeth, and Beth felt him swell inside her. She gasped as he thrust several times—hard, choppy pulses as he found his own release.

Out of breath, she dipped her head, intending

to rest her cheek on his shoulder. Instead, he lifted a hand and pressed it to her cheek, guiding her so that her forehead rested against his, her eyes looking into his own. It was more intimate than she should have been comfortable with, but as the endorphins flooded her system and left her completely blissed out, it felt strangely right.

She waited until he closed his eyes to close hers, still straddling him with his cock inside her. He'd claimed her entirely—in this moment, her body was his.

She'd think about that more later, but now, she let herself float away.

CHAPTER SIX

ANTICIPATION AND APPREHENSION tightened in Ford's gut as he walked the short distance from his motel to the garage, inhaling deep mouthfuls of the apple and smoke air of an early afternoon in fall. A few minutes ago he'd slung his laptop bag over his shoulder and looked around the small cube of his motel room. The sheets were on the floor, the pillows tossed halfway across the room. The heavy musk of sex was in the air, along with lingering hints of engine grease and vanilla.

It had made lust surge to his groin. Hell, he'd been half-hard since he'd woken up at four in the morning and turned to Beth, hungry for another helping of her body.

He'd gone hungry, because she'd been gone. He was normally a light sleeper, but after that insane orgasm he must have slept like the dead, allowing her to sneak out.

It was just as well. They'd both gotten what they'd wanted—some incredible sex.

The memory of her on her knees in front of him, his cock in her mouth as she let him boss her around, wasn't one he would soon forget. The way she'd responded to him, had urged him to let his dominance out, would be burned in his brain for a long time, even if it was something he should probably forget.

They'd had fun, but he still felt the stirrings of shame. He'd been rough with her—had pulled her hair, spanked her, played endlessly with that fascinating piercing of hers.

Nice men didn't do that. He supposed he should think of it like a diet. He'd cheated a little, had a serving of rich, sinful chocolate cake. Now it was time to go back to chicken and steamed veggies.

Was he really comparing sex to a bland meal? As he reached the end of the garage's driveway, he forced himself to chuckle. He liked the sex he usually had.

He liked chicken and veggies.

Not the same as cake, though.

He shook his head to clear his thoughts. What the hell was wrong with him? He'd never felt awkward during a morning after, probably because he usually only slept with nice women he was dating.

He'd never felt like this after sex. He wasn't sure what to do with it.

He paused at the end of the driveway, adjusting the strap of his laptop bag on his shoulder. Irritated by the state of his car, he hadn't paid that much attention to the structure the last time he'd been here.

Now he took in the large gardens, the wide expanse of grassy lawns—probably a bitch to keep up. In fact, both were looking pretty neglected. As was the house, two stories and spacious but covered in weathered brown wood, the roof sagging and missing shingles.

Still, his hotelier eye looked over it all and saw good bones. The house had once been something special, and he wondered how Beth had become a part of it. She'd mentioned sisters, but apart from that and the garage, he knew nothing about her.

He had no business wanting to know more about her. She wasn't the kind of woman he got involved with.

He'd never let go like he had last night. Real men shouldn't want the kind of things he'd let himself do, and yet he couldn't help his mouth watering with the hunger for more.

Get a grip, man.

Ford scowled at himself and started up the driveway. On the short walk here he'd passed several men begging at the side of the road, and more than a few businesses that were shuttered, even gutted and tagged with spray paint. It was clearly not a wealthy area of Boston. It was such a stark contrast to his plush waterfront condo that he'd felt the stirrings of guilt, but he shoved them away.

He'd worked hard for what he had. Why should he feel bad about it?

But did that mean that the people who lived here

didn't work hard? Before yesterday he might have actually made that generalization, but after seeing the operation that Beth ran, he knew that at least one resident of this area was hardworking.

Chirpy pop music blasted from the open garage this time. Man, her music taste was strange. Though when he cocked his head, he thought he recognized the song—from where, he had no idea. Yeah, one of those songs by that British boy band with all the hair.

Heavy metal. Sitar music. Boy banders in skinny jeans. Just a few more pieces in the puzzle that was Beth.

The bubbly music hid the female voices until he was framed by the garage door. He stopped short when he saw the three women lounging there, none of whom were Beth.

"Well, well." One of the woman pushed herself out of the ratty lawn chair she'd been sitting in, reaching for an open can of soda on one of the workbenches. She was tall and slender, with long blond curls that fell to her waist. Her torn jeans and white tank top revealed a fair amount of skin, and most of that skin was covered in ink—she even had a tattoo covering her collarbone and throat, one that looked like a lacy collar. At least twice as much ink as Beth. He wondered if this was Amy, the tattoo artist sister. "You need some directions there, honey?"

Honey?

"Easy, Ames." One of the other women was reclining in an old, torn armchair. Ford blinked when he looked at her—he couldn't help it. She was beautiful, even in denim overalls with—wow.

She was wearing overalls over just a bra, leaving her generous curves on more than full display. And she was knitting. He didn't know where to look.

"Why easy?" The first woman took a couple of steps in his direction, and he suspected that the sway to her hips was deliberate. "Maybe the lost little puppy is looking for a...meal."

Ford knew that he wasn't misinterpreting the double entendre.

"Because," the knitting woman started, smiling calmly up at Ford, "I bet this is what kept our Beth out of the house till all hours."

Setting down her knitting, she brushed pink-streaked chestnut hair back, pulling it up into a ponytail. Then she stretched, causing her curves to spill out of her overalls. She had some kind of tattoo stretching out of her cleavage.

The third woman said nothing, just beat her heels on the workbench she was sitting on. Average height, she had the leanest build of the sisters, emphasized by the skinny, ripped jeans and tight men's T-shirt that she wore. Her hair was cut in a sharp bob dyed inky black that brushed along a chiseled jawline and slightly pointed chin as she kicked.

Her caramel-colored eyes were fixed on Ford with more than a little suspicion.

"Mmm." The first woman, the blonde one—Amy?—looked Ford over slowly, and damned if she didn't make him squirm. "Interesting choice this time, Beth."

"I thought so. And he has a name. It's Ford." Without warning, Beth pushed herself out from beneath the clunky gray SUV that sat in the garage. Ford jolted—he'd been keeping an eye on the other women and hadn't noticed her work boots at his feet. Lying on her back on that rolling thing she used, she looked up at him with those intense eyes of hers, a small smirk playing around the corners of her lips. "Hello."

"Hi." Seeing her spread out there like that, beneath him, had interest stirring anew. He'd wanted to take her like that when he'd woken up in the early morning—to roll between her soft thighs and slide into her while she was sleepy and submissive.

He didn't like that she'd run out without saying goodbye. It must have shown on his face, some sign of his displeasure, because her posture changed, just ever so slightly, responding to him.

She ran her tongue over her lips, stare still fastened on his, and he remembered the way she'd looked when she'd ridden his cock—pure sex.

He wanted her again. Now.

"Found what you were looking for?" The woman in the bra and overalls picked up her knitting again, smirking at him over the top of it. The other two women laughed.

That was enough of that. Ford was never intimidated. He wouldn't let himself be now. Wordlessly, he extended a hand to Beth. With a bemused smile, she took it, seemingly entertained by the way the other women were talking to him.

When she was on her feet, she tugged to pull her hand away. He held tight, drawing her in closer, until there was only a ribbon of space between their bodies. Her eyes widened as heat passed between them, and he heard her soft exhale as he dipped his head.

"Thanks for last night," he whispered into her ear. A strand of purple had fallen loose of her braid, and he tucked it behind her ear, making sure that his lips grazed her cheek as she leaned back, savoring her small shudder.

What the hell was he doing? Looking for round two? What else could he want?

She arched an eyebrow at him, as if to ask if he was quite done, but when his gaze lowered, he saw that her nipples had bunched up tightly and were pressing against her thin T-shirt, under which she seemed to be naked. He couldn't hold back the smirk. She pressed her lips together and turned to the other women.

"Meet my sisters. The one hitting on you is Amy—she's the tattoo artist I mentioned. The one knitting is Meg, and the one sitting on the workbench is Jo." She gestured to each with a hand as she introduced them. Amy licked her lips. Meg smiled sweetly. Jo scowled.

He had no idea what to make of the lot of them.

"Your car is ready." Reaching into the pocket of the coveralls that she'd tied at the waist, she fished out his key ring, dangled it in front of him. She followed it with a total scribbled on a Post-it note. "Will that be cash or card? I don't take checks."

Last night he'd tasted her on his tongue, and now she was demanding that he pay up for the work she'd done. He wasn't put off—hell, no. He was a businessman.

It was sexy as hell.

"Credit will be fine." He didn't bother looking at the total. Handing her his card, he watched as she took it to her bench and ran it through one of the old-fashioned imprint devices. Her sister Jo nudged her with her foot, and when Beth looked up something wordless passed between them, ending only when Beth rolled her eyes.

Ford tracked her progress back to him. She was surprisingly graceful, even in the baggy coveralls and chunky boots. It reminded him of the way she'd moved last night, and his body tightened.

Her eyes darkened, and he knew that she'd noticed. A pulse passed between them.

Having sex hadn't caused the fire between them to burn out—no, it had stoked the flame. His focus narrowed until he saw nothing but her, the vanilla and grease scent now conditioned in him to make him hard.

"Didn't get enough the first round?" Her words were barely audible, a whisper against his lips. She hooked her index fingers in his belt loops, and awareness of the sexual tension between them was painted all over her face.

"You left before I was done with this tight little body of yours." Surely if he'd had another taste—or two—he wouldn't be craving her again so strongly now.

She smiled up at him, but her eyes narrowed. "Maybe I was done with you."

"I don't think so." Not with the way she was vibrating against him right now. So why had she left?

"Lunchtime, girls!" Another woman entered the garage, opening a worn wooden door that he thought probably led to the house. Of average height, she had birch-brown hair pulled back into a messy bun, with a striking streak of white at her right temple. She was wearing cutoff jeans that had faded to almost white, an equally well-worn T-shirt that boasted a silkscreen of a palm tree and a long, loose kimono-type garment with an earthy orange-and-white pattern. She looked directly at him, arching an eyebrow over a pair of bright blue eyes that looked exactly like Beth's.

"Who are you?" The question wasn't accusing, but still he felt compelled to answer.

"I'm...a customer of Beth's." He winced inwardly as he spoke, knowing that Beth wouldn't care for that description. Her expression didn't change, however, and he found that part of him didn't like that.

"He's where Beth was all night, Mamesie." Jo slid off the bench, casting him a challenging look. Wow, these women didn't give an inch.

"Given the way he's got his hands on my daughter, I gathered that," said the older woman. She smiled at him. "Well, he can come for lunch as well."

"Uh…" He didn't know how to respond to the unexpected offer. Beth released his belt loops as he stepped back. A derisive noise came from Jo.

The older woman—Mamesie—hummed as she looked him up and down. He found himself standing straighter under her eyes.

"Do you eat lunch?"

"Yes." He knew where she was going with this.

"Were you planning to eat lunch today?"

"Yes." His throat felt tight. Beth fascinated him. He still wanted her. But lunch with her family?

He didn't do that.

"Well, then you can eat lunch with us." Mamesie gestured for them all to follow her. Amy and Meg did immediately, but Jo lingered on the steps, watching him. When she was sure that he was looking back, she pointed at her own eyes with two fingers, then at him to indicate she was watching him.

He felt like he was caught in a windstorm, being pulled along through no decision of his own.

What the hell? He planted his feet. He was a millionaire. He owned a very successful chain of hotels. He didn't do things that he didn't want to do. He would just wait until the rest of the women had headed into the house, then get in his car and go. That was what he'd planned to do anyway, wasn't it?

Beth crossed her arms over her chest. A knowing

smile curved her lips—one that said she'd expected him to do just this.

That was why she'd left in the middle of the night—she'd wanted to beat him to the punch.

That didn't sit right with him. Besides, something about this woman fascinated him. Yeah, he didn't do family stuff, but it wasn't like she was expecting him to, right? Where was the harm? They both knew this wasn't a long-term deal. That didn't mean he had to pretend that he wasn't interested in her, which he most certainly was.

"All right." He enjoyed the look of surprise that crossed her face. "What's for lunch?"

CHAPTER SEVEN

THE LAST THING Beth had expected was for Ford to accept Mamesie's invitation to lunch, and she really didn't know what to think about it. He hadn't needed much convincing, either, which surprised the hell out of her. A guy like him—she didn't expect him to do family stuff.

Nothing about their opposites attract–style hookup was normal, so she supposed that lunch with her family while her body was still sore from the way he'd used it the night before wasn't that weird.

Still, she felt apprehension as she led the way into the house—not a common emotion for her. She wasn't ashamed of her home, not at all, but as she and Ford followed her mother and sisters into the well-worn house, she tracked his gaze, seeing things through his eyes.

When her dad had been alive, they'd had money. Not a ton of it, or they probably would have lived in a different part of the city, but they'd had enough to keep the house in good repair.

Then her dad had died overseas. He'd always been the primary source of income for the house—Mamesie made good money on her pottery when she sold it, but an artist's income was sporadic. Over the years they'd found ways to make the house their own on a budget, and the result was cluttered and cozy.

Beth liked to think of it as bohemian, but she suspected that when Ford looked at the scarves pinned to the walls, the worn rugs layered on the floors, the tables full of scented candles, he saw junk.

Didn't matter, she reminded herself. He wasn't the one who lived here.

"Mamesie's made soup." Pushing away that thought, Beth made a show of sniffing the air. "You're lucky. She makes the best soup in the South End."

"What's that other smell?" Coming up beside her in the tight hallway, Ford inhaled deeply. Beth ignored the sparks that danced over her skin as his pelvis brushed against the round curves of her ass. "Is it citrus?"

"Lemongrass." Beth gestured to a small diffuser that sat on a table. She was pleased with his comment, since the scent was her favorite. "Mamesie changes the oil in it depending on her mood."

"Smells great." He sniffed again, and she just blinked at him. The comment was not what she expected from the terse, tense man who'd stormed into her garage yesterday. She'd thought she had Ford Lassiter figured out, but it seemed like maybe she was wrong.

Unbidden, something fluttered in her midsection.

"Amy, Jo, set the table." When Beth led Ford into the cozy area that held the living room and dining room, they found Mamesie with brightly quilted oven mitts on, carrying a large pot of steaming soup from the kitchen. Setting it on the scarred wooden table, she wiped the sweat from her forehead with the sleeve of her kimono. "Meg, you get the bread. Beth, why don't you play us a little something while they set the table?"

"Play something?" Ford turned to Beth, surprise evident on his face. She couldn't help the quick, bright streak of pleasure at being asked to play.

Holding up her hands, she wiggled her fingers, smirking. "These babies are good for more than one thing."

His expression darkened, heated, and Beth felt an answering tangle of warmth tightening in her gut as she thought about how it had felt to have her hands on his body.

"Beth?" Mamesie cast her an exasperated look, and Beth flushed, just a bit. She and her sisters were open about their sexuality, and they'd learned it from their mother, but there were still some boundaries. She wasn't about to cross one now by jumping on Ford here in the living room, no matter how much the man could turn her on with a single look.

"What are we in the mood for, girls?" Gesturing Ford to the threadbare sofa draped in brightly patterned blankets, she crossed the room to her old but very well-loved piano. It had been a vintage piece, a garage sale find, when her father had purchased it for decoration, and now it was ancient. Beth had fallen in love with it at first sight, prompting their dad to sign them all up for lessons. Meg, Jo and Amy could plunk out a simple melody, but Beth was the one with the passion.

"What was it that you played a couple of nights ago?" Amy asked as she set mismatched silverware on the table. "That one by Sarah somebody?"

"'Sweet Ones,'" Beth answered as she ran her fingers lightly over the keys. "Sarah Slean."

Her breathing slowed as she seated herself on the bench. It was solid wood, but it was so comfortable for her that she swore the years had molded it to her curves.

The fluttering she'd felt at having Ford in her home eased, her world centering as she placed her fingers on the necessary keys.

She could feel Ford's eyes burning into her from behind as she started to play, but within a moment she was drawn completely into the music. Her body moved as she played, and sweat beaded on her brow—she'd always been an energetic musician. The energy that filled her demanded it, though, and when the cover song she was playing ended she segued right into another, one that she'd written herself that matched the tempo of the first song.

Coaxing the last notes from the battered instrument, she inhaled deeply, folding her hands in her lap.

"Nice one, Beth!" Amy hooted from behind her. "Did you write that?"

"I did." An uncharacteristic hint of shyness colored her words. She knew that she could play, was talented, even. But while she never minded playing one of her own compositions for her family, she rarely felt confident enough in their strength to play them for anyone else.

They were a part of her, something she'd given birth to. Someone could hate her tattoos, her hair, but if they hated her music, it would hurt.

Stretching for something to do with her arms, she twisted to look at Ford. He looked slightly taken aback, and she held her breath until he spoke.

"You're very talented." His tone indicated that she'd impressed him, and warmth suffused her. She shouldn't have cared about his opinion—she barely knew him—but she liked to at least try to be honest with herself. There was something here between them. Something more than sex. They were so different that she really didn't think it was going to go anywhere, but that didn't turn off the interest rising inside her.

She liked that she'd impressed him. Liked that he was here, in her home.

"Thanks." Rising from the piano bench, she sauntered across one of the worn rugs until she stood directly in front of him, her knees brushing against his own. His stare traveled the length of her body with intent, lighting her up from inside, and she sucked in a breath.

"Why aren't you doing something with your talent?" Her pulse skipped a beat when he took one of her hands and studied the faint smears of grease that never seemed to come off. "Why work as a mechanic when you can do something so fantastic?"

What?

Both flattered and stung, she tugged her hand back. He'd unknowingly just aired her deepest dream. The one that her life would never allow. "I like my job. I'm good at it."

"But—"

She shook her head, cutting him off again. She didn't want to talk about this. Thinking about what she really wanted hurt. "How would I make a living at playing the piano? A few bucks here and there while I chased gigs at restaurants full of snooty people? I need a steadier paycheck than that."

He didn't seem convinced, so she continued. "And like I said, I like what I do. I have passion for it."

It was true. She loved cars, loved picking them apart to discover what was needed to make them run again. She was good with her hands, and this was one more way to use them. "Isn't there more than one thing that you love?"

"No." Ford pulled back a bit, and puzzlement was clear on his face. She wasn't entirely sure that he was understanding what she was saying. "No, I really just work. My company is my life."

"That's sad." Stepping back, she led the way to the table, but he'd confused her as much as she'd confused him. He'd said that his company was his life, and she was inclined to believe him. But how could he live that way? Didn't he have a hobby? Friends? Something more than casual sex with a near stranger?

She didn't think he would appreciate it if he knew, but his words made her heart ache. He had what appeared to be a boatload of cash, but what good was it if all he did was work for more?

They were so different. And yet when they sat down beside each other at the table, and their hands brushed, something sizzled inside her. Beside her Ford shifted in awareness, and she felt her pulse quicken.

They were different, and yet that connection—that sexual tension—was undeniable.

She was willing to see where it could go. She wondered if he would be, too.

"Soup's up," Mamesie said. Beth busied herself by passing the pot to Ford first, since he was the guest. She watched him ladle some of Mamesie's Italian wedding soup into a green glazed-pottery bowl. She liked watching his hands, liked remembering what they'd done to her body.

"So. Ford, right?" Meg took the pot next, serving herself into a bowl of cherry red. "You must be rich."

"Margaret Marchande." Mamesie spoke sharply from the head of the table. "You're being rude."

Meg shrugged, grinning. "We're all wondering, with that Turbo sitting in the garage. That suit you're wearing. Though it looks a bit rumpled, hmm, Beth?"

Beth rolled her eyes. "Meg's obsessed with how the other half lives. Your half, I guess I should say."

Ford arched an eyebrow as he spooned up some soup and made a noise of pleasure. He didn't seem put off by the question. "I am wealthy, yes. I own a chain of hotels."

"What are you doing with our Beth, then?" Jo's words were more than a bit aggressive, but Beth was pleased that Ford barely blinked at her sister's sharp tone.

"I—"

"I think we know what he's doing with Beth." Amy cut him off, and Beth was disappointed that she didn't get to hear what he was going to say. Her youngest sister grinned over her own bowl of soup, and Beth frowned back at her. They all shared the same open attitude about sex, and they weren't shy about details with one another, either. But Amy's words stung a little.

Did her sisters really think it was impossible that a man like Ford would want to be with a woman like Beth for more than just sex? What the hell?

Underneath the table, Ford settled his hand on her thigh, squeezing gently. She wasn't sure if it was because he'd sensed her upset and was trying to soothe her, or because he'd craved the touch, but when his hand slid a few inches higher, she felt her breath hitch.

She'd thought that one time would be enough. But here she was, need gathering hot and tight for him again.

"I think that's enough of the grand inquisition." Pushing away her half-empty bowl, Beth stood. She wanted another taste of this man, and she wanted it now.

Ford had just finished his soup as well, so she stacked his bowl with hers, then tugged at his sleeve to get him moving. "Come on."

"Thank you for the hospitality." Ford nodded at Mamesie before Beth was able to tug him from the room. That he took the time to thank her mother did something funny to her insides.

Without another word, she pulled him from the room, ignoring her sisters' knowing laughter that followed her.

CHAPTER EIGHT

FORD FOLLOWED BETH'S curves back out of the garage like she was a piper and he was dancing to her tune. When he'd placed a hand on her thigh, he'd wanted her attention, but he hadn't expected her to all but melt into the touch.

She was so fucking sexy. No other woman had ever gotten him hot like this.

He paused just outside the door that divided the house from the garage. He wanted to just look at her, to try to analyze why her hair, her ink, her devil-may-care attitude got to him the way that it did.

He watched as she sauntered to the front of his Turbo. His pulse stuttered when she undid the knot she'd made at the waist of her coveralls. They fell to the stained concrete floor, leaving him with a killer view of her sweet ass in insanely tight little shorts.

This. This was why she was so sexy—her un-apologetic hunger. The way she wasn't afraid to get down and dirty, to push him to do the same.

The need to grab that tight little ass, to darken it

with his palm the way he had the night before, was nearly impossible to contain.

Hitching herself up onto the hood, Beth fisted her hands in the hem of her thin T-shirt. Tearing it up and over her head, she tossed it aside, then tugged the elastic from her messy braid. Inky black and violet rioted over her shoulders as she settled back onto her elbows, parting her thighs.

The silver bar nestled in one of her taut nipples glinted. Her breasts looked heavy and full, ready for his mouth. And when his gaze strayed between those sweet thighs, he saw that the crotch of those little shorts she was wearing was already damp.

"Fuck." He was off the stairs and to her before he could take his next breath. He put his hands on her knees and spread her legs farther, dipping his head to inhale her sweet scent.

"That's the idea, Sir Lassiter." She stretched out the *sir* on that velvet tongue of hers, and pure lust rocketed straight to his cock. "Fuck me. Now."

"Bossy little woman." Lifting his head, he feasted his gaze on those luscious tits. Needing to touch, he slid his hands up to cup them, catching the ripe nipples between forefingers and thumbs. She arched beneath the touch, falling back onto the hood of the car. Hooking her legs around his hips, she pulled his aching erection against her barely covered core, moaning when she rubbed over him.

He was going to have her again. Fuck, he needed to have her again. He braced his hands on the cool metal on either side of her, dipping his head to nip at her neck. "The garage door is open."

"So it is." She rocked her hips against him, and he saw stars. "In a few minutes, you're going to be fucking me hard, right here on your pricey little car. And anyone could walk by and see. Anyone at all."

Fuck, fuck, but that turned him on even more. He knew he had a bit of an exhibitionist streak, but he tried not to look at it too hard.

Right now, with her dirty words and her tight little body, she was urging him to grab that desire that he tried to deny with both hands. Demanding that he own up to his dirty side.

Cupping her breasts in her hands, she began to play with those tits of hers, undulating when she pulled on her piercing. His last shreds of sanity fled.

"I hope someone walks by." If he was going to do this, then he was going to do it right. Grabbing her just above the knees, he hauled her down the car's hood until her ass rested on the front edge. She gasped at the sudden movement, but the groan that followed it told him she was right there with him. "Undo my pants."

"Gladly." Extending her arms, she worked the button at his waist free, then slowly—maddeningly—lowered his zipper. Those wicked fingers of hers brushed against his rigid length, and he hissed at the sensation.

"Pull me out." She stroked down his length again, fingers teasing him through the thin cotton of his boxer briefs, and he delivered a sharp tap to her hip. "Now."

Working her hands inside his waistband, she circled his shaft, rubbing a thumb over the tip. He felt red-hot liquid bead beneath her touch as she tugged the elastic down beneath his erection.

He indulged himself with a look down at the length of her—naked breasts swollen and pink, dampness between her thighs, legs wrapped around his waist and hands in his pants.

So. Fucking. Hot.

She squealed when, without warning, he flipped her over. Pressing her hot body against the cool metal of the hood, he dragged the little scrap of spandex down around her knees. The fabric was tight, holding her legs together, which was just what he wanted.

Bending over, he covered her from behind. Even through the fabric of his shirt, he could feel her little vibrations of excitement. She was as into this as he was.

He pressed his weight down, trapping her against his car. Circling her wrists with his fingers, he pinned her against the sleek car, running his lips over the shell of her ear.

"You'd like it if someone came by, wouldn't you?" He gave one small thrust, rubbing his naked cock through her slick folds, and she laughed breathlessly, raising her ass for more contact. "What would turn you on the most?"

She parted her lips, but no sound came out. Her hot breath misted across the hood.

"Let me think." Rolling his hips forward again, he thrust through her slickness, and the feeling was so heady his entire body tightened. "A lot of men were watching you at the bar last night. Watching you dance, put on a show."

"They were," she agreed, rubbing back against him.

"I bet you'd just love it if some of those men were out for a walk right now. Maybe heading down the street on their lunch breaks." Beneath him she whimpered. "They hear that sexy little sound that you just made and come to see what's going on."

She rose up on her toes, pushing back against him.

"Yeah, I can just picture it." He could. "Five or six men, crowding into the garage. The noises that they hear, they wonder if maybe someone is hurt. Instead they see that hot little tease from the bar last night. She's bent over the hood of a car in her own garage, and she's about to get fucked."

"Oh my God," Beth hissed out between her teeth. "Please. Now."

He could see it in his mind's eye—the men that had watched her provocative dancing had wanted her. They wouldn't question their luck at the open garage door—they'd just enjoy the show.

Enjoy watching him fuck *this* woman. Him. Fuck Beth. The fact that it could actually happen, that someone could come along right now and watch them together, was the hottest thing he'd ever felt.

Jesus, who the hell was he? He'd never talked dirty like this. He'd wanted to, oh, hell yes, but the way he'd been raised, he'd always known he didn't want to be like his father. Didn't want to treat women like objects.

Was that was he was doing here?

Looking down at Beth, he took in her flushed skin, so hot in contrast with the sleek metal of his Turbo. She was stretched out for his pleasure, but there was no doubt in his mind that she was here because she wanted to be. Because it turned her on.

And so help him, but she demanded that he do what turned him on, too.

He couldn't hold back any longer.

Working his hand into one of his pockets, he pulled out the condom that he'd tucked there earlier. He hadn't been sure what to make of Beth's leaving in the night, but he'd have been lying to himself if he said he hadn't been hopeful.

Not wanting to take his other hand from her, he caught the foil packet in his teeth and pulled. The ring of latex fell onto her back, and he snatched it up, conceding that he needed both hands free to put it on.

"Yes." Her voice was raw. Dirty. "Hurry."

Pinching the tip, he rolled the condom down his length, his own touch feeling good on his engorged flesh. Catching the swell of her hip in one hand, he slid his sheathed cock through her cheeks one final time. "Ready?"

She nodded frantically, hips rocking.

He dipped a hand between her legs. She gasped when he tucked two fingers inside, and he exhaled loudly. She was soaked, and hot, and more than ready for him. And if she felt this fucking good on his fingers, then she was going to feel like heaven on his dick.

Placing the swollen head of his cock at her entrance, he thrust. Her moan mingled with the strangled sound from his own throat as he surged in to the hilt.

"Yes." Her voice was ragged with need. Her fingers scrabbled at the cool metal for something to hold on to. Her channel tightened around him in a snug embrace, and he saw stars.

"Better be quiet," he muttered as he rocked his pelvis, his hips still flush against her gorgeous heart-shaped ass, "or someone will come in, will see what a dirty girl you are."

"I am," she agreed, rising up onto her toes. "I'm so dirty. And so are you."

Her words spurred something on in him. With a guttural sound, he placed one hand flat on her back and started to thrust in earnest, pulling out slowly, then surging back in. She met his thrusts as best she could in her position, a small sound of pure pleasure falling from her lips every time he hilted inside her.

Sensation coiled tightly inside him, and he knew

he wasn't going to last long. Working his hand between Beth's soft abdomen and the hood of the car,
he found her swollen clit. Catching it between his
fingers, he rubbed. Her hips jumped as she absorbed
the pleasure.

She clenched around him as she gasped through
her climax, wringing his own release from him. He
collapsed over her, trying to brace his weight as he
pressed against her back so that he didn't crush her.

They were silent for a long moment, sweat and
heat sealing them together. Beneath him, Beth
laughed breathlessly.

"You've got some moves, Sir Lassiter." Sliding
out from beneath him, she rolled those skimpy little shorts back up. Her skin was glossy, her cheeks
flushed as she moved, completely comfortable in
her nakedness.

"Jesus." Legs shaking, he tucked himself back
into his pants, then raked a hand through his hair.
He knew he'd never forget the sight of her, topless
with legs spread on the hood of his Turbo. Daring
him to take what he wanted. "What was that for?"

Retrieving her T-shirt, Beth tugged it back over
her head, leaving the coveralls on the floor where
they lay. That silver bar in her nipple pressed against
the tissue-thin cotton, and he found he couldn't look
away.

Heading to the small, rusty fridge that stood by
the workbench, she pulled out two cans of Coke.

Studying him with those bewitching blue eyes, she walked back and pressed one into his hand.

"I felt like it." She smirked up at him as she popped the top on her can and took a long drink.

"I'm never going to look at the Turbo the same way again." He was pretty sure they'd just incinerated some of his brain cells, and she confirmed it when she searched his face and laughed.

"That look on your face. You look like you just got laid for the first time." She took another sip, then licked her lips. "But maybe it's just one of the first times that you really let yourself go."

"I don't know how to answer that." Discomfited, he cracked open his own can, hoping the combination of sugar and caffeine would jolt him back to reality. The way she was looking at him—it felt like she could see right to his very soul, like she had full access to all of those dark needs and wants that he tried so hard to keep hidden away.

"Ford." Placing her can on the workbench, Beth laid one of her hands on his cheek. "I don't get it. Why are you fighting so hard against what you like when it's what you obviously want?"

Those damn witchy eyes of hers. He couldn't deny those needs when she was looking right at him like that. Jerking back, he turned away from her, chugging his Coke and trying to cool off.

When he turned back, she was still waiting, the slightest hint of mockery on her face. Like instead of thinking that he was more of a man for denying his kink, she believed he was less of one.

It pissed him right off.

"So what do you do when you're dating someone?" She seemed genuinely puzzled. "Who are you then?"

"I—" How the hell was he supposed to answer that? He dated. He dated a lot, but he knew that his wealth attracted a lot of women who only showed him their best side.

Just like he did. The parallel wasn't lost on him, but damn it. He didn't want to be thinking about this, didn't want to have to explain himself. He would not be like his father, treating women like crap.

No matter how much a purple-haired siren tempted him.

"I don't date women who are into…this." The words came out harsh, but he couldn't think straight. "And that's fine, because this isn't the real me."

"I see." Beth crossed her arms over her chest. "So it was someone else who just bent me over the hood of your car and fucked me where anyone could have seen?"

He winced, guilt and shame rising at her words. He'd done just that. He'd treated her like an object. He was no better than his father.

"Gotcha." Her smile turning brittle, Beth sauntered over to her cluttered desk. Slamming a staple through a thin sheaf of paper, she crossed back to him and slapped it against his chest. "Here's your detailed service report. Have a nice day."

He took the paper, anger and something else warring inside him. She looked him over slowly, then snorted inelegantly.

"I feel sorry for you."

"What?" he sputtered, crumpling the report in his hands. "You're sorry for *me*?"

"Yup. It's a sad life you have if all you do is work and pretend to be someone you're not." She reached for her crumpled coveralls, and damn if his eyes weren't drawn to that freaking silver bar through her nipple. She noted the direction of his gaze and smirked.

"This isn't who I am." He crumpled the paper into a ball and threw it across the garage in frustration. "You bring this out in me!"

"Oh, no." She shook her head, her eyes emitting sapphire sparks. "Don't you blame me. This is who you are, Sir Lassiter. What you choose to do with it, though? That's up to you. But I'm not going to go along for the ride with someone who is going to treat me like a dirty little secret."

He sputtered again. She was putting words into his mouth, except that she was right. Silently, he watched as she climbed the steps back to the house.

And then she was gone, and he had no choice but to get into his car and go.

CHAPTER NINE

Now

BOSTON LOOKED NOTHING like Los Angeles, and Ford loved it.

The drive through the familiar streets, the New England architecture and the leafy greenery soothed his soul. He'd lived in California for two and a half years, and he'd enjoyed the sparkle of it all, the bright lights and eclectic people and towering palms.

But Massachusetts was home.

Working his black SUV through traffic to the South End, he made his way to his new home—a midsize two-story on a large lot. It was a far cry from the waterfront condo he'd once owned on the harbor, or the minimansion he'd inhabited in Los Angeles.

He was happier to be moving in here than he'd been in either of those other places.

For years he'd worked feverishly, building his hotel chain into a global dynasty. He'd been engaged to a woman who suited his life. He'd had everything he'd ever wanted.

He'd been greedy. And he'd lost it all.

A smile quirked the corners of his lips as he turned onto the run-down street. There, the Sold sign still on the lawn, was his new home.

He hadn't lost quite everything.

Slinging his laptop bag over his shoulder, Ford parked the Escape in the driveway and wrenched open the manual garage door, wincing at the screeching sound. He couldn't imagine wrestling with the thing in the middle of winter, so he'd have to look into installing an automatic one. Other than that, he didn't intend to add many other luxuries to the place. In truth, he could have afforded something in a nicer neighborhood. When the German hotel chain he'd partnered with—had trusted—had done a hostile takeover of his company, he'd still had a cushion in the bank. To many people in this neighborhood, it was probably even a small fortune.

To him, it was money to start over. To invest in something fresh. He didn't want to waste any of it on his personal life when it could be used for an investment opportunity.

He didn't know what that opportunity would be yet, but he'd know it when he saw it. He'd built his fortune the first time around by trusting his gut. He could do it again.

The front door creaked as he unlocked it and pushed it open. The smell of dust greeted him, and he could see the specks of it dancing in the white light of early afternoon.

He certainly hadn't splurged on any luxuries here. The flooring was a mix of worn linoleum and shag carpet straight from the '70s. He'd purchased the place furnished, and the olive-green couch had been shredded by cat claws.

The beige paint was peeling from the plaster walls. Peyton would have hated it.

As he set his laptop bag down in the front entry-way, Ford noted that thinking of his former fiancée didn't bring up anything more than a mild bitter-sweet sensation.

When he'd left Boston for California, he'd been... well, he'd been shaken by what had happened with Beth Marchande. The things she'd pulled from his very core and insisted that he acknowledge.

He'd thrown himself into work, searching for what he thought he wanted. He'd met Peyton Channing at the launch of his Beverly Hills location, and he and the sleek brunette socialite had hit it off.

They had fun together. They were friends. And the sex between them was...nice.

Still, when he'd lost his fortune, she hadn't known quite what to do. She had money of her own—she wasn't a gold digger—but something between them had shifted.

She no longer saw him as her equal. And he—well, he knew that he'd never really shown her who he was. They'd parted on good enough terms that he knew while he'd loved her, he'd never been *in* love with her.

Wading through the dregs of his life had been an eye-opener. He'd done everything he'd thought he was supposed to do, and look where it had landed him.

An international empire and a sweet vanilla woman hadn't fulfilled him. Moving home, searching for a new business that excited him, and acknowledging who he truly was—*that* was what got his blood pumping now.

Heading to the garage, Ford treated himself to a quick peek inside. There she was, his baby—his now fifteen-year-old Porsche Turbo. He really should sell her, add the money to his investment capital, but he couldn't.

The car was a symbol. He loved it, and it meant something to him, so it was a reminder to be present, to actually live his life instead of getting caught in the trappings of what he thought he should do.

Heading to the kitchen, he washed his hands and splashed water over his face. It smelled faintly of rust, and for some reason that made him grin.

This was his new life, and he couldn't wait to live it.

Mamesie's ancient Honda Civic turned over when Beth put the key in the ignition. She grinned as the old engine rumbled to life, a senior citizen protesting being coaxed from its nap.

The car hadn't wanted to start this morning, so

she'd slotted it into her day of appointments, after an
ancient pickup that belonged to a friend and a young
family's minivan.

The routine felt good. She liked having a structure to her day, enjoyed seeing tangible results from
her actions.

It gave her a purpose, something to cling to when
she thought that she might fall apart.

"Hey, baby girl." Pushing through the door from
the house, Jo shoved her hands into her pockets and
whistled a few notes. "How are you feeling? You've
been at that for a while."

Beth bit back a sharp retort. She loved all of
her sisters, but she and Jo had always had a special bond. That meant her older sister worried about
her, though, and fussed without meaning to.

She both appreciated it and resented it. Her sister
meant well, but sometimes it was hard enough for
Beth to get through the day without being bogged
down with worry. Someone else fussing over her
just made it worse.

Shaking it off, she climbed from behind the wheel
of her mother's sedan. "I'm fine. Mamesie's baby is
back up and running. I'm about to break for lunch."

"I was hoping you'd say that." Jo grinned and
hiked up her skinny jeans. "I'm starving. Let's go
to the Tearoom and grab some lunch."

"With what money?" Beth felt the familiar guilt
as she stripped off her coveralls and headed for the
industrial sink to scrub her hands with mechanic's

orange-peel scrub. They'd floated along just below the line of comfortable income after her father died, but Beth's illness had sunk them. They'd be paying off her medical bills for years, and it was going to take a miracle to keep their home in the meantime.

"I don't want to see that look on your face, baby girl." Stomping down the steps in her battered Doc Martens, Jo closed the space between them and crossed her arms over her chest. "I don't know how we can make this sink in. We're a family. We handle things together."

Beth pinched her lips together as she reached for a pair of worn jeans to pull on over her spandex shorts. She didn't want to have this argument again.

Especially since she knew Jo was right.

Instead, she tugged the elastic from the bottom of her braid, letting the waves shake free. Turning to her sister, she arched an eyebrow. "Yeah, yeah. Still. Where did you come up with the cash? Shouldn't you give it to Mamesie?"

"I scored a ghostwriting gig that paid up front." Jo scowled at her. "And of course I gave it to Mamesie. But I set aside twenty bucks to celebrate. And I choose to celebrate with you, so stop being crabby and let's go."

She was being crabby. She'd woken up in a mood that day and it had been hard to shake. She made a deliberate choice to start the conversation over and scurried to catch up with her sister's quick gait as Jo strode out of the garage and started down the street.

"Congrats on the ghostwriting gig." She nudged her sister with her hip, and Jo nudged her back, letting her know that everything between them was fine. "What's it for?"

Her sister grinned wickedly, her amber eyes sparking with amusement. "An erotic romance."

"No way." Beth choked out a surprised laugh. "Don't you usually get contracts for sci-fi?"

"I was getting bored of writing about blonde aliens with three boobs who want nothing more than to worship the human male who stumbled across them." Jo shrugged, her lips twisting sarcastically. "Figured I'd open up the parameters of what I was willing to do. Turns out there are a ton of these erotic romance authors who want to release a book every month but just can't write that fast. Enter Jo."

"Or Jo gets entered." Beth laughed when her sister snorted. "Seriously. How does this work. Do you get an outline like with the sci-fi? Are you going to… hmm, draw on personal experience?"

"Wouldn't you like to know, perv." Gesturing to the strip mall that was their destination, Jo sniffed at the air. "Hurry up. I'm dying for an order of pierogies."

Beth followed her sister into the Tearoom. Not much to look at, the café was an odd but delicious mix of Jewish deli and Ukrainian cuisine.

Her sister ordered a pierogi platter, and Beth's mouth watered as the cafeteria-style setup served a paper plate loaded with the potato-and-cheese-filled dough crescents, topped with fried onions, bacon and an artery-clogging scoop of sour cream.

She hesitated, tempted to get the same. Instead she ordered a spinach salad with dressing on the side.

She didn't particularly like spinach or salad, and she certainly wasn't trying to lose weight. But with her new lease on life, she'd decided to try to treat her body properly. And that meant chewing on chopped spinach and boiled eggs while Jo inhaled deep-fried mashed potatoes wrapped in dough.

Swallowing a particularly fibrous chunk of the spinach, she reached for her water, looking across the tiny eat-in area, into which were crammed eight small tables for two.

The water caught in her throat when she looked right into the face of Ford Lassiter.

"Holy shit." She dropped her fork. Jo swallowed a massive mouthful and swiveled in her seat to see what Beth was staring at. "What?"

"Don't do that!" To get her attention she stole her sister's fork, and Jo growled. "Simmer down. Just… stop looking."

"Well, what are you looking at?" Jo stole her fork back, her body still half turned in the seat. "The Jolly Green Giant? George Washington? Niall Horan?"

"Remember that suit I had a thing with a few years ago?" Beth reached for her bottle of water, since her throat was suddenly dry. "The one who came to lunch?"

"Uh-huh." Jo cranked her head around again as

Beth sighed with exasperation. "What was his name? Felix?"

"Ford." His head snapped up, and she realized that she'd spoken far too loudly. She smiled tentatively as storm-brown eyes focused in on her.

Ford Lassiter. Jesus, talk about a blast from the past. Unconsciously, she smoothed a hand over the kinky waves left by her braid. Did she have spinach in her teeth? She'd been under the hood of Mamesie's car for the last hour. What did she look like?

His brow furrowed, as though he was trying to place her. Her heart sank, and heated irritation surged in an attempt to burn away the disappointment.

Of course he didn't recognize her. They'd fucked twice, and it had been five years since.

She'd never forgotten him.

As she sat frozen, the puzzlement on his face quickly morphed into pleasure. He grinned and set down his sandwich.

"Beth?" Standing, he approached their table with an open expression, which both delighted and surprised her. "Wow. It's so good to see you."

He held out his arms for a hug, and after a heartbeat of indecision, she rose to welcome the embrace. Over the years she'd thought about this, about what might happen if she ever ran into Ford again. If he'd pretend he didn't know her. If he'd be embarrassed to admit their past to the fancy fiancée that was plastered all over the newspapers.

She'd never imagined that he'd be so openly delighted to see her. Warmth suffused her, and when she stepped into his arms for the hug, the heat cranked up to a roaring flame as her body pressed against his own.

He ran a hand down the length of her hair lightly, then pulled back. The spark in his eye told her that he felt it, too, that same attraction between them. That he still enjoyed the buzz of their chemistry.

She reminded herself that he was engaged.

"I'm sorry I didn't recognize you." He took a step back, but she could still feel the heat from his body. "You've changed your hair."

"Oh." Her hand went to the wild waves again. The length was much the same as it had been five years ago, but prescriptions had thinned it out in the meantime. It was now wavier, a bit wilder. And gone were the days of bright blues and purples and pink—she now settled for a cherry-red henna rinse on her natural light brown. No unnecessary chemicals for her. "Well, it's been a long time. And men are kind of stupid about hair."

He laughed, and she liked the sound. She smiled in return, and when their stares met she felt another little jolt.

Basic chemistry. It was there or it wasn't, and apparently the years hadn't dimmed the potent punch of attraction between them.

"We are pretty stupid about stuff like that." He looked down at her with a face that was still ridiculously gorgeous, and she felt a pulse of adrenaline. "But seriously. It's so great to run into you."

"I'm going to let you two catch up." Jo stood abruptly,

gathering up her empty plate and soda can. She waggled her eyebrows suggestively at Beth, who couldn't help grin in reply. "Nice to see you again, Felix."

Ford didn't correct her—he seemed to be too focused on Beth. Gesturing to her half-eaten salad, he cocked his head back to his own table. "May I join you? We can catch up?"

"Yes." Beth exhaled a breath that she hadn't known she was holding. The man still made her a little light-headed. "That would be great."

Ford grabbed his sandwich and soda. Beth stared at the bright red can, remembering how she'd once seduced him by stealing his Coke for a sip.

"You're in California now, right?" She blurted the words out as a distraction for herself, because she could almost taste the sugar on her tongue. "Are you just back for a visit?"

"Nope." Ford settled into his new seat but didn't dig back into his sandwich. "I've moved back."

A shot of adrenaline surged through Beth. "Did your fiancée move with you?"

Ford took a quick sip of his drink, looking at the can as he set it back down. Beth knew that he was thinking about the exact same thing that she was when his eyes darkened.

"No more fiancée." He swallowed, and she followed the motion of the muscles in his throat. "I'm back for good."

CHAPTER TEN

WHAT THE HELL was Beth Marchande doing back in Boston's South End?

The engine grease smeared on her right cheekbone was the obvious answer—she was working at her garage. But why?

After they'd parted ways, she'd found success with her music. He hadn't followed too closely because it wasn't his kind of thing, but he knew that she'd released a few albums of her original songs. She'd gotten some airplay.

He didn't know what had happened to her after she'd faded from the limelight. In truth, he hadn't wanted to look too closely, because it had been a reminder of what an asshole he'd been to her. But here she was, sitting across from him as he ate his first meal back in the city.

He watched as she picked at her salad. She looked good—great, even. She'd lost a bit of weight since he'd seen her last that she could stand to put back on, but her body was still sexy as hell. She was wearing ripped jeans and a simple black tank top, which showed the arm ink that had fascinated him before, and maybe a few new tattoos.

He tried not to look, but he couldn't help a quick peek at the gorgeous cleavage peeking out of her top. He wondered if she still had that mouthwatering silver bar through her nipple.

God, he hoped so.

"You look good, Beth." She looked up quickly. There was a bit of reserve around her that hadn't been there before, but it didn't hide the interest in her gaze. The chemistry between them was still there, and it was intense.

He really wanted to pursue it. He was free. Was she?

"I have a meeting in twenty minutes. I should get going." He didn't miss the flicker of disappointment in her eyes.

"I should get back to work, too." Smiling genuinely, she stood, packing up the remains of her meal. "It's been good to see you, Ford. Really."

"Wait." He caught her wrist as she turned away. His thumb rubbed once, gently, over the thin skin at the inside of her wrist, and her pulse jumped beneath his touch. She turned back, looking at him with a question in her eyes. "Are you free tonight?"

Heat slowly encased her, like warm oil poured on her skin at a massage. He wasn't asking because he wanted to meet up for an evening of pleasant drinks and chitchat.

He still wanted her. Wanted her again. Whatever the semantics were, it both turned her on and threw her off her game.

She'd never forgotten that night with Ford, not even when her life had fallen apart. Hell, sometimes she pulled the memory out as her own personal porn, remembering the way those bossy hands had felt all over her body.

She also remembered the hurt and confusion she'd pushed through after their encounter. The way her confidence had been shaken because he'd so vehemently denied that he wanted her and what she had to offer, even though she'd known even then that it was his issue, not hers. Was it wise to go there again?

Did she care? The potential for something good had been there. Something hot. It was here again now.

"Why are you in Boston?" The last she'd heard of him had been splashed across a glossy tabloid in the supermarket checkout. It had announced his merger with a massive German corporation and also his engagement to Peyton Channing, the more reserved little sister of notorious party-girl socialite India Channing. "You've really moved back? Why did you leave LA?"

"I take it you don't read the tabloids?"

She furrowed her brow. "Um, why?"

"Never mind." He barked out a laugh. "Anyway, it was front-page news for a while. I partnered with a German conglomerate to expand my hotel chain and was reckless with how much control I gave them. They booted me out. Lassiter Deluxe Hotels is no longer mine."

"Oh my God." Acting on instinct, Beth reached across the table to take his hands in hers with sympathy. "I'm so sorry."

"Don't be." To her surprise, he grinned at her. "It was the best thing that ever happened to me. I was forced to reexamine my entire life. What I found was that I didn't much like it."

"What wasn't to like?" Her voice was skeptical. "Boatloads of cash. A-list invites. Gorgeous woman wearing your ring."

"Does that sound like paradise to you?"

"Hell, no." She shuddered. "Well, maybe the cash."

"I still have some of that." He smirked at her expression. "Enough that I can take a step back and think about what I do want."

"And what is that?" She heard the rasp in her own voice, knew it was because he was winding her up. "What does Ford Lassiter want from life?"

"I want to invest the money I have left in a new business. Something that excites me." His wraith-like eyes studied her face. "And then there's the second part."

"Which is?"

"I don't want to pretend to be someone I'm not anymore." Catching her hand again, he kept his gaze on her face as he stroked his thumb over her palm.

She couldn't hold back the small shudder at the sensuous touch. "I've had a lot of time to come to terms with who I am. With what I want."

"And what do you want?" She ran the tip of her tongue over her lips. Her pulse picked up the pace.

"Can't give away everything right off." Releasing her, he picked up his soda and took a sip, grinning down at her.

"Tease."

"You have no idea." The air between them pulsed with promise. She realized that she was wet, just from their conversation.

"Can I take you for dinner tonight?" Dinner, she knew, would be more than that. A whole delicious course more.

He wanted her. She wanted him. Her body was on fire, and it infused her with a hint of the sass that had once come so easily to her.

He wanted her back? She wasn't going to make it a cakewalk for him.

"There's a place a few blocks over. Mamacita's." She sat back in her chair. "Ever heard of it?"

"Nope." His expression was amused. "But I have the miracle of GPS. What time?"

"Seven." She was pleased with herself. If he wanted to do this, he was going to have to sit through dinner at a place of her choosing. One that she guessed was a few thousand times more of a dive than anything he'd ever set foot in before. "Don't be late."

Tugging at the hem of her tank top, she watched as his gaze flickered down to her chest. She'd noticed his herculean effort to be polite earlier, but now she deliberately pulled the fabric snug, guessing that he was searching for the bump of her piercing.

She could tell the instant he found it, because he hissed out a breath. His gaze returned to her face, and he grinned at her.

"I have no intention of disappointing you like that."

Oh, yeah.

Leaning across the table, she picked up his can of Coke and slowly, deliberately took a sip.

It was answer enough.

CHAPTER ELEVEN

BETH LOOKED GOOD, and she knew it.

With one final, satisfied look at her reflection, she exited the bathroom that she shared with Meg— she was closer with Jo, but Meg and Amy were both bathroom hogs, so they'd split the difference. She'd made sure to tell her eldest sister that she needed the space for at least an hour this evening, and to Meg's credit, she hadn't knocked even once.

Still, Beth braced herself as she followed the sound of her sisters' voices to the kitchen. What would they think about this, her first date in…well. She hadn't been counting, but it was at least a year and a half. Since before she'd gotten sick.

Shoving aside her nerves, she entered the kitchen. Meg, Jo and Amy were seated around the kitchen island, and from the looks of it, Amy was kicking the older two's asses at Crazy Eight Countdown.

They all fell silent as Beth entered, and she winced. Here it came—the worries, the *gentle* questions. The smothering.

Two years ago, she would have flipped them the bird and told them where to go. Now, though? Now there was guilt. The feeling that she had to listen them all, had to take their fears on as her own because she owed them all so much.

Her illness had essentially tied them all to this house. Forever. How could she not feel guilty?

Her defenses started to rise as the other three stared at her. She got ready for the onslaught of concern.

It didn't come. Instead, the three women she was closest to in the world broke into applause.

"I knew I looked good, but I didn't know I looked that good." She grinned as she did a little spin. She wouldn't admit, even here, how long she'd spent deciding what to wear. In the end she'd settled on a little sundress that she'd picked up from her favorite thrift store a couple of months ago and hadn't yet worn. The skirt was short and flared, flirty with its multicolored paisley print. The top had thick straps, dipping into a low vee in both the front and the back.

The material was silky and thin. She'd chosen it both because it made her feel sexy, and because she knew that the thinness of the material would have Ford thinking about her nipple piercing all night.

She finished the look off with tan booties, a chunky white cardigan and just a bit of polish to her hair and nails. She'd pulled on a pair of the little spandex shorts she wore under her coveralls since the skirt was so short, but she'd left off the bra.

She felt damn good.

"You look good, baby girl." Jo looked up from her bowl of cold cereal to give her a thumbs-up while Amy continued to clap her hands with glee.

Meg squinted at her and fake frowned. "That's my eye shadow. But it looks so good, I won't yell."

"You guys are...excited for me?" This was strange. She wasn't quite sure what to make of it.

"Beth, it's been so long. *So* long. It's about time you got back out there." Amy stood up and tucked one of Beth's waves behind her ear.

"I know we all get a little overprotective." Meg and Amy arched eyebrows at Jo as she spoke, and she scowled in response. "Okay, *I* get a little over-protective."

"You think?" Amy muttered. Meg swatted her arm.

"We—*collectively*—" Jo glared at the other two "—have been waiting for this. You were given your life back. You need to live it."

Her sister's voice cracked on the last couple of words, and Beth's heart both swelled and broke at the same time. Wordlessly, she crossed the kitchen to her sister and wrapped her in a big hug. Meg and Amy followed, and within a minute they were all tearing up and laughing at the same time.

"Come on," Meg ordered, shooing the other two away. "I'll drive you."

"I can walk." Though when she looked down at her booties, she wasn't at all sure that she could.

"Let me be the big sister." Meg nudged her toward the back door. "Go."

Enjoying the freshness of the crisp air outside, Beth hauled herself up into Meg's van. Not quite Ford's Turbo, she thought wryly as she buckled herself in, but it would do.

"Have fun." Meg smiled at her when they pulled up in front of Mamacita's. Beth smirked, about to tell her just how much fun she intended to have, but the seriousness of Meg's expression made her stop. "I'm serious, Beth. You deserve this."

Reaching into her bag, she pulled out a small cardboard box and pressed it into Beth's hand.

"Ribbed for her pleasure." She snorted out a laugh. "Always looking out for me."

"Damn straight." Meg stepped on the gas, causing the van to roar and everyone within a half-block radius to stare. "There. Now you can make an entrance. Go!"

"Going!" Beth was still laughing when she entered the restaurant. It was small, dingy and packed with blue-collar types, but Mamacita herself made the best Mexican food on the South End.

The small size made it easy to spot Ford. Hell, she would have zeroed right in on him even if the place had been huge. Part of it was that she seemed to be connected to him with an invisible string whenever he was here, and part of it was that even in his jeans and plain black T-shirt, he would never blend in with the rough crowd.

He moved like a man who got what he wanted, when he wanted it. And as she moved through the room, he was the only one she could see.

"Sorry I'm late." Through the crowd, she slid into the booth across from him. His appreciative stare made the extra effort she'd put into her appearance worth it.

"I'd say you were worth the wait." He grinned at her. "I ordered you a margarita. I figured that's what you'd want here."

"What if I don't want what you have to offer?" Her voice was teasing, but she needed something to ease the tension before she combusted.

"You want it." The grin slipped from his face, replaced with pure heat. "You wouldn't have made the choice to come here otherwise."

"Touché," she conceded, leaning back in her seat. "However, in all fairness, I don't drink. Not anymore."

He cocked his head slightly, and she knew he was wondering why, but he didn't ask. Instead he signaled the waitress and ordered two glasses of Coke.

Beth didn't drink soda anymore, either, the sip of Ford's she'd had earlier not counting in her books. But tonight was a celebration of starts—a new beginning—so she decided to just go with it.

She expected him to cut straight to the heart of the matter—that they still wanted to be in each other's beds. To seduce her toward what she already knew they would be doing after they left here.

Instead, after they ordered, he led her into conversation. Date-type conversation. Bemused, she let him.

"So you really don't know what kind of business you're going to start up this time?" Her tortilla soup arrived, and she dipped her head to fan a breath over the fragrant steam. "And...wow. You seem so okay with being forced out of your own business. Are you really? Last time I saw you, you were all *my work is my life.*"

She grinned sheepishly when he winced. "Sorry. Foot in mouth. Am I poking at a sore subject?"

"No." He spooned steak, grilled peppers and cotija cheese into a tortilla to make one of the fajitas that he'd ordered. She found that she liked watching his hands. "The wince was because of what I sounded like back then. All work, no play makes Ford a dull boy."

"I wouldn't say there was *no* play."

Beneath the table, his knees brushed against hers. She held her breath, waiting—hoping—for him to place a hand on her bare knee. He caught her expression and, reaching under the table, grazed his hand lightly over the sensitive skin beside her kneecap.

Who knew that the knee could be an erogenous zone?

"Don't get me wrong. I raged for a while. Drank my way through half the bars in Los Angeles. Shoved money I no longer had at my lawyers to find a loophole." Reaching for his Coke, he took a sip and shrugged. "At the end of the day, it truly was out of my hands. I'd made some mistakes and had to live with the consequences. And after I finished cursing the world, I realized how much happier I was. I started following that path, and here I am."

"That's admirable." She wished she'd reached the same level of peace.

One day at a time.

"And what about you?" He took a bite of his fajita. "You were famous for a while there. I'm afraid I couldn't name one of your songs, but I know you were making some headway. How come you landed back here?"

Beth felt her smile freeze. She reached for her drink to cover it, sipping until she felt calm again. Getting sick certainly wasn't anything to be ashamed of. But everyone she'd known before getting sick looked at her just a little differently now.

Ford saw her as a woman—a healthy, sexual woman. She didn't want that to change, at least not tonight, so she shook her head to gloss over it. "I had some health problems. Once I stopped to take care of them, I realized that I didn't really miss it."

"Didn't miss touring? Or didn't miss music?" He fastened his gaze on her face. "I remember hearing you play. Watching you. Your whole body got into it."

"I didn't miss touring. Music is part of me. I still play." She poked her fork into her salad. "Now I just upload my songs to YouTube instead of playing them live. I'm happier this way."

It wasn't a lie. Still, she didn't add that touring would never be a good decision for her again. The constant travel and stress was hard on the body, and though she'd been healthy for a year now, she knew that could change in the blink of an eye.

She could tell that he knew there was something more, that he wanted to push, and she was grateful when he didn't.

"What about your sisters? Amy was a tattoo artist, right?"

"Yes. She still is. Meg works for a catering company, and Jo ghostwrites. Books, magazines, whatever comes her way."

"And you all still live at home?"

"We do." She sensed his curiosity. It wasn't unfounded—four grown women still living with their mother was, well, weird. "It works for us. It's our family home, and it's an old house. It eats up a lot of cash in upkeep, but we love it. If one of us moved out, though, the others wouldn't be able to afford it anymore. They'd have to sell. So we stay."

She had no idea what they'd do if any of her sisters got married. The husband to be might protest at moving into a house full of women.

"We get along well," she offered. Still, she saw the question on his face, and she guessed that he wanted to ask what had happened to the money she'd made on her albums and her touring.

Telling him it had all barely made a dent in her hospital bills was a story for another time.

He didn't press. Instead, they ate in comfortable silence for a few minutes. She enjoyed having the time to just watch him. He looked a little older, but that leonine power was still there, and this time it was more potent.

He was more confident in who he was. And it was freaking hot.

As they finished their meal and Ford paid the bill, she felt a clutch of excitement in her stomach. After lunch today, she'd gone back to her shop and mechanically worked her way through her afternoon's jobs. With busy hands, she'd had a lot of time to think about this.

Five years ago, they'd been careless with one another. With a second chance, she wondered if they were ready now.

She couldn't wait to find out.

"After you." He placed his hand at the small of her back to guide her from the restaurant—which, she was forced to concede, he hadn't blinked an eye at. His fingers were on skin bared by the deep vee of the back of her dress, and her senses hummed from the contact.

Following him outside, she stopped short when she saw the Turbo parked at the curb.

"Risky business, driving that thing in this neighborhood." Reaching out, she ran a hand over the sleek silver finish. Behind her Ford growled low in his throat, and she looked back over her shoulder to see heat painted over his features.

"I thought it was worth it," he said, closing the thin ribbon of space between them. His chest brushed her partially bare back, and she shivered. "I have some really good memories of this car. And you."

"I remember." As if she could forget. She touched herself to that memory more often than she cared to admit, the feeling of being trapped between the cool metal and Ford's hard thrusts a permanent part of her dreams.

One of his hands settled on her waist as he reached around her to open the passenger-side door. Without meaning to, she pressed back against him, and for a moment they just stayed like that, pressed together, absorbing each other's heat.

Hand still on her waist, he urged her to turn around. She gasped when he trapped her against the car with his lean hips, but he did nothing more than open her door for her.

"My place is close." His voice was raw with need, and she thrilled to it.

"Drive fast."

CHAPTER TWELVE

He drove as fast as he dared. Beside him in the car Beth was quiet, but he felt so much intensity, so much need, that there was no way she didn't feel it, too.

Pulling into his driveway, he contemplated getting out to wrench open that damn garage door so he could park the Turbo inside.

It would take too long, time that could be spent with his hands on Beth's soft skin. He'd risk it.

"Welcome to my palace." He held out his hand to help her from the low-slung vehicle. When she swung herself out, he caught a glimpse of the little black spandex boy shorts she was wearing.

Fuck.

He remembered those little shorts. He wanted to have those little shorts in his teeth.

"It's a dump," he warned her as he opened the creaky front door. She laughed, brushing his comment aside.

"My bedroom threatens to turn into a swimming

pool every time it rains. I wouldn't be worried about impressing me."

He shut the door behind them, and the only reason he didn't press her right up against it was because she'd kicked off her shoes and padded forward into his living room.

"Not too shabby, Ford." Bending to flick on a lamp, she treated him to another view of the shorts, this time hugging the sweet, heart-shaped ass from his fantasies. His cock had been at half-mast since he'd pressed her against the car back at the restaurant, and now all the blood in his head rushed to his swollen shaft.

"No need to try to impress me, either. The place is a wreck." Kicking off his own shoes, he followed her into the living room. His cock was straining at the zipper of his fly, but he liked the ache. The anticipation.

"Au contraire, my friend." Beth finished circling the room, stopping in front of a chair upholstered in a geometric print. She pointed to it. "This is a vintage Italian armchair. Midcentury. You could sell it for a few thousand dollars."

"That thing?" He cocked his head. He didn't see it.

"Yes, this thing." Sinking into it, she settled back with a happy sigh. "Don't listen to him. I know what a beauty you are."

"The beauty isn't the chair." And it wasn't. Even against the hideous print, she was stunning. The lamp cast a soft glow over her features, the reddish tint of her hair. He liked that she'd kept a natural look for tonight. As natural as a woman with tattoos sleeving her arms could look.

Opening her eyes, she peered up at him. He stepped farther into the room, standing in front of her. Bending, he placed his hands on her knees, then slowly urged his hands up, up beneath the silky fabric of her dress. He stopped midthigh, and her muscles tensed beneath his hands as he dipped his head to kiss her.

"Mmm." She sighed softly into his mouth, reaching up to work her hands through his hair. "Still got some moves, Sir Lassiter."

Sir Lassiter. He'd dreamed of hearing that from her lips for years. Hearing it again now was a punch of lust straight to the gut.

He wanted her. The need had only gotten better with time, and he wanted to drink her up.

"I could probably be persuaded to like this chair." Easing back, he settled his weight on an ottoman that sat across from it.

"Oh?" She smirked. "Do tell."

"What would you say if I told you to get naked and get back in it?" He noted her quick shudder of excitement.

"I'd wonder why you were asking instead of telling." Her eyes shot blue sparks, and he groaned.

She was challenging him. Asking if he really was ready to accept everything he'd wanted before but denied them both.

Leaning forward, he settled his elbows on his knees, watching her. He could never get enough of watching her.

"Get naked." His words weren't a question. "I want to watch."

She said nothing, simply pushed up out of the chair. As she turned, his stare feasted on the swirls of colorful ink on her back as she lifted the hem of her dress.

She tugged it up and over her head, then cast it to the floor. She was still facing away, but he was transfixed by her tattoo.

"This is new." He stretched his arm out to drag a single finger down her spine. The ink started at the nape of her neck, lines of music notes that tapered with the shape of her body, ending with a single note at the base of her spine. "It's fucking gorgeous."

"It's the score to one of my songs." She wiggled impatiently, drawing his attention to her ass. Pulling the ottoman closer, he cupped the plump cheeks in his hands, his thumbs grazing the insides of her thighs.

"Fuck," she hissed when he traced just the outside of her lower lips through the thin fabric of her shorts. "You're still good at that."

"I'm better." He repeated the move, enjoying the tremble in her thighs. Moisture dampened the tips of his fingers, and he inhaled the musky, salty scent. "Now turn the fuck around. You know what I want to see and you're hiding it."

She laughed breathlessly as she turned, too slowly for his liking. When she again faced him, her hands were covering her breasts.

"You're a brat." Placing his hands on her hips, he tugged her into the vee of his thighs. That close, he could feel the heat of her skin, and he felt wetness leak from the head of his cock. "I want to see those fucking amazing tits of yours. Show me."

Gaze glued to his, she slowly, deliberately dropped her hands. Her breasts bounced as they were freed, the jiggling of the plump flesh sending a surge of something almost painful through him.

Her right nipple was still pierced. But now, instead of the silver bar, the rosy tip was decorated with a delicate gold hoop.

"Fuck me." The words tore out of him, and then his hands were at her waist, tugging her to him. She gasped when his mouth closed over her nipple. He caught the ring in his teeth and tugged, just a bit, and she wobbled, her hands landing on his chest.

Sucking hard, laving the tip of her breast with his tongue, he urged her down until she straddled his lap. This brought her damp cleft into direct contact with his rock-solid shaft, and he thrust against her instinctively.

She ground down on him when he took her neglected nipple in his fingers, rolling and tugging until it was as swollen as the one in his mouth. He wanted to keep sucking, teasing, grinding—he wanted it all, but it had been five years. He wanted to make it worth the wait.

He pulled his mouth from her breast with a damp pop. Her nipple was red, engorged, wet from his mouth. Sometime soon he was going to play with those fantastic tits all night long. That was all he would do.

At the end of it he'd have her hold them together so he could fuck them. The image was so arousing he started to shake.

"Stand up." He wasn't even sure he was speaking English by this point. She whimpered at the order, rubbing her pussy over his erection until he saw stars. "Do it."

Chest heaving, and breasts jiggling along with it in a way that made his mouth water, she did. He took a moment to trace his fingers over the flock of birds inked onto her rib cage before pushing the ottoman back a foot.

"Lose the shorts." His hands were damp as he settled them on his knees. They were shaking a little.

What *was* this?

He thought she might argue. Instead she hooked her fingers in the waistband on the spandex. With a sensuous little sway, she pulled them down to midthigh, baring a plump, damp pussy that he'd missed for far too long.

"All the way." She kicked them off, standing in front of him naked. Her hair was loose and wild around her shoulders, the ink on her skin highlighting the curves of her body.

How had he ever thought that a woman like her shouldn't be sexy? She was the hottest fucking thing he'd ever seen.

"Sit down in that chair you love so much." Slowly, he undid the buckle of his belt. She did as he ordered, but her eyes were fastened on his fingers as he popped the button on his jeans.

His cock was escaping the confines of his boxer briefs, pressed up flat against his belly. Lifting his hips, he shoved his jeans and underwear down around his hips, freeing his erection fully.

Her stare was fastened to it.

"Hook your legs over the arms of the chair." She did, the crook of her knees settling on the top edge. She was completely naked, open wide to him, and his pulse stuttered.

"It's been far too long since I got to see you." She hissed in a breath when he fisted his erection in his hand. "I want to look my fill, so this is what we're going to do. You're going to play with those tits while I look, while I think about what I'm going to do to that tight little body of yours. I'm going to jerk off while I do it. But if you try to touch that pretty little pussy of yours, then I'm going to finish myself, and you won't get what you want."

"Jesus, Ford." Her breath was coming in pants. "You got good at this."

"Don't talk." Who was this person speaking with

his mouth? He was just saying what he wanted, but man, he was a filthy fucker.

This was who he was, and he was going to embrace it this time around. Why the fuck wouldn't he, when it felt so damn good?

Settling in on the ottoman, he moved his hand up and down his length. He could feel his pulse in his cock, and it jumped when Beth cupped her breasts in her hands and rubbed her thumbs over her nipples.

"Yeah. Like that." He jerked himself faster, felt pleasure tightening at the base of his spine. His gaze bounced between the clever fingers plucking at her nipples and the pink lips that looked so wet and ready for his cock.

He prayed that she could keep her fingers out of it, because he didn't know if he had the strength to follow through on his threat.

One of her hands started to travel south, splaying over the soft curve of her belly. Springing forward, he caught her wrist. She cried out as he hauled her up out of the chair, spinning her so that he could lay her out flat on the ottoman.

"I wanted to go slow this time, but you drive me to distraction, woman." Grabbing his T-shirt at the back of the neck, he tugged it up and off. "I'm going to fuck you now. I'm going to fuck you hard."

"Yes. Now!" She writhed where he'd laid her down. Working her way back until her long hair spilled over one end, she planted her heels on the other edge so that she was still wide-open to him. "I have condoms in my purse. Hurry the fuck up."

"Still bossy, I see." He swatted her hip before pulling his wallet from his pocket. "And I've got it covered."

He tore the condom wrapper open faster than he had when he'd lost his virginity, sheathing himself in the latex. Kneeling in front of her, he tucked two fingers inside her hot sheath to make sure she was ready.

She cried out, bucking against his hand. He ran his thumb over her clit and she ground against him, her pussy leaving dampness where it rubbed against his stomach.

"Get ready," he warned her, lining up the head of his cock with her lower lips.

"Fucking do it already!" She rolled her hips in response, begging him to come inside.

He did. Grabbing her by the hips, he surged inside. She was wet, she was hot, she was heaven on his cock. He pushed as far as he could, grunting when she clawed at his chest.

"I forgot how tight you are." Finding her clit again, he rubbed small tight circles until he felt her melt around him, letting him in the last inch.

In her to the hilt, he stopped, panting. She was splayed out before him, naked and open, hair damp with sweat, nipple ring glinting in the lamplight, thighs trembling around him.

Something in the area of his heart squeezed. He

wanted to panic, but her lips curved into a sexy little smile, and he knew that whatever the hell this was, she felt it, too.

"You feel incredible." Her voice was a whisper, barely audible over their combined panting. She gave a little wiggle that had his eyes rolling back in his head. "*Sir.*"

A sound somewhere between a growl and a groan tore from his throat. Clasping her thighs, he placed one of her bent knees on each of his shoulders. She was fully open to him, unable to do more than grab at his biceps as he started to thrust.

"Yes," she breathed against his shoulder as he rocked up into her. "God, I knew you'd be incredible when you finally let yourself go."

He'd show her letting go. One of her thighs slipped from his shoulder as he increased his pace. His pelvis made a smacking sound every time he seated himself inside her, and droplets of his sweat fell from his forehead to splatter wetly across her breasts.

Beneath him, she shuddered. He could feel her body tightening, straining toward release.

His thrusts became impossibly harder. She braced her foot on the floor with the leg that had slipped from his shoulder, and he tucked the other up close to her breasts, bent at the knee. Grasping either side of the ottoman to support his weight, he found himself almost fully on top of her. Her head fell back, over the edge of the upholstery, and her lips were parted.

Utter surrender. That was what she looked like

to him. She had no trouble giving in to what she wanted—she never had. And here, with her, all of those old voices that told him real men didn't want this—didn't want rough sex, didn't want to boss women around—were silenced.

His orgasm was close. He could feel the tide rising. Bracing himself on one elbow, body stretched out over hers, he pulsed once, twice, three times, shuddering through his release. He caught her nipple ring in his teeth as he shook, and her pussy clenched around him like a vise as she came, too.

Beth had convinced herself over the years that the sex she'd had with Ford couldn't possibly have been as good as she remembered. And it wasn't—it was better.

His weight sprawled out over top of her felt decadent. She couldn't help but laugh, and he joined her as he pressed his damp forehead against her breast.

"You just about killed me." He nuzzled against her nipple ring, and even though she'd just come, she felt a tight jolt that shot straight to her core. "Hell of a way to christen the place, though."

She nodded in agreement. As he peeled himself up off her, then helped her to a sitting position, she found her knees were wobbly. She brushed her hair out of her face as she tried to center herself again.

Instead, as Ford hitched on his jeans, then headed to kitchen to grab two bottles of water from the fridge, she found herself staring at him. This—them together again—felt so incredibly surreal that she kept questioning if it was all a dream.

A nagging little voice in her head tried to peck its way through her postcoital bliss. She hadn't been with anyone since she'd gotten sick, because she'd wanted to focus on herself, on staying healthy and enjoying the life she'd been given a second lease on.

Well. She'd learned the hard way that life didn't give a shit about what you'd planned or what you'd wanted.

She wasn't in any position to be thinking far down the road. She wasn't sure that she ever would be. But he was here right now, and this time he wanted the same thing she did—to act on that insane chemistry between them.

Ford returned from the kitchen and pressed a water bottle into her hand. When she smiled at him in thanks and their eyes met, something hot and sweet settled into her veins.

Something good, something real had just happened here. And she wanted to enjoy it for as long as she could.

CHAPTER THIRTEEN

BETH WAS STILL smiling two weeks later as she hovered outside Jo's door. When her sister didn't answer her knock, she shifted the scalding mug of coffee to the other hand and banged on the entrance with her fist.

The door shuddered as it finally flew open, revealing her sister's irritated face. A tuft of black hair stuck out over her ear and she had ink on her nose.

"I come in peace." Beth held her free hand up, palm out. "Thought you could use a caffeine fix, that's all."

"Thanks." Grabbing the mug, Jo took a large gulp, hissing at the heat. She followed it with a more cautious sip. "You didn't make this."

"Nope." Beth didn't drink coffee anymore, but when she had, she'd figured that the stronger, the better. She'd been really good at brewing what her sisters called sludge. "Meg brewed a pot, so I stole you a cup. I think she put cinnamon in it."

"You're a goddess." Jo took another sip, then gestured for Beth to come in. "I just finished this chapter. I'm due for a break."

Beth followed her sister into the room, grimacing as she did. The patchouli scent of the incense that was burning was strong enough to make her eyes water, and it was layered with the burning hint of too many electrical plugs and a staleness that said Jo hadn't left the room for a while. Without asking, she crossed the small room and cranked open the window, letting fresh air circulate.

Jo settled herself cross-legged on her unmade bed. Beth took the thrift-shop chair that was pulled up to the plywood slab and sawhorse that her sister used as a desk. Legal sheets covered in illegible, cramped handwriting covered the desk, and she caught a glimpse of some very naughty words on the screen of the old laptop before it went to sleep.

"The erotic piece?" She cocked her head toward the computer, wishing she'd brought herself some tea.

"You bet." Jo grinned, wrapping her hands around the mug. "I have three bicurious men and one very bad girl on the page right now. Swords are about to fly."

"Sounds titillating." Beth grinned. "Send me a copy when you're done. And give me some warning so I can buy some batteries."

"Don't be greedy. Save the batteries for those of us who aren't getting laid right now." Jo arched an eyebrow at her sister. "How's it going with Felix, anyway?"

"Ford," Beth corrected automatically.

"Well?" Jo sat back, clearly expecting details. Beth opened her mouth to reply but found herself hesitating.

The last two weeks had been, quite simply, amazing. The more than Ford embraced his kink, the better it got for both of them—he fucked her better than she'd ever had it before, and she was pretty sure it was the same for him. And more than that, she actually liked him. When they weren't rolling around naked, they actually had fun together. Despite their obvious differences, they had more in common than she ever would have guessed, from their mutual love of a nice sleek Porsche to the fact that they both enjoyed weird viral YouTube videos.

"The man is good with his hands," she finally admitted, drumming her fingers on her sister's desk. "You're right that I don't need the batteries."

"That's all you have to say about it?" Jo cocked her head. "You've had a smile on your face since you spotted him at the Tearoom. Obviously the sex is good. What gives?"

"Nothing gives." Beth made sure that her expression remained neutral. "We're having fun. I don't need him to propose or anything."

When her sister's toffee-colored gaze narrowed in on hers, Beth knew she wasn't fooling her. Jo knew her better than anyone else in the world.

But she didn't know everything. She didn't know that sometimes Beth couldn't sleep because of the oppressive guilt that weighed her down until she felt like she couldn't breathe.

Her family was in their current financial situation in because of Beth. For so long now, their lives had revolved around her health. She knew they only cared that she stayed well, not about the money, but knowing that she'd so dramatically changed the dynamic of their family was a cape of stress that she could never shed.

And over all of that was the fact that she could get sick again anytime. Logically, she knew that the guilt she felt was self-destructive, but she couldn't help it.

She was obsessive about monitoring her health so she didn't get sick again because she couldn't handle the thought of being a burden. Ford? The man had lost his empire. The last thing he needed was to be saddled with her, the possibility of more massive hospital bills an albatross around his neck.

They liked each other. They had fun together. They rocked each other's worlds. Why did it have to be more than that?

"You know, you make a point of proving that you can still do everything else you could before you got sick." Jo cast her a sidelong look. "So why would you hold back from someone who makes you feel good? If anyone deserves to be happy, it's you. Even if I find it questionable that you chose a guy named Felix."

Beth rolled her eyes, choosing to focus on that rather than what her sister was trying to say. She held back for a reason. It was her choice.

"I've got to get back to work." Jo stretched. "I need a massive amount of words today in order to get that story in on time."

"Give me your mug. I'll take it downstairs for you." Standing, Beth reached for the empty cup. The light from the window shifted, and the dark purple smudges beneath her sister's eyes became more pronounced.

Narrowing her eyes, she looked around the room. Jo hibernated when she was really into her work, but she usually surfaced at least once a day to shower and track down something to eat. It was Saturday and she hadn't seen Jo since... Thursday?

"Why are you working so hard on the weekend?" Setting the mug back down, she began to prowl around the room. The laundry hamper was overflowing, and the wastebasket was crammed full of empty Pringles cans and Starburst wrappers.

Having made the circle of the room, she stopped in front of her sister. Crossing her arms over her chest, she waited.

"I may have picked up an extra contract. Or two." Jo lifted her chin defiantly. "I'm just a little stressed. What's your point?"

"You're always really good about not taking on more than you can handle." Jo wasn't telling her something.

Beneath her stare, her sister squirmed, then finally huffed out a breath that sent her wayward tuft of hair dancing. "We have a balloon payment on our mortgage coming up. We're all trying to make a little extra this month."

What? No one had said anything about a big payment to her. Though when she thought of it, just last night Mamesie had enlisted her to help upload listings of her pottery to Etsy, when she normally only did it once a month. Meg had been working a lot of lunchtime functions as well as at night, which she didn't normally do, and Amy hadn't come home from her tattoo shop until eleven the night before.

Jo winced just as Beth put it together. "You didn't tell me on purpose."

The guilt was a fog, gathering thick and fast, so heavy that she couldn't see, couldn't breathe.

They hadn't told her because they didn't want to stress her out. Stress increased the chance of her relapsing.

She knew they didn't want her to relapse because they didn't want her to be sick again. But was there a small part in any of their minds that thought they *literally* couldn't afford for her to get sick again.

"I am not happy with you. With any of you." Beth rarely lost her temper—not the full-force tsunami of it, at any rate—but she could feel her rage bubbling up, about to boil over and scald anyone in its path. "You just finished telling me that I shouldn't let my illness change how I lived my life. That I can do everything I could before. Were you just trying to make me feel better?"

"Simmer down, princess. You know I wasn't." Jo planted her hands on her hips. "You almost died, Beth. Why the fuck can't you just let us take care of you once in a while?"

"Because I don't need to be taken care of!" She had so much to say, but most of it caught in her throat, choking her. She settled for an inarticulate growl before whirling on her heel and storming from the room. She slammed the door hard enough to make it shudder for good measure.

She met Meg coming up the stairs. Her sister wore a white blouse covered in fresh mustard stains and smelling of French fry grease. Now that she was looking for them, she saw that her oldest sister had dark shadows beneath her eyes as well.

"What the hell are you and Jo getting into it about?" Meg tugged the elastic from her tight ponytail, letting the length of stick-straight hair fall free. "I could hear you from the garage."

"How about the fact that my entire family thought I was incapable of contributing to a big payment we have coming up without breaking?" Beth spat the words out. She was pretty sure she'd never been so mad. Felt so betrayed.

Meg bit her lower lip and looked away.

"Yeah, that's what I thought." Beth shook her head with disgust. "I can't deal with any of you right now. I'm going out. Don't wait up."

CHAPTER FOURTEEN

FORD DIDN'T ANSWER his door when she rang the bell. She'd been over enough times in the last two weeks that she felt comfortable heading around the side of the house when she heard the buzz of some kind of power saw from the back.

She stopped dead when she entered the backyard and found her man stripped to the waist despite the chill in the late-September air. Safety goggles were strapped to his head, work gloves were on his hands and a sheen of sweat shone on his hard torso as he ran a two-by-four through a battered power saw.

She'd stormed out of the house knowing that she'd head to Ford's. She hadn't known exactly why, only that he was the one she wanted to help soothe her.

Finding him here looking he'd stepped out of a very dirty dream instantly turned her fury to lust. There were lots of ways to work off a mad, and this was her favorite one.

Unzipping her hoodie, she crossed the yard. She

watched the rock-solid planes of his biceps flex as he set aside the first piece of wood and lifted another.

With every other lover that she'd had, the desire, the wanting had faded a little every time. With Ford? Every time they had sex her need grew thicker, deeper.

Whether it was still just chemistry or if it was because she knew what he could do to her, she didn't care. But she wanted him right now, wanted to use the pleasure he could bring her to edge out the anger, even if just for now.

Closing the space between them, she waited for him to notice her. When he did he grinned, setting aside the piece of wood he was working on and powering down the saw.

"I was just cutting some replacement planks for the deck, but you're much more interesting." Tugging off his gloves, he tossed them to the ground, then drew her in for a kiss. Brushing his lips over hers, he pulled her in slowly, but she was impatient, rising to her toes and fisting her hands in his hair. When they broke apart, she saw the banked fire in his stare and smiled wickedly.

"You look like you're going to eat me alive." He tugged gently on a chunk of her hair, and the nerves in her scalp sparked to life. "Wanna share with the class?"

"I'm angry like I've never been angry before." She bared her teeth when he tugged again. The stiffening of his body against hers made her clarify. "Not with

you. But I need to burn it off." Tilting her head back
to expose the line of her throat, which she'd learned
was a huge turn-on for him, she gasped as he traced
his tongue down it. "Interested?"

In answer, he slid his hands down to cup her ass.
When he lifted her off her feet, she wrapped her legs
around his waist, her arms around his shoulders. Her
nails raked over the bare skin of his shoulders.

"I'm pretty sweaty. Want me to shower?" His
hands explored the curves of her ass through the
thin fabric of her yoga pants, paying particular attention to the cleft that divided her cheeks. She shuddered at the dark promise of his touch.

"Fuck, no." Rolling her hips against his taut stomach, she dipped her head. She ran her tongue over the
hard muscle of his shoulder, savoring the taste of salt.

"That's so hot." Striding with her across the deck
that he was working on, he propped her against the
door frame. Still cradling her ass in one hand, he
used the other to cup the breast with the piercing.
He growled as he rubbed a thumb over it, making
need tighten inside her.

"I think you've got yourself a little fetish there,"
she teased as she arched into his touch. "Never would
have guessed that piercings would turn your crank
when you first walked into my garage."

"I have a Beth fetish." Pressing his forehead to
hers, he looked into her eyes as he slid his hand inside
the camisole she wore under her hoodie. Tugging the

thin cotton of her bra beneath her breast, he plucked at the hoop, and she ground her hips into him.

"Now. I want you now." She clawed at his bare chest, knowing but not caring that she was probably leaving welts. "Damn it, Ford. I need this."

"You need what I tell you that you need." He sucked in a breath after he spoke, as if waiting to see her reaction. It did funny things to her insides to see him still finding his footing with what he wanted, who he really was.

And on a whole other level, his words made her so, so hot.

"I told you what I need." The words spilled out of her before she could think them through. Like he had, she paused, holding her breath to see what he thought about the new aspect she'd just added to their game.

They studied each other for a long moment, her bright blue eyes swallowed up by the intensity of his brown ones. There was time for either of them to back out, to make sure that this was what they both wanted.

"You'll get what I decide to give you." With agonizing slowness, Ford cupped his large hand around her throat gently. The spicy scent of cedar drifted to her nose, and she couldn't hold back the shudder.

"Thought so." He smirked. Balancing her with one hand, he threw the screen door open, carrying her through. The back door led to a small laundry room that had probably been in style when Mamesie was a baby, but when he tugged at her hair again and roughly settled her on the ancient washing machine, she thought she could make herself right at home.

"Bastard." Playing the game, she shoved at his chest. He caught her wrists, twisted them up and over her head, holding them with one large hand. Her chest was thrust forward, and he used his free hand to tug her camisole and her bra below both breasts. Dipping his head, he caught her nipple ring between his teeth and tugged, and she cried out.

"That's what I thought." With a smug smile, he did it again, and she felt the answering pull in her pussy. "Why are you fighting it? You want what I've got, baby."

"Is that the best you can do?" she panted.

His eyes glinted darkly as he reached behind her. Twisting a knob on the washer, he set the machine rumbling beneath her.

"You don't mind if I multitask, do you?" Splaying one hand over her naked breasts, he pressed her down against the vibrating surface. "Since you think you're running things here?"

"Oh, God." Her legs were splayed around his hips, her thinly clothed pussy pressed against the machine, and when he pushed her down the vibration woke up nerves that she hadn't even known she had. She tried to close her legs against the sudden onslaught of sensation, but only succeeded in hugging his hips.

"Still think you know best?" Dipping his head, he nipped at her lower lip, just enough to sting, then released her wrists. Splaying his hand over her belly, he slipped inside the waistband of her yoga pants, heading straight for her cleft and dipping three fingertips inside. "You're fucking soaked. Seems you like what I do just fine."

"Put your cock where your fingers are and maybe you can redeem yourself." A bolt of adrenaline followed her words as she sassed him. This was a game, a hot, filthy game, but the intensity on his face had her fully invested. "That's all I've asked for. Seems like a real man would give it to me."

She gasped when he abruptly slid his fingers from her pussy. Had she gone too far?

She felt the cold kiss of air between her legs as he yanked at her pants, hard. Using fingers still wet with her arousal, he ripped the seam of her pants, under which she wore nothing.

"You'll get it," he promised, releasing her. She cupped her own breasts, lifting them for his gaze as he quickly undid his belt and lowered the zipper of his jeans. "You'll get it when I'm damn well ready to give it to you."

She gasped when pressed a hand against her back, bending her forward so that her cupped breasts were against her knees. When he fisted his cock and slid the head into her cleavage, she thought she just might stroke out.

"Maybe I should just fuck these pretty tits instead of your pussy." He slid the hand from her back up to her hair, running his fingers through the silky strands. "Come all over this sexy little ring and leave you all hot and bothered."

"Do that and I'll just finger myself." He worked his cock a little farther into her cleavage, and she lowered her lips and ran her tongue over it. "You can't stop me."

She gasped when he pulled from between her breasts abruptly, yanking her back up to a sitting position. Pushing her legs so wide that her hips protested, he lined his erection up with the rip in her pants, and ran his head through the folds.

"Keep those clever little fingers of yours out of your pussy," he ordered as he wedged his swollen head against her slick entrance. "Your orgasms belong to me, and I won't have you keeping any of them from me."

"Now. For the love of God, Ford, fuck me now!" She dropped all pretense of the game, body wound so tight she thought that she might shatter. Digging her fingernails into his shoulders until he hissed, she rocked forward, taking him an inch inside her.

"Fuck." He exhaled slowly as she clenched around him. Her breath escaped her on a strangled cry when, with one thrust, he seated himself the rest of the way, stretching her wide-open.

"Yes," she hissed before sinking her teeth into his ear. "More. Now."

He said nothing. Instead, his hands slid to her hips, grabbing them tightly. He pulled her back an inch before slamming them together again, completely controlling her movements.

She wanted more. Bracing her hands on the surface of the washing machine behind her, she leaned back, changing the angle, allowing his solid erection to hit an even deeper spot inside her. Her head fell back, her lips parting as he stroked through her tight flesh.

"I wish you could see yourself right now." He slammed into her again, gaze fixed on the point where they were joined. "You look so dirty. Couldn't even wait to get naked. Demanded my cock and couldn't wait."

"I am dirty," she breathed, looking down the length of her own body. Her breasts bounced and jiggled with every movement, and the view between her legs was obscene, his cock stretching her wide, her pussy leaving him wet. "And you're dirty, too."

"Yeah." He shuddered out a breath, and she could see his excitement visibly rise, all from her words. "You'd better finger that pretty little clit of yours anyway, because I'm close."

"Yes, Sir Lassiter." He moaned, his pace increasing. Bracing herself on one hand, she slid the other over her belly and to the rip between her thighs. Circling the tight knot of flesh, the tips of her fingers brushed his cock as he moved, and they both clenched as need ratcheted higher.

"Come for me, Beth." His thrusts became sloppy, losing the rhythm as his movements turned frantic.

She circled her clit quickly, her legs trying to close as her excitement rose.

With his grip on her hips, he pressed her ass down harder on the rumbling washing machine. The vibrations shot through her flesh straight to her pussy, setting off a chain reactions of explosions inside her.

"Ah!" Her hoarse cry echoed off the ceiling of the small room. She clenched around him as he continued to work his way through her swollen flesh, her pleasure a razor-sharp edge that centered entirely on his cock.

He growled and shoved inside her with one fierce, final thrust. She felt the hot pulse of him between her thighs, vaguely registered that she probably shouldn't be feeling that, then decided she didn't care as his movements triggered an aftershock.

Wrapping her arms around his neck, Beth laid her head on his shoulder as she struggled to catch her breath. His chest heaved against hers, heat sealing them together.

"We have a problem." Running a hand down her spine, he looked down into her face cautiously. She nodded, shifting on the machine, wincing as she felt the sticky heat between her thighs.

"I'm on the pill." She swallowed hard. "And I'm clean."

"I am, too." He kept his stare centered on her face, and she felt her nervous pulse begin to slow. It was probably stupid, trusting him so soon.

But it wasn't really that soon, was it? They had

history. Plus, she'd been over here so much in the last two weeks, he wouldn't have had any time to fuck another woman. Not that she thought he would.

"So we're good." She ran a hand over her forehead, wiping away the sweat that slicked the skin there. "We probably shouldn't do that again, though."

"I don't know if I can go back to a condom after that." His words were raw and honest. "That was... God, but that was hot, Beth. I lost my mind a little at the end there. I wanted to mark you from the inside out."

"You say the sweetest things." She grinned and he laughed. Her mirth turned to a gasp when he slid his hands up her body, squeezing her breasts before easing out of her.

"I'm serious, though." Reaching for a pile of folded towels that sat on the dryer, he grabbed a facecloth. She was shocked when he rubbed it between her legs, cleaning her up before tossing the used cloth into the sink.

She hadn't expected that. But...it was nice to be taken care of.

"If you're on the pill. And we're both clean." Catching her head in his hands, he slid his palms over her cheeks slowly, stroking the lines of her cheekbones with his thumbs. "I don't want to pressure you. But I'd like to trust each other."

"Fuck, yes." A distant alarm bell rang in the far recesses of her mind, but she ignored it. This was a level of intimacy she hadn't been prepared for.

Right now she wanted it.

"It's going to be even harder to keep my hands off you now." Pressing a kiss to her lips, he twitched his lips in the direction of her clothing. "It probably doesn't bode well for the state of your wardrobe."

"But I feel better." Grinning, she let him help her off the washing machine. "If you find me picking fights with people, you'll know it's so I can come over here and take it out on you after."

"Want to talk about it?" She was startled again when he hooked his fingers in the waistband of her yoga pants and slid them down, helping her out of the ruined clothing. Sorting through another bin of clean laundry, he tossed her a pair of plaid flannel boxer shorts. "I don't have anything else that will fit you. You're going to have to do the walk of shame when you go home."

"There's no shame involved." Her voice was quiet, the words chosen carefully. Ford had come a long way from the man she'd first met, the one who had been terrified of who he was and what he wanted. Still, she saw those hints of uncertainty, of wonder far more often than she wanted, as though he couldn't really believe that this was what she actually wanted.

He met her gaze, then nodded. Message received. Satisfied, she started to strip off her camisole and bra, doing her best to hide her smile when he cocked his head at her questioningly.

"Not that I'm complaining," he said, stare fastened on her breasts as she bared them, "but I don't believe I tore those."

"They're all stretched out, though." Blinking at him innocently, she tossed them aside. "Can't go around in that."

"You're evil." Reaching for yet another piece of laundry, he handed her a pale blue button-down shirt. "There. If you walk around with those fantastic tits out, I'll be inside you again before you can count to three."

"That doesn't exactly give me a reason to get dressed," she pointed out, though she shrugged into the shirt. It was far too big, and she had to roll the cuffs up several times before her hands emerged.

"You can run around topless in a bit. Far be it from me to hold you back." He caught her attention by shoving his own pants down his hips. When they hit the floor, he stepped out of them.

"What are you doing?" She was thoroughly distracted by the sight of his now half-hard cock, which was still hanging out of his boxer briefs. She scowled her disapproval when he picked up a pair of athletic shorts.

"I was working on the house when you showed up and demanded that I let you ride me." He grinned when she rolled her eyes. "I've lost time, so you're going to have to help me make it up."

"Doing what?" He pulled the shorts up around his waist, but before he could tuck himself back in, she reached out and grabbed his waist. "Wait."

Treating herself to the fully lewd view, she tangled their fingers together, then lowered their hands to his still swollen member. Licking her lips, she clasped their twined hands around his length, helping him to tuck himself back into his underwear.

"You're so evil," he gasped when she kept her hand in his pants, their fingers still twisted together. Stare still fixed on the juicy head of his now rapidly hardening cock, she helped him to pump his own length several times, working him back to a full erection.

Then she quickly removed her hand and stepped back, busying herself with tying back her long tangles of hair. She hissed out a breath when, in retaliation, he slid one hand inside her borrowed shirt, tweaking her pierced nipple a handful of times until it was hard with arousal.

"Come on, my little nymphomaniac." He chucked her under the chin, then pressed a soft kiss to her lips. Her pulse sped.

She was starting to have feelings for him—too many feelings. She was going to have to think long and hard about that tonight.

But for now, she struggled to process what he was saying. When she understood, she thought he was joking.

"Let's go frame some drywall."

CHAPTER FIFTEEN

"MY SISTERS WOULDN'T make me do this."

Ford looked up from where he knelt on the living room floor. He was checking the frame he and Beth had just constructed, making sure all the measurements were correct before they lifted it up for installation.

She made quite a sight. Standing on a short ladder, her arms were above her head as she checked that the top plate they'd installed was secure.

She was still in his boxer shorts and shirt, but she'd refused to button it closed. He had a very nice view of her sexy-as-sin breasts, which he knew was supposed to torment him.

He was enjoying every delicious minute of it.

"You distracted me earlier." His tone sounded like butter wouldn't melt in his mouth. "This is your punishment."

"It's actually kind of nice." She spoke softly just before she climbed back down the ladder, and he wasn't sure that he'd heard her properly.

She met his gaze, and he knew that she'd meant for him to hear. He held his breath, searching for the right thing to say, not wanting to scare her off if she was ready to open up to him.

"Well, you're a mechanic. A musician. You like working with your hands."

"True." Crossing to him, she sank down cross-legged on the carpet and stole his bottle of water. He tried not to read into the intimacy of her action. "But I meant it's nice to be treated like I'm capable of doing something physical. Yesterday Amy caught me carrying a pickup motor, something I've done a million times before. She nearly shouted the house down."

"Is it because you were sick?" He kept his eyes on the pine frame, not wanting to spook her. "Is that why you were angry when you came over today? You had a fight with your family?"

"I had a fight with Jo." She toyed with the cap to the water bottle. A streak of her red-washed hair hung over her left eye, but she didn't bother to brush it back. "Look, you've been to our house. You know we're not exactly rolling in it."

"Hmm." He was noncommittal. He just wanted to keep her talking.

"Anyway. I've told you we all live together so we can afford to keep that house. Apparently we have a big balloon payment coming up, but no one told me. I found out by accident."

She shook the strand of hair out of her face. "They

kept it from me because they didn't want to stress me out and make me sick again."

"Beth, what happened to you?" His concern for her trumped worry over her family's financial state. "I wish you'd tell me."

She shook her head vehemently. "It's in the past. I'm fine now. That's all you need to know."

Her refusal to open up stung, he couldn't lie. She'd agreed to no more condoms, trusting him with her body, but she wouldn't share what had happened that had brought that reserve to the woman he'd known.

He could only hope she'd open up in time.

"What made you decide to come back to Boston?" Clearly she wanted to change the subject. Fine. He wouldn't push...for now. "You've told me some. But I'd like to hear more."

Walking on his knees to the next frame, he got out his measuring shape to double-check that it was the size he wanted.

"I wanted to come home." Satisfied with the measurements, he reached out a hand for the bottle of water she still held. Taking it back, he drained it in two swallows.

"When I went to Los Angeles, I was consumed with the idea of what my life should be. My hotels were doing so well, why shouldn't I live in the land of excess? Why shouldn't I spend my time with famous, pretty people?" Tossing the empty bottle aside, he leveled her with a look. "I suspect a shrink might discover that I was trying to build myself up into what I wanted to be because a certain woman with tattoos and a nipple ring had made me take a good hard look at who I really was, which sure as shit wasn't that."

She blushed, something he hadn't seen her do before. "I never meant to make you feel like crap."

"Sure you did." He grinned. "And I needed it. I might never have wound up back here if it wasn't for that, so don't feel bad. In fact, thank you."

She pressed her lips together but said nothing.

"Anyway. When I lost everything, I realized that I didn't even like California. Too hot. Too many people." He shrugged. "When Peyton and I broke up, there was nothing keeping me there anymore. I wanted to come home."

"If she ditched you because you lost your money, she never really loved you." Beth's words were both brutal and true. He barked out a laugh. He didn't need to even probe at his feelings for his former fiancée, because he already knew that he no longer had any.

"She did love me, in just the same way that I loved her." A primitive part of him beat its chest when he watched Beth's eyes narrow. "As friends. She didn't dump me because I'd lost my fortune. Not really. She had plenty of cash of her own. It was that she'd wanted the man she thought I was, not the one who emerged after the dust settled. She wanted someone to go to Hollywood parties with her, to stand by her side as an equal. And she equated money with that equality."

He shrugged. "It was never meant to be."

Beth was silent for a moment, apparently digesting that info. Then she scowled, and he didn't have the heart to tell her that the expression made her look cute. "She still better pray I never meet her. I can't guarantee there won't be a tire iron in my bag."

Surprised laughter exploded out of him; he couldn't help it. Jesus, but she was fantastic. Reaching for her, he tugged her across the short expanse of worn carpet that separated them and planted a firm kiss on her lips.

"What was that for?" She batted at him, but she was grinning.

"Your little violent streak makes me hot." He waggled his eyebrows lewdly. "Next time you go after someone with a tire iron, please let me watch. Please."

She tried to hold back her smile, but the corners of her lips quirked upward. "Yeah, yeah." Settling back into his arms, she sighed.

He held his breath.

"I guess this kind of reminds me of when I stopped touring." She sucked in a deep breath, then slowly exhaled. "You know, getting label attention, getting a record deal for my weird, quirky piano music? That was a one-in-a-million shot. I was so fucking lucky. There were thousands—probably hundreds of thousands—of people who would have done literally anything to be in my place.

"I enjoyed it at first. The attention, the chance to

share my music. The money—I was finally able to treat my sisters, Mamesie to a taste of the life that they deserved."

"But?" He was dying to hear the but.

She smiled wanly. "But touring really took its toll. The shows, the press—it was too much. I'm an introvert, you know."

He coughed. She glared.

"You don't have to be shy to be an introvert. I'm not shy, obviously, but being around so many people all the time—it drained me. So when I got sick, at first…at first I was relieved." Casting a sidelong look at him through her lashes, she was clearly waiting for him to judge her. It wasn't going to happen.

"Of course, then shit blew up in my face. I was forced to quit touring. All the money I'd made…well, it was needed for something else." He watched the shadows move across her face, the shutters coming down. She was glossing over what he most wanted to know—what had happened when she was sick—but he had no right to demand that information. Not yet. "But the truth is, that life that I had? Turned out it wasn't really what I wanted after all."

Shifting in his arms, she rose to her knees. Dipping her head to press a kiss to his lips, she smiled up at him with a hint of the shyness that she professed not to have. "So what I'm trying to say is, I get it."

He was a goner.

This woman had been through so much, and yet she was so strong. But even as he thought about that, the shadows of guilt that never quite left him grew darker, clinging to his skin.

She'd glossed over it, but he got the impression that her health still wasn't exactly what it could be.

He was rough with her. Jesus, not two hours ago he'd used her so thoroughly that he'd left the lightest shadows of bruises on her hips. He could see them now, soft violet against her ivory skin.

She wanted it that way. He wanted it that way. But in that moment, hot panic clawed at his throat.

A real man wouldn't bruise his woman. He wouldn't fuck her on top of a washing machine and forget to use a condom.

If he told her the thoughts clouding his mind, she'd call him a coward and accuse him of hiding who he really was.

She'd be right.

Holding on to that, he pulled himself from the mire of his own mind. He and Beth did these things because that was what got them off—got them both off.

He was not his father. He knew his father was into some kinky shit, though he'd always tried to ignore it, but it was the way the older man treated the woman in his life that had left a lasting impression on Ford. It didn't matter if they were wives, girlfriends, mistresses or strippers he'd brought home from his club. In his head, they were there to please him, and the second they didn't, they were gone. No regard for what they wanted or how they felt.

Ford supposed he was lucky he wasn't more fucked-up.

Damn it, he wasn't Bruce. He could be the man he really was—it didn't mean that he didn't treat women well, or care about what they wanted.

Hell, the reason he was able to even think that way was because he wanted to make one specific woman happy.

"I could fall in love with you." Maybe it was endorphins from the sex, maybe it was the vanilla and engine grease scent wafting from Beth's soft hair. He usually had more of a filter, considered big steps like telling someone something like that.

It was true, and he wanted her to know.

In his arms, she froze. He waited, holding his breath, suddenly feeling like he was in the back seat of a limo at prom, pants around his ankles, hoping that Jennifer St. Morrisette would actually let him lose his virginity to her.

Except worse. The waiting now was worse.

Slowly, Beth sat up. Turning to face him, he noted the sudden rush of rose into her cheeks, the widening of those sapphire-blue eyes.

"Thank you."

CHAPTER SIXTEEN

"EXCUSE ME, MISS. Where can I put my keys? I have an appointment for an oil change."

Beth froze at the sound of Ford's voice. She'd know it anywhere. Slowly, she turned around, eyeing the Turbo that he'd edged up the driveway.

"You don't have an appointment. Chevy Lattner has an appointment." As soon as she spoke, she heard it. Closing her eyes, she pressed a hand to her temple. "Ford, Chevy. Got it. Very clever."

"I wouldn't have had to be sneaky if you weren't avoiding me." Holding up a white plastic bag, he leaned a hip against his car. Her pulse quickened. "I brought dinner."

Why the hell did he have to look so damn good? Especially when she felt like crap? Yeah, she'd been avoiding him. She missed him like hell, but she knew it was the right thing to do.

He'd all but told her that he loved her. That was... bad.

"Ford, maybe we can have dinner next week." She

took a deep breath. "I don't have time right now. If you don't actually have an appointment, then I could use that time to get ahead on the rest of my work."

"Oh, I have an appointment. An oil change takes what, an hour? So I've booked an hour of time at Marchande Motors. If I don't get that hour, I'll be forced to leave a very nasty review on Yelp."

Beth rolled her eyes. He took advantage of her momentary softening to stride forward, close enough that she could feel the heat from his body. "Come on. You'd be eating dinner anyway, right? Eat it with me."

She pinched her lips together, unconvinced.

"I brought taco salad from Mamacita's." He smiled hopefully, and she couldn't help but melt just the tiniest bit.

Damn fool. What did he have to go and fall in love with her for, anyway?

Setting the bag of takeout on the workbench, he placed his index finger under her chin, tilting her face up for a look. She tried to jerk away—in her state of mind, it made her feel too exposed—but he just followed.

"You don't look good," he stated bluntly, making her scowl. "What the hell is going on?"

"Always with the sweet talk." Her words were dry. Jerking away from him, she tugged off her coveralls. She knew he wouldn't go away until she agreed to eat with him.

Tucking a finger into the strap of the tank top that she wore beneath them, he drew her to him. Her breath came more quickly at the proximity, her body scenting its mate.

"If you don't understand by now that I think you're the sexiest woman alive, I'll fuck you right here, right now to get my point across." His words were mild, but she felt a spark light in her belly at the threat. She wanted that. Fuck, yes, she did.

If he got inside her, she'd lose all perspective.

"I meant that you look pale. You've lost weight." She squawked with indignation when he ran his hands down her sides, brushing past her breasts to frame her waist. He scowled into her face. "And I could use those circles under your eyes as a landing pad for my spaceship. What the hell, Beth? Is this all because I told you I was falling in love with you?"

"No." Partly. His declaration had sent her into a blind panic. Not because she didn't want it, but because she did.

It made sense in her head, but she knew that as soon as she tried to explain, he'd refuse to accept it. And that didn't work for her.

"Then what gives?" Casting a sharp glance around the garage, she saw him take note of the pile of invoices, the parts stacked on the floor. The man wasn't an idiot, and she watched him connect the dots. "You're working yourself into the ground so that you can contribute to that balloon payment."

"We're all pulling double time to make that bill." Jerking out of the circle of his arms, she bent to pick up her coveralls. When she stood, she noted that he was staring at her ass. Normally noticing that would set her on fire.

Now? The set of his lips told her that he'd noticed that her little spandex shorts had gotten a little baggy.

"You're going to make yourself sick." He blanched as soon as he spoke, and she exhaled a breath of pure fire. He held up a hand to placate her, asking her to hold on.

"I didn't mean it like that." His eyes narrowed. "Whether you had to watch yourself or not, I'd be on your ass about this. You're working too hard. You're not sleeping, obviously not eating. That's enough to run anyone down."

She lifted her chin. No way was she going to admit that he was right. Rigidly, she pointed at the takeout bag. "You brought food, right? So let's eat. Then I can get back to work."

"I don't think so, babe." He moved so fast that she didn't see him coming. Like a linebacker, he tackled her, lifting her up and over his shoulder, hefting her like a sack of potatoes.

"Oh, I don't think so." Her words were full of venom. "Put me the fuck down, Ford. Now."

In response, he cupped her ass in both hands. She gasped as he made a thorough examination. "Needs to be fattened back up. Don't worry, I'd still hit it."

Outrage choked the words in her throat as he balanced her over his shoulder with one hand and snatched the takeout bag with the other. She slammed her fist against the broad muscles of his back as he carried her up the steps and through the door that led to the house.

Mamesie and Jo were in the kitchen when Ford came storming through with her over his shoulder. Mamesie's full lips parted with surprise, but Jo cocked her head, and Beth could see a smidgen of respect on her sister's face. She narrowed her eyes, but before she could yell at her sister, Ford had carried her to the stairs.

At the top, he paused, and she smirked. "I'm not telling you which one. Put me down."

She felt him shrug, which moved her body up and down. "Process of elimination, then."

Why was he being so stubborn?

"Nope." He opened and closed Jo's door, then Meg's. The third one he grunted, then hauled her in, shutting the door behind them. Bracing herself to be thrown on the bed, she was surprised when he instead slid her gently down in front of him, settling her on her bed softly.

Drawing her knees up to her chest, she hugged them tightly and looked up at him with curious eyes. "How did you know this one was mine?"

He snorted softly, settling himself beside her. He pointed at each object as he listed it. "Poster of dude playing the piano. Poster of chick playing the piano. Stack of those little booty shorts you love so much."

"I don't think I'm the only one who loves them." She sniffed, eyeing him from the corner of her eye. "And for your information, those posters are of Lang

Lang and Martha Argerich. They're arguably the
best contemporary pianists of our time."

She watched as he studied the posters, then turned
back to her with a sly grin. "I still like Coldplay."

"Coldplay has its merits." When he undid the sack
of takeout, she accepted the cardboard container that
he handed her, even though the spicy scent made
her stomach roll. "Chris Martin is no Lang Lang,
but he's talented."

Ford handed her a plastic fork, nudging her container open. "Your music wasn't classical piano,
though, right? Not the stuff you wrote."

"I thought you didn't listen to my music." She
smirked. "Since it reminded you of what a bastard
you'd been to me."

"That was then." He shrugged simply, opening a
foil wrapper that contained his burrito. "I've checked
out your YouTube channel."

"You what?" She sat up straighter. It was insane
that those simple words made her feel so exposed,
since the entire point of a YouTube channel was to
get her content out there for others to find. Still, the
thought of Ford listening to something that she'd
birthed from within herself...

She wondered if he realized that the song she'd
posted this week was about him.

"You have almost a million subscribers to your
channel." Finished with his burrito, he removed a
foil packet of tortilla chips and a plastic container of

salsa. "Doesn't that help with your finances some? You make money off views, right?"

She appreciated that he hadn't tried to offer them money. She knew that what he had now was a drop in the bucket compared to his former fortune, but if he had enough that he was searching for a new investment, then he had at least six figures more in his bank account than she did in hers.

But he wasn't trying to give her charity. He wasn't trying to take things over. He was treating her like she was capable. And she appreciated it more than he could possibly know.

"Views are monetized, yes." She poked at her salad. He glowered until she scooped a bite into her mouth. "Thing is, I don't have the time to put up that much content. Just one song every month or two."

She chewed. She loved the taco salad from Mamacita's, but it tasted like dust in her mouth. She'd lost weight because she just hadn't been hungry much lately.

"And of those million subscribers, only a small fraction actually watch the new video when it's released." She shrugged. "It works for me, but no, it doesn't add much to the bank account."

He seemed to accept that, polishing off the chips and salsa while she struggled to eat half of her salad. When she'd eaten enough to suit him, he tugged the container from her hands, closed it and set it on her bedside table.

"Shirt off."

She felt her face form the lines of what her sisters called her *what the actual fuck* look.

He waited, and she shook her head.

"I have to get back to work. I don't have the time for this." She crossed her arms over her chest when he tugged at the hem of her tank. "Plus I can't say I'm in the mood after you told me I looked skinny and tired and hauled me through my own house."

"Beth." He fixed her with that intense stare of his, his expression serious. "Take off your shirt."

Damn it.

Part of the chemistry between them was rooted in the way they played with their power exchange. And even though she wasn't feeling particularly sexual at the moment, she found herself doing what he asked, tossing the tank top aside.

"Bra, too." Not waiting for her this time, he reached behind her back and unhooked the plain purple cotton garment. Sliding it down her arms, he pulled it off.

She expected him to cup her breasts, to toy with the piercing that he loved so much. She wasn't sure what to think when, instead of playing with her, he eased her back on her bed.

"Roll over onto your stomach." He patted her lightly on the ass. "Do you have any lotion? Oil?"

Huh?

"I have some sweet almond oil in my bedside drawer." She gestured lazily, but the prone position was somehow making her sleepy, despite the fact that she hadn't been sleeping well at all lately.

"Perfect." Retrieving the bottle, he squirted some into his hands, cupping it in his palms to warm it up. "I know you've been dying to try anal sex. No time like the present."

"Jackass." Still, she couldn't help the soft laugh, even as she tried to get her stomach to settle from the food she'd forced into it.

"Be nice, or I won't do this." Tipping his palm over above her back, he drizzled the warm oil down her spine. With a flat hand, he slicked it over her skin, then nudged her over so that he could climb onto the narrow bed and straddle her hips.

"Haven't had many boys in your room, huh?" She felt him shifting above her, trying to get comfortable. "How do you sleep on this thing?"

"Well, unlike you, I don't sleep crossways and spread-eagle." Pillowing her head on her hands, she moaned as traced a line beneath her shoulder blades with his thumbs. "And I've had plenty of boys up here. It works. You just have to get all nice and...tight."

"Temptress." Still, the hands stroking over her back continued what they were doing, the touches meant to soothe rather than arouse. He worked at a tight spot at the base of her neck, and she pushed into the good kind of hurt that his fingers found.

"Your hands are swollen." He worked his way down her arms, and she could hear the frown in his voice as he worked on her grease-smudged hands. "I told you you've been working too hard."

"They are?" She hadn't noticed, and an alarm bell started to ring in her head. His soothing touches quickly melted her concern.

"Yeah." Finished with her hands, he worked his way back up her arms. Sliding his hands into her hair, he started to rub the muscles of her scalp in a way that made her go cross-eyed with pleasure. When he stopped, she gurgled a protest. "Hey."

"You're warm, too. Way warmer than usual." He stopped rubbing her back, and she could all but hear his thoughts racing. "Are you sure you're feeling okay?"

"Yes." The response was automatic, but she found herself quickly scrolling through her mental check-list. Swollen hands, slightly feverish. Weight loss and fatigue, a stomach that struggled to digest what she'd put into it.

Damn it. How had she been so stupid?

She hadn't been feeling great for the last week, but she'd really thought she was just working hard and stressed about money. For all the attention that she paid to trying to keep herself healthy, she hadn't considered that what she'd been experiencing was a flare-up.

"What is it?" Ford rolled her over suddenly, and she struggled to smooth her features into blankness, even though her heart started to beat triple time.

She wasn't special. She was one of thousands of

people who had lupus, a condition in which her body basically attacked itself.

But not all of those people had almost died from a sudden, wicked onslaught of symptoms. Not all of them had lost their careers and saddled the people they loved with such massive burdens that they feared they might never crawl out from beneath them.

This—this was why she couldn't let herself get too attached to Ford. She already fought not to buckle under the guilt every single day of her life. She couldn't add to it with another person that she was dragging down into the dirt.

More than that, what if she actually did die next time? It was too late for her not to love her family, and her family to love her in return.

But she didn't need to add anyone else to that list.

"I'm fine." Closing her eyes, she let Ford pull the covers up around her as she feigned sleepiness. "Thank you for this. I just need some sleep—you were right."

"Good girl." The bed dipped beneath his weight, and an invisible fist squeezed her heart when he pressed a soft kiss to her forehead. "I'll talk to you later. Get some sleep."

With her eyes squeezed shut, she waited until she knew he'd gone, then sat straight up in her bed. Holding out an arm, she examined the pale skin.

Yup. There was the start of the nasty rash. She hadn't been paying attention. Her mouth was dry and her joints were stiff and sore, though she'd chalked that up to the physical labor she'd been doing.

How could she have been so *stupid*?

She needed to go to the ER to get checked out. The memory of the last time this had happened flashed in her mind's eye—the time her symptoms had come on so strong and fast, her body deteriorating so quickly that she almost died. Her pulse started to thunder, fear of a repeat making her nauseous.

But…a trip to the ER cost money. Money they didn't have, especially right now. She winced as she thought of the balloon payment—of how deeply they were all rooted in this home.

She hadn't had a flare-up since that first time because she took excellent care of herself. She ate well, exercised, took handfuls of prescribed vitamins and supplements. There was no way it could be as serious this time, and if she dragged her ass to the ER when it wasn't really necessary, she'd collapse beneath the weight of the guilt.

She'd be fine. She just needed some rest.

Arranging herself on her pillow, she ignored how painful it was to move her limbs. Gulped some water from the bottle on her nightstand to counteract the dry mouth.

If she'd been awake for it, she would have been surprised at how quickly the fatigue dragged her down into sleep.

"Baby girl, I thought you said you had an eight o'clock oil change this morning." Jo pushed into Beth's bedroom, the words piercing through her feverish dream. She jolted awake, staring wide-eyed at her sister as her brain struggled to work.

She couldn't move. Everything hurt. And something was wrong with her breathing. Her mouth opened, her chest moved, but she just couldn't get enough air.

She watched, paralyzed, as her sister's eyes widened in terror. Jo bolted across the room, gathering her in her arms, pressing on her back and chest as if trying to force the air into Beth's lungs. Beth felt her sister shake against her, or maybe it was her shaking. The voice that echoed around the room in a scream, though, that wasn't hers, because she couldn't draw in enough air to make a sound.

"Mamesie! Meg! Amy! Help!"

CHAPTER SEVENTEEN

THE NEXT MORNING, Ford drove the streets of Boston's South End, unable to settle. Something was up with Beth.

Something more than her being spooked at the fact that he'd told her he could fall in love with her.

He thought of the way she'd looked yesterday, the weight she'd lost apparent in her sunken cheeks. Her skin had been so pale that it was almost transparent.

She'd brushed aside his concerns about her temperature and swollen hands, telling him she hadn't been sleeping very well and was just tired.

His instincts said it was more than that. She'd shared that she'd been sick, sick enough that it had forced her to change her life.

But she still hadn't trusted him enough to tell him what, exactly, had happened. He'd wanted to wait for her to open up to him, to give her that respect.

Something wasn't right.

He ignored the blaring horns and screeching tires of the car between him as he swung the SUV to the side of the road. Lifting his hips, he worked his phone from his pocket. Pulling up his browser, he tapped out the words with his thumb.

beth marchande illness

The first few news articles that came up were fairly generic, with headlines like Local Girl Cancels Piano Tour Due to Health Reasons. While Beth had achieved something that very few people did—a recording contract—she still hadn't been that big a name. Piano enthusiasts knew of her, as did people who were into cutting-edge music, but she hadn't achieved the widespread popularity of the Gagas and Katys and Rihannas of the world.

His frustration grew as he scrolled through. Finally, on the tenth entry, he saw words that caught his eye—words she'd written, it looked like. An entry on the front page of her website, which was no longer actively updated.

Clicking on it, he was greeted with a breathtaking image. There was his girl, her sleek curves outlined in a fitted black sheath that formed a sexy V in the front. The sheer black sleeves of the jacket she wore over it muted the prismatic colors of her ink, but the bright hues still shone through.

She was seated on the bench of a piano—a fancy one to his eye, not that he really knew the difference—with her legs crossed demurely, one hand resting lightly on the keys. Her legs were bare, the tattoo work there peeking out teasingly from between the satin ribbons that wound from her high-heeled pumps to wrap temptingly over her calves.

Her hair had been tamed back into a sleek bun, but he smiled when he noted that it was cotton-candy pink. She smiled brightly out at the camera, a young woman with the world at the tips of her fingers, but he frowned, tracing his fingers over the image of her face.

Some makeup artist had worked their magic, smoothing out Beth's naturally rosy skin, doing that stripy thing Peyton used to do—was it called con-touring?—and adding smoky stuff to her brilliant blue eyes to make them pop. Her lips were glossed a bright red, her eyebrows penciled in dramatically.

She looked gorgeous. Stunning.

But he liked her better in her coveralls with grease on her nose.

Scrolling down, he found the message on the homepage—a note from Beth to her fans.

I know many of you are disappointed that I've can-celed the remainder of my tour. I'm very sorry to have to announce this, but due to an emergency with my health, I will not be rescheduling these dates or booking any other tours in the near future. I do not make this announcement easily, and I want to thank all of you for participating in this beautiful mu-sical journey that I've been on for the last few years.

Bless,
Beth

The message was vague, just as she had been with him, but as he scrolled down to the comments he started to get more information. There were the inevitable nasty comments from the trolls. As he read some of the shit that people had thrown at her, his temper rose.

One long comment caught his eye, and as he read it, he found himself freezing.

PIANOGRRL94:

My sister is an ER doc in Cincinnati and I got the scoop. Beth was admitted in the morning before that first show she canceled and was moved to the intensive care unit. She was diagnosed with an autoimmune disorder called lupus.

KEYKEYSKEYS:

So? Lots of people have autoimmunes. My brother-in-law has Crohn's but he still gets his ass out of bed and goes to work every day. She's a lazy bitch

ADAM4732:

So is she going to reschedule her shows?

PIANOGRRL94:

You guys are assholes. She was admitted because

her entire body shut down. I guess she'd been ignoring that she felt sick because she thought she
just had concert fatigue. She almost died. Like, my
sister didn't think she was going to make it. It's not
advisable for her to tour anymore.

ADAM4732:

Why is your sister telling you this? Isn't there patient
confidentiality shit that she's supposed to have?

PIANOGRRL94:

Whatever, guys. Just though you might want to
know.

Beth had almost died.

Things began to click into place. The way she
no longer drank, her inexplicable devotion to sal-
ads. The shroud of reserve that seemed to cover her
at all times.

She was having a setback—he would have put
every dollar that he had left in the bank on it. But
why on earth wouldn't she just tell someone or go
to the hospital? Why would she try to convince him
that she was fine?

The balloon payment.

"Well, fuck." Beth was nothing if not stubborn,
determined to prove that she was still capable of everything she'd been able to do before she got sick.

She'd been so angry at her family for trying to cover for her, to make the payment without her, that she'd gone and made herself sick over it.

Anger and frustration radiated up his spine, exploding through his fingers as he pulled up his contacts and hit Beth's name. Putting it on speakerphone, he pulled away from the curb and started to drive, hanging a quick U-turn in the middle of the busy street, leaving honking and swearing behind him.

"What?" It wasn't Beth that answered, but one of her sisters.

"I think Beth's sick again," he blurted out. "I think she's hiding it because she'd worried about money."

"No shit, Sherlock." It was Jo, he was pretty sure. The acid in her tone was her signature, but it didn't melt away the worry that was there as well. "We're at Boston Medical Center. She didn't get up for her first appointment today, so I went into her room and she wasn't breathing."

"What?" Ice was a frigid spike that slammed into the length of his spine. "No. What's happening?"

"She's in the ER." Jo's voice was tight, and Ford felt her pain as well as his own. "It's…they say it's not as bad as it could be. I don't know what she's told you—"

"She refused to tell me shit, so I just looked it up." He didn't even feel guilty. "I know what happened before. I know that she almost…died."

"Yeah." On the other end of the line, Jo's voice

shook. "It's not that bad this time. We just can't believe she hid it from us. I can't believe I didn't see."

"She didn't want you to see." Ford sighed, taking
one hand from the wheel to wipe the sweat on the
thigh of his jeans. "Look, I'm on my way."

She thought that Jo might tell him not to come—
not that he would listen—but instead she made a
humming sound.

"Good."

"This is unacceptable, Elizabeth Serena Marchande."

"I'm sleeping." Beth squeezed her eyes shut. The
touch of her mother's familiar hand on her brow had
them flying open again.

The women of her family were gathered around
her hospital bed in a tight ring. All of them were
pale, clearly having lost sleep over the last twenty-
four hours, and not a single one of them was smiling.

"Beth." Pulling up a hideous olive-green chair
to the bed, Meg sank down into it, leaning forward
to clasp her sister's hand. "What the hell were you
thinking?"

She'd been thinking that she was avoiding placing
a bigger financial burden on her family, and yet here
they were. Another hospital bill and stress.

Sister of the year award did not go to her.

"Do you have any idea how scared I was when
I went into your room yesterday morning?" Normally Jo would be the one right beside her, soothing
her and offering comfort. Instead, her fiercest sis-

ter was standing at the end of the bed with her feet planted shoulder-width apart. Her arms were crossed over her chest, and her expression was terrifyingly blank. "I thought you were dying. *Dying*, Beth. Do you understand?"

"I—" She had no words. No excuse. She'd been trying to do the right thing, and yet she'd fucked it right up.

"Hi." Ford poked his head into the room. Her heart leaped at the sight of him, sinking again when she saw the ferocity on his face. She swallowed past a suddenly thick throat as her family greeted him, let him into the room, then filed out to give them some privacy. She was more than a little shocked by the courteous nod that he and Jo cast each other's way as they passed.

Great. She'd made a mess of her entire family, but her closest sister and her boyfriend had bonded over it. Fan-fucking-tastic.

Ford circled her bed, settling himself in the chair Meg had vacated. Beth studied him with trepidation.

Was he her boyfriend? If not, what was he? They hadn't been back together for very long, and yet she felt as though he carried a piece of her heart around in his pocket.

It was terrifying.

"Before you say anything, you should know that I went digging online. I know about your lupus." Beth winced. Ford shook his head. "I wish you'd shared that with me. Beth, you almost died."

"You think I don't know that?" Her voice was rough, groggy from all of the medications that were currently pumping through her system.

"Beth." He caught her hand. She tried to yank it back, but instead he laced their fingers together. "Talk to me."

She pressed her lips together. She hated this. Hated it all.

"Forget the guilt over the money part." She choked out the words. "This is how I feel. When you have a brush with death, and you survive, it's a new beginning. Treatment has been successful, so it's like... it's like people expect that that chapter of your life is over. They'll treat you with kid gloves, but the focus is on picking up and carrying on. Moving past it."

She swallowed, trying to find the right words.

"There can't be a return to normal because normal is gone. I'm not the same person I was before. I monitor myself constantly, and yet I'm in denial." She waved a hand around the room. "Like, hello. I've been waiting for the other shoe to drop, and I still missed it somehow."

"Oh, baby." He tried to tighten his hold, but she tugged her hand away. The simple touch was too much.

"Survival is a lonely place," she started, looking down at her own hands, which she twisted in the sheets. "But for me it's the way it has to be. You say you're falling in love with me, but how can you fall in love with all of this? I could get sick again, really sick, at any time. I got my life back, and I want to live it, but how can you treat me normally now? You'll be monitoring my every movement, since I've proven I can't take care of myself. That's no way to live."

"Do you think less of me for losing my money?" Sitting forward, he braced his hands on his knees, wraithlike eyes fixed on her figure.

"What?" She shook her head. "Of course not."

"You don't think I'm less capable because I did some really stupid things?" His voice was mild.

She got the point. Pinching her lips together, she studied his face. Her entire life, people had called her stubborn.

Turned out she had nothing on Ford Lassiter.

"Get some rest, baby girl." Extending one of his arms, he tugged her hand into his again, holding it tightly. "I'm not going to let go."

CHAPTER EIGHTEEN

"YOU HAVE AN appointment to change a transmission," Ford reminded Beth as he pressed a light kiss to her lips. She moaned and twined her arms around his neck, rocking her hips into his until he saw stars. "You're the one who wanted to go back to work already."

"I know, I know." Rising onto her toes, she slid her lips down the column of his throat. Growling, he pressed her back into his front door, covering her still too-thin frame with his body. "I had to run over and see you quickly between appointments, though. I'm missing you."

"Missing me or my cock?" Grinning, he turned her so that her breasts were pressed against the door. She was in her standard uniform of tank top and tight little shorts underneath coveralls that she'd tied around her waist.

They hadn't had sex in the full week since she'd been released from the hospital. First, it had been because the doctors hadn't allowed any strenuous exercise—she needed to rest.

Now it was because they hadn't had time. Beth had filled her schedule back up with appointments, desperate to make up the cash they needed for that big payment.

At least she was eating again, and sleeping because she'd been prescribed something for it. She was still too skinny, but she'd put on a couple of pounds, which was a relief to them all.

"How much more time do you have?" Growling with frustration, he clasped her waist, sliding his hands up to cup her breasts, toying with her piercing through her shirt the way he knew she liked. She pushed her ass back into his pelvis, rubbing it over his growing erection.

"Five minutes," she panted, placing her hands flat on the door. The sight of that, of her choice to assume a position she knew really did it for him, had his arousal cranking up to scorching levels.

Not enough time to get them both off. But at least he could send his girl off with a smile on her face.

"Keep your hands where they are." Leaving her bent over, he undid the knot she'd made at the waist of her coveralls. Letting them fall to the floor, he gathered the back of her little shorts in his fist, tugging until the elastic material slid between her cheeks.

"What will get you off right now?" Sliding his other hand over her stomach, he grabbed the front of her shorts as well. Alternating where he pulled, he tugged the taut material back and forth through her dampening cleft, and her hips rocked with the rhythm.

"Just…treat me like I won't break." She dipped her head, her loose waves of hair falling into her face. "Whatever you want, just be rough."

The remaining blood from his brain drained south. He was hard as stone, and the need to sink inside that sinful cleft of hers was blinding.

No time. But he could make her feel good.

"Don't move." Letting go of her shorts, he left them as they were, where they'd ridden up and were wedged into the cleft of her ass. It left her round cheeks open to his view.

He hesitated for a moment. Those cheeks weren't quite as round as they usually were, and he reminded himself that she was still on the mend. If he was rough with her, would it hinder her healing?

"Come on already." She canted her ass back at him, impatience thick in her voice. "Three minutes. Should I do it myself?"

"You little brat." Growling, he lifted his hand and brought it down on her right cheek. She cried out, the sound swallowed by the audible smack of his palm on her ass.

"Is that what you wanted?" He delivered a second smack to her other side, then a series of lighter ones between her legs, right over her center. Her body tightened as he slid fingers between her legs, pushing beneath the stretched-out fabric of her shorts.

"You know it is." She clenched around him as he

tucked his fingers inside her. Closing the space between them, he covered her body from behind with his own, using his free hand to work into her bra and pluck at her pierced nipple.

She was right. He'd developed a bit of a fetish about it. If he had his way, he'd convince her to do her other one, too.

"I wish I could be inside you right now." Knowing the words would bring her closer, he pistoned his fingers between her legs while roughly pinching the small gold hoop in her nipple with his fingers. "My cock is so hard it hurts, wanting to be inside you. This will just have to hold us both until we have time."

Scissoring the fingers inside her, he found the soft, fleshy spot that always made her scream. This time was no different, and when he rubbed the pad of a finger over it, she exploded around him, crying out and rubbing her breast into his palm hard, begging for him to tug on it.

When her shudders subsided, she kept her palms flat on the door, panting to try to catch her breath. Withdrawing his fingers, he hugged her from behind, pressing his lips to the back of her neck.

"I love you, Beth." His voice was rough, his body tense as he waited for her reaction. Or for her to fucking thank him again, like on that episode of *Friends*, Ross with that girl he'd met in China. "You don't have to say it back. But I wanted you to know, I'm not falling anymore. I'm fully there."

Placing her hands over his, where they were clasped at his waist, she was silent for a moment—long enough that his nerves began to flock through his veins like migrating birds. Then she purred, a sound of pure satisfaction, tilting her head back to look him in the eyes.

"I love you, too." She swallowed, and he watched the line of her throat as she turned in his arms. "It scares the shit out of me, but you already knew that."

Rising to her tiptoes, she pressed a kiss to his lips. "And with that chitchat, I've got to go."

"One more thing." He ran his hands through his hair as she straightened her shorts, tugging her coveralls back up. "And hear me out."

Looking up from the knot she was tying, she arched an eyebrow.

"I know you're still stressed about money. And I know that there's a good chance you guys aren't going to make that payment." Her face fell, and he swore.

He hating seeing her unhappy. He wanted to do everything he could to keep her from being that way. Which, actually, was where this idea had sprung from.

"You'd better not be offering to pay it for us." The fire that sparkled in her eyes was blue flame. While she was in the hospital, he'd actually considered offering.

He didn't much like his chances among all five Marchande women on the warpath. They were proud;

he understood that. He wouldn't insult them when he knew there was no way they'd say yes.

Which had birthed his idea.

"So first, let me remind you of some of my credentials." Straightening, he held up a hand to tick them off on his fingers. "I started Lassiter Hotels at the age of twenty-three. I used my own money because I wanted to be more than a trust-fund kid. I made my first million by age twenty-five and grew a single hotel into a global conglomerate."

"Uh-huh." Her voice was wry, but he saw the flicker of curiosity on her face. "Is this your idea of sexy talk?"

"Shush." She snorted, and he took it as a sign to continue. "I also went on to lose most of it, but I've been looking for a new opportunity. Not necessarily the one that would make me the most money, but one that felt right."

"Keep going."

"There are a lot of hotels in Boston. A lot of motels, a lot of B-and-Bs. But today people are so overly stimulated by devices and social media that they're wanting something simpler. A more authentic experience."

"You sound like a commercial." She rolled her eyes. "Get on with it."

"The very first time I visited your garage, I noticed that you have a large, rather oddly shaped lot. There's a lot of wasted space. Space that could be used." Normally in a sales pitch he pulled out all the stops, but right now he stopped. "Now, if you hate this idea, or your family hates it, that's fine. I'll think of something else. But I wanted to present this to you."

"Can't hate it if you don't get on with it." She tapped a finger on the door. "I have about thirty more seconds."

"Microhotels are the next big thing." He paused, searching for the right words. "What I'm proposing is that I lease a share of your land from you to build one of these. It will simply look like another house on the grounds but will be able to accommodate sixteen or so guests at a time. And I think you'd be solidly booked."

Beth furrowed her brow, trying to take it all in. "Who owns the structure then, if it's on our land? What happens if we hate it? Who runs it?"

"Those are all details to be discussed," he started, feeling the familiar thrill of a new project creeping into his veins. "But my suggestion is I—or rather, the company I will set up—will assume responsibility for building a plan that you approve of, on land that I lease a share of for a five-year term, to be renegotiated at that time. At the end of that term, the deal can be renewed or canceled. If it's canceled, you would have the option to purchase the structure at wholesale, and I guarantee you, by that time you'll have made plenty to do so."

Beth's face was expressionless, but he knew she was turning it over in her head. He wasn't expecting her to tackle him into a hug, pressing her lips into his neck.

"I like it. I mean, I have to think about it. And tell the others and see what they think." Her eyes were bright, and he knew she was imagining the possibilities. "But if it will help us keep our house...wow."

Pulling back, she looked at him, and he was alarmed to see a sheen of tears in her eyes.

"Oh, God, don't cry." Alarm coursed through him. "I can't handle it if you cry."

"I'm not crying." With a giant sniff, she slid from his arms and opened the door. Looking back over her shoulder, she grinned. "You're kind of awesome, you know that?"

"I'll show you how awesome I am later." Propping open the screen door, he sank a hand into her hair and kissed her deeply, sweeping his tongue over hers. "I bought something I think you're going to like. Hint, it involves some clamps and your very pretty nipples."

"Fucking tease." She pushed through the door, then stopped short. "Um, hello."

"Well, hello there." A man in an impeccable suit stood at the top of the steps leading to Ford's house. An Armani suit, Ford recognized at first sight.

The man was almost as tall as Ford, and they shared the same lean build, the same thick golden hair, though his was sprinkled with salt and pepper. Looking past the man to the curb, Ford noted the sleek black town car that no doubt had a driver whose name the man didn't know, instructed to wait there for however long the man felt like leaving him there.

"Hello, Ford." The man smiled down at Ford, and Ford felt barriers that he'd only recently let down slamming back into place. "Aren't you going to introduce me to your lady friend?"

"This is Beth." He ran a hand down her back, a gesture of possession. Holding on to her, he smiled, but the movement felt stiff, frozen.

"Beth. This is my father."

"Aren't you going to invite me into your...home?" Bruce Lassiter rocked back on his heels, his expression as he looked at the house Ford had purchased showing exactly what he thought of it, which wasn't much. Beth had had to leave, and Ford was incredibly glad. "I had planned to drive the Beamer, but when I discovered which neighborhood you lived in, I thought better of it. Imagine leaving that parked on one of these streets."

"Why are you here, Dad?" Crossing his arms over his chest, Ford shut the screen door behind him. There was no need to let his father inside—it would only invite more disapproval.

Bruce heaved a great sigh, as though Ford was a great trial to him. He probably was, but what Bruce didn't understand was that the feeling was mutual.

"My own son has been back in Boston for almost two months and hasn't come to see me." Bruce's words were an arrow, their aim true. "So I came all the way to the South End to see you. Try to talk some sense into you."

"We're not doing this again." Ford sighed, tilting his head up to the sky. Overcast and crammed with dense clouds, it was going to storm later. If the man upstairs favored him, the clouds would burst now and free him from this conversation.

"I just don't understand why you would live like this." Bruce cast his stare down the street, fixating on Ford's neighbor two houses down, who had a car on blocks parked in the middle of the lawn.

"Well, you've never understood me, so that's nothing new."

"Ford." Bruce fixed him with an exasperated stare. "I worked very hard to give you a life of leisure. You've never had to work, and I've never understood why you feel the need to drive yourself so hard. Let alone to live like...this."

Ford pinched the bridge of his nose.

"Especially now." Bruce was on a roll. "You have a trust fund waiting for you. What the hell are you doing in this shithole? Go back to LA and that woman you were engaged to. Or find a younger version. But I won't have a son of mine living like this."

"Dad, any success you've had is because it was handed down to you from Grandpa." A man not much better than Bruce, in Ford's opinion. "And I hate to break it to you, but I like it here."

And he really did. He never would have imagined it, but he was enjoying the physical labor of fixing up his own home. He liked looking at things after and knowing he'd put his own sweat into its creation.

"You've always been a little snot." Bruce smiled, but it was like ice. "So sure you were better than me."

"I've made it my life's mission to be better than you." The words were true, but they hurt Ford to say. He'd made his peace with the fact that he and his father would never see eye to eye, but he still had love for the man. Somewhere. You know, really deep down. "I wanted to work for a living. I wanted to prove that I could set a goal and turn it into reality. And heaven knows I wanted to treat women better than you ever have."

"That's why you bought clamps for your girlfriend's nipples?" Bruce laughed, tucking his hands into his pants pockets. "You can't fool me with this one, son. You're as kinky as your old man. Have been since you knew what sex was. Movies with some pain? Something rough? Yeah, you liked those. You think I didn't notice?"

Ford felt like he was fourteen again, watching one of those movies while his dad was nearby. It was nearly impossible to block the humiliation.

"And that girlfriend of yours? She looked like the type who likes it rough." Bruce smirked. "Don't tell me you don't give it to her good. The apple doesn't fall far from the tree."

"Get out." Nausea was bitter, coating Ford's throat. "I'm not going to stand on the steps of my own damn house that I bought with my own fucking money and listen to this shit. Don't come here ever again."

"Wouldn't dream of it." Holding out the paper bag he'd been clutching since his arrival, Bruce set something down on the step. "Brought you a little taste of the good life as a reminder. Wasted on you."

Ford pointed down the stairs. Bruce went, but Ford could hear his mocking laughter even after he'd gone.

CHAPTER NINETEEN

FINISHED WITH HER work for the day, Beth had come inside to grab a quick shower before she headed back to Ford's. Her body still tingled from his touch, and she felt a thrill of anticipation every time she wondered what he might have in store for her that night.

Her piano caught her eye as she walked through the house. She liked to play every day, but it had been over a week since she'd touched it.

Lifting the cover, she settled onto the bench. Stroking her fingers over the old keys, she paused for a moment then, grinning, started into a rendition of Coldplay's "Clocks."

She'd have to play it for Ford next time he came over. Which would probably be soon, if her family reacted to his idea the way she anticipated they would.

In her pocket she felt her cell phone buzz with an incoming call. She was tempted to let it go to voice mail, since she was just getting into the song, but if it was one of her family members checking on her, they'd freak out if she didn't answer.

"Hey, Ames." Her youngest sister's tattoo shop showed on the call display. As she'd guessed, one of her family members was checking up on her. "I finished work and I'm fine. Promise. Going to make some dinner, have a shower, head to Ford's."

"About that," Amy started. In the background Beth could hear the whine of the needles that Amy's other artists used. "Ford is here."

"What?" Beth frowned. "He doesn't strike me as the type to get ink."

"I had the same thought." Her sister's voice was not amused. "He's so drunk he might black out, though, so I'm assuming that has something to do with it."

"I just left his house two hours ago. He was fine," Beth protested, then thought of the sharklike man Ford had introduced her to. "Shit. His dad showed up just as I was leaving. It's got to have something to do with that. I'll come get him."

"Tank's already loading him into his van," Amy said. "He'll get him in the door, if you could just meet them there."

"On my way." Sliding her phone back into her pocket, Beth hesitated, then grabbed the keys to the sporty little Toyota sitting in her shop. She'd just serviced it, but her client, a friend from high school, wasn't picking it up until morning.

Beth didn't think Natalie would mind. It was an emergency. So she slid into the little red car, barely noticing the familiar smell of the cleaner she'd used to wipe down the dashboard—Natalie's daughter always had sticky fingers.

Ford wasn't the kind of guy to get sloppy drunk. He liked to be in control.

What the fuck had happened?

"He's in the tub." Beth had only met Tank, one of the artists who worked at Amy's shop, a handful of times. At six and a half feet tall and built like a linebacker, he lived up to his name. Beth didn't have to ask how he'd hauled a man who wasn't small himself all the way to the bathroom. "You'll want to help him shower. He reeks."

"Thanks, Tank." Beth shook his hand, giving it a squeeze. "Your next oil change is on me."

"I'll hold you to it." He jerked a thumb at his van, which was covered with spray-painted art. "The beast is making a clunking noise. I'll pop in next week."

Entering Ford's house, Beth closed and locked the door behind her. As she tossed her jacket on the bench where she always did, it occurred to her how comfortable she was here. Comfortable enough to let herself in and head to the en suite, which was where she assumed Tank had deposited Ford.

The medicinal aroma of scotch was strong enough to make her feel drunk just from breathing the air. Gagging for a moment, Beth blinked down at where Ford was reclining, fully clothed, in the ancient avocado-green tub.

"This is not a good look for you." Dropping to her knees, she started to tug his T-shirt over his head. He grunted but let her undress him like a rag doll.

Unable to get him upright, she ran a hot bath for him. She ran soap over his body, into his hair, aware that his eyes were on her the entire time. He seemed slightly more sober when she tried to get him to stand up after, though he still wobbled when she toweled him off and dragged him to the bed.

"Let's sleep it off, Sir Lassiter." Arranging his naked frame on the sheets, she pulled the quilt over him, then stripped and climbed in on the other side. There wasn't a point in trying to get him to talk while he was still so drunk, so she'd wait until morning.

She was surprised when he rolled onto his side, facing her.

"My dad sucks," he slurred, reaching out to cup her cheek. He missed, stroking his hand over her nose and mouth instead. "All of him sucks. Not all of me sucks, but he reminded me of a part that sucks today."

"Figured there was a reason for the scotch spree." She pursed her lips. "Why scotch, dude? You're going to feel like shit in the morning."

"My dad knows I'm kinky." Ford frowned, trying to focus. "Picked up on it when I was a teenager. He likes it. He's proud of it. Said the apple doesn't fall far from the tree."

Beth's stomach rolled.

"I shouldn't treat you like that." She watched him

swallow—he needed some water. "Shouldn't be that kind of man."

Temper licked along her skin—not at Ford, but at the asshole who had spawned him. Ford was still settling into being comfortable with who he was. This was the last thing he needed.

She opened her mouth to argue, but Ford's eyes were already closed. He'd rolled onto his back. She thought he was already asleep, but he said one thing before he started to snore. One little thing, but it made her blood chill.

"I'm not good enough for you."

Ford smelled coffee before he even opened his eyes.

He needed some. Preferably a bucketful to soak his head in.

He pushed himself to a sitting position, yelping when the white light of morning blinded him. Stabbing pains pierced his skull, and he clutched his head in his hands, willing the pounding drums to stop.

There was a glass of orange juice and two tablets of aspirin on his bedside table. Beth. The woman was a fucking goddess.

Staggering into the bathroom, Ford brushed the fuzzy feeling from his teeth, then showered away the alcoholic sweat. Pulling on the first shirt and track pants he found, he stumbled into the kitchen.

Beth was sitting at his table, playing with her phone while she sipped tea from a mug. His mug, one that said Lassiter Hotels.

He needed to get rid of that.

She watched as he seated himself beside her. Assuming the piece of dry toast was for him, he choked it down silently, aware that she had her eyes on him the entire time.

"Better?" she asked when he pushed the plate away. Cautiously, he took stock, then nodded. He wasn't great, but he'd do.

It wasn't until he chugged his own mug of coffee that his vision cleared enough for him to really look at Beth. She was there, which was definitely something, but her manner was...off. Stiff.

What the fuck had he done?

"Do you remember last night?"

He winced, rubbing his hand over the top of his head. "Yeah. It's hazy, but yeah. Right up until you hauled my ass into bed."

"Mmm-hmm." She set her mug down with a sharp click. "Do you remember what you said to me?"

"Ah...no." *Fuck.*

"I see." Nodding, she folded her hands together, then seemed to change her mind, holding one hand up as she ticked items off a list. "You told me your dad was an asshole. Granted, I only met him for a moment, but the way he stared at my tits made me inclined to agree."

Ford's stomach sank.

"Since we're not the sum total of our parents, that didn't bother me very much. What *did* get under my skin was when you compared yourself to him. Specifically, when you told me that you weren't worthy of me because you were a bad, bad man for being kinky like dear old dad."

"I—" The words brought it back. The humiliation that had come rushing in when his dad had mocked him for thinking that he'd distanced himself.

The sinking sensation that Bruce was right—that even after all the effort he'd put into it, he was cut from the same cloth.

"He's not wrong." Whether it was the shitty way he felt, the way the sun was still streaming into his eyes and blinding him, or the fact that he was just emotionally bankrupt after the night before—he said it, and he didn't even feel like taking it back. "Jesus, Beth. You, of all people, I shouldn't be fucked-up and rough with."

"Are you fucking kidding me?" She slammed her hands on the table, sending the coffee mugs flying. "Me, of all people? What the fuck does that mean?"

"You know what it means." He couldn't stop the words from flying out of his mouth, maybe because they needed to be said, his deepest fears seeing the light of day. "It means that I don't want to be responsible for sending you to the hospital again because I'm a perverted fucker!"

"I suppose it's missed your attention entirely that I like the fact that you're a perverted fucker." When he didn't answer, Beth stood, shaking her head. "I'm out of here."

He wanted to go after her, wanted to hold her

down and claim her with his body until neither of them had any doubt about what they both really wanted.

So close on the heels of the shit with his dad, the thought both aroused him and made his stomach turn. He let Beth make her way to the front door, misery seeping from every pore.

Before she left, she turned around, glaring at him with those fierce blue eyes. She pointed with her index finger, and he couldn't look away. "I have a disease that affects my life. Yup, I do. You have daddy issues. We're both kinky as fuck, and we both need to get the hell over it. When you sort that shit out, you know where to find me."

Fuck, fuck, fuck.

CHAPTER TWENTY

HER SISTERS WERE being twitchy. All of them.

The three women were lounging around the garage as Beth checked the brake pads of an old beater some high school student had dragged in. He wanted the thing to run for a big date but couldn't afford the service. She'd traded him for some work around the garage and was pleased with the way her space sparkled.

An engine sounded outside, and her sisters all tensed. Beth looked around, wondering what she was missing that they were obviously clued in to.

The engine noise drew closer, and suddenly her sisters were on her. Meg ran a brush through the length of her ponytail, Amy scrubbed grease from her nose with a clean rag and Jo unzipped her coveralls so that they fell to the ground and Beth was obliged to step out of them, leaving her in a shirt and her shorts.

"What the hell, guys?" She tried to jerk away, but they clung to her like pandas to bamboo. Finally satisfied, they pulled away, letting her turn to greet the newcomer.

A shiny silver Porsche Turbo sat in the garage. It had a gigantic purple bow on it, and Beth's pulse went from zero to sixty as Ford swung himself out from behind the wheel.

She hadn't seen him, heard from him, even heard *about* him since she'd left his pathetic, hungover self sitting at his breakfast table. When she left she'd felt confident that he would get his shit together, but just this morning a tendril of worry had snaked its way into her gut, making her wonder if maybe he hadn't been able to overcome his mixed feelings about who he was and what he wanted.

"Got to get to work!" Amy held a condom in front of Beth's face, then tucked it into the waist of her shorts before scampering up the steps to the house. Meg followed her, laughing. Jo moved more slowly, and when she reached the top of the stairs Beth was amused to see her point to her eyes, then to Ford's again, mimicking the gesture she'd given him the first time he'd been over since he'd been back.

The garage was quiet with the chatter of her sisters suddenly gone—almost too quiet. Beth could hear the sudden thundering of her heart as she turned to face the man she loved, hoping, praying that things were going to be okay.

He stared right back. Finally, she cleared her throat and pointed at the Turbo. "What's with the bow?"

"You know how much I love this car," Ford
started, closing the distance between them. He
stopped with a thin ribbon of space still between
them, and Beth yearned to press her body against
him, to take in his heat. To take in *him*.

"I might have an inkling." For something to do,
she ran a hand over the sleek silver hood.

"I love you more." Startled, she turned her gaze
back to him. His expression was dead serious, his
hands held out for her. Slowly, cautiously, she took
them, a shudder of relief working through her at the
feel of his skin on hers.

Looking from him to the car, she understood.
"You are not giving me a Porsche. *Your* Porsche.
No way."

"I needed something to demonstrate how I feel.
How stupid I've been." He grinned crookedly, one
side of his mouth curling up higher than the other.
"It's this or a ring, baby. I figured you'd choose the
car."

"Holy shit." She knew she was gaping; she
couldn't help it. "You're insane. And playing dirty."

"I sure am. I'm a little messed up," he admitted, pulling her against him. Burying his face in her
hair, he inhaled deeply, and she melted against him.
"Look, I'm not miraculously all better. I have issues.
You do too, you know."

She sniffed but said nothing.

"But I know one thing with absolute certainty.
I want you in my life." Grasping her chin, he tilted

her face so she looked at him. "Do you feel the same way?"

She wanted to make him work for it after what he'd put her through, but she didn't have the heart. Swallowing past a sudden burning lump of tears, she nodded, unable to speak.

He grabbed the end of her ponytail, wrapping it around his hand. She gasped when he tugged her head back, his smile turning from relieved to wicked. "Besides, when you finally agree to that ring, the Turbo will at least be in the same house again."

"You're so bad." She gasped when he tugged again, dipping his head to sink his teeth into the cord of her neck. She hissed out a breath when his free hand cupped her breast firmly, pushing her back until her ass hit the front hood of the Turbo. Wet heat rushed between her legs as he eased her back onto the hood, the way he had so many years before.

"Like it or not, it seems that I am," he agreed, sliding his hand down between her legs. She cried out when he rubbed his fingers over her clit, through her shorts.

"And I'm going to spend the rest of my life proving to you just how bad I can be. 'Cause that's what we both want."

* * * * *

COMING SOON!